Destined

BY P. C. CAST AND KRISTIN CAST

The House of Night

MARKED

BETRAYED

CHOSEN

UNTAMED

HUNTED

TEMPTED

BURNED

AWAKENED

DESTINED

HIDDEN

REVEALED

REDEEMED

The House of Night Novellas

DRAGON'S OATH

LENOBIA'S VOW

NEFERET'S CURSE

THE FLEDGLING HANDBOOK

A HOUSE of NIGHT novel

Destined

P.C. & KRISTIN CAST

www.atombooks.net

ATOM

First published in the United States in 2011 by St Martin's Press
First published in Great Britain in 2011 by Atom
This edition published in 2013 by Atom

5 7 9 10 8 6

A CIP catalogue record for this book
is available from the British Library.

ISBN 978-0-349-00120-3

Typeset in Minion Pro
Printed and bound by CPI Group (UK) Ltd, Croydon, CR0 4YY

Papers used by Atom are from well-managed forests
and other responsible sources.

 MIX
Paper from
responsible sources
FSC® C104740

Atom
An imprint of
Little, Brown Book Group
Carmelite House
50 Victoria Embankment
London EC4Y 0DZ

An Hachette UK Company
www.hachette.co.uk

www.atombooks.co.uk

For Allie Jensen, with love and appreciation.
Our magick works because you *are* magick!

ACKNOWLEDGMENTS

Thank you to our Atom team at Little, Brown, UK. Especially our editor and friend, Samantha Smith.

As always, we appreciate our agent and friend, Meredith Bernstein, without whom the House of Night would not exist.

We appreciate Will Rogers High School and how cool they are to let us crawl around their awesome building and turn it into fiction. (No, none of the gorgeous art deco building was *really* harmed during the writing of this book!)

Speaking of awesome and gorgeous—a giant THANK-YOU to our hometown community. We love how supportive T-Town is of the HoN! These folks are particularly covered with awesomesauce: The Ambassador Hotel and the Chalkboard restaurant, Moody's Fine Jewelry, Starbucks at Utica Square, Miss Jackson's, The Dolphin, The Wild Fork restaurant, Little Black Dress, the Gilcrease and Philbrook Museums, and Street Cats. And thank you to our dedicated, wonderful fans who have be coming to Tulsa on HoN trips! Our fans rock!

And last but totally NOT least: *Thanks, Josh!* for the Okieisims, but mostly for *taking the reins.*

PROLOGUE

Zoey

I think my mom is dead.

I tested the words silently. They felt wrong, unnatural, as if I was trying to comprehend the world turning upside down or the sun rising in the west.

I drew a deep, sobbing breath and rolled onto my side, reaching for another tissue in the box that was on the floor next to the bed.

Stark muttered and frowned and moved restlessly.

Slowly and carefully, I got out of bed, grabbed Stark's giant sweatshirt from where he'd tossed it, pulled it on, and curled up on the beanbag chair that sat near the wall of our little tunnel room.

The beanbag made that smushy noise that always reminds me of the balls in those inflatable kid party houses, and Stark frowned and mumbled something again. I blew my nose. Quietly. *Stop crying stop crying stop crying! It won't help. It won't bring Mom back.* I blinked a bunch of times, and wiped my nose again. *Maybe it had just been a dream.* But even as I thought the words my heart knew the truth. Nyx had pulled me from my dreams to show me a vision of Mom entering the Otherworld. That meant Mom had died. *Mom told Nyx that she was sorry for letting me down,* I reminded myself as tears leaked down my cheeks again.

"She'd said she loved me," I whispered.

I had hardly made any noise, but Stark tossed and turned restlessly, and muttered, "Stop!"

I clamped my lips together, even though I knew my whisper wasn't what was messing with his sleep. Stark was my Warrior, my Guardian, and my boyfriend. No, boyfriend is too simple a word. There's a bond between Stark and me that goes deeper than dating and sex and all the stuff that comes and goes with normal relationships. That's why he was so restless. He could feel my sadness—even in his dreams he knew I was crying and hurt and scared and—

Stark pushed the blanket off his chest and I could see that his hand was clenched into a fist. My gaze went to his face. He was still asleep, but his forehead was furrowed and he was frowning.

I closed my eyes and drew a deep, centering breath. "Spirit," I whispered. "Please come to me." Instantly I felt the element brush against my skin. "Help me. No, actually, help Stark by shielding my sadness from him." *And maybe,* I added silently, *you could help shield some of my sadness from me, too. Even if it's just for a little while.* I drew another deep breath as spirit moved within and around me, swirling over to the bed. Opening my eyes I could actually see a ripple in the air surrounding Stark. His skin appeared to glow as the element settled against him like a diaphanous blanket. I felt warm and glanced down at my arms and saw that the same soft glow was resting against my skin. Stark exhaled a long sigh with me as spirit worked a little soothing magick, and for the first time in hours I felt a little, tiny bit of my sadness lift.

"Thank you, spirit," I whispered and crossed my arms, hugging myself tight. Wrapped in the comforting touch of the element I felt closest to, I was actually a little sleepy. It was then that a different kind of warmth penetrated my consciousness. Slowly, not wanting to disturb the comforting spell the element was working, I unwrapped my arms from around myself and touched my chest.

Why is my seer stone warm? The small, round stone was dangling from its silver chain, resting between my breasts. I hadn't taken it off since Sgiach had gifted it to me before I'd left the beautiful, magickal Isle of Skye.

Wonderingly, I pulled the stone out from under the sweatshirt, running my fingers over its smooth, marble surface. It still reminded me of a coconut-flavored Life Saver, but the Skye marble glittered with an unearthly light, as if the element I had invoked had made it alive—as if the warmth I felt was because it pulsed with life.

Queen Sgiach's voice echoed through my memory: *"A seer stone is in tune with only the most ancient of magicks: the kind I protect on my isle. I am gifting you with it so that you might, indeed, recognize the Old Ones if any still exist in the outside world . . ."*

As her words replayed in my mind the stone turned slowly, almost lazily. The hole in its center was like a mini-telescope. As it shifted around I could see Stark illuminated through it, and my world shifted, too, narrowed, then everything changed.

Maybe it was because spirit was so close to me at that moment, but what I saw didn't feel anything like the mind-blowing first time I'd looked through the stone on Skye and had ended up passing out.

But that didn't mean it was any less unsettling.

Stark was there, lying on his back, most of his chest bare. The glow of spirit was gone. In its place I saw another image. It was indistinct, though, and I couldn't make out his features. It was like someone's shadow. Stark's arm twitched and his hand opened. The shadow's hand opened. As I watched the Guardian sword—the massive long sword that had come to Stark in the Otherworld—took form in Stark's hand. I gasped in surprise and the phantom-like Warrior turned his head in my direction and closed his hand around the sword.

Instantly the Guardian sword shifted, changed, and became a long black spear—dangerous, lethal, tipped in blood that looked way too familiar to me. Fear spiked through me.

"No!" I cried. "Spirit, strengthen Stark! Make that thing go away!" With a noise like the beating wings of a giant bird, the apparition disappeared, the seer stone went cold, and Stark sat straight up, frowning at me.

"What are you doing over there?" He rubbed his eyes. "Why are you making so much noise?"

I opened my mouth to try to explain the bizarre thing I'd just seen when he sighed heavily and lay back down, flipping open the covers and motioning sleepily for me. "Come here. I can't sleep unless you're cuddled up with me. And I really need to get some sleep."

"Okay, yeah, me, too," I said, and on shaky legs I hurried to him and curled against his side, my head resting on his shoulder. "Hey, uh, something weird just happened," I began, but when I tilted my head so that I could see into his eyes, Stark's lips met mine. The surprise didn't last long, and I slid into the kiss. It felt good—so good to be close to him. His arms went around me. I pressed myself against him while his lips followed the curve of my neck. "I thought you said you needed some sleep." My voice sounded breathless.

"I need you more," he said.

"Yeah," I said. "Me, too."

We lost ourselves in each other then. Stark's touch chased away death and despair and fear. Together we reminded each other of life and love and happiness. Afterward we finally slept and the seer stone lay cold and forgotten on my breast between us.

CHAPTER ONE

Aurox

The human male's flesh had been soft, pulpy.

It had been a surprise how easy it had been to destroy him—to end the beating of his feeble heart.

"Take me to North Tulsa. I want to go out into the night," she'd said. That was the command that began their evening.

"Yes, Goddess," he'd responded instantly, coming alive from the corner of the rooftop balcony that he'd made his own.

"Do not call me Goddess. Call me . . ." She'd looked contemplative. ". . . Priestess." Her full lips, slick and reddened, turned up. "I believe it is best if everyone should simply call me Priestess—at least for a short while."

Aurox had fisted his hand over his heart in a gesture he instinctively knew was ancient, though it somehow felt awkward and forced. "Yes, Priestess."

Priestess had brushed by him, gesturing imperiously for him to follow her.

He had followed.

He'd been created to follow. To take her orders. To obey her commands.

They'd entered something Priestess had called *car,* and the world had flown. Priestess had commanded him to understand the workings of it.

He'd watched and learned, just as she'd commanded.

Then they'd stopped and exited the car.

The street had smelled of death and rot, corruption and filth.

"Priestess this place is not—"

"Protect me!" she'd snapped. "But do not be protective *of* me. I will always go where I wish, when I wish, and do exactly what I wish. It is your job, no, your *purpose* to defeat my enemies. It is my destiny to create enemies. Watch. React when I command you to protect. That is all I require of you."

"Yes, Priestess," he'd said.

The modern world was a confusing place. So many shifting sounds. So much he did not know. He would do as Priestess commanded. He would fulfill his reason for creation and—

A male had stepped out, blocking Priestess's way.

"You way too pretty to be in this here alley so late with nothin' but one boy keepin' ya company." His eyes widened, as he took in Priestess's tattoos. "So, vampyre, you stoppin' here to get you a little snack from this boy? How 'bout you give me that purse then you and me, we'll talk 'bout what it's like to be with a real man?"

Priestess sighed and sounded bored. "You're wrong on both counts: I am not simply a vampyre, and this is no boy."

"Hey, what you mean by that?"

Priestess ignored the man and looked over her shoulder at Aurox.

"*Now* you should protect me. Show me what kind of weapon I command."

He obeyed her without conscious thought. Aurox closed on the man with no hesitation. In one swift movement, Aurox plunged his thumbs into the man's staring eyeballs, which made the screaming begin.

The man's terror washed over him, feeding him. As simply as drawing a breath, Aurox inhaled the pain he was causing. The power of the man's terror swelled through him, pumping hot and cold. Aurox felt his hands hardening, changing, becoming *more*. What had been normal fingers became claws. He pulled them from the man's eyes when the blood began to seep from his ears. With the borrowed power of pain and fear, Aurox lifted the man, slamming him against the wall of the nearest building.

The man screamed again.

What a wonderful, terrible thrill! Aurox felt more of the change ripple through his body. Mere human feet became cloven hooves. The muscles of his legs thickened. His chest heaved and split the shirt he had been wearing. And most wonderful of all, Aurox felt the thick deadly horns that swelled from his head.

By the time the man's three friends ran into the alley to help him, he had stopped screaming.

Aurox dropped the man to the filth and turned to place himself between Priestess and those who might believe they could cause her harm.

"What the fuck?" The first man skidded to a halt.

"I ain't never seen nothin' like that," said the second man.

Aurox was already absorbing the fear that was beginning to radiate from them. His skin pulsed with the cold fire of it.

"Is they horns? Ah, hell no! I'm outta here." The third man turned and scurried back the way he had come. The other two began to back slowly away, eyes wide, shocked and staring.

Aurox looked to Priestess. "What is your command?" In some distant part of his mind, he wondered at the sound of his voice—how it had become so guttural, so bestial.

"Their pain makes you stronger." Priestess looked pleased. "And *different, more fierce.*" She looked at the two retreating men and her full upper lip lifted in a sneer. "Isn't that interesting . . . Kill them."

Aurox moved so quickly the nearest man had no chance to escape. He gored him through his chest, lifting him so that he writhed and shrieked and soiled himself.

This made Aurox even more powerful.

With a mighty toss of his head, the skewered man flew into the building to land, crumpled and silent, beside the first man.

The other man didn't run away. Instead he pulled out a long, dangerous looking knife and charged at Aurox.

Aurox feinted to the side and then, when the man overcompensated, he stomped a cloven hoof through his foot, ripping off his face as the man fell forward.

Breathing hard, Aurox stood over the bodies of his vanquished enemies. He turned to Priestess.

"Very good," she said in her emotionless voice. "Let us leave this place before the authorities descend."

Aurox followed her. He walked heavily, his hoofs gouging furrows in the dirty alley. He fisted his claws at his side as he tried to make sense of the emotional storm that flowed through his body, taking with it the power that had fueled his battle frenzy.

Weak. He felt weak. And more. There was something else.

"What is it?" she snapped at him when he hesitated before entering the car again.

He shook his head. "I do not know. I feel—"

She laughed. "You don't *feel* at all. You're obviously overthinking this. My knife doesn't feel. My gun doesn't feel. You're my weapon; you kill. Deal with it."

"Yes, Priestess." Aurox got in the car and let the world speed past him. *I do not think. I do not feel. I am a weapon.*

Aurox

"Why are you standing here *looking* at me?" Priestess asked him, staring at him with eyes of green ice.

"I await your command, Priestess," he said automatically, wondering how it was possible to have displeased her. They had just returned to her lair at the top of the magnificent building called Mayo. Aurox had walked to the balcony and simply stood there, quietly, gazing at Priestess.

She blew out a long breath. "I have no command for you at this moment. And must you always stare at me?"

Aurox looked away, focusing on the lights of the city and how they glittered alluringly against the night sky.

"I await your command, Priestess," he repeated.

"Oh, by all the gods! Who would have known the Vessel created for me would be as mindless as he is beautiful?"

Aurox felt the change in the atmosphere before Darkness materialized from smoke and shadow and night.

"Mindless, beautiful, and deadly . . ."

The voice rang in his head. The enormous white bull formed fully before him. His breath was fetid, yet sweet. His gaze was horrible and wonderful at the same time. He was mystery and magick and mayhem together.

Aurox dropped to his knees before the creature.

"Get off your knees. Get up and go back there . . ." She waved her hand in a dismissive gesture toward the shadows that edged the far recesses of the rooftop.

"No, I'd rather he stayed. I enjoy gazing on my creations."

Aurox didn't know what to say. This creature commanded his attention, but Priestess commanded his body.

"Creations?" Priestess put a special emphasis on the last part of the word as she moved languidly toward the massive bull. "Do you often make gifts like this to your followers?"

The bull's laughter was terrible, but Aurox noticed Priestess didn't flinch at all—that instead she seemed to be drawn closer and closer to the creature as he spoke.

"How interesting! You are actually questioning me. Are you jealous, my heartless one?"

Priestess stroked the bull's horn. "Do I need to be?"

The bull nuzzled her. Where his muzzle touched Priestess the silk of her gown shriveled, exposing smooth, naked flesh underneath.

"Tell me, what do you believe is the purpose of my gift to you?" The bull answered Priestess's question with one of his own.

Priestess blinked and shook her head, as if she was confused. Then her gaze found Aurox, still on his knees. "My lord, his purpose is protection, and I am ready to do as you bid to thank you for him."

"I will accept your lush offerings, but I must explain to you that Aurox is not simply a weapon of protection. Aurox has one purpose, and that is to create chaos."

Priestess inhaled a deep, shocked breath. She blinked rapidly, and her gaze went from the bull to him, and then returned to the bull.

"Truly?" she asked in a soft, reverent voice. "Through this one creature I can command chaos?"

The bull's white eyes were like a sick, setting moon. *"Truly. He is, indeed, one creature, but his power is vast. He has the ability to leave disaster in his wake. He is the Vessel that is the manifestation of your deepest dreams, and are they not for utter and complete chaos?"*

"Yes, oh yes," Priestess breathed the words. She leaned against the bull's neck, stroking his side.

"Ah, and what is it you will do with chaos now that it is at your command? Will you take down the cities of humans and rule as vampyre queen?"

Priestess's smile was beautiful and horrible. "Not queen. Goddess."

"Goddess? But there is a Goddess of Vampyres. You know that all too well. You used to be in her service."

"You mean Nyx? The Goddess who allows her minions free choice and a will of their own? The Goddess who will not intercede because she believes so strongly in the myth of freewill?"

Aurox thought he could hear a smile in the beast's voice, and wondered how that was possible. *"I do mean Nyx, Goddess of Vampyres and Night. Would you use chaos to challenge her?"*

"No. I would use chaos to defeat her. What if chaos threatens the very fabric of the world? Would Nyx not step in and defy her own rules to save her children? And by doing so wouldn't the Goddess rescind her edict that grants humans freewill and betray herself? What would happen then to her divine reign if Nyx changes what is destined to be?"

"I cannot say, as that has never before happened." The bull snorted as if in amusement. *"But it is a surprisingly interesting question—and you know how much I enjoy being surprised."*

"I only hope that I can continue to surprise you over and over again, my lord."

"Only is such a small word . . ." the bull said.

Aurox continued to kneel on the rooftop long after Priestess and the bull had departed, leaving him discarded and forgotten. He stayed where he had been left, staring up at the sky.

CHAPTER TWO

Zoey

"A short bus? Really?" All I could do was shake my head and stare at the squatty yellow thing that said HOUSE OF NIGHT in fresh black letters across its side. "I mean, it's nice that my call to Thanatos worked so fast and we're being allowed to go back to school, but *a short bus?*"

"Twin! They sent the retard bus for us!" Erin said, giggling.

"Twin, that's really mean," Shaunee said.

"I know, Twin. I can't believe Neferet's so f-ing evil she sent the retard bus for us," Erin continued.

"No, I don't mean Neferet's being mean. I mean it's mean to say *retard,*" Shaunee explained, rolling her eyes at her Twin.

"I think Shaunee's correct, *and* you should consider expanding your vocabulary. You're using *mean* too many times; it's redundant," Damien said.

Shaunee, Erin, Stevie Rae, Rephaim, and I stared wide-eyed at Damien. I knew we were all thinking it was great to hear him obsessing about vocabulary again, but we didn't want to say anything because we were all scared he might burst into tears and retreat back into the soggy depression that had been haunting him since Jack's death.

Aphrodite and Darius chose that moment to emerge from the depot's basement and as per usual, Aphrodite bridged the gap between decorum and disaster by invoking her one tried and true rule: Care About How It Looks.

"Oh, for shit's sake. I'm not getting in *that.* The short bus is for 'tards," Aphrodite said with a snort and a hair toss.

"Y'all, it's not that bad. I mean, obviously it's a new bus. Check out the fresh black House of Night lettering," Stevie Rae said.

"It might as well say Social Suicide," Aphrodite said, frowning at Stevie Rae.

"I'm not lettin' you rain on my parade. I *like* school," Stevie Rae said. She stepped up into the bus, grinning at the Son of Erebus Warrior who had, unsmilingly, opened the door for her.

"Priestess." He greeted her somberly with a nod, and then, totally ignoring our own Son of Erebus Warrior, Darius, he looked at me and, with even a more clipped nod said, "Zoey, I am to notify you and Stevie Rae that there will be a school Council Meeting, which will convene in a thirty minutes. You are both to attend."

"Okay, well, Stark's letting everyone else know you're here, so we'll be ready to leave in just a sec," I said, smiling at him like his face didn't look like a storm cloud.

"Hey, y'all, it still smells new!" Stevie Rae yelled. I could see her short blond curls bobbing as she gawked around inside. Then she popped back out and skipped down the stairs to take Rephaim's hand and grin up at him. "Wanna sit in the backseat with me? It's real bouncy!"

"Seriously," Aphrodite said. "That bus is perfect for you; you're a retard. And I hate to be the one to break it to you—oh wait, that's a lie; I don't really hate it—but even though the Vamp High Council has clearly put the pressure on Neferet and forced her to bus us back to the House of Night, birdboy is still not welcome there. Did you forget in the afterglow of whatever you two could have been doing in the one-point-two seconds between sunset and now that he wasn't a bird?"

I saw Stevie Rae tighten her hand clamp on Rephaim. "I'll have you know it's been more than one-point-two seconds since sunset, none of your business what we've been doin', *and* Rephaim's goin' to school. Just like the rest of us."

Aphrodite's blond brows went up to her hairline. "You're not kidding, are you?"

"No," Stevie Rae said firmly. "And you should understand that better than anyone else."

"Me? Understand? What in the hell are you talking about?"

"You're not a fledgling, red or regular. You're not a vampyre. You're maybe not even a human."

" 'Cause she's a hag," I heard Shaunee whisper.

"From Hell," Erin whispered back.

Aphrodite narrowed her eyes at the Twins, but Stevie Rae wasn't done.

"Just like Rephaim, you're something that's not quite normal, but Nyx has given her blessing to you—*even* if none of the rest of us understands why the heck she'd do that. Anyway, you're goin' to school. I'm goin' to school. So's Rephaim. The end."

"Stevie Rae has a point," Stark said as he joined us in the parking lot outside the depot, the rest of the red fledgling kids trailing along behind him. "Neferet's not gonna like it, but Nyx forgave and blessed Rephaim."

"In front of the entire school," Stevie Rae added quickly.

"They know that," Rephaim murmured to her. He looked from her to the rest of us, his gaze finally settling on me. "What do you think?" he surprised me by asking. "Should I try to go to the House of Night, or would that just be causing trouble for no reason?"

Everyone gawked at me. With a quick glance at the stony-faced Son of Erebus Warrior in the bus, I said, "Uh, would you guys go ahead and get on the bus? I need to talk to my . . . uh . . ." I trailed off with a gesture that took in Aphrodite, Stevie Rae, and the rest of my closest friends.

"Your circle," Stevie Rae said, smiling at me. "You're goin' to talk to your circle."

"And their accoutrements," Damien added, nodding at Aphrodite, Darius, and Kramisha.

I grinned. "I like that! Okay, would you guys get on the bus while I talk to my circle and their accoutrements, please?"

"I ain't sure I like being called *accoutrements,*" Kramisha said, narrowing her eyes at me.

"It means—" Stevie Rae began, but Kramisha interrupted her with a shake of her head. "I know what it mean. I'm sayin' I ain't sure I like it."

"Could you journal about it later and right now shut up and follow Zoey so we can get this over with?" Aphrodite said while Kramisha sucked air and glared. "And for the record," she pointed at everyone except Darius. "You are a Nerd Herd. I am your token Popular and Perfect."

The Twins looked like they were taking verbal aim at Aphrodite so I said, "Guys, focus. Rephaim's question is important." Thankfully, that shut everyone up and I motioned for my circle, accoutrements, and Aphrodite to follow me down the sidewalk and out of hearing range as the red fledglings clambered into the bus and I frantically tried to think about Rephaim's very important question.

My mind felt mushy. Last night had been awful. I glanced at Stark and felt my cheeks getting warm. Okay, well, not all of it had been awful, but still, hard questions filled my head. I mentally shook myself. I wasn't just a kid anymore. I was the first Fledgling High Priestess and all these guys looked up to me and expected me to Know the Right Answers (well, to everything except geometry, Spanish translations, and parallel-parking issues).

Please, Nyx, let me say the right thing. I sent up a quick, silent prayer, then met Rephaim's gaze and realized suddenly it wasn't *my* answer we needed.

"What do you want?" I asked him.

"Well, he wants—" Stevie Rae began, but my raised hand silenced my BFF. "No," I said. "This can't be what you say Rephaim wants, or even what you want for him. I need Rephaim's answer. So, what it is? What do you want?" I repeated.

Rephaim met my gaze steadily. "I want to be normal," he said.

Aphrodite snorted. "Sadly, normal plus teenager equals going to stupid school."

"School isn't stupid," Damian said, and then he turned to Rephaim. "But she's right about the normal part. Going to school is what normal kids do."

"Yep," Shaunee said.

"Sucks, but yep," Erin said. "Although it is an excellent fashion parade."

"Right you are, Twin," Shaunee said.

"What does that mean?" Rephaim asked Stevie Rae.

She smiled at him. "Basically that you should be goin' to school with us."

He smiled back at her, love and warmth filling his face. When he looked from Stevie Rae to me, that wonderful expression was still there, and I couldn't help smiling back at him.

"If normal means going to school, then that's what I would really like to do. If it doesn't cause too much of a problem."

"It'll cause problems, make no mistake about that," Darius said.

"You don't think he should go?" I asked.

"I did not say that. I agree with you that it is his choice, his decision, but Rephaim, you should understand that it would be easier if you chose to stay here—out of the way—at least until we see what Neferet and Kalona's next moves will be."

I thought I saw Rephaim cringe at the mention of his dad, but he nodded and said, "I do understand, but I'm tired of hiding alone in the darkness." He looked down at Stevie Rae again and then back at us. "And Stevie Rae may need me."

"Okay, you know this whole 'let's let the birdboy decide' and 'Stevie Rae may need me' stuff is all real happy-schmappy in theory, but in reality we're gonna be walking onto a campus where the batshit crazy High Priestess hates us, and will use anything she can to bring us, and by that I mean you specifically, Z, down. Not to mention Dragon, the *Leader* of the Sons of Erebus Warriors, is definitely not acting right since his mate was killed by the guy we're bringing back onto campus. Neferet's going use Rephaim against us. Dragon is going to back her. Shit is going to hit the fan."

"Well," I said. "It won't be the first time."

"Uh, may I say something?" Damien's hand was raised like he was in class and wanted to be called on.

"Yes, honey, and you don't have to raise your hand," I said.

"Oh, okay, thanks. What I wanted to say is we need to remember that when Nyx appeared at the House of Night, forgave and blessed Rephaim, she basically gave us permission to include Rephaim in our world. Neferet can't go against that—at least not openly. And neither can Dragon. How much they don't like it is beside the point."

"But they did go against it," Stark said. "Neferet asked Dragon if he'd accept Rephaim, and he said no, so she kicked him off campus. Stevie Rae called bullshit on that, and that's why we all ended up leaving."

"Yeah, and just because the High Council managed to pressure Neferet into letting us come back to class, it doesn't mean we're really going to be accepted. I can promise you that she and Dragon, and probably a lot of other people aren't going to be cool with this." Aphrodite fluttered her fingers at Rephaim.

Damien spoke before I could say anything. "Well, the truth is neither Neferet nor Dragon can supersede the Goddess's wishes."

"Super what?" Shaunee asked.

"Seed who?" Erin added.

"It means to replace," Stevie Rae explained for Damien. "And that's a real interestin' point, Damien. No one can supersede the Goddess, not even a High Priestess."

"Can you imagine what the tight-assed High Council would say about that?" Aphrodite rolled her eyes. "Litter of kittens—they'd have several litters of flying kittens. Each."

I blinked and had the sudden urge to hug Aphrodite. Well, the urge passed quickly, but still.

"Aphrodite," I said. "You are a genius! And so is Damien."

"Of course I am," Aphrodite said smugly.

"You're going to tell on Neferet and Dragon to the High Council, aren't you?" Damien said.

"I think 'telling on' them is not the right way to put it. Uh, you have your laptop with you, don't ya?" I asked.

Damien patted the man purse slung over his shoulder. "Of course. It's in my satchel."

"Man purse," Shaunee said.

"Just sayin'," Erin added.

"It's a European satchel," Damien said firmly.

"If it has feathers . . ." Erin said.

"And quacks . . ." Shaunee said.

"Whatever it is, I'm glad it means you have your computer with you." I jumped in before Damien could big word them. "You do have Skype downloaded on it, don't you?"

"Yes," he said.

"Good. I need to borrow it for the Council Meeting, if that's okay with you?"

"No problem," Damien said, raising his brows questioningly at me.

"What are you thinkin'?" Stevie Rae asked his question for him.

"Well, when I talked to Thanatos about helping us get back to school, I didn't mention that little thing about the fact that we're kinda, sorta branching off with our own House of Night here, but that we'll still be going to class and such at our original House of Night."

"We're gonna have to think of a great new name for our place," Shaunee said.

"Ooooh! Right you are, Twin," Erin said.

"Hey, it's the depot, so how about the Pot Lot House of Night," Shaunee said.

I looked at them. Shook my head and said a firm, "No to the Pot Lot." Then I went back to my original point. "But I do need to do a whole Skype conference with the Vamp High Council to get permission for what we want to do. A school Council Meeting seems a good time to do that, especially since I'm sure Neferet will love it if I ask that she bear witness to my call."

"Z, that sounds like a crap plan. Neferet *will* love talking to the High Council and figuring out a way to twist everything you say to make you look like Insane Teenager," Aprodite said.

"That's kinda my point," I said. "I'm not gonna be Insane Teenager. I'm gonna be the Fledgling High Priestess who gives the High Council all the details about the amazing, miraculous gift Nyx has given our Red High Priestess's Consort, Rephaim, and that he's super excited to be starting school at the Tulsa House of Night. I'm sure they'll even want to congratulate Neferet on being such an awesome High Priestess who can handle all the changes going on here."

"That's devious. I like it," Aphrodite said. "You put Neferet and even Dragon in a position where if they say 'hell no we're not accepting the birdboy,' or even bitch and complain a little about it, they look massively bad—what with Nyx showing up and miracling."

"This still isn't going to be an easy road," Stark said.

Rephaim met his gaze steadily. "No matter how rough it is, it's a better road than the one that leads to darkness and hatred and death. And I think you know exactly what I mean."

"I do," Stark said, returning his gaze unflinchingly.

"So do I," Stevie Rae said.

"Me, too," I added.

"We're in agreement then. Rephaim returns to the House of Night with us," Darius said.

"Okay, wait. Does this mean we have to get in the damn short bus?" Aphrodite asked.

"Yes!" we all said together.

Laughing and feeling lighter than I had in days, I clambered on the short bus with my friends, and bumped my shoulder against Stark as we took our seats. He barely glanced at me. It was about then that I realized he really hadn't had much to say to me (or anyone) since we'd woken up. Remembering how close we'd been—how he'd touched me and made the world seem all right again—had me chewing my lip and feeling super confused. I snuck another glance at him. He was staring out the window. He looked tired. Really tired.

"Hey, what's up with you?" I asked as the bus bounced its way along Cincinnati Street heading toward midtown

"Me? Nothin'."

"Seriously, you look really tired. Are you feeling okay?"

"Zoey, you woke me up and kept me up through most of the day yesterday. Then you made that call to Thanatos to get the whole 're-turn to school' thing in motion, which was not exactly a calm, quiet conversation. I'd just got to sleep when you yelled whatever and woke me up again. Making love was great." He paused and for a second smiled and looked almost normal. Then he opened his mouth and ruined it by saying, "Afterward you did some serious tossing and turning before you passed out. I couldn't get back to sleep. So I'm tired. That's all."

I blinked at him. Twice. And tried not to feel like he'd just slapped me in my face. Keeping my voice down because I didn't want to deal with all my friends knowing, I said, "Okay, putting aside the whole I-had-to-call-Thanatos-to-get-us-back-to-school thing, which is what I shoulda done 'cause I'm the High Priestess in charge, and the fact that *you* came on to *me* when all I meant to do was cuddle and sleep, *my mom is dead, Stark.* Nyx let me see her enter the Otherworld. As of right now I don't know how or why that happened. I'm trying like hell to act semi-normal. I haven't even talked to my grandma yet."

"That's right, you haven't. I told you that you should have called her right away—or at least called your mom. What if it was all just a dream?"

I looked at Stark in utter disbelief, struggling to keep my voice and my emotions under control. "You are the one person in this world who should understand better than anyone else that I can tell the difference between *really* seeing the Otherworld and dreaming it."

"Yeah, I know, but—"

"But are you saying I should have gone through all of that and not disturbed your precious sleep? Well, except to have sex with you!"

I clamped my mouth shut and tried to look normal when I saw Aphrodite turn around and glance back at me with a question mark on her face.

Stark blew out a long breath. "No, that's not what I mean. I'm sorry, Z." Then he took my hand in his. "Seriously. I'm sounding like a jerk."

"Yeah, you are," I said.

"Sorry, again," he said, and then he butted my shoulder with his. "Can we rewind this conversation?"

"Yeah," I said.

"Here goes—I'm tired and it's making me stupid. And about your mom, we don't know what really happened and I think it's freaking both of us out. But no matter what I love you, even if I'm a jerk. Okay? Better?"

"Okay. Yeah. Better," I said.

Still letting him hold my hand I looked out of the window as we took the left on Fifteenth Street, passed Gumpy's Garden, which always made the air smell like piñon wood, and traveled down

Cherry Street. By the time we were on Utica, and passing Twenty-first, I was completely distracted by worry about my mom and my grandma—and wondering if maybe Stark could be right to question what I thought had been my vision. I mean—I hadn't heard from Grandma. What if it had all been a bad dream . . .

"It's always so pretty." Damien's voice drifted back from the front seat he'd automatically chosen as his own. "When you look at it from here, it's so hard to believe that such horrible, heartbreaking things could happen there."

I heard the sob in his voice, squeezed Stark's hand once before letting it go, and then lurched up the aisle to sit beside Damien.

"Hey," I said, sliding my arm through his. "You have to remember that wonderful, heartmaking things happen there, too. Don't ever forget that's where you met Jack and fell in love with him."

Damien stared at me and I thought he looked sad but really, really wise.

"How are you doing without Heath?"

"I miss him," I said honestly. Then something made me add, "But I don't want to be like Dragon, eaten up by sadness."

"Me, either," Damien said softly. "Even though sometimes it's hard not to be."

"It hasn't been very long."

Clamping his lips tightly together, as if to keep himself from crying, he nodded his head.

"You'll get through this," I said. "And so will I. We will. Together," I said firmly.

Then we were going through the iron gate that had the crescent moon crest on the middle of it, and driving around to the side entrance of the school.

"School Council Meeting begins at seven thirty," said the Son of Erebus Warrior as the bus came to a halt. "Classes begin at eight o'clock sharp, just like they should."

"Thank you," I said to him like he'd actually been friendly (or at least respectful). Then I glanced at my phone: 7:20 P.M. Ten minutes until the meeting and forty before school started. I stood up and looked back at the group of obviously nervous kids.

"Okay," I said. "Just go to your old homerooms and wait there for what to do next. Stevie Rae, Stark and I are going to the Council Meeting and, as they'd say on the Isle of Skye, get Rephaim's and your permanent schedules sorted."

"How 'bout me? Ain't I comin' to the Meeting?" Kramisha asked. "It's usually borin', but I bet today it'll be better than usual."

"You're right," I said. "It's about time they started to automatically include you, along with Stevie Rae and me."

"Where do I go?" Rephaim asked from the back of the bus.

I was thinking, trying to figure out where the heck he should go when Damien stood up beside me. "You can come with me—at least for today. If that's okay with Zoey and Stevie Rae."

I smiled at Damien. I don't think I'd ever been so proud of him. Everyone would be worried about him and handling him like he could break down into hysteria at any second, so if he latched onto Rephaim, no way would anyone question him—they'd be too scared of upsetting Damien.

"Thank you," I said.

"That's a real good idea, Damien," Stevie Rae said.

"All right. Try to act normal," I said. "And I'll see you guys back here after school."

"My first hour was Spells and Rituals," I heard Aphrodite mutter to Darius. "And there's that new vamp teaching it who looks like she's twelve. This should be fun."

"Remember," Stevie Rae said, giving Aphrodite a hard look she totally ignored, *"be nice."*

We filed off the bus. I could see how difficult it was for Stevie Rae to let Rephaim go with Damien. We didn't really know what he could be walking into, but we did understand that the chances of him being accepted and treated like the normal kid he longed to be were slim to none.

When Stevie Rae, Stark, and Kramisha and I were alone I said, "Ready to enter the lion's den?"

"I'm thinkin' it's more like headin' into a nasty wasp nest," Kramisha said. "But I'm ready."

"Me, too. Let's cowboy up and get this done."

"Deal," I said.

"Deal," they repeated.

And we walked into a future that was already making my stomach clench and feel like a raging IBS episode was going to hit me at any moment.

Ah, hell.

CHAPTER THREE

Kalona

He didn't have to fly long to find his sons. Kalona followed the thread that connected him to his offspring. *My loyal children,* he thought as he circled the tree-covered rolling hills of the less populated and heavily wooded land that was just a short distance southwest of Tulsa. At the very topmost part of the highest of the ridges Kalona dropped from the sky, easily navigating between the thick, winter nude branches to stand in the middle of a small clearing. Around him, built into the trees themselves, were three wooden structures, crude but sturdily made. Kalona's sharp gaze saw into the windows of the structures where scarlet orbs glowed in his direction.

He opened his arms. "Yes, my sons, I have returned!" The sound of wings was balm to his soul. They burst from the raised shacks and knelt around him, bowing low and respectfully. Kalona counted them—seven.

"Where are the others?"

All of the Raven Mockers stirred restlessly, but only one face tilted up to meet his gaze and only one hissing voice responded.

"Wessst hiding. Lossst in the land."

Kalona studied his son, Nisroc, cataloguing the differences between this Raven Mocker and the one who used to be his favorite child. Nisroc was nearly as evolved as Rephaim. His speech was almost human. His mind was almost sharp. But it had been that *almost,* that fine line between them, that had made Rephaim the son upon which Kalona had depended and not Nisroc.

Kalona clenched and unclenched his jaw. He had been foolish to lavish such attention on Rephaim alone. He had many sons from which to choose and to show favor. It was Rephaim who had lost when he'd chosen to leave. Rephaim had but one father, and he would find poor substitute in an absent goddess and a vampyre who could never truly love him. "It is good that you are here," Kalona said, cutting off thoughts of his absent son. "But I would have preferred that all of you stayed together and awaited my return."

"Hold them, I could not," Nisroc said. "Rephaim dead—"

"Rephaim is not dead!" Kalona snapped, causing Nisroc to shudder and bow his head. The winged immortal paused and regained control of his temper before he continued. "Though it would be better for him if he were dead."

"Father?"

"He has chosen to serve the red vampyre Priestess and her Goddess."

The group of Raven Mockers hissed and cringed as if he had struck them.

"Posssible? How?" Nisroc said.

"It is possible because of females, and their manipulations," Kalona said darkly. He knew all too well how one could fall prey to them. He'd even been brought low by . . .

In sudden realization, the immortal blinked and spoke, more to himself than his son, "But their manipulations do not last!" He shook his head and almost smiled. "Why did I not consider it sooner? Rephaim will tire of being the Red One's pet, and when he does he will realize what a mistake he has made—a mistake that is not entirely his and his alone. The Red One manipulated him, poisoned him, turned him against me. But it is only temporary! When she rejects him, because ultimately she will, he will leave the House of Night to return to my—"

Kalona broke off his words, deciding quickly. "Nisroc, take two of your brothers with you. Return to the House of Night. Watch. Be vigilant. Observe Rephaim and the Red One. When opportunity arises speak to him. Tell him that even though he has made this terrible mistake and turned from me . . ." Kalona paused, clenching and unclenching his jaw, utterly uncomfortable with the sadness and loneliness that washed over him whenever he thought too long about Rephaim's choice. The winged immortal ordered his thoughts, commanded his feelings, and continued giving Nisroc direction. "Tell Rephaim that even though his misguided choice was to leave me, there is still a place awaiting him at my side, *but* that place would be better served if he remained at the House of Night, even after he wants to depart."

"He spiesss!" Nisroc said, and the other Raven Mockers mirrored his excitement with their distinctive croaks.

"He does, but at the moment he may not know he spies," Kalona said. Then he added, "You understand, Nisroc? You are to watch him. To remain unseen by all except Rephaim."

"Not to kill vampyresss?"

"Not unless you are threatened—then do as you will, without being taken *or killing any High Priestess*," Kalona said slowly and distinctly. "It is never wise to needlessly provoke a goddess, so Nyx's High Priestesses are not to be killed." He frowned at his son, remembering his other child who had almost killed Zoey Redbird not long ago—and who had died for it. "Do you understand my command, Nisroc?"

"Yesss. Tell him I will. Rephaim to watch. Rephaim to ssspy."

"Do so, and return before dawn lightens the sky. Fly high. Fly fast. Fly quietly. Make yourselves like the night wind."

"Yesss, Father."

Kalona glanced around, nodding at the thickness of the surrounding woodland, and appreciating the fact that his children had found a high, isolated spot in which to nest.

"Humans, they do not come here?" he asked.

"Only huntersss, and they no more," Nisroc said.

Kalona raised his brows. "You killed humans?"

"Yesss. Two." Nisroc moved, agitated and excited. "Against rock we threw them." He pointed a little way ahead of them and, curious, Kalona strode forward to look down on the steep side of the ridge where the massive power lines that carried electric magick for the modern world stretched before him. The humans had cleared the area surrounding the tall pylons so that the land fell away from him in a wide ribbon that stretched to the horizon. The clearing had left exposed jagged outcroppings of huge chunks of Oklahoma sandstone, clean and lethal and jutting toward the sky.

"Excellent," Kalona said, nodding in appreciation. "You made it look like an accident. That was well done." Then he turned back to the clearing and the Raven Mockers who clustered there with all of their attention focused solely on him. "This place is well chosen. I want all of my sons around me here. Nisroc, go to the Tulsa House of Night. Do my bidding. The rest of you fly to the west. Call to your brothers—call them here to me. Here we will wait. Here we will watch. Here we will make ready."

"Make ready? For what, Father?" Nisroc asked, cocking his head.

Kalona thought about how his body had been entrapped and his soul ripped from him and sent to the Otherworld. He thought about how after he'd returned she'd lashed him, enslaved him, and treated him as if he'd been her property to command

"We make ready for Neferet's destruction," he said.

Rephaim

Everyone looked at him with suspicion. Rephaim hated it, but he understood it. He'd been an enemy. He'd killed one of their own. He'd been a monster.

The truth was he could still be a monster.

As third hour began and a professor who called herself Penthasilea read from and then spoke about a book written by an ancient vampyre named Ray Bradbury entitled *Fahrenheit 451*, and the importance of the freedoms of thought and expression, Rephaim tried to school his new human features into a semblance of attention and interest, but his mind kept slipping away. He wanted to listen to the professor and have nothing more to worry about than what she called "deciphering symbolism," but the change from boy to raven obsessed him.

It had been as painful and terrifying as it had been thrilling.

And he remembered almost nothing of what had happened to him after it.

Image and sensation were all that remained with him from the day and his transformation into a raven.

Stevie Rae had gone with him up from the deep, earthen tunnels to the tree nearest the depot—the one that, not so long ago, had served as an escape route for them from the blistering sun.

"Go back inside now. Dawn is breaking," he'd said to her, touching her cheek gently.

"I don't wanna leave you," she said, throwing her arms around him and hugging him close.

He'd only allowed himself to return the embrace for a moment, then he'd gently unwound her from around him, and guided her firmly back to the shadowed, grated entrance to the basement.

"Go below. You're exhausted. You need to sleep."

"I'm gonna watch until you're, uh, you know. *A bird.*"

She'd whispered the last part as if not saying it aloud would change whether it was so. It was probably foolish, but it made him smile.

"It does not matter whether you say it or not. It's going to happen."

She'd sighed. "I know. But I still don't wanna leave you." Stevie Rae had reached forward, out into the lightening morning, and taken his hand. "I want you to know I'm here for you."

"I do not believe a bird knows very much of the human world," he'd said because he hadn't known what else to say.

"You're not gonna be just any bird. You're gonna turn into a raven. And I'm not a human. I'm a vampyre. A red one. Plus, if I don't stay here how are you gonna know what to come back to?"

He'd heard a sob in her voice that had made his heart ache.

Rephaim kissed her hand. "I'll know. I give you my oath. I'll always find my way home to you." He'd been about to give her a little shove through the entry to the basement when a sickening pain had torn through his body.

Looking back on it he realized he should have expected it. How could it not be painful to change form from a human boy to a raven?

But his world had been filled with Stevie Rae and the simple but complete joy of taking her in his arms, kissing her, holding her close . . .

He'd not spent time considering the beast.

At least he'd be prepared next time.

The pain had ripped him. He'd heard Stevie Rae's scream echo his own. His last human thought had been worry for her. His last human sight had been of her crying and shaking her head back and forth. She'd reached for him as animal had completely replaced human. He remembered spreading his wings as if he was stretching after being imprisoned in a tiny cell. Or a cage. And flying.

He remembered flying.

At sunset he'd found himself cold and naked beneath the same tree beside the depot. He'd just pulled on his clothes that had been left neatly folded for him on a little stool when Stevie Rae burst from the basement.

With no hesitation she'd hurled herself into his arms.

"Are you okay? Really? Are you okay?" she kept repeating as she'd studied him and felt his arms as if searching for broken bones.

"I am well," he'd assured her. It was then he'd realized she was crying. He cupped her face in his hands and said, "What is it? Why do you weep?"

"It hurt you so bad. You screamed like it was killing you."

"No," he'd lied. "It wasn't so bad. It was just surprising."

"Really?"

He'd smiled—*how he loved to smile*—and pulled her into his arms, kissing her blond curls and reassuring her. "Really."

"Rephaim?"

Rephaim was wrenched back to the present by the sound of his name being called by the professor.

"Yes?" he responded with his own questioning tone.

She didn't smile at him, but she also didn't taunt or admonish him. She simply said, "I asked what you believe the quote on page seven means. The one where Montag says Clarisse's face has a light that is like a 'fragile milk crystal' and the 'strangely comfortable and rare and gently flattering light of the candle.' What do you think Bradbury is trying to say about Clarisse with these descriptions?"

Rephaim was absolutely astounded. A professor was asking him a question. *As if he was just another daydreaming fledgling—normal— the same—accepted.* Feeling nervous and completely exposed he opened his mouth and blurted the first thing that came to his mind.

"I think he's trying to say this girl is unique. He recognizes how special she is, and he values her."

Professor Penthasilea's brows lifted and for an awful heartbeat Rephaim thought she might ridicule him.

"That is an interesting answer, Rephaim. Perhaps if you kept your mind more on the book and less on other things, your answers would go from interesting to incredible," she remarked in a dry, matter-of-fact voice.

"Th-thank you," Rephaim stuttered, his face feeling warm.

Penthasilea nodded her head slightly in acknowledgment before turning to a student sitting more toward the front of the class and asking, "What about her final question to him in this scene: 'Are you happy?' What significance does that have?"

"Good job," Damien whispered from his desk beside Rephaim.

Rephaim couldn't speak. He only nodded and tried to understand the sudden lightness of spirit he felt.

"You know what happens to her? This special girl?" The whisper came from the fledgling sitting directly in front of Rephaim. He was a short, muscular male with a strong profile. Rephaim could easily see the disdain in his face as he glanced at him over his shoulder.

Rephaim shook his head. No, he did not know.

"She's killed because of him."

Rephaim felt as if he'd been kicked in his gut.

"Drew, did you have a comment about Clarisse?" the professor asked, raising her brows again.

Drew slumped nonchalantly forward and lifted one shoulder. "No, ma'am. I was just givin' the birdboy some insight to the future." He paused and glanced over his shoulder before saying, "The future of the book, that is."

"Rephaim." The professor spoke his name in a voice that had gone hard. Rephaim was surprised to feel the power of it against his skin. "In my classroom all fledglings are equal. All are called by their correct names. His is Rephaim."

"Professor P, he's no fledgling," Drew said.

The professor's hand came down on the top of her podium and the entire room vibrated with sound and energy. "He is *here*. As long as he's here, in my classroom, he will be treated as any other fledgling."

"Yes, ma'am," Drew said, bowing his head respectfully.

"Good. Now that that is straight let's discuss the creative project you'll be doing for me. I want you to bring alive your choice of one of the many symbolic elements Bradbury uses in this wonderful book . . ."

Rephaim held very still as the class's attention was pulled from him and the Drew fledgling back to the book. *She's killed because of him* was playing round and round inside his mind. Drew's meaning was clear. He hadn't been speaking of a character in a book. He'd meant Stevie Rae—that she was going to be killed because of him.

Never. Not as long as he drew breath would he allow anything or anyone to harm his Stevie Rae.

When the bell rang to release them from class, Drew met Rephaim's gaze with unflinching hatred.

Rephaim had to hold himself back from attacking him. *Enemy!* his old nature shrieked. *Destroy him!* But Rephaim ground his jaw and returned Drew's gaze without blinking as the fledgling brushed roughly past him.

And it wasn't just Drew's eyes that stared at him with hatred. *All* of them were sending him glances that ranged from hostile to horrified to frightened.

"Hey," Damien said, walking out of the classroom with him. "Don't let Drew bother you. He used to have a thing for Stevie Rae. He's just jealous."

Rephaim nodded and waited until they were outside and had drawn beyond hearing distance of the rest of the students. Then, quietly, he said, "It isn't just Drew. It's all of them. They hate me."

Damien motioned for him to follow him a little way off the path, then he stopped and said, "You knew it wouldn't be easy."

"That is true. I just—" Rephaim stopped himself and shook his head. "No. It is simply true. I knew it would be a difficult thing for others to accept me." He met Damien's gaze. The fledgling looked haggard. Grief had aged him. His eyes were red and puffy. He'd lost the love of his life, yet here he was showing Rephaim kindness. "Thank you, Damien," he said.

Damien almost smiled. "For telling you this wouldn't be easy?"

"No, for showing me kindness."

"Stevie Rae is my friend. The kindness I show is for her."

"Then you are a remarkable friend," Rephaim said.

"If you really are the boy Stevie Rae thinks you are, you'll find that when you're on the side of the Goddess, you'll make a lot of remarkable friends."

"I am on the side of the Goddess," Rephaim said.

"Rephaim, if I didn't believe that I wouldn't be helping you, no matter how much I care about Stevie Rae," Damien said.

Rephaim nodded. "That's fair."

"Hey, Damien!" One of the red fledglings, an unusually small boy, hurried up to them, giving Rephaim a look, then adding a quick, "Hey, Rephaim."

"Hi, Ant," Damien said.

Rephaim nodded, uncomfortable with the whole greeting process.

"I heard you had fencing this hour. Me, too!"

"I do," Damien said. "Rephaim and I were just—" He paused and Rephaim watched several emotions pass his face, ending with embarrassed. He sighed heavily before saying, "Um, Rephaim, Dragon Lankford is the fencing professor."

Then Rephaim understood.

"That's, uh, not good," Ant said.

"He may still be at the school Council Meeting," Damien said hopefully.

"I think it best that I stay here, whether Dragon is absent or not. If I come with you it will only cause . . ." Rephaim's voice ran out because all he could think of were words like: chaos, trouble, and disaster.

"Unpleasantness." Damien filled in the silence for him. "It would probably cause unpleasantness. Maybe you should skip fencing for today."

"Sounds smart," Ant said.

"I'll wait for you." Rephaim motioned vaguely to the tree-filled area around them. They weren't far from one of the school walls where, just inside the stone façade there was a particularly large oak under which sat a wrought iron bench. "I'll be sitting there."

"Okay, I'll come by and get you after class. The next hour is Spanish. Professor Garmy is nice. You'll like her," Damien said as he and Ant started toward the field house.

Rephaim nodded and waved and made himself smile because Damien kept glancing worriedly over his shoulder at him. When the two fledglings were finally out of sight, Rephaim walked to the bench and sat heavily down.

He was glad for the time alone, when he could be unguarded— could let his shoulders slump and not worry about having others stare at him. He felt like such an outlander! What had he been thinking when he'd said he wanted to be normal, to go to school like everyone else? He wasn't like everyone else.

But she loves me. Me. Just as I am, Rephaim reminded himself, and thinking it made him feel a little better—a little lighter of spirit.

Then, because he was alone, he said it aloud.

"I am Rephaim, and Stevie Rae loves me just the way I am."

"Rephaim! No!"

The whispery, semi-human voice came from the branches of the oak. With a terrible sense of dread Rephaim looked up to see three Raven Mockers, three of his brothers, perched there staring down at him in shock and disbelief.

CHAPTER FOUR

Zoey

Okay, I know I'm a teenager and all, but I suck at using Skype. Actually, I'm kinda moronic about technology in general. Casting a circle—yep. Communing with any of the five elements—definitely. Figuring out how to synch my iPhone with a new computer—uh, probably not. Just thinking about tweeting gave me a headache and made me really miss Jack.

"Here, it ain't that hard. You just gotta click that." Kramisha reached over my shoulder and snagged the magic mouse. "And then that, and that's it. We's all on Skype and the camera's workin' now."

I looked up to see Stevie Rae and everyone else, including Dragon, Lenobia, and Erik all gawking at me.

Stevie Rae, at least, grinned and mouthed a quick, *"Easy-peasy."*

"What exactly is the point behind—" Dragon began, but Neferet's entrance to the Council Room cut him off. And, thankfully, it was at that moment that the commanding voice of the Leader of the Vampyre High Council carried clear and strong through Damien's computer.

"Merry meet, Zoey Redbird," Duantia said. "I am pleased to speak with you again."

I fisted my hand over my heart and bowed respectfully. "Merry meet, Duantia. Thank you for making time for this call."

"Merry meet, Duantia," Neferet said, stepping up beside me and bowing formally. I saw her shoot a quick, questioning look at Dragon before she smiled silkily and continued. "I must apologize. I knew nothing about this call. I was only expecting a simple school Council

Meeting." Then she skewered me with her emerald eyes. "Are you responsible for this, Zoey?"

"Yeah, definitely. I would have told you earlier, but you just now got here," I said, smiling and sounding super cheerful. Before Neferet could respond I turned my attention to Duantia. "I wanted to make sure the High Council heard all the details about Nyx's amazing appearance at the school yesterday and," I paused, nodding to Neferet as if I was including her, "I knew Neferet would be eager to share with you as well."

"Actually, we know very little, which is one of the reasons I was looking forward to this call." Duantia looked from me to Neferet. "I tried to contact you during the day, after I instructed Dragon to allow the red fledglings and Zoey's group to begin attending classes today, but I could not reach you, High Priestess."

I could feel Neferet bristle, but she only said, "I was secluded in deep prayer."

"All the more reason for this call," Duantia said.

"What Nyx did was a miracle." I gestured for Stevie Rae to come into camera range. "This is Stevie Rae, the first Red High Priestess."

Stevie Rae fisted her hand over her heart and bowed deeply. "I'm real pleased to meet you, ma'am."

"Merry meet, Stevie Rae. I have heard much of you and the red fledglings. And, of course, I have already met the Red Warrior, Stark. Nyx is, indeed, generous with her miracles."

"Um, thank you, but, well, us bein' red and all isn't the miracle." Stevie Rae glanced at me and added, "Well, at least it's not the miracle Zoey's talkin' 'bout." She cleared her throat and then said, "Nyx's miracle has to do with my Consort, Rephaim."

Duantia's eyes widened. "Is that not the name of one of the creatures called Raven Mocker?"

"Yes." Dragon's voice was as hard as his face. "It is the name of the creature who killed my Anastasia."

"I do not understand," Duantia said. "How could that abomination be called Consort?"

Quickly, before Neferet could chime in something awful I started babbling, "Rephaim used to be a Raven Mocker, and Dragon is right, back then he did kill Anastasia." I glanced up at Dragon, but it was real hard to meet his eyes. "Rephaim asked Nyx's forgiveness for that."

"And for everything bad he'd done when he was Kalona's son," Stevie Rae added.

"Blanket forgiveness is—"

Neferet began, but I cut her off saying, "Blanket forgiveness is a gift that can be given by our Goddess, which is exactly what she did last night," I said. Then I looked at Stevie Rae. "Tell the High Council Leader what you did."

Stevie Rae nodded and swallowed hard, then she said, "A few weeks ago I found Rephaim almost dead. He'd been shot from the sky. I didn't turn him in." She looked from the computer screen and Duantia up to Dragon and said pleadingly, "I didn't mean to hurt anyone or do anythin' wrong."

"That *abomination* killed my mate," Dragon said. "The same night he was shot from the sky and should have died."

"Professor Lankford, please allow the Red High Priestess to continue her confession," Duantia said.

I saw Dragon's jaw clench and his lip lift slightly in a sneer, but Stevie Rae's words drew my attention back to her.

"Dragon's right. Rephaim would have died that night if I hadn't saved him. I didn't tell anyone about him. Well, except my momma, and that was later. Anyway, I took care of him instead. I saved his life. And then he saved my life in return—twice. Once from the white bull of Darkness."

"He faced Darkness for you?" Duantia sounded shocked.

"Yes."

"Actually, he turned away from Darkness for her." I took up the story. "And last night he asked forgiveness from Nyx and pledged himself to her path."

"Then the Goddess made him a boy!" Stevie Rae said with such enthusiasm that even Duantia's lips twitched up in a smile.

"Only from sunset to sunrise," Neferet added, in a throw-cold-water-on-the-moment voice. "During the day he is condemned to be a raven—a beast—with no memory of his humanity."

"That was his consequence for the bad stuff in his past," Stevie Rae explained.

"And now, during the time he's a boy, Rephaim wants to come to school like any other fledgling," I said.

"Remarkable," Duantia said.

"The creature does not belong at this school," Dragon said.

"The *creature* isn't at this school," I said. "The *boy* is. The same boy Nyx forgave. The same boy Stevie Rae has chosen as her Consort. The same boy who tried to swear himself into your service."

"Dragon, you rejected him?" Duantia asked.

"I did," Dragon said tightly.

"And that is why I expelled them all," Neferet said in a calm, reasonable, *adult* voice. "My Sword Master cannot tolerate his presence, and rightly so. When Zoey's group decided to turn their allegiance from us to Stevie Rae and the Raven Mocker I saw no choice except that they all had to go."

"He isn't a Raven Mocker anymore." Stevie Rae sounded totally pissed-off.

"And yet he is still the being who murdered my mate." Dragon's voice was a lash.

"Hold!" Duantia's command shot from the computer. Even from thousands of miles away and through Skype, the power in her voice was a tangible presence in the room. "Neferet, let me be certain that I am absolutely clear about last night's events. Our Goddess, Nyx, appeared at your House of Night and forgave the Raven Mocker, Rephaim, and then gifted him with the form of a human boy during the night, and as penance cursed him with a bestial form of a raven during the day?"

"Yes," Neferet said.

Duantia shook her head slowly. "Neferet, there is a part of me—the remnants of a very young me, mind you—that understands your response to such unusual events, though you were mistaken. Simply put, you cannot expel a group of fledglings who have done nothing more than stand by their friends. Especially not *this* group of fledglings," Duantia said. "*This* group has been far too goddess-touched to be cast away."

"That kinda brings up the second thing I need to talk to you about," I said. "Because of the differences between red fledglings and regular fledglings, it's really better that they were expelled." I frowned. "Wait, that didn't come out right."

"What she means is we can't rest right unless we're underground," Stevie Rae explained for me. "And there isn't much underground here."

"So during daylight they'd like to stay in the tunnels under the Tulsa depot, and at night during the week they'd like to be bussed here for classes. There aren't very many red fledglings in Stevie Rae's group, and except for me no blue fledglings left the school at all, so I'm thinking between me, a Red High Priestess, and two Changed Warriors, we should be able to handle ourselves okay over there." I fixed my face into a giant smile and beamed up at Neferet. "And I know Neferet is such an awesome High Priestess that she'll be able to handle all the changes going on over here."

There was a long silence during which Neferet and I locked gazes. Finally Duantia said, "Neferet, what say you?"

I caught a glimpse of smugness in her expression before Neferet turned to the camera. "After listening to your wisdom, Duantia, I do see that I made my decision too hastily last night. As someone who is, myself, newly forgiven by Nyx, I can only strive to emulate the Goddess's benevolence. She clearly has special plans for Zoey and her group. Perhaps a resting place separate from us would be best. Of course they must still abide by the rules of this House of Night, and acknowledge me as their rightful High Priestess."

"Uh, not necessarily," I said, ignoring Neferet's piercing look and concentrating on Duantia. "The time I spent on Skye with Queen Sgiach really meant a lot to me. She and I got close. Sgiach even said she'd like me to mentor under her, that she would start opening up Skye to the modern world. Right now I can't be on Skye with her, but I'd still like to follow in her footsteps." I drew a deep breath and finished in a rush, "So, I want to officially declare the Tulsa Depot outside of the jurisdiction of the House of Night, like Sgiach has declared Skye." I looked directly at Neferet. "And just like Sgiach, I won't get in your business if you don't get in mine."

"You dare declare yourself a queen?" Neferet sounded stunned.

"Well, I didn't. But Sgiach did and so did her Guardian. Plus, Stark has been accepted as a Guardian. In the Otherworld he had the sword and everything. He's my Warrior, so kinda by default that means I'm being declared a queen. A little one, though," I added.

"This does not feel right to me," Neferet said.

"I agree with Neferet," Dragon said.

I stared at him, trying to telegraph: *Really? Are you really saying you agree with Neferet after all you know about her?* But Dragon looked past me as if he couldn't see me.

"I must consult the High Council on this matter, Zoey Redbird. We do not support the idea of vampyre queens. Vampyres are Priestesses and Warriors and Professors, and the various life paths that spring from those callings. That has long been our tradition."

"But Sgiach is a queen," I insisted. "She has been for centuries. That has to be long enough to be a tradition, too."

"Not a vampyre tradition!" Duantia's raised voice made the little hairs on my arms lift. The Leader of the High Council drew a deep breath, obviously steadying herself, before she continued in a calmer tone. "Sgiach is barely considered vampyre. She has maintained her existence separate from us for many centuries. We have an uneasy truce with her by default. We cannot enter her isle. She will not leave it." Duantia paused and lifted a brow. "Has that changed, Zoey? Is Sgiach planning on leaving Skye?"

"No," I said. "But she did tell me she was going to consider taking in students again."

"Allowing outsiders to come and go from Skye would be extraordinary." The way Duantia said it made me think she didn't believe "extraordinary" was synonymous with "a good thing."

"I believe opening up to outsiders is something we all must do in these changing times," Neferet said.

Everyone stared at her. Even Duantia was speechless.

"Because I feel so strongly about it I have decided to open the doors of my House of Night in the form of some of the more menial jobs, to local humans. I think it wise and responsible, especially in these hard economic times. I hope Sgiach follows suit."

"That is an excellent idea, Neferet," Duantia said. "As you are aware, humans have had a steady presence here on San Clemente Island for the past several centuries." The Vampyre High Priestess smiled. "Since we have become civilized and modern."

"As the Tulsa House of Night would like to become, as well," Neferet said.

"Well, then. That is decided. The Tulsa House of Night will employ local humans. Rephaim, the red fledglings, and Zoey's group of students will attend school at the Tulsa House of Night while resting in the tunnels under the depot during the day. I will make a note to speak to the Tulsa City Council about the purchase of the depot."

"And what of Zoey's status as queen and the depot's allegiance to me and this House of Night?" Neferet asked.

I held my breath.

"As I already ruled, I will consult the full High Council on a matter as serious as a young and gifted fledgling being considered a queen, even if just a queen in training. Until a decision can be made, Zoey Redbird and the Tulsa Depot are to be an extension of the Tulsa House of Night."

"And thus I remain their High Priestess," Neferet said.

Stevie Rae cleared her throat. Our eyes turned to her. "Uh, not to be mean or anything, but if Z's not gonna be called queen, and we have to have a High Priestess, I'm next in line. My red fledglings need someone like them to understand them. And that's me. So, call us a branch of the House of Night if ya want, but if there's a High Priestess over us, then she's gonna be me."

"You make a valid point, young Priestess," Duantia said with no hesitation, which made me wonder if she'd just been waiting for Stevie Rae to object. "Stevie Rae, until the matter of Zoey Redbird's standing is settled, you are acting High Priestess of the depot extension of the Tulsa House of Night."

"Thank you, ma'am," Stevie Rae said. "And I didn't mean to sound disrespectful."

Duantia's sharp features softened as she smiled. "You did not sound disrespectful. You sounded like a High Priestess. Now, if there are no further items of business, I will adjourn to update the other Council Members on these events and decisions."

"I'm done," I said.

"Yep, me, too," Stevie Rae said.

"I believe what we have already accomplished is quite enough for one day," Neferet said.

"Excellent. Then I bid you farewell, and wish you all to blessed be."

The computer made the weird Skype cutoff noise and the screen went blank.

"Well, that was quite interesting," Lenobia said.

I realized after she'd spoken that she hadn't said anything for the entire Skype call. It made me wonder about her. I mean, she'd clearly been on my side before against Neferet, but then again, so had Dragon.

"Yes, interesting is one word to describe what that was," Neferet said.

"Congratulations, High Priestess," I said to Stevie Rae.

"Yeah, congrats," Erik said.

"You was already our High Priestess, but it's nice they made it official," Kramisha said.

"I don't want him in my class." Dragon spoke abruptly, totally cutting through the well-wishing.

I started to open my mouth to defend Rephaim's right to go to fencing class or whatever, even though it still felt really weird to be defending Rephaim at all, but Stevie Rae's response surprised and silenced me.

"I think you're right. I know this is hard for you, Dragon. How 'bout I ask Darius and Stark to teach some extra classes on knife stuff and whatnot? Rephaim can take those classes."

"That is actually a good idea," Lenobia said. "As every fledgling must take some sort of self-defense class, with the unexpected addition of the red fledglings your classes will be overfilled."

"Yeah, we was supposed to be dead. Bein' undead will screw up class size for sure," Kramisha said.

Neferet sighed heavily and then said, "Every fledgling must take a self-defense class because of the attack of the Raven Mockers. Am I the only one who sees the terrible irony in what all of you are saying?"

"I see it—and more," Dragon said.

"And I see that you keep stirrin' the shit pot," Stevie Rae said. She'd turned and was standing toe-to-toe with Neferet. She didn't blink. She didn't back down. My BFF looked tough and strong and way older than her years.

Stevie Rae looked like a High Priestess.

A High Priestess who was making dangerous enemies.

"Duantia decided Rephaim and the rest of us can stay," I said as I stood up, stepping between Stevie Rae and Neferet. "I think what we need to do is to figure out a way we can do that without causing a bunch of stress and trouble." I looked at Dragon, trying to find within his anger-filled eyes the wise, kind Sword Master I'd known. "We've all had enough of that to last us a long time, don't you think?"

"I'll be in the field house with the normal fledglings," Dragon said and then he pushed through the room.

"Stevie Rae, you can tell Stark and Darius that they may hold class in the stables," Lenobia said.

"I'm glad to hear you're in such an accommodating mood, Professor Lenobia," Neferet said. "The first of the humans I am hiring will be a stable hand to aid you with all of the—" she paused and her gaze cut to Stevie Rae, Kramisha, and me. "*Sewage* in the stables."

"Manure." Lenobia's reply was swift. "I don't have sewage in my stables. I have manure. And I don't need any help with it."

"Ah, but you will accept the help, because it is the right thing to do, and because the High Council just endorsed it. Won't you?"

"I will do what I believe is right."

"Then you will do as I expected." Neferet turned a dismissive back to Lenobia. "Zoey and Stevie Rae, the red fledglings should resume the class schedule they were following before they died," she said matter-of-factly. "And you two should join them. Whether you're abnormally Changed," she flicked her fingers at Stevie Rae, "or just abnormal fledglings," she shifted her attention to Kramisha and me, "it matters little. You need to be in class. You're all much too young to be truly interesting without being better educated. Second hour should be underway by now. Get to class. This Council Meeting is now adjourned."

Without so much as a "blessed be" she swept from the room.

"She is one hot mess," Kramisha said.

"Crazy times ten," Stevie Rae said.

"But Neferet is a known entity. We understand that when we're dealing with her, we're dealing with a High Priestess who has gone wrong and who is utterly mad," Lenobia said slowly. "It's Dragon that I'm most worried about."

"Then you are with us?" I asked the Horse Mistress.

Lenobia's gray eyes met mine. "I told you once that I've battled evil. I bear the scars of that encounter, both physically and emotionally, and I will never allow evil and Darkness to decimate my life again. I'm with you," she nodded in turn to Stevie Rae and Kramisha, "and you and you because you're on the side of the Goddess." Then she turned to Erik, who was standing, but who hadn't made a move to leave the room. "And where are you in all of this?"

"I'm the Tulsa House of Night's Tracker."

"We know that, but what side does that put you on?" Stevie Rae asked.

"I'm on the side that Marks kids and changes their destinies." Erik evaded.

"Erik, someday you're gonna have to take a stand," I told him.

"Hey, just because I'm not battling toe-to-toe with Neferet doesn't mean I haven't taken a stand."

"No, it just means it's a weak one," Stevie Rae said.

"Whatever! You don't know everything, Stevie Rae." Erik stormed from the room.

Kramisha snorted. "That is a waste of one pretty boy."

It made me sad, but I couldn't disagree with her.

"I'll begin sectioning off space in the arena for Warrior classes," Lenobia said. "If you round up the two Warriors and let them know they're going to be professors, or at least temporary professors."

"Shouldn't be hard to find them," I said. "Stark and Darius are probably in the field house playing with their swords."

"I'll come with you," Stevie Rae said.

"I guess I'll go to second hour," Kramisha said with a heavy sigh.

As Stevie Rae and I left the room, she snagged my arm and slowed me down so that we were walking by ourselves. "Hey, you know that just 'cause the High Council and them are callin' me the High Priestess at the depot, it doesn't mean that I want to be the boss of you or anythin' like that."

I blinked in surprise at her. "Yeah, of course I know that. And anyway, you're a great High Priestess, and that means you won't be a bossy pain in the butt."

She didn't laugh like I thought she would. Instead she tugged on one of her curls, a definite sign she was stressing. "Okay, that's nice to say and all, but I've only been a High Priestess for, like, two seconds. I need to be sure you'll help me."

I hooked her arm with mine and bumped shoulders with her. "You can always be sure of me. You know that."

"Even after Rephaim?"

"Even after Loren and Kalona and Stark?" I countered with.

She started to grin. "You always gotta one-up me, don't ya?"

"Sadly, I think I three-uped you," I said, which did make her laugh, but made me sigh.

We left the part of the House of Night that held the tower-like media center and took a left on the sidewalk that wound around to the field house and stables. It was a cold night, but it was super clear. The sky was filled with stars, which were really easy to see through the winter branches of the big oaks that dotted the campus grounds.

"So, he's cute, huh?"

I pretended clueless. "Who? Stark? Definitely."

She knocked her shoulder into mine. "I'm talkin' 'bout Rephaim."

"Oh, *him*. Yeah, I guess he's okay." I hesitated, and almost didn't ask, but then I decided to go ahead. I mean, we were BFFs. And BFFs could ask each other anything. "So, did you see him turn into a bird?"

I could feel the tension that entered her body, but she sounded almost normal when she said, "Yeah, I did."

"What was it like?"

"Awful."

"Did he, uh, stay around? Or did he fly right off?" I couldn't help it. I was totally, morbidly, car-wreck curious.

"Flew right off. But as soon as the sun set he came back. He says he'll always find his way back to me."

"Then he will," I said, hating to hear the worry in her voice.

"I love him, Z. He really is good. I promise."

I was opening my mouth to tell her I believed her when a shout interrupted me. For a second I didn't understand what the voice was saying, all I reacted to was the danger in it. Stevie Rae understood, though.

"Oh, no! It's Dragon! He's calling Warriors to him!"

She dropped my arm and began to run toward Dragon's voice. With a terrible sense of foreboding, I sprinted after her.

CHAPTER FIVE

Rephaim

"Why are you here?!" Rephaim shouted at the three Raven Mockers perched above him. He looked hastily around. If he'd had time he would have breathed a sigh of relief that this part of the campus remained empty; all the fledglings had found their way to second-hour classes. "You must go before anyone sees you," he said in a much quieter voice.

"Rephaim? How?"

Though there were three Raven Mockers in the tree, only one of them was actually speaking. Of course Rephaim recognized him instantly as Nisroc, one of the more human-like of his brothers.

"I chose the path of Nyx. The Goddess forgave and accepted me, and when she did she changed my form to completely human." Rephaim wasn't sure why he didn't add "at night." What he was sure of was that anything he told Nisroc would be reported directly back to his father.

"Forgivenessss? Why?"

Rephaim stared at his brother, almost overwhelmed by pity. *He doesn't realize there is any other way than that which our father leads him, and he doesn't understand that what he does in Kalona's name is wrong.*

"Nisroc, when we—" Rephaim paused. *No,* he thought, *I can only speak for myself.* "When *I* harmed others, when I killed and raped and took whatever I wished simply because I could—that was wrong."

Nisroc cocked his head back and forth. His other brothers, two of the nameless, bestial horde that did their father's bidding, hissed softly, disturbed but not high enough evolved to comprehend why.

Finally his brother said, "Father'sss command. Not wrong."

Rephaim shook his head. "Even Father can be wrong." He drew a deep breath and added, "And even you can choose a different path."

The two nameless ones stopped hissing and stared at him in shock. Nisroc narrowed his scarlet colored, human eyes. "She did thisss. The female. As Father sssaid!"

"No one did anything to me. I decided for myself." Then with a start of fear, realization hit him. "Nisroc, the Red One, Stevie Rae, she didn't *make* me do anything. I *chose* her and her Goddess. You can never harm the Red One. Ever. She belongs to me. Do you understand?"

"Yours. High Priestessss to kill we cannot." Nisroc repeated as if by rote, but Rephaim saw the hard, mean glint in his glowing eyes.

"You need to leave. Now," Rephaim said. "You can't let anyone see you, and you can't return."

"First, Father's messsssage." Nisroc dropped from the thick middle branches of the oak, landing in front of Rephaim, followed by the other two Raven Mockers, who flanked him. "By Father's ssside you will be. But here. Watching. Waiting. Ssspying."

Rephaim shook his head again. "No. I will not spy for Father."

"Yesss! As Father willsss!" Nisroc spread his wings, an action mimicked by the other two Raven Mockers. Highly agitated, he bobbed his head and fisted his hands.

Rephaim didn't feel threatened. The physical danger he was in didn't register in his mind. He was too used to his brothers—too used to being one of them. No, it was more than that. Rephaim was too used to being their leader to fear them.

"No," he repeated. "It's not as Father wills for me anymore. I've changed. Inside and outside. Go back to him. Tell him that." Rephaim hesitated and then continued, "Tell him my choice stands."

"Hate you, he will," Nisroc said.

"I know that." Rephaim felt the hurt of it deep inside him.

"Hate you, I will," Nisroc said.

Rephaim frowned. "You don't have to."

"I mussst."

Slowly, Rephaim reached out, offering his forearm to Nisroc in the traditionally respectful greeting and parting gesture between Warriors. "You don't have to. We can part as friends, as brothers."

Nisroc paused, cocking his head side to side. His narrowed eyes relaxed. His aggressive stance shifted. He began to move, to speak, but Rephaim would never know his brother's true intent because at that moment Dragon Lankford's cry of "Sons of Erebus! To me!" shattered the night and the Sword Master descended upon them.

Rephaim experienced an instant of body-numbing panic. He stood frozen in the middle of chaos as his brothers, hissing and snarling, met Dragon's attack. He watched with the terrible, fatalistic knowledge that very soon Warriors would begin spilling from the field house, swords drawn and arrows notched. They would join Dragon and utterly overwhelm his three brothers.

"Dragon, no!" he cried. "They weren't attacking!"

From the midst of battle, Dragon Lankford's voice carried to him. "You are either for or against us! There is no middle ground."

"There *is* middle ground!" Rephaim yelled back, holding his arms wide as if in surrender. "It is where I stand!" He took a step toward Dragon. "They weren't attacking!" he repeated. "Nisroc, brothers, stop fighting!"

Rephaim believed Nisroc actually hesitated. He was quite certain his brother was listening to him, understanding, wanting to retreat. Then Neferet's voice sliced through the night.

"Aurox! Protect! Destroy!"

Neferet's creature exploded into the scene.

He came from the wall side of the grounds, facing Rephaim. At first he appeared to be human. He had a human male's form, youthful and unmarked as a fledgling or a vampyre. But his movements were too fast to be human. In a blur he struck. Attacking from behind he grasped the closest Raven Mocker by his upraised wings and in a single, horrible motion ripped them from his body.

Over his centuries of existence Rephaim had seen terrible things—he'd committed vile, dark deeds. But somehow seeing from his new, human point of view made the violence he was witnessing more awful. His scream echoed his brother's as the Raven Mocker's body fell to the ground, writhing in agony and spurting blood.

It was then that Aurox began to change. Even though Rephaim watched it happening he could hardly comprehend it.

Its body became bigger, thicker.

It grew horns.

Its fists solidified.

Its skin rippled, shifted, pulsed as if something beneath was trying to come forth.

It bent and, almost gracefully, twisted off his brother's head.

Even Dragon Lankford paused in his attack to stare.

Forcing his mind to think through the shock and horror, Rephaim shouted at Nisroc. "Go! Fly away!"

With a cry of despair, Nisroc, followed by one brother, lifted from the blood-soaked ground.

The transformed creature bellowed and leaped, trying, futilely, to knock them from the sky. When he crashed back to earth, his massive cloven hooves biting into the winter grass, he turned blazing moon-colored eyes on Rephaim.

Wishing he had wings or a weapon, Rephaim crouched defensively and readied himself for the creature's onslaught.

"Rephaim! Watch out!"

He heard her voice and his fear spiked hot and thick as Stevie Rae, followed closely by Zoey, ran toward him.

The creature lowered its head and charged.

Zoey

I was close behind Stevie Rae as we ran up on the fighting. Jeesh, all I can say is that it was disgusting and horrifying and totally confusing.

I could hardly tell what was happening. Two Raven Mockers were screaming and flying away overhead. I could see the headless (eesh!) body of another Raven Mocker twitching and oozing seriously odd-smelling blood at Dragon's feet. Rephaim stood a little away from them, as if he'd been watching but not involved in the fight. Somehow Neferet was there, too, looking super crazy and smiling in a very weird way.

In the middle of the whole thing was a creature that was kinda human and kinda not. The instant I saw him the middle of my chest started to feel hot. I reached up and felt the hard, hot marble circle that hung from a silver chain around my neck. "My seer tone," I muttered to myself. "Why again? Why now?"

As if in answer, my gaze was drawn to the bizarre creature. He had horns and hoofs, but his face was guy-like. His eyes were glowing. He'd been trying to grab a Raven Mocker out of the sky, but when he failed, he turned his attention to Rephaim, lowered his head, and charged.

"Rephaim! Watch out!" Stevie Rae yelled and sprinted toward him. She flung out her arms and I could hear her asking earth to come to her.

"Spirit!" I called, trying to keep up with her. "Strengthen Stevie Rae!" I felt the element respond as it swirled past me into Stevie Rae, along with her own element, earth. Like she was throwing a big ball, she heaved, and a glowing green wall cascaded like reverse waterfall from the earth upward, blocking Rephaim from the charging creature.

The creature hit the green wall and bounced, falling onto his back. Stevie Rae, strong and straight and proud, stood next to Rephaim. She took his hand. She raised her other hand, and when the creature tried to get up she made a smacking motion and said, "No! Stay down." A wave of glowing green washed against him, pinning him to the ground.

"Enough!" Neferet said, marching over to the creature. "Aurox is not the enemy here. Free him immediately."

"Not if he's gonna charge Rephaim," Stevie Rae said. She turned to Dragon and asked, "Was Rephaim in league with the Raven Mockers?"

Without even a glance at Rephaim, Dragon said, "He was talking with them, but he did not attack with them."

"*They* did not attack!" Rephaim said. "They were here to see me— nothing more. You attacked them!"

Dragon finally looked at Rephaim. "Raven Mockers are our enemies."

"They're my brothers." Rephaim's voice sounded incredibly sad.

"You're going to have to decide whose side you're on," Dragon said solemnly.

"I have already done that."

"And that is something the Goddess seems to believe as well," Neferet said. "Aurox," she spoke to the creature who was still lying on his back, encased in the power of the earth, "the battle is over. There is no need to protect or attack." She turned her emerald gaze to Stevie Rae. "Now, release him."

"Thank you, earth," Stevie Rae said. "You can go now." With a wave of her hand the green glow evaporated allowing the creature to stand.

Except a creature wasn't what was left standing. A boy stood there—a beautiful, blond boy who had eyes like moonstones and a face like an angel.

"Who's that? And what the hell's going on with all that blood?" Stark's voice, suddenly beside me, made me jump.

"Oh, for shit's sake. It's a dead Raven Mocker," Aphrodite said as she and Darius and what seemed like most of the school crowded around us.

"And it's a very pretty human kid," Kramisha said, giving him a look.

"He's not human," I said, holding onto my seer stone.

"What is he?" Stark asked.

"Old magick," I said as the puzzle pieces in my mind fitted together.

"This time you are correct, Zoey." Neferet stepped up beside the guy and with a flourish announced, "House of Night, this is Aurox—the gift Nyx gave me proving her forgiveness!"

Aurox stepped forward. His strange-colored eyes met mine. Facing the crowd, but looking only at me, he fisted his hand over his heart and bowed.

"No damn way is he a gift from Nyx," Stevie Rae muttered.

For once agreeing with Stevie Rae, Aphrodite snorted.

All I could do was stare. All I could feel was the heat from the seer stone.

"Zoey, what is it?" Stark said softly.

I didn't answer Stark. Instead I forced my gaze from Aurox and faced Neferet. "Where did he really come from?" My voice was hard and strong, but I felt like my stomach was trying to turn inside out.

Somewhere in the back of my mind I could hear the buzz and whispers of the kids around me, and I knew forcing a confrontation with Neferet here and now wasn't smart. But I couldn't stop myself. Neferet was lying about this Aurox thing, and for some reason that was all that mattered to me.

"I already told you where he came from. And, Zoey, I must say this is exactly why you need to be back in school, attending class and refocusing on studying. I do believe you have lost the ability to listen."

"You said he's old magick." I ignored her passive-aggressive crap. "The only old magick I know of is on the Isle of Skye." *And that,* I told myself, *was what I'd seen the night before when I'd looked through the stone at Stark—the old magick of the Guardian Warriors that still clung to him from the Isle of Skye.* Mind whirring, but still confronting Neferet I continued, "Are you telling me he came from the Isle of Skye?"

"Silly child, old magick isn't restricted to an island. You know, you might think twice about believing everything you hear, especially when it's coming from a vampyre who calls herself Queen and hasn't left an island in centuries."

"And you still haven't answered my question. Where did he come from?!"

"What magick could be older than that which comes from the Goddess herself? Aurox is my gift from Nyx!" Neferet looked knowingly at the crowd and laughed off my questioning as if I was nothing more than an irritating child and they were all in on the adult joke with her.

"What was he changing into?" I couldn't stop myself, even though I knew I was coming off as totally snotty and bitchy, like I was one of those girls who always has one more thing to say—and that one more thing was always negative.

Neferet's smile was magnanimous. "Aurox was changing into the Guardian of the House of Night. You didn't think you were the only one who was worthy of a Guardian, did you?" She spread her arms wide. "We all are! Come, greet him, and then let us get back to class and to that on which the House of Night was founded, the business of learning."

I wanted to scream that he was no Guardian! I wanted to scream that I was sick of Neferet twisting my words. I couldn't stop staring at Aurox as the fledglings (mostly girls) began approaching him, careful to step around the disgusting blood and Raven Mocker remains.

Actually, I didn't know why, but I just wanted to scream.

"You won't win this one," Aphrodite said. "She's got the crowd and the pretty boy on her side."

"That's not what he is." Still clutching my burning seer stone I turned away from the ridiculous scene and started walking back to school. I could feel Stark looking at me, but I kept my eyes straight ahead.

"Z, what is your problem? So he's not just a pretty guy. That's so awful?" Aphrodite said.

I stopped and turned to face them. They were all there, trailing along after me like baby ducks: Stark, Aphrodite, Darius, the Twins, Damien, Stevie Rae, and even Rephaim. It was to Rephaim I addressed my question, "You saw it, too, didn't you?"

He nodded soberly. "If you mean his change, yes."

"Saw what?" Stark asked, sounding exasperated.

"He was turning into a bull," Stevie Rae said. "I saw it, too."

"That pretty white boy was turnin' hisself into a bull? That ain't right," Kramisha said, peeking back at the crowd we'd left behind.

"White boy—white bull," Stevie Rae said. Then, sounding a lot like me she added, "Ah, hell.

CHAPTER SIX

Erik

He'd been walking slowly back to the drama room, wishing hard that instead of entering a class he was going to be making a grand entrance to a movie set in L.A., New Zealand, Canada . . . Hell! Anywhere but Tulsa, Oklahoma! He'd also been wondering how he'd gone from the hottest fledgling on campus and the next Brad Pitt according to the top vampyre casting agent in L.A., to a Drama Professor and a vampyre Tracker.

"Zoey," Erik mumbled to himself. "My shit started to go downhill the day I met her."

Then he felt crappy about saying that, even if there was no one around to hear him. He really was okay with Z. They were kinda even friends. What he wasn't okay with was all the crazy stuff that went on around her. *She's a damn freak magnet,* he thought to himself. No wondered they'd broken up. Erik was no freak.

He rubbed the palm of his right hand.

Several fledglings rushed past him and he reached out and snagged one kid by the scruff of his plaid school jacket. "Hey, what's the rush and why aren't you in class?" Erik scowled fiercely at the kid, more because he was pissed that he sounded like one of *those* teachers, the get-back-to-class-young-man kind, than that he actually cared where the fledgling was going.

Annoying Erik even more, the kid cringed and looked like he was going to piss his pants.

"Somethin's going on. Some fight or somethin'."

"Go on." Erik let go of him with a little push and the kid scampered off.

Erik didn't even consider following him. He knew what he'd find. Zoey in the middle of a mess. She had plenty of people to help get her out of her mess. She wasn't his damn responsibility, just like ridding the whole damn world of Darkness wasn't his damn responsibility.

It was as he reached for the doorknob of his classroom that his right palm began to burn. Erik shook it. Then he stopped and stared.

The spiral labyrinth-like mark had become raised, like a fresh brand.

Then the compulsion hit him. Hard.

Erik gasped, turned, and started jogging toward the student parking lot and his red Mustang. As the urge increased to a level that was feverish, he couldn't stay quiet and thoughts burst from him in jagged pieces of sentences.

"Broken Arrow. Twenty-eight-oh-one South Juniper Avenue. Walking. In thirty-five minutes. Gotta get there. Gotta be there. Shaylin Ruede. Shaylin Ruede. Shaylin Ruede. Go go go go go . . ."

Erik knew what was happening to him. He'd been prepared. The House of Night's last Tracker, who called himself Charon, had told him exactly what to expect. When it was time for him to Mark a fledgling his palm would burn; he would know a place, a time, and a name; he would have an uncontrollable compulsion to go there.

Erik had thought he'd been ready, but he hadn't realized the depth of the yearning that would come over him—the singular power of the focus that pounded through him in time with the pulse beat he felt hot and urgent in his palm.

Shaylin Ruede would be the first fledgling he would ever Mark.

It took him thirty minutes to get from midtown Tulsa to the little condo complex tucked within the quiet suburb of Broken Arrow. Erik pulled into a visitor's spot in the parking lot. His hands were shaking as he got out of his Mustang. The compulsion pulled him to the sidewalk that ran in front of the complex, parallel to the street. The condo complex had soft white lights that looked like giant opaque fishbowls resting on wrought iron poles, so pools of cream illumination were thrown on the sidewalk. Mature cedars and oaks lined the street side of the walkway. Erik glanced at his watch. It was 3:45 A.M. A weird time and place to Mark a kid. But Charon had told him the Tracker compulsion would never be wrong—that all he had to do was to follow it, to let his instincts lead him, and he'd be fine. Still, there was absolutely no one around and Erik was starting to panic when he heard a small *tap-tap-tap-tap*. In front of him a girl turned the corner from inside the complex and came into view. She moved slowly down the sidewalk, coming toward him. Each time she walked through the bubbles of light, Erik studied her. She was small—a petite girl with lots of dark brown hair. So much hair, in fact, that he was actually distracted for a moment by how thick and shiny it was and he didn't notice anything else about her—until the tapping sound broke into his consciousness. She was holding a long white cane that she kept continually sweeping in front of her, *tap-tap-tapping*, so that it was by sound and touch that she navigated her way. Every few feet she stopped and gave a terrible, wet cough.

Erik knew two things at once. First, this was Shaylin Ruede, the teenager he was meant to Mark. Second, she was blind.

He would have stopped himself if he could have, but no mortal power and, according to Charon, no magickal power, either, could take Erik from this kid until after he'd Marked her. When the girl was just a few feet in front of him he raised his hand, palm out, and pointed at her. He opened his mouth to speak, but she beat him to it.

"Hi? Who is it? Who is there?"

"Erik Night," he blurted. Then he shook his head and cleared his throat. "No, that's not right."

"You're not Erik Night?"

"Yes. I mean no. Wait, that's not right, either. This isn't what I'm supposed to be saying." His hands were shaking and he felt like he was going to be sick.

"Are you okay? You don't sound so good." She coughed. "Do you have the same flu I have? I've felt awful all day."

"No, I'm fine. It's just that I have to say something else to you, and it's not supposed to be my name or anything like that. Oh, man. I'm really messing this up. I never screw up lines. This is all wrong."

"Are you practicing for a play?"

"No. And you don't even know how ironic that question is," he said, rubbing his sweaty face and feeling confused.

She cocked her head to the side and frowned. "You aren't going to mug me, are you? I know it's late and all, and I'm blind and not supposed to be out here by myself. But it's the easiest time of day for me to go on a walk alone. I don't get much alone time."

"I'm not going to mug you," he said miserably. "I wouldn't do that."

"Then what are you doing out here, and what have you messed up?"

"This is so not going the way it's supposed to!"

"And kidnapping me won't do you any good. I'm living here with my foster mom. She doesn't have any money at all. Actually, since I've been working after school at the South BA Library down the street, I have more money than her. Uh, not that I have any of it with me at this second."

"Kidnap you? No!" Then Erik doubled over, holding on to his gut. "Crap! Charon didn't tell me it'd hurt if I didn't do it."

"Charon? Are you in a gang? Am I supposed to be an initiation sacrifice?"

"No!"

"Good, 'cause that would really suck." She smiled in his general direction, and then started to turn back the way she'd come. "Okay, well, then. If that's all. It was nice to meet you, Erik Night. Or at least I think that's your name."

With a huge effort, Erik straightened up enough to lift his hand again, palm out. "This is what I'm supposed to be doing." In a voice that was suddenly filled with magick and mystery and purpose, Erik Night intoned the ancient Tracker words, *"Shaylin Ruede! Night has Chosen thee! Thy death will be thy birth! Night calls to thee; harken to Her sweet voice. Your destiny awaits you at the House of Night!"*

All of the heat that had been building in his gut, making him feel sick and confused and too hot shot out of his palm. He could actually see it! It smacked right into Shaylin's forehead. She made a small, surprised, "Oh!" sound and dropped gracefully to the ground.

Okay, he knew he was supposed to be very vampyre-like and melt into the shadows and return to the House of Night, letting the fledgling find her own way there. Charon told him that's how it was done. Or at least that's how it was done in the modern world.

Erik thought about melting into the shadows. He even started to back away, and then Shaylin lifted her head. She'd fallen in the middle of a splotch of light, so her face was illuminated. She looked absolutely perfect! Her full pink lips tilted up in a surprised smile and she was blinking as if to clear her vision. If she hadn't been blind he would have sworn she was staring at him with those huge black eyes. Her pale skin was flawless, and in the middle of her forehead her new Mark seemed to glow a bright, beautiful scarlet.

Scarlet?

The color jolted through him and he started to move to her saying, "Wait, no. That's not right." At the same time Shaylin said, "Ohmygod! I can see!"

Erik hurried over to her and then stood helplessly, not sure what to do, as she collected herself and got to her feet. She was a little wobbly, but she was blinking and staring all around them, a huge smile filling her pretty face.

"I can really see! Ohmygod! This is incredible!"

"This isn't right. I've so messed this up."

"I don't care if you messed up or not—thank you so much! I can see!" she shouted and threw her arms around him, laughing and crying at the same time.

Erik kinda patted her back. She smelled sweet, like strawberries or maybe peaches—or some kind of fruit. And she felt really soft.

"Oh, god! Sorry." She suddenly released him and took a step back. Her cheeks were pink and she wiped her eyes. Then those wet, dark eyes widened at something over his shoulder and he spun around, hands up and ready to knock the crap out of someone. "Oh, no. Sorry again." Her fingers rested on his arm for just a second as she took a slow step past him. He looked down at her to see that she was gawking at a big, old oak. "It's so beautiful!" With steps that were becoming surer with each stride, she walked to the tree and pressed her hand against it. Staring up into the branches, she said, "I had images in my mind. Things I remember from before I lost my sight, but this is so, so much better." She wiped her eyes again and then her bright eyes came back to him, and they widened even more. "Oh, wow!"

In spite of the weirdness of everything, Erik couldn't help smiling back at her with his hundred-watt movie star grin. "Yeah, before I was zapped into being a Tracker I was on the road to Hollywood."

"No, I'm not wowing about how hot you are, even though you are hot. I suppose," she said quickly, still staring at him.

"I am," he assured her, reminding himself that she was probably in some kind of shock.

"Yeah, well, what I mean is that I can *really* see you."

"Yeah, and?" *Goddess, Shaylin Ruede, Marked or unMarked, was one strange girl.*

"I lost my sight when I was a just a kid, right before my fifth birthday, but I seriously don't remember being able to see the insides of people. And I think if that was common I'd at least have heard about it on the Internet."

"How can you use the Internet if you're blind?"

"Really? Are you really asking that? Like you don't know about stuff for disabled people?"

"How could I? I'm not disabled," Erik said.

"Again, really? That's not what the inside of you says."

"Shaylin, what the hell are you talking about?" *Was she a crazy kid? Had his messing up the Tracker stuff made her not just a red fledgling, but a crazy red fledgling? Crap! He was in so much trouble!*

"How do you know my name?"

"All Trackers know the name of the fledglings they're sent to Mark."

Shaylin touched her forehead. "Oh, wow! That's right! I'm going to be a vampyre!"

"Well, if you live. Actually, I'm not sure what's going on. You have a red Mark."

"Red? I thought fledglings have blue Marks and, eventually, blue tattoos. You do." She pointed at his tattoo, which framed his Clark Kent blue eyes like a mask.

"Yeah, well, you should have a blue tattoo. But you don't. It's red.

And could we go back to the stuff you were saying about seeing inside me?"

"Oh, that. Yeah, it's amazing. I can see you, and then I can also see all kinds of colors surrounding you. It's like what's inside you is glowing around you." She shook her head, as if in wonder, staring even harder at him. Then she blinked, frowned, and blinked again. "Huh. That's interesting."

"Colors? That doesn't make any sense." He realized she was clamping her lips together, as if she didn't want to say any more, which for some reason really annoyed him, so he asked, "What colors are around me?"

"Lots of pea green all mixed with something watery. It reminds me of the mushy peas some places try to give you when you order fish and chips, not that that makes any sense whatsoever."

Erik shook his head. "None of this makes any sense. Why the hell do I have mushy pea color around me?"

"Oh, that's the easy part. When I focus on it I can see what it means about you." She closed her mouth then and shrugged. "Plus you have some little bright specks that show up once in a while, but I can't tell what color they are and only a little of what they mean. Sounds crazy, right?"

"What does the pea green and the watery stuff say about me?"

"What do you think it says?"

"Why are you answering my question with a question?"

"Hey, you just answered my question with a question," Shaylin said.

"I asked you first."

"Does that really matter?" Shaylin asked.

"Yes," he said, trying to keep a handle on his temper, even though she was annoying the living crap out of him. "What does the pea color mean?"

"Fine. It means you've never had to work very hard at getting what you want."

He scowled at her.

She shrugged. "You're the one who asked."

"You don't know shit about me."

Shaylin suddenly looked pissed. "Oh, please! I don't know why, but I do know I know what I'm seeing."

"Hey, it's not like I have to be dripping in mushy peas for you to figure out this smile has taken me places," Erik said sarcastically.

"Yeah, well, explain to me why I also know the gray, foggy-looking stuff means something has made you sad." She put her hands on her hips, squinted her eyes, stared at him. Hard. Then she nodded, like she was agreeing with herself. Looking smug she added, "I think someone close to you just died."

Erik felt like she'd smacked him in the face. He couldn't say anything. He just looked away from her and tried to think through a wave of sadness.

"Hey, I'm sorry."

He looked down to see that she'd hurried up to him and put her hand back on his arm. She didn't look smug anymore.

"That was really wrong of me," she said.

"No," he said. "You weren't wrong. A friend of mine did just die."

She shook her head. "That's not what I meant. I was wrong to have said it like that—all mean-girl. That's not who I am. That's not how I am. So, I'm sorry."

Erik sighed. "I'm sorry, too. None of this happened like it was supposed to."

Shaylin touched her forehead gingerly. "You've never Marked someone with red?"

"I've never Marked anyone beside you," he admitted.

"Oh, wow. I'm your first?"

"Yeah, and I messed it up."

She smiled. "If me being able to see is a mess-up, I'm all for it."

"Well, I'm glad you can see, but I still need to figure out how that happened." He gestured at her red Mark. "And this." Erik waved his hand around him. "The pea stuff."

"The pea stuff came from you, but there's other colors there, too. Like when you said sorry I could see—"

"No!" he held up a hand, cutting her off. "I don't think I want to know what else you can see."

"Sorry," she said softly, looking down and scuffing the toe of one shoe through the winter-brown grass. "I guess it is really weird. So, what happens next?"

Erik sighed again. "Don't be sorry, and there's nothing wrong with weird. I'm sure Nyx has a reason for giving you this gift, and this red Mark."

"Nyx?"

"Nyx is our Goddess. The Goddess of Night. She's awesome, and sometimes she gives her fledglings cool gifts." As he spoke Erik felt like a total ass. He had to be the crappiest Tracker in House of Night history. He'd turned a blind kid into a red fledgling who could see inside stuff, and he was just now telling her about their Goddess. "Come on." He didn't care if Charon would approve or not—he wasn't following the damn script anyway. He might as well go for broke and screw everything up. "Show me where you used to live. Pack a bag or whatever. You're going to come with me."

"Oh, yeah. To the House of Night in Tulsa, right?"

"Actually, no. First I'm going to take you to a red fledgling High Priestess. Maybe she can figure out what I did wrong."

"Hey, she's not gonna try to 'fix' me by making me blind again, is she?"

"Shaylin, as much as I hate to admit it, I don't think it's you who needs to be fixed. It's me."

CHAPTER SEVEN

Zoey

"Zoey, did you hear me?"

I realized that while I'd been maniacally brushing Persephone, Lenobia had come into the stall and had been talking at me. Well, I mean I realized she'd been saying words. Out loud. To me. But I hadn't really heard them. I sighed and turned to face the Horse Mistress, leaning against the mare's warm, sturdy side and trying to draw calmness and energy from her familiar presence. "Sorry, no. I wasn't paying attention. I'm super distracted. What were you saying?"

"I was asking what you know about this Aurox boy."

"Nothing except that I can promise you he's not just a boy," I said.

"Yes, word's already spread around campus that he's a shape-shifter."

I felt my eyes get really big. "Seriously? There are such things? Like Sam and his crazy white trash mom and brother?"

"Sam?"

"*True Blood,*" I explained. "They're shape-shifters. They can change into anything they've seen. I think. Although I don't think they can change into inanimate stuff. Jeesh, I need to read those books to get the real deal. Anyway, again, *there are such things*?"

"A, I don't watch TV. I never got into the habit. I'll have to read the *True Blood* books, too."

"Actually, they're the Sookie Stackhouse books by a cool human author named Charlaine Harris." I registered Lenobia's look and hastily added, "Sorry, sorry, that's really not your point. What's your B?"

"My B is back to your original question, there are a lot of *things* out there—in this world as well as the Otherworld."

I swallowed hard. "I know that. Especially the Otherworld part."

"That said, many cultures have evidence of shape-shifters in their legends and mythology. It only stands to reason that at least some of those stories are based on truth."

"I can't figure out whether that's good or bad," I said.

"I think the best we can hope for is that it's like the rest of us— good or bad based on the individual. Which leads me to my next question. Along with campus gossip about Aurox and his ability to at least appear to be able to change form, word has it that you had a pretty strong reaction to him. Is that true?"

I felt my cheeks getting hot. "Sadly, yes. I made a fool out of myself in front of most of the school. Again."

"Why? When you know better then anyone how dangerously manipulative Neferet can be, why would you confront her publicly like that?"

"Because I'm a moron," I said miserably.

"No." She smiled kindly. "You're definitely not a moron, which is why I wanted to talk with you about this—alone. I think you should play down your reaction to Aurox, maybe even to your closest friends. Keep what you're feeling to yourself. Put on your poker face."

"Poker face? Sorry, I only know how to play Candyland."

"It means to keep your reaction to what you're seeing and how you feel about it secret from everyone watching you."

"Why?" She really had my attention now. It wasn't like Lenobia (or any *sane* vampyre) to ask a fledgling to keep secrets.

Her eyes met mine and I was struck anew by their unusual gray color. It was almost like she'd harnessed storm clouds within them.

"I learned young that evil sometimes likes to be bragged about, even when it would be best if it kept a low profile. It has been my experience that Darkness's true struggle isn't against Light and the strength of love and truth and loyalty. I think evil's greatest threat comes from its own pride and arrogance and greed. I've yet to see a bully who doesn't gloat, or a thief who doesn't brag. That's why they get caught. Darkness could get a lot more of its destructive work accomplished if it was more, shall we say, *circumspect*."

"But it's in Darkness's nature to brag and gloat, so Darkness understands it when someone calls attention to its actions and stuff," I said, finally getting her point. "Which means when someone who is trying to fight for good stays quiet, and watches and waits for the right time to act, evil is thrown a curve ball."

"And caught unaware by the strength that comes from honesty and serenity and quiet determination," Lenobia said.

I drew a deep breath, looked around to make sure no one was lurking outside Persephone's stall, and then spoke softly to Lenobia. "From the second I saw Aurox my seer stone got hot. The only two other times that's happened has been when old magick has been present." I hesitated, then admitted, "Last night I looked through the seer stone and saw something weird around Stark. It kinda freaked me out."

"What did Stark say about it?"

"I, uh, haven't told him."

"You haven't? Why not?"

"Well, first because I got distracted by him." I hurried on, knowing that I was probably blushing. "And since then I don't know why I haven't said anything." I thought about the almost-fight we'd had on the way to school. "No, wait, I do know why. Ever since the whole Otherworld thing things haven't been the same between Stark and me. Some of that's good—we're really close most of the time. But some of it's weird, too."

Lenobia nodded. "That's understandable. An experience the magnitude of what the two of you went through should change the dynamics of a relationship. And glimpsing some old magick attached to Stark could simply be a remnant of his time in the Otherworld." She smiled. "I imagine if you could look through the seer stone at yourself you might see—"

"Oh, hell no! I don't want to see anything hanging around me!"

Lenobia's smile faded. "You sound frightened."

"I'm freaked, that's for sure. I think I've had enough of old magick and the Otherworld and all that goes with that stuff for a good long while."

"Ah, I understand. If Aurox carries traces of old magick, that's why his presence affected you so much."

"He definitely made me feel funny, even before I saw him change into a bull."

"Funny? Like you were frightened then, too?"

"Yeah, but I also had a weird surprised feeling, like my intuition was seeing something that my mind couldn't handle. And then I got super anxious. There's something wrong about that guy, Lenobia, and that something is real, real old."

"But do you see that he looks like a handsome teenager to the rest of the world?"

"Yeah, I guess." Then I snorted. "I'd like to take him to Skye and find out what *that* part of the 'rest of the world' sees when they look at him."

"Your seer stone came from Skye?"

"Yeah, the Queen gave it to me. She said if old magick is around when I look through it, I can see it." I thought about Stark and shadows and creepiness. "Dealing with what I can see with my own eyes is way more than enough for me. I don't want to look through the seer stone again." I shook my head, ashamed of my weakness. "I'm sorry. I'm such a big baby. I shouldn't be so darn scared. I should have looked through the stupid stone at Aurox."

"And what would have happened had you seen something terrible? Can everyone who looks through the stone see old magick?"

"No." I wiped tears from my cheeks. "It's a gift only certain High Priestesses have."

"So, if you'd seen something of Darkness through the stone, told everyone, and relied on the stone to show them what you were seeing, you would have had no real proof?"

"Yeah, that's about it. I was and am screwed."

"No, you were and are wise to listen to your instincts. Something is very wrong with this pawn of Neferet's. You knew that from the first instant you saw him, and because you knew it you couldn't just stand there and shut your mouth and pretend to be a vapid child."

I made an internal note to look up vapid or ask Damien for a quick definition.

Lenobia wasn't finished. She continued earnestly, "I want you to spend some time thinking about Aurox. Note how you feel and exactly what you observe the next time you see him—but note those things silently. Keep your poker face on. Don't let anyone know what's going on underneath that pretty little teenage façade."

"You don't think I should look at him through my seer stone?"

"Not until you're no longer so frightened of what you might see. When your instincts tell you the time is right, then and only then is when you should look."

"What about Stark?" I held my breath.

"Stark is pledged to you and our Goddess. I think it's a good thing that old magick clings to him. Stop worrying about your Warrior—he can sense it and that won't help him."

"Yeah, okay, that makes sense. So, being super relieved that I don't have to look through the seer stone doesn't make me a big ol' baby or a coward?"

She smiled. "No, nor a moron, either. You're a young fledgling High Priestess, the first one in history, and you're simply trying to find your path in a very confusing world."

"You're really smart," I said.

Lenobia laughed. "No, I'm really old."

Then I laughed, too, because even though I was pretty sure she was like a hundred or so, Lenobia looked about thirty years old. "Well, you look twenty-something," I lied, "which only makes you kinda old, not *really* old."

"Twenty-something! With an ability to dissemble like that, you'll do just fine keeping your thoughts about Aurox to yourself," Lenobia said. Then I swear she giggled, which actually did make her look super young. "Twenty-something! I haven't been that for more than two hundred years!"

"What's your secret? Botox and lip injections?" I asked, giggling with her.

"B negative and sunscreen," she replied.

"Hey you two, sorry to interrupt." Stevie Rae's curly blond head popped into view as she peeked into the stall.

"You aren't interrupting, Stevie Rae," Lenobia said, still smiling. "Come, join us. We were just talking about aging gracefully."

"My mama always said eight hours of sleep, drinking lots of water, and not havin' any kids was a better anti-aging recipe than anything a doctor or L'Oréal could ever cook up." She grinned at Lenobia and then gave Persephone a worried glance. "And thanks for askin' me to come in, but I'll stay out here. I don't like horses much. No offense; they're real big."

"No offense taken," Lenobia said. "Do the Warriors need something?"

"Uh-uh. The arena is great for classes. They're havin' a bunch of guy fun, which means they're hittin' each other with wooden swords and shootin' arrows at things while they yell a lot." The three of us rolled our eyes. "But your cowboy is here, so I came to get ya."

"*My* cowboy?" Lenobia looked totally confused. "I don't have a cowboy."

"Well, he has to be yours 'cause he just showed up outside the corral entrance with a giant horse trailer sayin' he's reportin' for work and askin' where he can unload his stuff," Stevie Rae said.

Lenobia blew out a long sigh. Obviously annoyed she said, "Neferet. This is her doing. He's the first of the local humans she's hired."

"I do not get what Neferet's up to," Stevie Rae said. "I know dang well she hates humans and doesn't give a rat's ass about whether the local folks like us bein' here or not."

"Neferet's up to causing problems," I said.

"And she started with me because she knows I've sided with you," Lenobia said.

"Chaos." As I said the word I felt the truth of it. "Neferet wants to cause chaos in our lives."

"Then let's give this cowboy a warm welcome, make him feel at home, and show him how *unchaotic* and downright boring working at my stables can be. If we do that, maybe, just maybe, he'll decide to move on to more exciting pastures and Neferet will turn her attention elsewhere."

Like she was on a mission, Lenobia marched out of Persephone's stall. Stevie Rae and I shared a look.

"No way am I gonna miss this." I gave Persephone's warm flank a parting pat and tossed the curry brush into the tack bin.

Stevie Rae linked her arm through mine as we followed Lenobia. "What I didn't tell Lenobia is how dang cute her cowboy is," she whispered to me.

"Seriously?"

"Just you wait and see."

Now I was super curious, and I picked up the pace, hurrying through the arena sand and barely waving at Stark, who was handing a bow to Rephaim. Stevie Rae tried to blow him a kiss, but I kept her moving so basically all she did was giggle and wave. I tried to ignore Stark's scowl and focused on *not* leaking any of the curious, excited, and downright confused feelings I was having.

I didn't exactly know why, but I absolutely did not want Stark asking me questions about Aurox.

"There, that's him. The tall, non-vampyre in a cowboy hat over there by the door." Stevie Rae pointed to the wide side doors to the arena. They'd been rolled open. Just outside was a big horse trailer and one of those massive trucks Oklahoma guys liked to buy and drive and practically live in so much. Standing in front of the trailer was a super tall man. And Stevie Rae had definitely been right. He was seriously cute, even for an older guy.

"He looks like someone who should be on the Western Channel," I said. "Playing one of those olden-day cowboy heroes."

"Sam Elliott, that's who he looks like."

"Huh?" I gave her a question mark look.

She sighed. "He was in a bunch of cowboy movies. You know, like *Tombstone*."

"You watch cowboy movies?"

"I used to, with my momma and daddy, especially on Saturday night before bedtime. So?"

"So nothing."

"Do *not* tell Aphrodite," she said.

"Do not tell Aphrodite what?" Aphrodite asked.

Stevie Rae and I jumped as she seemed to materialize out of the air behind us.

"Don't be creepy and lurky," I said.

"I'm not. I'm just naturally graceful. It's because I'm delicate boned," she said. Then she turned her icy blue gaze on Stevie Rae. "Again—do not tell Aphrodite what?"

"That Lenobia's cowboy is super hot," Stevie Rae said.

Aphrodite gave her a look that said she was a crappy liar, which she was, but her gaze was already snagged by the man's broad-shouldered silhouette.

"Ooooh! That's Lenobia's . . ."

"Employee." I provided the word, even though Aphrodite was paying no attention to me. "He's supposed to be working for Lenobia."

"He's hot," Aphrodite said. "Not like Darius hot, but still. H.O.T."

"I told y'all. And he's so tall he makes Lenobia look even teenier than she is."

As Stevie Rae, Aphrodite, and I wandered into hearing distance and tried (unsuccessfully) not to be too obvious in our group gawk, the cowboy tipped his hat to Lenobia and in a perfect Oklahoma twang said, "Howdy, ma'am. I'm the new stable manager. I'd 'preciate it if you could point me to the man in charge."

I couldn't see Lenobia's face but I watched her back straighten.

"Uh-oh," Stevie Rae whispered.

"So much for the whole warm welcome thing," I said low enough that only Aphrodite and Stevie Rae could hear me.

"John Wayne just totally fucked up," Aphrodite said.

"I am Lenobia." Her voice carried easily to us. I didn't think she sounded pissed. I thought she sounded like an ice storm. "I am the *woman* in charge of these stables and your new boss." There was a kind of uncomfortable silence when Lenobia didn't offer a hand for him to shake.

"Brrr," Aphrodite whispered. "She just reminded me of my mom, and for John Wayne that's not a good thing."

"Sam Elliott," Stevie Rae whispered.

Aphrodite furrowed her brow at my BFF. I suppressed a sigh of hopelessness.

"He doesn't look anything like John Wayne." She continued her stage whisper. "But he looks *just like* Sam Elliott."

"You watched too much regular TV when you were a kid, probably after you had dinner as a family on Saturday nights. Pathetic."

Aphrodite gave Stevie Rae a dismissive shake of her head. I was thinking about how bizarre it was that Aphrodite knew about Stevie Rae's family stuff when the three of us turned our attention back to The Cowboy Show.

The man tipped his hat to Lenobia again, this time he smiled and even standing as far away as we were I could see that his eyes were sparkling. "Well, ma'am, seems I got me some misinformation. Glad that was cleared up quick. My name is Travis Foster, and I'm pleased to meet ya, boss lady."

"And you don't mind finding out your boss is a lady?"

"No, ma'am. My momma was a lady and I never worked harder or happier than when I worked for her."

"Mr. Foster, do I remind you of your mother?"

I thought Lenobia's voice could have frozen water, but Travis didn't seem to notice. Actually, he looked like he was enjoying himself. He cocked his hat back on his head and looked down at Lenobia, like the question had been serious instead of sarcastic. "No, ma'am, not yet you don't." Lenobia didn't say anything else and I was just getting that squirmy, embarrassed feeling that awkward conversations with adults can bring about when Travis kinda shrugged, hooked a finger in the belt tab of his Wranglers, and said, "So, Lenobia, could you show me where my mare and I are gonna bunk?"

"Mare? Bunk?" Lenobia said.

"This is some great shit. I wish I had popcorn," Aphrodite said.

"She's gonna burn him with her laser vision," I said.

"Lenobia has laser vision?" Stevie Rae asked.

Aphrodite and I looked at Stevie Rae like she'd just asked if we thought Lindsay Lohan was really rehabbed.

"How 'bout I watch and not talk," Stevie Rae said.

"Thank you," Aphrodite and I said together, which made her glare at me before the three of us returned to gawking and eavesdropping.

"Well, ma'am," Travis drawled. "I told y'all's High Priestess when she hired me that my mare and I come as a package deal, and I'd need to stable her here. Since I just wrapped up a season managing the stables at Durant Springs, I'd need a place to lodge, too." He paused, and when Lenobia didn't speak he added, "Durant Springs is in Colorado, ma'am."

"I know where it is," Lenobia snapped. "What makes you think you can stay here on campus? We have no accommodations for humans."

"Yes, ma'am, that's what the High Priestess said. Since the job needed to be filled right away, I told her I'd get along just fine bunking with Bonnie until I could find a place nearby."

"Bonnie?"

Travis rearranged his hat, the first sign he might possibly be uncomfortable. "Yes, ma'am. My mare's name is Bonnie." As if on cue, there came a giant *thud!* from inside the horse trailer. He moved to the rear doors while he continued to explain to Lenobia. "I'd 'preciate it if ya let me unload her. It's a long way from Colorado for a big girl."

"Do you think his horse is fat?" Stevie Rae asked quietly.

"Bumpkin, I thought you weren't going to talk," Aphrodite said.

"I think he just got his foot in the door," I said. No way was Lenobia gonna let a tired horse be hauled away to goddess only knew where.

"Unload your mare. You and I will discuss your accommodations after she's comfortable," Lenobia said.

I noticed that Travis had already been undoing the series of levers and chains that held the horse trailer's door shut, so we only had to wait a few seconds for the ramp to open.

"Come on, big girl. Baaack," Travis said in a voice that had gone from polite and at times slightly amused, to warm and gentle and sweet.

Then his horse backed out of the trailer and gasps of shock and awe came from all around us. I took my eyes from the horse long enough to see that Stevie Rae and I weren't the only gawkers. Darius, Stark, Rephaim, and most of the fledglings had somehow meandered their way over to us.

"That can't be a horse," Stevie Rae said, and even though we were several yards away from the animal, she actually took a step back.

"Holy shit. It's a dinosaur," Aphrodite said.

"I'm pretty sure it's a horse," I said, studying her. "But it's a really, really big one."

"Oh, a Percheron! She's exquisite!" Lenobia said.

Everyone stared as petite Lenobia walked up to the huge mare with no hesitation whatsoever. Totally dwarfed by the hulking equine, the Horse Mistress lifted her hand, just slightly. The mare watched her for an instant and then dropped her nose, blowing against Lenobia's palm. Lenobia, grinning like a girl, caressed the mare's gigantic muzzle and crooned to her, "Oh, you are indeed a bonnie, bonnie girl." She looked from the horse to the cowboy. The ice in her voice had totally thawed and I thought she was practically gushing. "I have not seen a Percheron since my voyage from France when I was a girl, and that's more years ago than I care to admit. There was a matched pair of the big beauties on the ship with me. I've remembered them fondly and since have been intrigued by draft horses. She's a lovely dappled gray. I imagine she'll continue to lighten as she gets older. I can tell that she's just turned five a month . . ." Lenobia paused, cocked her head, and stared into the horse's eye before continuing. "No, she turned five two months ago. She's belonged to you for her entire life, hasn't she?"

I saw Travis blink in surprise. His mouth opened, then closed, then opened again. He cleared his throat. "Well, yes, ma'am." He paused and reached up to pat Bonnie's ginormically thick neck like he needed to anchor himself to something to get his sense back. I knew why he was suddenly so messed up. Everyone who had ever watched Lenobia around horses knew why. When she communed with horses Lenobia changed from really pretty to utterly, totally gorgeous, and she was doing some serious communing with the big mare, so she'd turned the full wattage of her horse adoration onto the cowboy. It wasn't that he was the intended recipient of her super attractiveness, he was just getting the fallout. But it was some serious fallout.

Travis cleared his throat again, moved his hat around, and then said, "Her momma died right after Bonnie was born—freak lightning strike in the middle of a pasture. I bottle-raised her."

Lenobia turned her gray eyes on the cowboy. She looked surprised, like she'd forgotten he was there. Her horsey adoration blinked off like she'd thrown a switch. "You did a good job. She's big, easily over eighteen hands. Well muscled. In excellent condition." Even though what she said was complimentary, her tone sounded more annoyed than nice. It was only when she glanced up and smiled at the mare that her voice and expression shifted back to adoration and true pleasure. "You are a clever girl, aren't you?" Lenobia said to Bonnie, who was standing without fidgeting, ears flicking all around, gawking at all of us about as much as we were gawking at her. "*And* you're confident enough to be well behaved, even in a curious, new environment." Lenobia looked from the mare to the cowboy and her expression froze over to cool cordiality. She gave one short, decisive nod. "Well then, that is that. You and Bonnie may follow me. I'll show you where you'll be stabling—the both of you."

Lenobia turned and began striding back across the arena. When she reached the halfway point she stopped and addressed all of us. "Fledglings and vampyres, this is Travis Foster. He'll be working for me. His mare's name is Bonnie. Show her the respect she deserves as a fine example of the majestic Percheron breed. Warriors, please note her size and the way she carries herself. Her ancestors were warhorses of old."

I looked at the cowboy and saw him smile and nod at Lenobia's comment and pat the big mare affectionately before he threw an equally affectionate look the Horse Mistress's way. Lenobia didn't look at him at all. Instead she narrowed her eyes and included the entire group of us in her glare. "And now you can all stop staring and get back to work." Then Lenobia marched from the arena and into the stables without so much as a glance back at Bonnie and Travis, who followed her like they were moths and she was a super shiny light.

"That has interesting possibilities," Aphrodite said.

"No kidding, that mare is totally cool looking. I mean, *big*, but still totally cool," I said.

Aphrodite rolled her eyes. "I'm not talking about the horse, Z."

I was frowning at Aphrodite when Damien hurried up to us. "Zoey, good, there you are. You need to come back to the main building."

"You mean after sixth hour? It's almost over," I said.

"No, honey. I mean now. Your grandma's here, and I'm pretty sure she's been crying."

CHAPTER EIGHT

Zoey

My stomach clenched and I felt like I was gonna puke. "Okay, I'm coming," I told Damien. "But I'd appreciate it if you would come with me." When he nodded somberly I looked at Stevie Rae and Aphrodite. "You guys, too. 'Kay?"

"'Course we'll come with you," Stevie Rae said.

For once Aphrodite didn't gripe about Stevie Rae answering for her. She just nodded and said, "I'm in."

I was turning to look for Stark when he was suddenly there beside me. His hand trailed down my arm until our fingers met and threaded together. "Is it about your mom?"

I didn't trust my voice, so I just nodded.

"Your momma? I thought Damien said your grandma's here," Stevie Rae said.

"He did." Aphrodite spoke before Damien could. She was studying me with a look that made her appear older (and nicer) than she was. "Is it about your mom?" she asked.

Stark glanced at me and I gave another little nod. Then he said, "Zoey's mom's dead."

"Oh, no!" Damien said, tears instantly coming to his eyes.

"Don't, okay?" I said quickly. "Let's not do this here. I don't want everyone watching me."

Damien pressed his lips together, blinked hard, and nodded.

"Come on, Z. Let's all go see your grandmomma." Stevie Rae went to my other side and put her arm through mine. Aphrodite grabbed Damien's hand, and they followed us from the arena.

All the way there I tried to get myself ready for what Grandma would tell me. I suppose I'd been trying to get myself ready to hear what Grandma would tell me ever since I woke up from my dream visit to the Otherworld where I witnessed Nyx welcoming my mom's spirit there. The truth that I realized as I entered the main school building and approached the front lounge was that I'd never be ready to hear this news.

Just before we walked through the final set of doors Stark squeezed my hand. "I'm right here, and I love you."

"I love you, too, Z," Stevie Rae said.

"Me, too," Damien said and then he sobbed just a little.

"You can borrow my two-carat diamond stud earrings," Aphrodite said.

I stopped and looked back at her. "Huh?"

She shrugged. "That's as close to a declaration of love as you're gonna get from me."

I heard Stevie Rae expel a huge sigh and Damien's forehead squidged as he looked disbelievingly at her.

But I simply said, "Thanks. I'll take you up on it," which made Aphrodite frown and mumble, "Goddess, I hate being nice."

I untangled myself from Stevie Rae and Stark and pushed open the double doors. Grandma was alone in the room and sitting in a wide leather chair. Damien had been right; Grandma had been crying. She looked old and very, very sad. As soon as she saw me she stood up. We met in the middle of the room and clung to each other. When she finally stopped hugging me, Grandma stepped back just far enough to look into my face. She kept her hands on my shoulders. They felt warm and solid and familiar, and somehow that touch made the knot in my stomach bearable.

"Mom's dead." I had to say it before she did.

Grandma didn't look surprised that I'd known. She just nodded and said, "Yes, *u-we-tsi-a-ge-ya*. Your mother is dead. Did her spirit come to you?"

"In a way. Last night, while I was asleep, Nyx showed me Mom entering the Otherworld."

I felt the shudder that passed through Grandma's body in her hands. She closed her eyes and swayed. For a second I was afraid she was going to faint, and I covered her hands with mine. "Spirit, come to me! Help Grandma!"

The element I have the strongest connection with responded immediately. I felt it swirl through me and into Grandma, who gasped and stopped swaying, but she didn't open her eyes.

"Air, come to me. Please surround Grandma Redbird and let her breathe in strength." Damien stepped up to my side and touched Grandma's arm once, softly, as a sweet, impossible breeze stirred around us.

"Fire, come to me. Please warm Zoey's grandma so that even though she's sad, she'll not be cold."

I blinked in surprise as Shaunee joined Damien. She, too, touched Grandma for a second, then she smiled through wet eyes and said to me, "Kramisha told us you needed us."

"Water, come to me. Wash through Z's grandma and please take some of her sadness with you." Erin took her place beside Shaunee, touching Grandma's back. Then, just like her Twin, she smiled through tears at me. "Yeah, we didn't even have to read her poem. She just told us to get here."

Grandma's eyes were still closed, but I saw her lips tilt up ever so slightly.

"My poem was good, though." Kramisha's voice came from somewhere behind me.

Through Aphrodite's snort, Stevie Rae said, "Earth, please come to me." She went to my other side, and slid her arm around Grandma. "Let Z's g-ma borrow some of your power so that she can be okay again real soon."

Grandma drew three long deep breaths. As she let the last one out, she opened her eyes and, even though there was still sadness in them, her face had lost the scary, gaunt old person look it had when I'd first seen her. "Tell them what I do, *u-we-tsi-a-ge-ya*."

I wasn't sure what Grandma was up to, but I nodded. I knew she'd make me understand, and I was right. She went to each of my four friends. Starting with Damien, she touched his face and said, "*Wado, Inole*. You have strengthened me." As she moved to Shaunee I explained to my friends, "Grandma is thanking you by naming you the Cherokee word for each of your elements."

"*Wa-do, Egela.* You have strengthened me." Grandma touched Shaunee's cheek and went to Erin. "*Wa-do, Ama.* You have strengthened me." Last, she touched Stevie Rae's cheek, still wet from tears. "*Wa-do, Elohine.* You have strengthened me."

"Thank you, Grandma Redbird," each of the four of them murmured.

"*Gv-li-e-li-ga,*" Grandma said, repeating in English. "Thank you." She looked at me. "I can bear to tell it now." She stood in front of me and took both of my hands in hers. "Your mother was killed at my lavender farm."

"What?" I felt the shock of it move through me. "I don't understand. How? Why?"

"The sheriff is saying it was a robbery, and that she just got in the way. He says from what they took, my computer and television and my cameras, and the random violence of the crime, that they were probably addicts stealing so they would have money for drugs." Grandma squeezed my hands. "She'd left him, Zoeybird, and come to me. I was at a powwow. I was not there for her." Grandma's voice stayed steady, but tears welled and then spilled from her eyes.

"No, Grandma, don't blame yourself. It wasn't your fault, and if you'd been there I would have lost both of you—and I couldn't stand that!"

"I know, *u-we-tsi-a-ge-ya,* but the death of a child, even one that has been lost to her parent, is a heavy burden."

"Was it—did she—did Mom suffer?" My voice was barely above a whisper.

"No. She died quickly." Grandma spoke without hesitation, but I thought I saw something pass through her eyes.

"You found her?"

Grandma nodded, tears spilling more and more quickly down her cheeks. "I did. She was in the field just outside the house. She was laying there and she looked so peaceful that at first I believed she was sleeping." Grandma's voice caught on a sob. "She was not sleeping."

I held tight to Grandma's hands and spoke the words I knew she needed to hear. "She's happy, Grandma. I saw her. Nyx took the sadness from her. She's waiting for us in the Otherworld, and she has the Goddess's blessing."

"*Wa-do, u-we-tsi-a-ge-ya.* You give me strength," Grandma whispered to me as she hugged me again.

"Grandma," I said against her cheek. "Please stay with me, at least for a little while."

"I cannot, *u-we-tsi-a-ge-ya.*" She stepped back, but kept hold of my hand. "You know I will follow our people's tradition and mourn for seven full days, and this is not the right place for me to mourn."

"We're not stayin' here, Grandma," Stevie Rae said, wiping her face with her sleeve. "Zoey and our whole group have moved to the tunnels under the Tulsa Depot. I'm their official High Priestess, and I'd really like it if you'd come stay with us—for seven days or seven months—for as long as you want."

Grandma smiled at Stevie Rae. "That is a generous offer, *Elohine,* but your depot is not the right place for me to mourn, either." Grandma met my eyes and I knew what she was going to say before she spoke. "I must be on my land, at the farm. I must spend the next week eating and sleeping very little. I must focus on cleansing my home and my land of this horrible deed."

"All by yourself, Grandma?" Stark was there beside me, a warm, strong presence. "Is that safe after what happened?"

"*Tsi-ta-ga-a-sh-ya,* do not let my looks deceive you." She called Stark rooster, her pet name for him. "I am many things, and not one of them is a helpless old woman."

"I'd never think you were helpless," Stark amended. "But maybe it's not a good idea for you to be alone."

"Yeah, Grandma. Stark has a point," I said.

"*U-we-tsi-a-ge-ya,* I must cleanse my home, my land, and myself as I mourn. I cannot do that unless I am at peace with the land, and I will not stay inside the house until it is thoroughly cleansed and the seven days have past. I will be camping in my backyard, in the meadow by the stream," Grandma smiled at Stark, Stevie Rae, and the rest of my friends. "I do not believe you would fare so well exposed to the sunlight for that time."

"Well, Grandma, I—" I began, but she stopped me.

"This I must do myself, *u-we-tsi-a-ge-ya*. I do have something to ask of you, though."

"Anything," I said.

"In seven days will you come to the farm with your friends? Will you cast a circle and perform a cleansing ritual of your own?"

"I will." I nodded, and my gaze took in the friends who surrounded me.

"*We* will," Stevie Rae said. Her words were echoed by the kids who stood beside and around me.

"Then that is how it shall be," Grandma said firmly. "The Cherokee tradition of mourning and cleansing will be coupled with vampyre ritual. It is good that it is so, as my family has expanded to include so many vampyres and fledglings." Her eyes shifted around my group. "I ask one more thing. That each of you think bright thoughts of me, and of Zoey's mother, for the next seven days. It does not matter that Linda faltered in life. What matters is that she is remembered with love and kind thoughts."

"We will," and "Okay, Grandma," sounded around me.

"I will go now, *u-we-tsi-a-ge-ya*. Sunrise is not far away, and I would greet the dawn on my land." Keeping my hand in hers, Grandma and I walked to the door. As she passed my friends, each of them touched her and said "Good-bye, Grandma," which had her smiling through her tears.

At the doorway, we had a little bubble of privacy and I hugged her again, saying, "I understand why you have to, but I really wish you wouldn't go."

"I know, but in seven days—"

The door was pulled open and Neferet was suddenly there, looking somber and deceptively beautiful. "Sylvia, I have heard of your loss. Please accept my sincere sorrow that it was your daughter who was killed."

Grandma had tensed at the sound of Neferet's voice and stepped out of my embrace. She drew a deep breath and met the vampyre's gaze.

"I accept your sorrow, Neferet. I do feel the sincerity in it."

"Is there anything the House of Night can do for you? Is there anything you need?"

"The elements have already strengthened me, and the Goddess has welcomed my daughter to the Otherworld."

Neferet nodded. "Zoey and her friends are kind, and the Goddess is generous."

"I don't believe it was kindness or generosity that was behind the actions of Zoey and her friends or the Goddess. I believe it was love. Do you not think so, High Priestess?"

Neferet paused as if she was actually considering Grandma's question, then she said, "What I think is that you *could* be right."

"Yes, I could be. And there is one thing I need from the House of Night."

"We would be honored to aid a Wise Woman in a time of need," Neferet said.

"Thank you. I would ask that Zoey and her circle be allowed to come to my land in seven days to perform a cleansing ritual. That would complete my mourning and wash my home free of any lingering evil."

I saw something pass within Neferet's gaze—something that, for just a moment, might have been fear. But when she spoke her expression and her voice mirrored only polite concern. "Of course. I freely give permission for this ritual."

"Thank you, Neferet," Grandma said, and then she hugged me one more time and kissed me softly. "In seven days, *u-we-tsi-a-ge-ya.* I will see you again then."

I blinked fast, holding back my tears. I didn't want Grandma's last view of me to be about snot and bawling. "Seven days. I love you, Grandma. Don't ever forget that."

"I could no more forget that than I could forget to breathe. I love you, too, daughter."

Then Grandma turned and walked away. I stood in the doorway, watching her straight, strong back until the night blanketed her from me.

"Come on, Z." Stark slid his arm around my shoulders. "I think we've all had enough school for one day. Let's go home."

"Yeah, Z. Let's go home," Stevie Rae said.

I was nodding, getting ready to tell them okay when I felt a sudden warmth building in my chest. At first it confused me. I lifted my hand to rub the spot and touched the hard circle that had begun radiating heat.

And then Aurox stepped into view. He was with Dragon Lankford.

"Zoey, I heard the news about your mother. I am sorry," Dragon said.

"Th-thank you," I muttered. I didn't look at Aurox. I remembered Lenobia's words, that I needed to keep a poker face around him, but I felt too raw, too wounded to do anything except blurt at Stark, "I want to go home, but first I need a minute to myself." Before he could even say okay, I moved out of his encircling arm and pushed past Dragon and Aurox.

"Zoey?" Stark called after me. "Where are you—"

"I'll just be by the fountain that's in the courtyard next to the parking lot," I said over my shoulder to him. I could see he was frowning worriedly at me, but I couldn't help it. I needed to Get Out Of There. "Come get me when the bus is loaded and ready to go. Okay?"

I didn't wait for his reply. I put my head down and hurried along the sidewalk that ran beside the main school building. Almost jogging I turned right and went straight to the iron bench that was beneath one of the circle of trees that framed the fountain and the little garden-like area the fledglings called the professors' courtyard because it sat next to the part of the school that housed them. I knew if someone was looking out of the large, ornate windows I'd be seen, but I also knew all of the professors should be finishing up sixth hour in their classrooms, which meant it was the one place on campus at this particular time that I could pretty much count on being alone.

So I sat there, in the shadow of a big elm, trying to control my thoughts. Aurox's presence messed with my mind, and I didn't know why. *Right now, right at this second, I don't even care. Mom is dead. Whatever Neferet and Evil have planned for me, they can just back the hell off. Everyone can just back the hell off.* My thoughts felt mean and tough, but the tear that was sliding down my face told a different story.

Mom isn't in the world anymore. She's not at home waiting on the step-loser and puttering around the kitchen. I can't call and have her get mad at me and then lecture me for being a crappy daughter. It was a weird feeling, being momless. I mean, she and I hadn't been close for more than three years, but still it'd always been in the back of my mind that someday she'd come to her senses, leave that idiot she'd screwed up and married, and go back to being Mama.

"She had left him," I said. "I need to remember that." My voice hitched, but I cleared my throat and spoke out loud again to the night. "Mama, I'm sorry we didn't get to say good-bye. I love you. I always have. I always will." Then I put my face in my hands, gave in to the terrible storm of sadness that had been building inside me, and I began to sob.

Aurox

The fledgling called Zoey—the one with the odd tattoos that covered not just her face, but her shoulders, hands, and as Neferet had told him, some parts of the rest of her body, too—made him feel strange.

Neferet had said Zoey was her enemy. That made Zoey his enemy as well. She who was his mistress's enemy was a danger—that danger must be why he felt an oddness when she was near. Aurox noted the direction Zoey went as she hurried away. He should note everything about her. Zoey was dangerous.

"Neferet, I need to speak with you regarding the new classes that are being taught in Lenobia's arena," Dragon Lankford was saying.

Neferet's cold green eyes turned to Dragon. "It was decided by the High Council that these fledglings stay, at least for the time being."

"I understand that, but—"

"But would you rather have the Raven Mocker in your class?" Neferet snapped.

"Rephaim isn't a Raven Mocker anymore." The Red High Priestess spoke up quickly in her mate's defense.

"And yet he calls those creatures, those Raven Mockers, brother," Aurox said.

"Indeed, Aurox, that is a relevant observation," Neferet said without looking at him. "As you are Nyx's gift to me I think it is important that we listen to your observations."

"What in the Sam Hill is the point? They *are* his brothers. He's not tryin' to hide that." Shaking her head, the Red High Priestess met his eyes. Aurox saw sadness and anger there, though the emotions weren't strong enough for him to feel them—for him to draw power from them. "You shouldn't have killed that Raven Mocker. He wasn't attacking anyone."

"You think we should wait for the creatures to slaughter another one of us before we move against them?" Dragon Lankford said.

The Sword Master's anger was more tangible and Aurox absorbed some of the strength of it. He felt it boil through his blood—pulsing—feeding—changing.

"Aurox, you are not needed here. You may go on about your duties. Begin here at the main school building and move around inside the perimeter of the campus. Patrol the grounds. Be quite certain none of the Raven Mockers return." His mistress glanced at the Red High Priestess and added, "My command is to attack only those who threaten you or the school."

"Yes, Priestess." He bowed to her and then backed from the doorway and walked out into the night as he heard the Red High Priestess still defending her mate. *She, too, is an enemy, though my mistress says of a different kind—a kind that may be used.*

Aurox contemplated the intricacies of those who opposed Neferet. She'd explained to him that someday soon all of these fledglings and vampyres would either submit to her will, or be destroyed. His mistress looked forward to that day. Aurox looked forward to that day, too.

He stepped off the sidewalk, moving to his right toward the edge of the main school building. Aurox kept away from the flickering gaslights. Instinctively he preferred the deeper shadows and darker corners. His senses were always alert, always searching. So it was strange that the tissue startled him. It was a simple rectangle of white. It floated on the wind, fluttering before him almost like a bird. He stopped and reached out, plucking it from the night.

So strange, he thought, *a floating paper tissue.* Without conscious thought, he tucked it into the pocket of his jeans. Shrugging off the odd, foreboding feeling, he kept walking.

Her emotions hit him after he'd taken two more steps.

Sadness—deep, pressing grief. And guilt. There was guilt there in her feelings, too.

Aurox knew it was the young fledgling High Priestess—the Zoey Redbird. He told himself he approached her only because it was wise to observe one's enemy. But as he got closer—as her feelings flooded him—something unexpected happened within him. Instead of absorbing her emotions and feeding off them, Aurox absorbed them and *felt.*

He didn't change. He didn't begin to morph into the creature of great power.

Instead, Aurox *felt.*

Zoey's grief drew him forward, and as he stood in the shadows that surrounded her and watched her sob, her emotion flowed into him, gathered and pooled in a small, quiet, hidden place deep inside his spirit. As Aurox absorbed Zoey's sadness and guilt, loneliness and despair, something stirred within him in response.

It was utterly unexpected and completely unacceptable, but Aurox wanted to comfort Zoey Redbird. The impulse was so foreign to him that it shocked him into moving instinctively, as if his subconscious directed his body.

He stepped out of the darkness at the same moment she moved, pressing the palm of her hand to a place in the middle of her breast. She blinked, obviously trying to see through her tears, and her eyes found him. Her body straightened and she looked on the verge of bolting.

"No, you need not leave," he heard himself saying.

"What do you want?" she said, and then she hiccuped another small sob.

"Nothing. I was passing. You were weeping. I heard."

"I want to be alone," she said, wiping at her face with the back of her hand and sniffling.

Aurox did not realize what he did next until he, along with the girl, were both looking at his hand and the tissue he'd pulled from his pocket to offer to her.

"Then I will leave you, but you need this," he said, sounding stiff and foreign to his own ears. "Your face is very wet."

She stared at the tissue for a moment more before taking it, then she looked up at him. "I snot when I cry."

He felt his head nod. "Yes, you do."

She blew her nose and wiped her face. "Thanks. I never have a Kleenex when I need one."

"I know," he said. Then he felt his face flush hot and his body go cold because there was absolutely no reason why he should say such a thing. He had no reason to talk to this fledgling enemy at all.

She was staring at him again, with an odd expression on her face. "What did you say?"

"That I must go." Aurox turned and moved quickly away into the night. He expected the emotions she had made him feel to fade, to flow from him, just as the emotions of others had after he'd absorbed them, used them, cast them aside. But some of Zoey's sadness stayed with him, as did her guilt and, most peculiarly of all, her loneliness stayed with him pooled in a deep, hidden abyss in his soul.

CHAPTER NINE

Zoey

I stared after Aurox for a long time.

What the hell?

I blew my nose again, shook my head, and looked at the wet, wadded mess of Kleenex in my hand. What game had Neferet's creature been playing? Had she purposefully sent him out here after me to offer me a Kleenex and mess with my already totally messed-up head?

No, that couldn't be right. Neferet didn't know that Aurox giving me a Kleenex would remind me of Heath. No one would know that except Heath. Well, and Stark.

So it had to just be a weird coincidence. Sure, Aurox was some kind of creature of Neferet's, but that didn't mean he was immune to the effects of girl tears. He was a guy—at least I was pretty sure he was a guy. And anyway, he might not be one hundred percent one of Neferet's mindless minions. He might be an okay guy—or at least he might be kinda okay when he wasn't changing into a killing machine that looked like a bull. Hell, Stevie Rae had found a good Raven Mocker. Who knows what—

And then I realized what I was doing. I was Kalona-ing him. I was seeing goodness where there was none.

"Oh, hell no! I am soooo not going there," I chastised myself aloud.

"Not going where, Z?" Stark walked into the courtyard, a box of Kleenex in his hand. "Hey, looks like you were snot prepared for a change," he said, gesturing to my wadded mess of a tissue.

"Uh, I'll take another one. Thanks," I said, plucking a couple of tissues from the box and wiping my face again.

"So, where are you not going?" He sat down beside me on the bench. His shoulder brushed mine and I leaned into him.

"I'm just reminding myself not to let the crazy stuff that goes on around here make *me* crazy—or at least crazier."

"You're not crazy, Z. You're going through some hard things, but you're gonna be fine," he said.

"I hope you're right," I muttered and then another, even more depressing thought struck me. "Um, did you tell the rest of the guys not to treat me all weird because of my mom?"

"I didn't have to tell them. They're your friends, Z. They're gonna treat you like they care about you, not weirdly," Stark said.

"I know, I know I just . . ." My voice trailed off. I didn't know how to sift through and put into words the pain and guilt and terrible alone feeling not having a mom had left with me.

"Hey." Stark stopped and looked down at me. "You're *not* alone."

"Are you listening to my thoughts? You know I don't like it when—"

He took my shoulders in his hands and gave me a little shake. "It doesn't take an Oath Bound Warrior's link to know you're feeling all by yourself. I don't know any other kid whose mom is dead, do you?"

"No. Just me." I bit my lip to keep from bawling. Again.

"See, it's not tough to figure you out." He kissed me then. Not with a hot, open mouth, I-want-in-your-panties kiss. Stark's kiss was soft and sweet and reassuring. When his lips left mine he smiled into my eyes. "But, like I said before, you're gonna come through all of this just fine and *not* crazy because you're smart and strong and beautiful and basically covered with awesomesauce."

I giggled unexpectedly. "Awesomesauce? Did you seriously just say that?"

"Hell yes I just said it! You *are* awesome, Z."

"But awesome*sauce*?" I giggled again, and felt my stomach begin to unclench. "That's the dorkiest thing I think I've ever heard you say."

He clutched his chest like I'd just stabbed him. "Z, that hurts. I was trying to be romantic."

"Well, at least you tried," I said. "Please tell me you didn't make that word up all by yourself."

"Nah." He gave me his cute, cocky grin. "I heard a bunch of third former girls say I was covered with it when they were watching me shoot my arrows in the arena last hour."

"Reallly?" I raised a brow and gave him the stank eye. "Third former girls?"

The cocky part of his grin faded. "I meant to say *unattractive* third former girls."

"I'm sure that's exactly what you meant to say."

His eyes sparkled. "Jealous?"

I snorted and lied. "No!"

"You don't have to be jealous. Ever. Because you're not just covered with awesomesauce. You're what awesomesauce is made of."

"Are you sure?"

"Yep."

"Promise?"

"Yep."

I leaned against him. "Okay, I believe you, dork." I rested my head on his shoulder and he put his arm around me. "Can we go home now?"

"Absolutely. Your short yellow limo is loaded and waiting for you." He stood up and pulled me to my feet. Hand in hand we walked toward the parking lot. I snuck a sideways glance at him. He looked pleased with himself (and totally hot). Obviously his dorky word game had been part of his plot to pull me out of the pit of depression I'd felt myself falling into.

Stark would have felt it, too, and not because he was "listening" inappropriately to my thoughts—because he was my Guardian and my Warrior and much, much more.

I squeezed his hand. "Thanks."

He glanced at me, smiled, then lifted my hand to his lips. "No problem. Just wait 'til you hear the word I'm thinking up to describe your boobs. This time it'll be totally made up. I don't need the help of any unattractive third formers for this."

"No. Just no."

"But you might need more cheering up."

"Nope. I'm a-okay. Boob talk is *so* not necessary."

"Well, remember that I'm here if you need me," he said, grinning again. "Ready, willing, and able."

"That's a comfort. Thanks."

"All part of my Guardian job description," he said.

I lifted both of my brows this time. "Did you actually get a job description?"

"Kinda. Seoras said, 'Take care o' yur queen or I'll be finishin' the wee scratchin' I started on yu,'" he said, sounding freakishly like the ancient Scottish Guardian.

"Wee?" I shuddered, remembering the bloody knife wounds that had been slashed all across his chest. How could I ever forget? Even if they weren't still fresh pink scars, despite the healing power of my elements and my blood. "Wee is definitely not how I'd describe them."

"Ach, well, lassie. It wasna much more than pussy scratches."

I felt my eyes go wide, and then I punched him on his arm. "Pussy!"

He rubbed his arm, and in his regular voice said, "Z, it means cat in Scotland. Really."

"You." I scowled at him. "Are a guy."

For some goofy reason that made him laugh, and he put his arms around me, enfolding me in a giant hug. "Yeah, I'm a guy. *Your* guy. And I want you to remember that beyond all this stuff," he paused, pulled back far enough so he could gesture at the House of Night and the short bus that waited a little way from where we were now standing, "and my Warrior stuff, and even my Guardian stuff, I love you, Zoey Redbird. And I'll always be there for you when you need me."

I stepped back into his arms and breathed a long sigh of relief. "Thank you."

"There she is!" I heard Kramisha's voice shouting and I sighed, pretty sure I was the "she" she was talking about. I looked up and, sure enough, Kramisha was standing in front of the loaded short bus with Stevie Rae, Aphrodite, Damien, the Twins, Erik, and a red fledgling I didn't recognize. Keeping Stark's hand in mine I walked the rest of the way to the bus.

"I'm sorry 'bout your momma. That's bad," Kramisha said in greeting.

"Um, th-thanks," I stuttered, and had just started thinking that I was going to have to come up with a non-awkward way to respond to people who were telling me they were sorry my mom was dead when

Kramisha continued with, "Z, I know it ain't good timin', but we got us a problem."

I stifled another sigh. "We, as in me, or we as in you?"

"We think this problem might spill over onto all of us," Stevie Rae said.

"Great," I said.

"Zoey, this is Shaylin." Erik introduced me to the unfamiliar girl, who was studying me like she wished she had me under a microscope. Jeesh, it was a pain to meet new kids.

"Hi, Shaylin," I said, trying to sound normal while I ignored her stare.

"Purple," she said.

"I thought Erik said your name was Shaylin," I said, even though I wanted to shriek *Yes! It's me! The one with the weird tattoos!*

"My name is Shaylin." She gave me a really warm, really nice smile. "You're purple."

"She's not Purple, she's Zoey," Stark said, sounding as confused as I felt.

"You're also flecks of silver." Shaylin finished staring at me and then turned her gaze to him. "You're red and gold and a little black. Huh. That's weird."

"Okay, I'm not—"

"Oh, for shit's sake," Aphrodite interrupted, pointing at Shaylin. "This new kid's name *is* Shaylin, and she's not calling you colors, she's *seeing* your colors."

"My colors? I don't have a clue what that means," I said, frowning at Aphrodite and then giving Shaylin a big question mark look.

"I don't really know what it means, either," Shaylin said. "It just happened to me, right after I was Marked."

"I think Shaylin has been gifted with something called True Sight," Damien said. "It's rare. I think there's something about it in the *Advanced Fledgling Handbook,* but I only peeked at one of those." He looked embarrassed and apologetic. "I didn't really study it."

"Damien, you're only a forth former. It wasn't part of your classwork," Stevie Rae said.

"Hello, talk about homework obsessed," Erin muttered.

"Seriously," Shaunee added.

"Look." I raised my voice so everyone would gawk at me instead of launching into the bickering I was pretty sure was getting ready to start. "I don't know what True Sight is, but if it's a gift, and I'm assuming you mean from Nyx, then why is that a problem?" I said.

"She's a red fledgling," Aphrodite said.

"So? There's a whole short bus full of them," I said, gesturing behind them.

"Yeah, and each of us had to die and then un-die before we got us these." Kramisha pointed at the red outline of a crescent moon on her forehead.

I stared at her, then at the new kid, and then my mind caught up with my eyes. I looked at Erik. "You just Marked her in red?"

"No. Yes." Erik shook his head and looked worried as hell. "I didn't mean to. I Marked her. Okay, yes, it didn't go exactly according to plan, but that was because she was blind, and that surprised me." We all stared at him and he ran his hand through his thick, dark hair. His shoulders slumped. Then he added, "I messed up, and that's why she's a red fledgling and can see our colors."

"You didn't mess up, Erik." It looked like Shaylin started to reach out to pat Erik's arm, but halfway through the motion changed her mind. Her gaze moved to me and she continued, "Before he Marked me I was blind. I've been blind since I was a kid. The second he Marked me I could see again, and that's not a mess up. That's amazing."

"Ah! I knew I felt a new fledgling!" At the sound of Neferet's voice we all jumped like she'd Tasered us. She was hurrying toward us, her long green velvet gown sweeping the ground and making it appear as if she was gliding instead of walking (which was super creepy). "Merry meet, I am Neferet, your High Priestess." She turned her attention briefly to Erik, and I could see displeasure flash in her eyes. "Professor Night, you should not have brought the child here." Neferet reached Shaylin and made a graceful, apologetic gesture to her. "Young fledgling, the Tracker should have instructed you to come to the female dormitory where you will join the rest of the—" She broke off when she finally saw Shaylin's Mark.

"Yeah," I said, unable to keep my mouth shut any longer. "She's red. Which means she *is* in the right place."

"And I'm her High Priestess. Not you," Stevie Rae finished for me.

"Oh! You're . . . oh, I don't feel well!" Shaylin was staring at Neferet when she suddenly collapsed. Erik caught her before she conked her head on the ground, managing to look scared and hero-like at the same time. (Seriously, he's an excellent actor.)

"She's been through a lot," Aphrodite said, stepping up to stand toe to toe with Neferet. "She needs to go home. To the depot. With us. Now."

I held my breath as Neferet's eyes narrowed and her gaze flicked around at each kid in our group. All vampyres are intuitive, but Neferet is more than that. She can read minds. Well, most fledglings' minds—or at least the surface of their thoughts. I sent a quick, silent prayer up to the Goddess: *Please let each of them think about everything and anything except the fact that this new kid may have True Sight—whatever that is.*

Suddenly Neferet's suspicious expression changed. She laughed. She actually laughed. I had no idea how it was possible, but her laugh sounded horrible and mean and sarcastic. How could laughter be so awful?

"She was blind. That's why she's been Marked red. She's broken. She just didn't have to die to get that way. Well, at least not yet she hasn't died."

Kramisha was standing beside me, so I saw her little jerk of fear. So did Neferet. The pretend High Priestess smiled at our Poet Laureate. "What is it? Did you actually believe that red outline guaranteed you the Change?" She cocked her head to the side, reminding me of a reptile. "Yes, I can sense your shock and fear. You hadn't thought of that. Your body can still reject the Change."

"You don't know that for sure." Stevie Rae stepped closer to Kramisha.

"Don't I?" Again, Neferet's laugh was mean and awful. She jerked her chin at Shaylin, who was still passed out in Erik's arms. "That one feels odd to me." She shifted her gaze to Aphrodite. I saw Aphrodite put her fists on her waist, as if bracing herself for a physical blow. "A little like you feel, and you're not even a fledgling anymore."

"No, I'm not. But I am happy with what I am. How about you, Neferet?"

Instead of an answer, Neferet said, "Take the new fledgling with you. You're right about one thing, Aphrodite. Her home is with you and the rest of the misfits, not here. What in the name of all the gods will Nyx come up with next?"

And then, laughing, she turned her back dismissively on us and slithered away.

When she was out of hearing range I let out a long breath. "Good job, all of you, in not thinking about the True Sight thing."

"She scares me," Kramisha said in a voice that sounded very, very young.

Stevie Rae put her arm around Kramisha. "It's okay to be scared of her. That'll just make us fight harder against her."

"Or run faster," Erik said grimly.

"Some of us aren't running away," Stevie Rae said.

"Are you sure?" Shaylin said.

"Hey, are you back with us?" Erik asked.

"Actually, I never went anywhere. Um. You can put me down now. Please."

"Oh, right. Yeah." Erik gently put her down. He kept a hand on her arm, as if to be sure she wasn't going to wobble and fall, but she stood there looking pretty darn steady.

"So, you faked a faint. Why?" Aphrodite asked the question before I could.

"Well, it wasn't hard." Shaylin looked at Kramisha. "I agree with you. She scares me." Then she continued. "I acted like I passed out because it was either that or run screaming away from her." She shared a look with Erik. "Yeah, I agree with you, too." Then she shrugged a shoulder. "But she said she's a High Priestess. I don't know much about vampyres, but everyone knows High Priestesses are in charge. Running screaming away from one my first day as a fledgling didn't seem like a good option."

"So you figured you'd play opossum," Stevie Rae said.

"Play what?"

"That's a bumpkin way of saying that you pretended to be out of it so Neferet would leave you alone," Aphrodite said.

"Yeah, that's exactly what I did," Shaylin said.

"Not a bad plan," Stark said. "Meeting Neferet and being Marked all in one day sucks for you."

"What did you see?" My question seemed to take everyone except Shaylin by surprise. She met my gaze and held it steadily as she answered me. "Right before I went blind I was at Nam Hi, that big Vietnamese grocery store on Twenty-first and Garnett, with my mom. They had whole fish for sale in a giant bin of ice. They scared me so bad I remember all I could do was stand there and stare at their milky, dead eyes and their horrible slit open bellies."

"Neferet's dead fish belly color?" Stevie Rae asked.

"No. Neferet's color is the same color as dead fish eyes. That's her only color."

"That can't be good," Kramisha said.

"What can't be good?" Darius asked as he joined our group, taking Aphrodite's hand. She leaned into him and said, "Darius, stud Warrior, meet Shaylin, newly Marked red fledgling who didn't die to be red and who has True Sight. She just 'saw'"—Aphrodite air quoted—"Neferet and apparently her true color is like dead fish eyes."

Darius didn't miss a beat. He just gave the new kid a little bow and said, "Merry meet, Shaylin," which either showed the Warrior had impressive control or was just more proof that our lives had become totally bat-poop crazy.

"We need to learn more about True Sight," Damien said. "It's sixth former and beyond level information. Do you know anything about it?" he asked Darius.

"Not a lot. I focused mostly on knives, not vampyre sociology," Darius said.

"Well, I have the stupid advanced handbook," Aphrodite said. When we gave her a group gawk she frowned. "What? I was a sixth former before *this* happened." She pointed at her unMarked forehead. "Sadly, I had to rejoin my old schedule today." When we all kept staring without speaking she rolled her eyes. "Oh, for shit's sake, I have homework, that's all. The book's in my extremely attractive Anahata Joy Katkin bag in the retard bus."

"Aphrodite, stop sayin' retard!" Stevie Rae shouted at her. "I swear you need to check out www.r-word.com. Maybe you'd learn that some people get their feelin's hurt by the r-word."

Aphrodite blinked several times and then scrunched her forehead. "A Web site? Seriously."

"Yes, Aphrodite. Like I have tried to tell you a bazillion times, using the r-word is demeaning and just plain mean."

Aphrodite sucked in a deep breath and let it out in a rant: "What about having a site for the c-word—which demeans *half of the world*? Or, wait, no. Let's keep it the r-word site only make the r-word rape, which does more than just hurt upper middle class mommies' feelings. Or—"

"Seriously." I stepped between them. "We get it. Can we go back to Shaylin and the True Sight issue?"

"Yeah, whatever," Aphrodite said, flipping back her hair.

"Aphrodite's mean, Z, but she makes a good point," Erin said.

I glared at Shaunee who only nodded enthusiastically, but didn't chime in. My head felt like it was going to explode. "Ah, hell," I said, throwing up my hands in frustration. "I can't remember what we were saying before the retard part."

"Information about True Sight is on the bus," Rephaim said, surprising all of us. He smiled shyly. "I didn't really understand much of the rest of the conversation. I also got that Aphrodite is mean, but I already knew that."

Beside me Stark turned a bark of laughter into a cough.

I sighed.

"Okay, let's get on the bus and get back to the depot. Aphrodite and Damien, meet me in the kitchen with the advanced handbook." I paused and glanced at Stevie Rae, who was still holding Rephaim's hand. "You wanna join us after, um, you know, the sun rises and such?"

"Z, you don't have to tippie-toe around it. Yes, Rephaim's gonna change into a bird when the sun comes up, and I'd like to be with him 'til then." She glanced up at Rephaim who was smiling down at her like it was his birthday and she was some super amazing present he'd just opened.

"Seriously?" I heard Shaylin ask Erik.

"Yeah. It's a long story," Erik said.

"No wonder his color's so weird," she said.

I was curious about Rephaim's color, but I knew now was not the time to ask her a bunch of questions, so instead I just said, "Kramisha, would you please figure out where Shaylin will be staying?"

"I ain't sharin' my room," Kramisha said. Then she gave Shaylin an apologetic look. "Sorry. I don't mean no offense."

"That's fine. I've had to have people around me ever since I went blind. I'd rather have my own room, too."

Kramisha smiled. "That's right. I like me an independent woman, and I'll help you find a room of your own."

"Deal," Shaylin said.

"Er." Erik cleared his throat to get our attention. I thought he looked nervous and unusually unsure of himself. "How about I follow the bus in my car, and Shaylin comes with me? I can fill her in on some of the stuff like Rephaim and the whole red fledgling thing in general on the way."

"Trackers are just supposed to track and Mark," Aphrodite said.

"Yeah, and fledglings are supposed to be Marked with a blue crescent, and then Change or die," he countered.

"I think it's okay that Erik follows us," Stevie Rae said, which surprised me because I knew she wasn't exactly an Erik fan. "What do you think, Z?"

I shrugged. "Okay with me."

Erik gave a little nod and then he and Shaylin headed for his car in the parking lot.

"Are we ready to go?" Darius asked.

"I guess, or at least we will be as soon as our ever-so-friendly driver gets here," I said.

Darius smiled. "That would be me. "I told Christophe I'd handle the drive back and forth to the depot from here on."

I couldn't resist a look at Aphrodite. Her face was frozen and her eyes looked huge.

"Hey, Aphrodiky is going out with a bus driver!" Shaunee said.

It looked like Erin had some smart-ass comment she was going to add, but Aphrodite closed the space between her and the Twins. "Darius isn't a bus driver. He's a Son of Erebus Warrior. He *can* kill you, but he's honorable and good so he won't. I, on the other hand, am not honorable or a Warrior. I *will* kill you, or at the very least mess you up so bad you won't make the next Miss Jackson's trunk sale."

The Twins sucked air and I quickly said, "All righty then, let's all go back to the depot. Looks like we have some studying to do." I grabbed Aphrodite's wrist and practically dragged her to the bus. She jerked away from me, but was still following when I started to climb the stairs. Then an orange ball of fur hurled herself into my arms. "Nala!" I yelped, almost dropping her in surprise. "Oh, baby girl! I've missed you so much." I petted her and kissed her and laughed when she sneezed on me and then started to grumble in her old lady voice, *"mee-uf-owing"* even while she was purring like crazy.

While I was cuddling Nala there was a terrible screeching sound from the bowels of the bus, and suddenly Aphrodite was pushing past me yelling, "Maleficent! Mommy's here!" It seemed to rain white fur. The kids on the bus jerked legs and arms out of the way as the ugliest, most smoosh-faced, huge, hateful cat in the universe padded down the aisle hissing and yowling. Aphrodite stooped, picked her up, and began telling her how beautiful and wonderful and smart she was.

"That cat ain't right," Kramisha said, peeking over my shoulder. "But Aphrodite ain't right, either, so I guess it works out just fine." Her gaze went from Maleficent to Nala, who was still grumbling at me. "Actually, a whole bunch of these cats ain't normal."

"Whole bunch?" I looked up over Nala's furry orange head and, as I suspected, the yellow mini-limo was full of red fledglings *and* cats. "When did this happen?"

"They was here when we got here," Kramisha said. "Like I said—they ain't normal."

"Huh, well. I suppose this means the depot really is our new home," I said, feeling for the first time that it could be true.

"Z, home is where you are," Stark said, reaching over me and scratching Nala on her head.

I smiled at him and felt warm inside—almost warm enough to make me forget about moonstone-colored eyes and the fact that people around me kept dying . . .

CHAPTER TEN

Kalona

"What did you just say to me?" Kalona bellowed at the Raven Mocker, who cringed away from him.

"Rephaim issss a human boy," Nisroc repeated. His less-evolved brother, the one who had escaped the changeling creature's wrath, moved restlessly, backing up behind him.

Kalona paced around the clearing between the hunting blinds. It wasn't yet dawn, but the other Raven Mockers, the ones who had returned from searching out their brothers from the Oklahoma countryside, were already huddled inside the tree houses, hiding, escaping, cringing away from the possibility of prying eyes. He'd stood out there, watching each of them return, looking for something that he was loath to admit to himself. He'd been looking for humanity—for a son to talk with, to share with, to plan with. But all he'd been met by were sniveling, cringing beasts. *Rephaim was the most human of all of them,* Kalona had been thinking, for what seemed like the thousandth time, when Nisroc had landed in the clearing minus one son and with unbelievable news of another.

Kalona rounded on Nisroc. "Rephaim cannot have a human form. It is impossible! He is a Raven Mocker, as are you, as are your brothers."

"The Goddessss," Nisroc hissed. "Ssshe changed him."

An odd, bittersweet feeling came over Kalona. Nyx had changed his son from beast to human—gifted him with the form of a boy.

She'd forgiven Rephaim? How could that be?

Almost at a loss for words, the immortal blurted, "You spoke to Rephaim?"

Nisroc bobbed his enormous raven's head up and down. "Yessss."

"He actually said he is in Nyx's service?"

"Yessss." Nisroc bowed to him, but his eyes were bright and sly. "For you he refused to sssspy."

Kalona gave him a sharp look and then glanced at the battered Raven Mocker who stood innocuously behind him, suddenly realizing there was only one brother when there should have been two.

"Where is—" Kalona had to pause to remember which of his sons was missing. "Maion? Why did he not return with you?"

"Dead." Nisroc pronounced the world flatly, with no emotion.

"Rephaim killed him?" Kalona's voice was as cold as his heart.

"No. The creature. Killed him it did."

"What creature? Speak clearly!"

"The Tsi Sgili's creature."

"A vampyre?"

"No. First human, then bull."

Kalona's body jerked in surprise. "Are you quite sure? The creature took on the form of a bull?"

"Yesss."

"Did Rephaim join with it to attack you?"

"No."

"He fought beside you against it?"

"No. Nothinng he did," Nisroc said.

Kalona's jaw clenched and unclenched. "Then what stopped the beast?

"The Red One."

"Then did she and Neferet battle?" Kalona snapped the questions, silently cursing himself for sending lesser beings to witness what he should have seen.

"No. No battle happened. We flew."

"Yet you say the bull was Neferet's creature."

"Yesss."

"Then it is true. Neferet has given herself over to the white bull." Kalona paced again. "She has no idea of the forces she is awakening.

The white bull is Darkness in its purest, most powerful form." Somewhere deep within Kalona something stirred, something that had not surfaced since he'd fallen. For a brief moment, just the length of a heartbeat, the ancient Warrior of the Goddess of Night, the winged immortal who had defended his Goddess against the onslaught of Darkness for uncounted centuries, had an automatic desire to go to Nyx—to warn her—to protect her.

Kalona shook off the ridiculous impulse almost as quickly as he'd felt it. He began pacing again. Thinking aloud he mused, "So Neferet has an ally that ties her to the white bull, but she must be disguising him as something else to the House of Night, or you would have seen at least the beginnings of a major battle."

"Yessss, her creature."

Kalona ignored Nisroc's repetitive comments and kept reasoning aloud. "Rephaim has entered the service of Nyx. She has gifted him with a human form." His jaw clenched and unclenched. He felt doubly betrayed—by his son and by the Goddess. He'd asked, practically *begged* Nyx to forgive him. And what had her answer been? *"If you are ever worthy of forgiving, you may ask it of me. Not until then."*

The memory of his sojourn in the Otherworld and his glimpse of the Goddess caused a terrible ache in his heart. Instead of feeling it—thinking of it—acting on it—Kalona opened the gates to the anger that always boiled just below the levees in his soul. As anger flooded through him it washed away any other gentler, more honest, feelings.

"My son needs to learn a lesson about loyalty," Kalona said.

"Loyal I am!" Nisroc cried.

Kalona's lip curled up contemptuously. "I don't speak of you. I speak of Rephaim."

"Ssssspy Rephaim will not," Nisroc repeated.

Kalona cuffed him and the Raven Mocker stumbled back against his brother. "Rephaim has done much more than spy for me in the past. He has been a second pair of fists, a second pair of eyes, almost an extension of me. It is habit that has me searching the sky for him. I am finding habit is a hard thing to break. Perhaps Rephaim is finding it difficult as well." The winged immortal turned his back on his sons and stared off to the east, over the wooded ridges, toward sleeping Tulsa. "I should visit Rephaim. We do, after all, have a common enemy."

"The Tsi Sgili?" Nisroc asked, subservient and docile.

"That's right. The Tsi Sgili. Rephaim would not call it spying if we were serving a common goal—to depose Neferet."

"Rule in her stead you would?"

Kalona turned amber eyes to his son. "Yes. I would always rule. We rest now. At sunset I depart for Tulsa."

"With ussss?" the Raven Mocker asked.

"No. You remain here. Continue to gather my sons. Stay hidden and wait."

"Wait?"

"For my call. When I rule those who remain loyal to me will be by my side. And those who have not will be destroyed, no matter who they are. Do you understand, Nisroc?"

"Yessss."

Rephaim

"Your skin is so soft." Rephaim ran his fingertips down the curved slope of Stevie Rae's naked back, marveling at the joy it gave him to be able to hold her in his arms and press his body—his fully human body—against hers.

"I like it that you think I'm so special," Stevie Rae said, smiling up at him a little shyly.

"You *are* special," he said. Then he sighed and began to gently untangle himself from her. "It's close to dawn. I have to go above ground."

Stevie Rae sat up and hugged the thick comforter that covered the bed in her surprisingly pretty little tunnel room to cover her bare breasts. She blinked big blue eyes at him. Her hair was tousled and curly and framed her face making her look like a young, innocent maiden. Rephaim pulled on his jeans, thinking she was the most beautiful thing he'd ever seen. And her next words pierced his heart.

"I don't want you to go, Rephaim."

"You know I don't want to, either, but I must."

"C-can't you just stay here? With me?" she asked hesitantly.

He sighed and sat on the edge of the bed they'd so recently shared. He took her hand in his and threaded their fingers together. "Would you cage me?"

He felt her body jerk as if in shock—or was it revulsion?

"No! I didn't mean it like that. I just thought, well, that you could maybe try bein' here for a day. I mean, what if we just kept holdin' hands, like this, until you were done changin'?"

He smiled sadly at her. "Stevie Rae, a raven doesn't have any hands. These," he pressed his palms against hers, "will very shortly be claws. I will, very shortly, be a beast. I will not know you."

"Okay, so, what if I kept my arms around you? Maybe you wouldn't be scared then. Maybe you'd just curl up beside me and stay here and sleep, too. I mean, ya have to sleep sometime, don't ya?"

Rephaim thought about it before he answered her, and then began to slowly try to explain the unexplainable. "I must sleep, but Stevie Rae, I do not remember anything from the time I'm a raven." *Anything except the agony of the physical change and the almost unbearable joy of the wind against my wings*—but he could not tell Stevie Rae either of those things. One would hurt her. One could frighten her. So instead of the raw truth, he told her a version of it that seemed more civilized, more understandable. "A raven is not a pet. It is a wild bird. What if I panicked and in trying to escape I somehow wounded you?"

"Or yourself," Stevie Rae said solemnly. "I get it. I really do. I just don't like it much."

"I don't, either, but I think that's the point Nyx was making. I'm paying the consequences for my past actions." He cupped her sweet, soft cheek in his palm and pressed his lips to hers murmuring, "It is a price I willingly pay because the other side of it, the good side of it, gives me the hours we steal together when I am human."

"We don't steal them!" Stevie Rae said earnestly. "Nyx gifted you with them for the good choices you've made. Consequences go both ways, Rephaim. They can be good and bad."

Somehow that made his heart feel lighter and he smiled, kissing her again. "I'll remember that."

"I want you to remember somethin' else, too. You did a good thing today when you didn't turn your back on your brothers." Her fingers plucked at a blond curl, and he knew whatever she was saying was hard for her, so even though he needed to get free of the tunnels, to get above to the waiting sky, he remained sitting there beside her with her hand in his while she continued. "I'm sorry your brother got killed."

"Thank you," he said quietly, hardly trusting his voice.

"They came to the House of Night to get you to leave with them, didn't they?" she asked.

"Not really. Father did send them to find me, but not to take me away." Rephaim paused, not sure how to explain the rest to Stevie Rae. The two of them hadn't talked about his brothers when they'd finally been alone—they'd been too eager to touch, to be close, to love.

Stevie Rae squeezed his hand. "You can tell me. I trust you, Rephaim. Please trust me, too."

"I do!" he exclaimed, hating the hurt he saw in her eyes. "But you have to understand that even though Father has disowned me, that changes nothing here." He touched his chest over his heart. "I will forever be his son. I'll walk the path of the Goddess. I'll fight for Light and what is right. I'll love you. Always. But you must understand that somewhere inside me I'll always love him, too. Becoming human has taught me that."

"Rephaim, I have to tell you somethin' that might sound mean, but I think you need to hear it."

He nodded. "Go ahead. Tell me."

"Before I was Marked I went to school with this girl name Sallie. Her momma took off and left her and her daddy when she was about ten 'cause she was basically just a downright nasty ho slut and she didn't want the responsibility of raisin' a kid. It hurt Sallie real bad when her momma left, even though her daddy tried to do his best for her. But the worst part of the whole thing was that her momma wouldn't stay gone. She'd come back and, as my momma used to say, stir the shit pot."

He gave her a questioning look, and Stevie Rae said, "Sorry, that means her momma came back around just to mess with her—to keep Sallie's life all filled with stupid drama and such because she was selfish and mean and uber screwed up."

"What happened to this Sallie girl?" Rephaim asked.

"When I got Marked and left school she was on her way to bein' as uber screwed up as her momma 'cause she didn't have the strength to tell her momma to stay away. Sallie still wanted her momma to be a good person, to love her and care about her, even though that just wasn't possible." Stevie Rae drew a deep breath and let it out in a long sigh. "What I'm tryin' to say, and probably not doin' it very well, is that you're gonna have to decide whether you want to be as messed up as your daddy, or if you want to really start a new life."

"I've already chosen a new life," he said.

Stevie Rae met his eyes and shook her head sadly. "Not all of you has."

"I can't betray him, Stevie Rae."

"I'm not askin' you to. All I'm askin' you to do is to not let him stir your shit pot."

"He wanted me to spy for him. That's what he sent my brothers to tell me. I told Nisroc no." Rephaim said the words quickly, as if by doing so he could get rid of their bitter taste.

Stevie Rae nodded. "Yeah, see, shit pot stirring."

"I do see it, even though it isn't an easy thing to look at. Can we not talk about him for a while? All this is new for me. I need to figure out how to find my place in this world." Rephaim stared into Stevie Rae's kind eyes, willing her to understand. "I've been with Father for hundreds of years. It's going to take some time for me to get used to not being by his side."

"That makes sense. How 'bout this: I'll tell Zoey and the rest of the gang that your brothers were there to let you know Kalona would take you back if you said you'd made a mistake. You said no, so they were just leavin' when Dragon and that Aurox guy saw you. That's the truth, right?"

"Yes. What about the rest of it, the part about Father asking me to spy for him?"

"Well, I can tell you that I'll bet everyone pretty much figures

Kalona would try to use you against us if you let him. You're not letting him, so I don't think spelling it out for them is a big deal."

"Thank you, Stevie Rae."

She smiled. "No problem. Like I said, I trust you."

He kissed her again, but about then he began to feel an already all-too-familiar prickling over his skin, as if his feathers were forming, growing, pressing to be free. "I must go." And this time he began to move quickly from the room. He could hear her start to get off the bed behind him and when he looked back she was pulling on her T-shirt and looking around for her jeans. "No," he said more firmly than he'd intended, but the pain had already begun through his body and he knew he hadn't much time. "Don't come with me. You have to meet with Zoey."

"But I can after—"

"I don't want you to see me become a beast!"

"I don't care about that," she said, looking like she was on the verge of tears.

"But I do. Please. Do not follow me." Without another word he ducked under the blanket that served as a door covering to Stevie Rae's room. By the time he'd reached the metal ladder-like stairs that led up from the tunnels and into the basement, Rephaim was running. Sweat poured from his body and he had to grit his teeth not to cry out with the burning agony of the change that was gripping him. He sprinted through the basement and flung open the grate just as the sun slipped free of the horizon and with a scream that turned into the cry of a raven his body shifted form and the dark raven who had no memory of the boy launched himself into the seductive, waiting arms of the morning sky.

Stevie Rae

Stevie Rae didn't go after him, but she did finish getting dressed. She wiped her eyes, too, before she left her room and turned in the opposite direction Rephaim had taken and headed for the hub of the depot tunnels—the little cul-de-sac-like area they'd turned into a kitchen and computer hub. *Mountain Dew,* she thought as she stifled a yawn. *I need me some caffeine and sugar.*

She rounded the corner and smiled sleepily at Damien, Zoey, Aphrodite, and Darius. The four of them were sitting around a table loaded with books in the center of the kitchen.

"There's lots of pop in that fridge," Zoey said, waving at one of the two big side-by-side refrigerators.

"More than just brown?"

"There's brown and green and clear. Oh, and some Orange Crush because Kramisha said she thinks it's healthy," Z said.

"Which is bullshit," Aphrodite said before upending a bottle of Fuji water. "Choose water. Anything else will make you fat. Well, except for blood." She paused and her beautiful face squeezed into an *ick* look. "I don't know about the calorie count in it, and since I un-fledgling-ed I don't even want to think about it."

Stevie Rae pulled open the fridge and gawked at the loaded insides. "Where did all this stuff come from?"

Zoey gave a little sigh. "Kramisha. She said instead of going to third hour she 'field-tripped'"—Z air quoted—"to Utica Square and just happened to run into some night shift guys stocking the shelves at Petty's grocery store."

Stevie Rae peeked around the arm of the fridge at Z. "Uh-oh. She red vamp zapped them?"

"She definitely zapped them," Damien said. "Which is how all this food got delivered down here. She even talked them into bringing this table from one of their food sample setups."

"She didn't eat them, did she?" Stevie Rae asked, crossing her fingers behind her back.

"No, but she didn't pay them, either," Aphrodite said. "She just made them do her bidding and then leave and forget all of it. I think I'm taking her with me to New York City next time Yoana Baraschi has a trunk show."

"No," Zoey said. "Just no." Then she looked at Stevie Rae. "Are you really awake? Stark and all the red fledglings, including Miss Kramisha Make-Them-Do-My-Bidding are sound asleep."

Stevie Rae grabbed a Mountain Dew and joined them at the table, sitting heavily and yawning. "Yeah, barely. It's easier to stay awake during the day down here, but I gotta tell ya, I'm pretty dang tired. Stark's asleep already?"

"Yeah." Stevie Rae thought Z looked worried. "He's been having problems sleeping since, well, you know—he came back from the Otherworld. So when he passes out I just let him alone."

"It'll take a while, but he'll be back to normal soon," Stevie Rae said.

"I hope so," Zoey said and chewed at her lip.

"Speaking of boyfriends, is yours a bird?" Aphrodite asked her.

"Yes." Stevie Rae gave her a narrowed-eye look. "And I don't wanna talk about it."

"But we do need to know exactly why the Raven Mockers were at the school today," Darius said, not unkindly, "And since Rephaim is unable to answer our questions we're hoping you can."

"I thought this meeting was about the True Sight stuff," Stevie Rae said, feeling immediately defensive of Rephaim.

"It is, but it's also a catch-up meeting," Damien said. "I think we need one, don't you?"

There was just no way to argue with Damien, especially when he had that sweet, concerned look on his face. Stevie Rae met his eyes. "Yeah, I think we do. So, to start with, how are you holdin' up?"

Damien blinked several times, like he was surprised by the question, which made Stevie Rae feel like crap. Had everydangbody forgotten Damien had lost his boyfriend just days ago?

"It was better being at school today. It felt like a step toward normal." Damien spoke slowly and carefully, as if he had to think about each word. "But I missed Jack a lot. Actually, and I know this might sound crazy, but I kept expecting to see him around every corner in the hallway."

"That's not crazy," Zoey said. "I keep expecting to see Heath, too. It's hard and just plain wrong when someone dies too soon." Everyone watched the different expressions play across Z's face, and then she added, "My mom, too. I know I've been at the House of Night since last year, and even before that she and I hadn't been close for a while, but it's hard to really get that she's dead. So I understand what you mean about Jack."

"That makes it better, too," Damien said. "The fact that you guys understand what it's like to lose someone close to you." He smiled at Stevie Rae. "So, my answer to your question is that I'm holding up as well as can be expected."

"Good. Next question, or actually back to the original question," Aphrodite said. "What were the birdboys doing at the House of Night?"

"Kalona sent 'em. They were supposed to tell Rephaim that his daddy will take him back as soon as he admits he made a mistake choosing me and the Goddess." Stevie Rae shook her head. "Sometimes I think Kalona's just plain dumb."

"What do you mean?" Z asked.

"Heck, Rephaim hasn't even been my official boyfriend for a month. You'd think his daddy'd at least give us a chance to have our first fight before he was all 'oooh, you've made a mistake.'"

"What exactly was Rephaim's response?" Darius asked.

"Well, what do you think it was? Jeeze Louise, he's still here." Stevie Rae felt her anger build. "He told them to tell Kalona that he hadn't made a mistake and he wasn't comin' back. Period. The end."

"Yeah, but is it?" Aphrodite said.

"Is it what?" she asked.

"Is it the end? Isn't Kalona going to keep hanging around, trying to get Rephaim to see the light or whatever?"

"So what if he does? Rephaim isn't on his team anymore. He hasn't been for a long time."

"So you say."

"So he says!" Stevie Rae felt like she was going to explode. "So his dad says. So his brothers say. So even Nyx says! The dang Goddess herself showed up and forgave him. What the hell does Rephaim have to do to prove to you guys he's changed?"

"Hey, no one's saying Rephaim has to prove anything," Zoey said, sending Aphrodite a *you're not helping* look. "But we do need to know if something is up with Kalona and the Raven Mockers."

"Z, nothin's up with them. Well, except that it really hurt Rephaim that that dang bull kid killed one of 'em. Seriously, guys, his brothers weren't doin' anything except talkin' to him. Dragon showed up, pissed of course, but we all get that because of Anastasia. Still, the Raven Mockers were just defendin' themselves. Aurox is the one we should be askin' questions about."

"Yeah, except that we don't have Aurox answers here—and we should have Rephaim answers," Aphrodite said.

"I gave you his answers." Even as weak and tired as she felt because it was past sunrise, Stevie Rae automatically began pulling power from the earth. Not that she'd really hurt Aphrodite, but the girl definitely needed a good smack.

"Hey, you're glowing green," Z said.

"Well, I'm pissed!" Stevie Rae saw Darius move closer to Aphrodite, which really annoyed her. "You know what, Darius, you need to check yourself. We're all on the same side here, but that doesn't mean we can't get pissed at each other once in a while."

"I think we can all understand that. Isn't that right, Darius?" Damien said in his calmest, most soothing voice.

"Yes, of course," Darius said.

Aphrodite snorted.

"So, basically, Rephaim said no to Kalona and the Raven Mockers were just the messengers," Z said. "Right?"

"Totally right," Stevie Rae said.

"Okay, let's move on to True Sight." Zoey looked at Damien. "Want to summarize what you've found out?"

"Yeah, but it's not much. There's only a short reference to it in the advanced handbook. Basically, it's rare and it hasn't happened for a long time. Like as in more than a couple hundred years. It's frustrating because there isn't a lot of documentation about it, but from what I could find it seems that a fledgling or vampyre gifted with True Sight—and they're usually vampyres, by the way—has the ability to see the truth about people."

"That's a handy little gift," Aphrodite said.

"You'd think so, but the problem is that the 'seeing' is only as accurate as the person with the gift," Damien said.

"Huh?" Zoey said.

"Okay, it's like this: Shaylin has to be good at using her gift. She has to understand what she's seeing and interpret it accurately," Damien said.

"And if she doesn't, it's just a bunch of colors?" Zoey said.

"Worse," Damien said. "Because with True Sight it's never just a bunch of colors. We all know she's seeing inside someone's soul." He shook his head. "In the handbook there were excerpts of stories about how True Sight has been misunderstood and misused. It can be bad, really bad."

"How about guidelines or rules or whatnot?" Z asked.

"None. It's different for everyone who has the Sight," Damien said.

"So we're just shootin' in the dark," Stevie Rae said, feeling totally overwhelmed. "Again."

"I think that depends entirely on what kind of person Shaylin is," Damien said.

"She's buddied up to Erik, which isn't a great sign," Aphrodite said.

"Hey, some of us who used to be buddied up with Erik have turned out okay," Zoey said. "And plus, a girl who can see his true colors could be really good for him."

Aphrodite snorted. "If she can actually translate them correctly—or whatever you want to call it."

"I want to believe that she can," Damien said.

"Yeah, me too," Stevie Rae said, but who she was really thinking about was Rephaim and Kalona. *Please, Nyx, let Rephaim be able to see the truth.* As she sent up the fervent but silent prayer, her eyes lifted and she met her BFF's gaze.

"I want to believe, too," Zoey said softly as if she could read Stevie Rae's mind.

"Well, I want to believe that when I step out of this room and down the hall I'm going to be instantly transported to a suite at the Ritz-Carlton on Grand Cayman Island. I understand the rest of you are sun challenged, but I could use a little shake and bake." Aphrodite paused and gave Darius a sexy grin. "I'll take care of the baking part if you can handle the shaking."

Stevie Rae stood up and yawned. "Okay, before y'all get totally gross I'm gonna go pass out. I'll see everybody at dusk."

"Ugh, school and no Ritz. Double ugh, reality," Aphrodite said. "Goddess, I'm glad tomorrow is Friday." She raised a blond brow at Zoey. "I can promise you I'm doing some serious shop and redecorate this weekend. Battling evil, Darkness, or whatever is just gonna have to wait."

"Hey, speaking of rooms, does anyone know where Erik put Shaylin?" Stevie Rae asked around another huge yawn.

"Elizabeth No Last Name's room," Damien said.

"Kinda creepy," Stevie Rae said.

"It's not like she's using it," Aphrodite said.

"I'm going to bed," Z said. " 'Night guys."

Everyone called "night" to her, but Stevie Rae watched her walk slowly away down toward Dallas's old room that she and Stark were making their own. Her steps were slow and her shoulders were slumped, as if she was trying way too hard to carry way too much weight on them.

Stevie Rae sighed. She knew exactly how Z felt.

CHAPTER ELEVEN

Lenobia

Lenobia sniffed the air. Mixed with sawdust, leather, sweet feed, and horse was something else—something smoky and vaguely familiar. She gave Mujaji—her favorite mare, a solid black quarter horse—a final stroke of the soft curry brush and, following her nose, left the stall. She turned down the long, wide hallway that was lined on either side with roomy stalls. Her nose led her exactly where she'd expected it to—the big foaling stall that was near the tack room. Moving quietly Lenobia told herself she wasn't really sneaking up on him. She was just being sure she didn't spook his mare.

Travis's back was to her. The cowboy was standing in the middle of the stall. In one hand he was holding a thick, smoking stick of dried herbs. His other hand was passing through the light-colored smoke, wafting it around and over him. Bonnie, his big Percheron mare, was standing in front of him, dozing with one leg cocked. She only twitched an ear slightly when he moved to her and passed the smoking herb all along the outline of her very large body. He went from Bonnie to the cot he'd set up for himself in the far corner of the stall, giving it the same smoke-out treatment he'd given the mare and himself. It was only as he began to turn from the cot that Lenobia stepped back out of his view. Pondering what she'd seen, Lenobia went out the side door of the stable and walked a few feet to a bench where she sat, breathed in the stillness of the cool night, and tried to sift through her thoughts.

The cowboy had been burning sage. Actually, Lenobia was pretty sure from the scent that it had been white sage. *Excellent for cleansing a space.* But why would an Oklahoma cowboy have been doing that?

Human behavior? What did she know of it? She'd had only the most perfunctory contact with them for . . . Lenobia considered twisting the slim gold band that held the heart-shaped emerald around and around the ring finger of her left hand. She knew exactly how long it had been since she'd been close to a human, specifically a human man—two hundred and twenty-three years.

Lenobia looked down at her ring finger. There wasn't much light. Dawn was just beginning to turn the sky from black to blue-gray, and she could almost see the pure green of the emerald. In this light its beauty was illusive, shadowy—like memories of faces from her past.

Lenobia didn't like to think of those faces. She'd learned long ago to live in the here and now. Today was struggle enough. She looked to the east and squinted against the growing light. "Today is also happiness enough. Horses and happiness. Horses and happiness." Lenobia repeated the three words that had been her mantra for more than two hundred years. "Horses and happiness . . ."

"The two have always gone together for me."

Even as Lenobia's brain processed that it was the human cowboy who had spoken, and not some dire threat, her body was whirling around and crouching defensively—and there came the shrill scream of a mare's battle cry from within the stable.

"Whoa, easy there," Travis said as he held his hands up, showing they were empty and took a step back from her. "I didn't mean to—"

Lenobia ignored him, bowed her head, drew a deep breath, and said, "There is no danger. I am well. Sleep, my beauty." Then she lifted her head and her gray eyes skewered the man. "Remember this: do not sneak up on me. Ever."

"Yes, ma'am. Lesson learned, though I didn't mean to sneak up on you. Didn't think that there'd be a vampyre out here at this time a day."

"We don't burn up in the sunlight. That's a myth." Lenobia was thinking about whether he needed to know that red vampyres and fledglings *did*, but his response made her lose her train of thought.

"Yes, ma'am. I know that. I also know that sunlight is uncomfortable for you, which is why I thought I'd be alone if I came out here and, well, smoked this," Travis paused and took the slim cigar from the front pocket of his fringed leather coat, "by myself and watched the sunrise. I didn't even see you sittin' there 'til you spoke." His smile was charming and it warmed his eyes, gave them a sparkle which changed their ordinary brown to a lighter hazel color—something Lenobia hadn't noticed happening before. Seeing it now made her stomach tighten. She looked away from his eyes quickly, and had to mentally shake herself to focus on his words. "You sayin' horses and happiness made me speak without thinkin'. Next time I'll clear my throat or cough or somethin' before."

Feeling strangely disconcerted by him, Lenobia asked the first question that came to mind. "Why do you know things about vampyres? Have you been the mate of a vampyre?"

His smile grew. "No, nothin' like that. I know a little 'bout you because my momma liked you."

"Me? Your mother knows me?"

He shook his head. "No, ma'am. I didn't mean you. I meant vampyres in general. See, my momma had a friend who'd been Marked when they were kids. They stayed in touch—used to write letters—lots of letters. They kept writing up until the day my momma died."

"I'm sorry about your mother," Lenobia said, feeling awkward. Humans lived such short lives. They could be killed so easily. Strange that she'd almost forgotten that about them. Almost.

"Thank you. It was the cancer. Took her fast. She's been gone five years now." Travis looked away toward the rising sun. "Her favorite time of day was sunrise. I like to remember her then."

"That's my favorite time of day, too," Lenobia surprised herself by saying.

"That's a nice coincidence," Travis said, turning his gaze to her and smiling. "Ma'am, can I ask you a question?"

"Yes, I suppose so," Lenobia said, taken off guard more by the smile than the question request.

"Your mare called to you when I scared you."

"You didn't scare me. You startled me. There's a large difference between the two."

"You could be right, there. But as I was sayin', your mare called to you. Then you spoke and she quieted, though there's no way she could hear you from out here."

"That's not a question," Lenobia said dryly.

He raised his brows. "You're a smart lady. You know what it is I'm wonderin'."

"You want to know if Mujaji can hear my thoughts."

"I do," Travis said, studying her and nodding his head slowly.

"I'm not accustomed to talking with humans about the gifts of our Goddess."

"Nyx," Travis said. When she just stared at him he shrugged and continued, "That's your Goddess's name, isn't it?"

"It is."

"Does Nyx care if you talk to humans about her?"

Lenobia studied him closely. He didn't appear to be anything except authentically curious. "What would your mother's answer to that question be?"

"She'd say that Willow wrote to her about Nyx a lot and the Goddess didn't seem to mind at all. 'Course Willow and I don't write, and I haven't heard from her since she came to my momma's funeral, but then she seemed pretty healthy and definitely hadn't been smote by a goddess."

"Willow?"

"They were children of the 1960s. My momma's given name was Rain. Are you gonna answer me or not?"

"I'll answer you if you answer me a question in turn."

"Done," he said.

"My gift from Nyx is an affinity for horses. I can't literally read their minds, just like they cannot literally read mine, but I do get images and emotions from them, especially horses I'm closely connected to like my mare Mujaji."

"And you got stuff, images and such, from Bonnie about me?"

Lenobia had to force herself not to smile at his eagerness. "I did.

She loves you quite a lot. You've cared for her well. She has an interesting mind, your Percheron mare."

"She does—hardheaded sometimes, though."

Lenobia did smile then. "But never mean spirited, even when she forgets she weighs two thousand pounds and almost steps over the top of mere humans."

"Well, ma'am, I do believe Bonnie will step over the top of mere vampyres, too, if given half a chance."

"I'll remember that," she said. "And now my question. Why were you smudging?"

"Oh, you saw that? Well, ma'am, my daddy's part Muscogee, that's probably Creek Indian to you. I have a few of his habits—smudging a new place is one of them." He paused and gave a little half laugh. "And here I was thinkin' you'd ask me why I took this job."

"Bonnie already gave me that answer."

She was pleased to see his eyes widen in surprise. "You said you couldn't get thoughts from horses."

"What I got from Bonnie is that you've been traveling restlessly for some time. That tells me we're just the next stop on your life journey."

"Is she fine with it? I mean, it's not hurtin' her, right?"

A little warmth for the cowboy seeped into her veins and pulsed through her body. "Your mare is fine. She's happy as long as she's with you."

He tilted his hat back and scratched his forehead. "Well, that's a relief. It has been hard for me to settle since my ma's death. The ranch just ain't the same without—"

Not far away from them the peaceful morning was shattered by engines and shouting.

"Well, what in the hell?"

"I have no idea, but I'm going to find out." Lenobia stood and began striding toward the sounds of chaos. She noticed Travis stayed right beside her. She glanced at him. "When Neferet interviewed you did she happen to mention some pretty rough things have happened recently at this House of Night?"

"No, ma'am," he said.

"Well, you might want to rethink accepting this job. If you're looking for peace, this is definitely the wrong place for you."

"No, ma'am," he repeated. "I've never run from a fight. Don't seek them out, neither, but when they find me I don't run."

"Too bad you cowboys don't carry six-shooters anymore," she muttered.

Travis patted the side of his coat and smiled grimly. "Some of us still do, ma'am. Oklahoma has the good sense to be a conceal/carry state."

Her eyes widened slightly. "I'm glad to hear it. Just a quick tip: if it has wings like a bird, but red eyes that look human, get ready to shoot it."

"You ain't kidding, are you?"

"No."

Together they followed the noise around the lightening campus and approached the central grounds of the school. As they reached the beautiful front lawn, both of them slowed and then stopped. Lenobia shook her head. "I don't believe it."

"You don't want me to shoot them, do ya?"

She scowled. "Not yet I don't." Then she marched into the middle of the caravan of trucks and flatbeds and lawn equipment and men—decidedly *human* men—and joined the blurry-eyed, bed-headed, but really angry female vampyre who was facing all of them down.

"Are you deaf or stupid? I said you're not touching my grounds, and you're especially not touching my grounds at this ridiculous time of the day when professors and students are trying to sleep."

"Gaea, what's going on here?" Lenobia put a restraining hand on the vampyre's arm because she looked like she was going to hurl herself at the poor, confused, clipboard-holding man who had unwisely stepped up as leader of the group. He was staring at Gaea with a mixture of horror and awe, which Lenobia understood. Gaea was tall and slender and unusually attractive, even for a vampyre. She could have been a fabulous successful model, had she not been perfectly content tending to the earth instead.

"These *men*," Gaea made the word sound as if it tasted bad, "just showed up and started to attack my grounds!"

"Look, missus, like I said before, we were hired yesterday to be the new lawn service for the House of Night. We weren't attacking anything—we were mowing the grass."

Lenobia bit back a cry of utter frustration. Instead she asked the man, "And who hired you?"

He looked down at his clipboard. "Name the boss gave me was Neferet. Is that you?"

Lenobia shook her head. "No, but it is the name of our High Priestess." She turned to the grounds manager. "Gaea, did you not receive the information that Neferet was going to be hiring humans to work at the House of Night?"

"I got that information. I just didn't get the information that the humans would be usurping *my* position!"

Of course you didn't, Lenobia thought grimly, *Neferet didn't want either of us to be prepared for what she was doing, and you're as protective of your grass and shrubs and flowers as I am of my horses, which is something our manipulative High Priestess is very aware of.* Lenobia shook her head, annoyed at Neferet's checkmate. "No, Gaea," she explained in her most reasonable voice. "You aren't being usurped. You're being helped."

Lenobia saw the struggle in Gaea's eyes. Obviously she, like Lenobia herself, hadn't wanted human help at all, but going against an edict created by their High Priestess and sanctioned by the Vampyre High Council would create dissension in the school.

And the ancient vampyre truth was that they shouldn't be showing any dissension in front of humans.

"Yes, well, I can see that." Lenobia let some of the tension drain from her body as Gaea chose to follow the ancient vampyre truth over pride and power. "I was just caught unaware. Thank you, Lenobia, for helping me see this situation more clearly." Then she turned to the man and the workers who were milling nervously behind him. Gaea smiled and Lenobia watched the men's faces go slack and round-eyed as the full force of her beauty hit them. "I do apologize for the initial confusion. It seems there has been a mistake in communication. Shall we discuss exactly what your job is going to entail, and how it would be best if . . ."

Lenobia unobtrusively retreated as Gaea launched into a lengthy explanation about timing and grass cutting and the phases of the moon. Travis, once again, fell into step beside her.

He cleared his throat.

Without looking at him, Lenobia said, "Go ahead. Say whatever it is you want to say."

"Well, ma'am, seems to me there's an awful lot of job confusion going on at this school."

"Seems the same to me," Lenobia said.

"Your boss doesn't appear to be—"

"Neferet is *not* my boss," Lenobia interrupted.

"All right, I'll rephrase that. It appears *my* boss has been doin' a lot of hiring without tellin' the people those hirings most affect anything about it. So, I'm wonderin', does this have anything to do with the rough times you mentioned before?"

"It might," Lenobia said. By this time they'd made their way back to the main door that led to the stables. She stopped and faced Travis. "You should get used to not being surprised by confusion and chaos. There can be a lot of both around here."

"But you're not going to give me specifics. Am I right about that?"

"You are," Lenobia said.

Travis cocked his hat back. "How 'bout elaboratin' on those birds with the red eyes?"

"Raven Mockers," Lenobia said. "That's what they're called. Horses don't like them; they don't like horses. They've caused problems here lately."

"What are they?" Travis said.

Lenobia sighed. "Not human. Not bird. Not vampyre."

"Well, ma'am, sounds like they're not good in general. Do I shoot if they come around the horses?"

"Shoot if they attack the horses." Lenobia met his gaze steadily. "My general rule is: protect the horses first, ask questions later."

"Good rule," Travis said.

"I think so." Lenobia nodded her head in the direction of the stables. "Do you have everything you need in there?"

"Yes, ma'am. Bonnie and me don't need much." He paused and

then added, "Will you want me to change my sleeping hours around to match yours?"

"Well, I'll want you to change your sleep pattern, but you'll be matching the entire school, not just me," Lenobia said quickly, wondering why what he said had embarrassed her. "And you'll be surprised how quickly Bonnie will adapt to the night and day switch."

"Bonnie and I have done our fair share of night riding."

"Good, then you're already a little prepared for the change." There was an awkward moment when they both just stood there, and then Lenobia said, "Oh, my quarters are up there." She pointed to the tall second story over the stables. "The rest of the professors are back there." Lenobia jerked her chin toward the main campus building. "I prefer to be closer to the horses."

"Seems you and I see eye to eye on at least one thing."

She raised her brows in a silent question.

Travis smiled. "Preferring horses." He opened the door for her.

Lenobia went into the stables and they walked together for a little way until they reached the stairwell that led to the upper level. "I suppose I'll see you at dusk," she said.

Travis tipped his hat to her. "Yes, ma'am, you will. Good night to you."

"Good night," Lenobia said, and then hurried up the stairway feeling his eyes on her back long after she was out of his sight.

CHAPTER TWELVE

Aurox

Aurox followed his Priestess from the professors' building out into the waning sunlight of evening. Though it was winter, and the light held no warmth, and, truth be told, little light, she cringed as if it caused her pain. He watched her pull the cowl of her green robe more fully over her head so that it fully swathed her face.

"Sunlight!" Neferet made the word sound as if it tasted bitter. "I shall make them pay for causing me to take this trip in the sunlight." She glanced at him before donning dark, mirrored glasses. "Actually, you shall make them pay for me."

"Yes, Priestess," he said automatically.

Imperiously, she walked out to the large black vehicle she'd commanded he learn how to drive and stood before the door, waiting for him to open it, which he did quickly. Aurox noted that even in the daylight hours Neferet cast a shadow that was preternaturally dark. *Darkness always travels with her,* he thought.

After he'd turned on the vehicle she punched a button in the rearview mirror and a voice asked, "Yes, Neferet, where may OnStar take you today?"

"Will Rogers High School, Tulsa, Oklahoma," she said in response to the voice, then to him she commanded, "Follow their directions exactly."

"Yes, Priestess," was all he was required to say.

From the moment he'd parked in front of it, Aurox had found the light-colored brick and stonework building pleasing to his eye. He followed Neferet inside, entering the first of its gleaming, wide hallways and he was taken aback by the feel of the place. It was almost as if the building was sentient. It had a wise, listening quality that Aurox found surprisingly calming.

But how could that be? How could a building make him feel anything?

There had been only one elderly security guard. He'd approached Aurox and Neferet, walking slowly and with a limp, more curious and polite than cautious.

"May I help y'all?"

"Yes, does the school have an underground area? A large basement or tunnel system?" Neferet had asked, pulling back her hood and taking off her dark glasses.

The guard's eyes had widened first at her beauty and then fixated on her sapphire-colored tattoo.

"We have some old tunnels in the basement that haven't really been used since bomb shelter days. That is, other than as a hidey-hole from a tornado now and then. Why do you—"

"How do you reach the tunnels?" Neferet cut him off.

"I'm sorry, I'd need to get administrative permission for any—"

"That won't be necessary." This time she added a seductive smile to her words. "I'm simply compiling historical information about the school building. The tunnels are still accessible, aren't they?"

The man looked equally as confused by her question as he was dazzled by her smile. "Oh, yes. They're easy to get to. Just follow this here main hall 'til you pass the library." He gestured to their right. "There're stairs in the corner of the intersecting hallway. Take them down a flight. The access is through an old music room about midway through the next hall on the right. I got the master key right here. I don't suppose it'd hurt anything if I gave you a quick look. It's not like classes are going on right now or—"

"Incapacitate him, but do not kill him," Neferet had ordered. "Oh, and give me that key."

Aurox hit him hard enough to make him unconscious. He didn't believe the old man was dead, but he wasn't certain. There was no time to check. He handed Neferet the jangling keys and she began hurrying in the direction the man had unwisely indicated. She paused when she came to the large room on their left, glancing in the windows of the closed doors. Aurox looked with her. It was an elegant room. Large, decorative lights hung over tables and bookshelves.

Strange that Aurox perceived a waiting quality from within.

"Library," she said. "All this Art Deco architecture is utterly wasted on human teenagers." Neferet dismissed the building's beauty and majesty. She nodded at the intersecting hallway ahead of them. "This is the correct way."

Almost reluctantly, Aurox followed her.

"This a school, just as the House of Night is a school?" Aurox had to give voice to some of the questions that were circling around his mind.

Neferet didn't even glance at him. "It is a human school—a public school. *Not* like the House of Night." She shuddered delicately. "I can practically see the hormones and testosterone. Why do you ask?"

"I am simply curious," he said.

She did look at him then, briefly. "Do not be."

"Yes, Priestess," he said softly.

They wove their way farther within the quiet building, and the hall became less and less touched by sunlight. The shadows around Neferet stirred as she stopped in front of a door with musical notes painted on it. "This is it," she said, as she unlocked the door, and stepped into a dingy area that smelled of dust and neglect. To their left was a room filled with metal stands and chairs. Before them was a cluttered area that led into more darkness. Neferet hesitated and made a low sound of frustration. "I grow weary of searching."

Neferet lifted her right hand, pressed the sharp nail of her left middle finger against her palm, slicing open a wound that wept red.

> *"To the red ones I command you lead me;*
> *my blood your payment will be."*

With a sense of fascination Aurox watched Darkness release from within the shadows beneath and around Neferet as well as the corners of the room. Questing tendrils slithered to her. Twining around her body they crawled up her skin to the blood that pooled in her palm. Darkness fed there, causing Neferet to shiver and moan as if in pain, though the Priestess did not close her hand. Did not pull away.

It made Aurox *feel*. Part of him felt excited as he anticipated a battle to come and welcomed the rage and power that battle would evoke. But another part of him felt revulsion. Darkness pulsed around Neferet, malevolent and sticky and dangerous. Aurox was pondering the different feelings when Neferet shook off the tendrils and licked her wound closed.

"You have fed.
I will be led."

The singsong rhyme of Neferet's spell brushed power against Aurox and he shivered as Darkness writhed and then skittered off leaving a thin ribbon-like trail that was blacker than a new moon night as its signpost.

"Come," Neferet said.

Aurox did as he was commanded.

They followed the ribbon into the seemingly abandoned hallway, which began to slope down and down, tunnel-like. Eventually they came to a space that widened and dead-ended. There Neferet paused.

Aurox scented them before he saw them. Their odor was vile, rotten, filthy. *Death*, he thought. *They smell of death.*

"Unacceptable," Neferet said angrily under her breath. "Utterly unacceptable." She strode into the underground room, went to the wall, and flipped a switch. A single bare bulb cast a sickly yellow light.

Aurox thought it looked like a nest.

Mattresses were piled against one another. Bodies were curled around each other under blankets. Some were naked. Some were clothed. It was difficult to see where one ended and another began. One head lifted. The vampyre's tattoos were red and they looked remarkably like the tendrils of Darkness that had led them to him. His gaze was hard. His voice angry.

"Kurtis, take care of whoever is bothering us."

A large mound moved sluggishly and a thick broad forehead appeared from the other end of the nest. This one had a red crescent outlined on his forehead—a fledgling.

"It's barely even day. Just zap 'em with electricity or somethin' and—"

"And what?" Neferet's voice was ice. "Kurtis, you were stupid and bumbling before you died. Now you're stupid and bumbling and you stink." Neferet glanced at Aurox. "Throw him against the wall."

Aurox moved to do her bidding, but slowly, giving the fledgling time to feel fear. Aurox fed from that fear, and as his body shifted, changed, grew into something else, something more powerful, the fledgling's fear shifted, changed, grew into delicious terror. With a roar Aurox lifted the boy from his nest and hurled him into the wall. There was a sick cracking sound and the boy lay still.

"Whoa! Whoa! Wait a second. Neferet! I didn't know it was you." The red vampyre stood, shirtless, hands out, facing the Priestess. Aurox felt his fear. It felt good.

He took a step toward the vampyre. His hooves rang against the cold cement floor.

"Halt for now, Aurox," Neferet commanded. She turned her back to him and concentrated on the vampyre and his nest. "Did you really believe you could hide from me, Dallas?"

"I wasn't hiding from you! I didn't know what to do—where to find you."

"Don't lie to me." Neferet's voice had gone soft and in that softness Aurox heard a black, endless danger. "Don't ever lie to me."

"Okay, okay. Sorry," the vampyre said hastily. "I guess I just didn't think."

The nest of fledglings had been stirring, awakening as their vampyre and Neferet had been speaking, and now Aurox could see faces, wide-eyed with fear, staring from Neferet to him.

He longed to crush those staring faces under his hooves.

A rattling cough came from the nest.

Neferet sneered. "How many of you are there?"

"After the depot when Zoey and her assholes fought us, ten are left besides me." He glanced at Kurtis. "And him."

"He isn't dead. Yet," Neferet said. "So there are eleven fledglings and one vampyre. How many of your fledglings have begun coughing?"

Dallas shrugged. "Two, maybe three."

"There are too many of them. They need to be around vampyres or they will die. Again," she added with a cruel smile.

From the fledgling nest more fear washed over Aurox. He ground his teeth together, fighting the urge to feed from it.

"Will you come around us then? Like you used to?"

"No. I've had a change in plans. It's time you joined me. All of you joined me."

"You mean at the House of Night? That's impossible. We're not what we used to be and we don't want to—"

"What you *want* is of no consequence to me unless you obey me. And if you do not obey me you will die."

The vampyre seemed to stand straighter. His anger burned brighter, as did the single electric bulb. "I won't die. I've already Changed. Some of them might," he gestured to the fledglings that crouched all around his feet, "but I say that's survival of the fittest."

"You're not as smart as I remembered, Dallas. Let me speak plainly and simply then so even you can understand: if you and your fledglings do not obey me *you* will be the first to die. My creature will kill you. Now. Or whenever I command him to. Make your choice."

The bulb's light dimmed. "I choose to obey you," Dallas said.

"Wise choice. I want you cleaned up and back at the House of Night in time for classes tonight."

"But how—"

"Use the school's showers to wash the stench off yourselves. Steal clothing. Clean clothing. Or buy it. At seven thirty, just before classes begin, a House of Night bus will be waiting down the street at the east entrance to the University of Tulsa. You'll board it. You'll resume classes. You'll sleep at the House of Night." Neferet paused, waving a hand dismissively. "I'll have windows covered or open a basement or something. But you will live at the House of Night."

"How will we satisfy our hunger?"

"Carefully. And what you cannot satisfy carefully you will control, at least until the world has turned and changed to embrace your needs."

"I don't get it! Why do you even want us there?"

"Rephaim, the Raven Mocker you failed to kill more than once, has been gifted with a human form during the night and has mated with Stevie Rae. He is allowed to attend the House of Night, along with Aphrodite, and the other red fledglings—Stevie Rae's red fledglings."

"I'm supposed to go to school with him? And her? Together?"

The bulb glowed brightly again.

"You hate them, don't you?"

"Yes."

"Good. That is the reason I want you there—want you all there."

"Because we hate them?"

"No, because of what your hatred, controlled by me, will cause," she said.

"And what's that?" he asked.

Neferet smiled. "Chaos."

They left shortly after Neferet finished instructing the vampyre called Dallas in the ways he could and could not cause chaos. Apparently, his purpose was much like Aurox's purpose—Neferet commanded and controlled his violence and held his allegiance. He was not to kill—yet. And always, always, there was the underlying thread of seeding dissent and discontent and hatred.

Aurox understood. Aurox obeyed.

When Neferet commanded that he control the beast within him, he obeyed and followed her from the rotting nest up through the cool, clean corridors of the school.

At the front door the old guard lay where Aurox had left him.

"Is he alive?" Neferet asked.

Aurox touched him. "Yes."

Neferet sighed. "I suppose that is for the best, even though it's slightly inconvenient. You'll need to go back downstairs and tell Dallas I want the old man's memory wiped clean. Tell him to implant the suggestion that he was wounded when the school was robbed."

She tapped her chin, considering, and looked down the hallway at the glass cases that held memorabilia and the library beyond with its neat rows of books and gleaming, ornate light fixtures. "No, I have a more amusing idea. Tell Dallas to make the human believe he was wounded when the school was vandalized. Then on the way out, I want you to smash the cases and destroy the library. Do it quickly. I'll be waiting outside. And I do *not* like to be kept waiting."

"Yes, Priestess," he said.

"As I said, this architecture is wasted on human teenagers . . ." She laughed as she left the building

Hastily he retraced his path back to the underground lair. As soon as Dallas caught sight of him, the vampyre stood and faced him, putting himself between Aurox and the fledgling pack. The red vampyre's grimy arm lifted to rest on a metal box that was bolted to the cement wall. Aurox felt the power that thrummed there, coiling, waiting to do his bidding.

"What do you want?" Dallas asked.

"Neferet sent me with a new command for you."

Dallas took his hand from the metal box. "What does she want me to do?"

"There is a guard who is unconscious near the entry to the school. Priestess does not want him to remember our presence. Instead he is to believe vandals attacked him."

"Yeah, fine. Whatever," Dallas said, then before Aurox could turn away he asked, "Hey, what the hell are you?"

The question surprised Aurox. His answer came automatically. "I am Neferet's to command."

"Yeah, but *what* are you?" asked a dark-haired fledgling girl who was peering at him from behind Dallas. "I saw you. You were changing into something with horns and hooves. Are you some kind of demon?"

"No. Not a demon. I am Neferet's to command." Aurox turned away then, leaving them behind, but he could not leave their words behind. They followed him down the hallway. *He's a freak,* they whispered. *Something not right.*

He used a desk made of wood and steel to smash and destroy the treasures in the clean, wide hallway. He shattered the ornate fixtures that hung from the room filled with books. While he did that Aurox fed from the fear and anger that lingered in his body. When those emotions were used up he channeled the fear the red vampyre and his fledglings were evoking from the old man as the fledgling he'd wounded drank his blood and the others looked on laughing. When they finished with the guard and wiped his mind clean, Aurox used the vestiges of the disgust the fledglings felt for him to fuel the power he needed until that emotion, too, was gone. Then he unearthed the only emotions he had left. The emotions he'd not fed from, but instead had somehow kept, and claimed as his own. So it was washed in Zoey's loneliness and sadness and guilt that he finished vandalizing the school and then, changing back to the shell of a boy, Aurox walked heavily from the destruction he had caused and made sure Neferet waited no longer.

CHAPTER THIRTEEN

Stark

Stark's dream started okay. He'd been on an awesome beach with white sand around him and clear blue water before him. The sun hadn't burned him at all. Actually, it was just like before he'd been Marked and the sun had felt great on his face and shoulders. He was shooting arrows at a big round bull's-eye target that magickally absorbed them and then made them reappear in the sand beside him so that he could continue to shoot and shoot and shoot.

He was just thinking how really great the dream would be if Zoey showed up on the beach in a bikini.

Or maybe it would be a European beach and Zoey would show up in a *topless* bikini. Now that would be even better.

And then, like what happens a lot in dreams, the scene shifted and all of a sudden Zoey was there, only they weren't on the beach. She was there, curled up in his arms, warm and soft and smelling really good.

"Hey," she said, smiling up at him. "You're awake and the sun hasn't set yet."

"Yeah." He grinned at her. "Let me show ya how awake I am." He kissed her and she tasted sweet. Her body fit with his perfectly. She made that little sighing moan she made when she was really feeling good.

But just as he was really getting into the dream Zoey pulled back from him. He looked questioningly at her, thinking maybe it was going to be an awesome-beyond-awesome dream and she'd do a sexy little strip for him. Then he saw the look on her face. It was wide-eyed terror.

"Stop them!" she yelled. "Stark! Guardian! Help me!"

She was reaching for him as dark, snake-like tendrils dragged her away.

Stark leaped up and the Guardian Sword appeared in his hand. He ran to her, vaulted over her fallen body, and landed smack in the middle of the tendrils of Darkness. Swinging the Guardian Sword he slashed through them over and over again, but where he cut one, two grew to take its place, and both reattached like Velcro to Zoey's body.

"Stark! Oh, Goddess! Help me!"

"I'm trying! Zoey, I'm doing my best!" But he was making no difference against Darkness. By now, Z was wrapped completely, cocooned like something a giant spider would snack on, and she was conscious and screaming for him to save her.

Stark fought and fought, but there was nothing he could do, and as Darkness pulled her from him, he saw Neferet, the puppet master commanding the black, sticky strings. She stood just out of his sword reach and laughed as she tightened the threads around Zoey until his love, his queen, was strangled, killed, and then absorbed by her enemy.

In the dream Stark stood there, sobbing and lost without his Zoey. In his mind he heard a voice strong and clear: *This will happen unless Zoey Redbird publicly breaks from Neferet. She must stand up to the Tsi Sgili and stop these pretenses of a truce between them.*

Stark, still shocked and broken from the dream loss of his queen, only heard the words and not the voice. He didn't think of where the message came from—only the warning itself.

He took a deep breath and woke with Zoey safe, warm, and willing in his arms, and she smiled up at him saying, "Hey, you're awake and the sun hasn't set yet." A terrible, portentous chill shivered through his body. It had been more than a dream—he knew it. Which meant the warning was more than just words—it was prophecy. Stark filled his arms with Zoey, pressing her hard against his body.

"Tell me you're okay. Tell me you feel fine."

"I will if you stop smothering me," she choked out.

He loosened his grip with one of his arms, with the other he ran up and down her back as he looked over her shoulder, being sure there were no tendrils there—no sticky memories from his dream.

"Stark, hey stop." She grabbed his hand and stared into his eyes. "What the heck is wrong?"

"Massively bad dream. Like of apocalyptic proportions. And then I woke up and you were saying the exact same words you said to me in the dream right before Darkness got you."

"First, eew, Darkness getting me is disgusting. How'd it happen?"

"You don't want to know," he said.

"Yes, I most certainly do. It could be a prophetic dream, and if it is I need to know what to avoid."

"Yeah, that's what I was thinking, too. Actually, I was trying *not* to think that, but you're right." He leaned back and ran his hand through his hair, trying to shake off sleep and foreboding. "It might be prophetic and you could need to know; Darkness got you like Shelob got Frodo, only worse," he said.

Stark watched Zoey's face drain of color. "As a girl who is deathly afraid of spiders, I don't know how that dream could be much worse."

"Make the spider Neferet and its web Darkness."

"Okay, well, you're right. That is worse." She gave him what he knew was a brave smile. "But you saved me, right?"

He didn't say anything. He couldn't.

"Hello, big strong Guardian! You. Saved. Me. Right?"

"No," he admitted. "I tried, but the Darkness Neferet controlled was too much for me."

"Well, hell," Zoey said. "I hate when that happens." Then she shook her head and added firmly, "Hey, it didn't *really* happen. For now at least it's just a dream."

"Too damn many things that seem like they could only happen in dreams have turned out to be real," he said grimly. "And there was something else. Someone was telling me that what I dreamed would really happen unless you start standing up to Neferet."

Zoey frowned. "Hey, I do stand up to Neferet! All the darn time. And what do you mean 'someone' was telling you that? Was it Nyx? Did the Goddess speak to you?"

Stark thought back, trying to recall the dream voice, but even though the horror of it was fresh, the specifics were already fading back into his subconscious. "I can't really remember, but I don't think it was Nyx's voice, or at least not a voice of hers I recognized."

"I think you'd know for sure if it'd been the Goddess. Plus, like I said, I do stand up to Neferet, so I don't know what your dream voice was talking about."

"Actually, right now you are kinda in a truce with her," Stark said slowly.

"I supposed that depends on your definition of truce. If it means I-can't-kick-Neferet-out-of-the-House-of-Night-'cause-the-High-Council-forgave-her, then yeah, we're in a truce."

"Hey." He touched her cheek. "I didn't mean to piss you off. That dream scared me, that's all."

She snuggled into his arms and he felt the tension in her body begin to relax. "You didn't really piss me off. You just surprised me. I mean, I thought you and I were on the same page about Neferet."

"We are." He held her tight. "We know Neferet's evil and crazy, and we know all of us on Nyx's side have to watch out for what-the-hell-ever she's gonna do next."

Zoey shuddered and buried her face in his shoulder. "Makes me want to run back to Skye."

"Makes me want to take you back to Skye." He hesitated and almost didn't say anything else, but something in the back of his mind wouldn't allow him to let it go. "The dream, Z. Darkness got you and I couldn't save you. I think it was a warning; I really do. And the most sense I can make of it is that you've got to keep standing up to Neferet."

"I will," she said, tilting her head back to look at him. "You look tired and you're up early."

He gave her his cocky smile. "I'm up early so that you and I can spend some quality time alone before we have to catch the short bus, and I may look tired, but I'm not *that* tired." He slid his hand up under the big, baggy T-shirt she was wearing and tickled her ribs with a light caress. Zoey giggled. He caught the sweet, happy laugh with his lips and turned it into a long, hot kiss. And then his hand quit tickling and almost all of the worry his dream had caused disappeared as he loved her . . . almost . . .

Zoey

"Ah, hell," I muttered as Darius pulled the bus into the long driveway that wound through the rear of the House of Night and led to the parking lot. We'd just turned onto campus and I saw Neferet, Dragon, and five Sons of Erebus Warriors standing there as if they were a weird vampyre welcome wagon. "Slow down," I told Darius. "We need to get ready for this."

"Yeah, it don't look good," Kramisha said.

"Wow, you would not believe all the colors." Shaylin was gawking open-mouthed out the window at the group of professors. "Eek, and there's the Dead Fish Eye Lady, so gross!"

"Dead Fish Eye Lady—I like that," Aphrodite said. "It suits her."

"Dead Fish Eye Lady is super intuitive," I was reminding everyone, even though I was speaking specifically to Shaylin.

"And we all decided it's best if she doesn't know much about Shaylin's gift," Stevie Rae said, walking up from her seat with Rephaim in the back of the bus. "Z, you want to call spirit and ask it to help shield Shaylin's thoughts, at least until we get past Neferet right now?"

"Yeah," I said. "Sounds like a good idea." I drew a deep breath and whispered, "Spirit, come to me." I felt the air over my skin stir with the power of the element. "Shield Shaylin. Keep her thoughts private."

"Oooh!" Shaylin giggled as the element washed over her. "That's so cool, and you're super purple when you do that."

"Thanks, I guess," I said. The new kid was definitely weird, but she seemed nice enough. I glanced back at the rest of the bus, picking out the Twins and Damien. "You guys keep your elements close, too."

"I think whenever Neferet is around it's an excellent opportunity for all of us to focus our thoughts on academics," Damien said.

We stared at him.

"Academics?" Shaunee asked.

P. C. CAST and KRISTIN CAST

"Like homework and whatnot?" Erin added.

"Or are you talking about the fashion show that really is school to us?" Shaunee said.

"We're confused," Erin concluded.

Damien sighed dramatically. "Academics—as in school*work*. For instance, when Neferet is near you should practice memorizing the definitions for your vocabulary words." He looked down his long nose at the Twins. "You two should start with the word *miscreants*."

"I have sort of no idea what that means, Twin. What about you?" Erin asked.

"Don't have a clue, Twin," Shaunee said.

"Be still, brain-sharers. Queen Damien has a point. We haven't been around Neferet like this in a while. Everyone needs to focus and keep their thoughts busy—and not busy on our business. Busy on stupid school business." Aphrodite glanced at Rephaim. "Can Neferet read your mind?"

Rephaim looked surprised by the question, but hardly hesitated before saying, "She cannot."

"You know that for sure?" I asked.

"Yes," he said.

"How?" Aphrodite asked.

"He doesn't have to explain that to you," Stevie Rae said.

"Yeah, he does." Stark spoke before I could say anything. "Stevie Rae, you're going to have to stop being so defensive about Rephaim. He used to be on Neferet's side. He might have info we could use."

"I was never on Neferet's side." Rephaim's voice was as hard as the gaze he leveled on Stark. "I was on Kalona's side. As were you."

That totally shut Stark up, and I took the opportunity to step between them and say, "Whatever the specifics, what we mean is that you were on an opposite side, and that might help us now." He looked at me and his gaze softened, though his expression was still guarded.

"I know Neferet can't read my mind because she didn't know about Stevie Rae and me." He took Stevie Rae's hand. "I tried not to think about you when she was near, but I couldn't help myself. I thought of you. Often."

Stevie Rae grinned and went up on her tiptoes to kiss him.

"Ugh," Aphrodite said. "So, moving on quickly before I puke, it's for sure that Neferet can't read my mind, Zoey's mind, or birdboy's mind. The rest of you need to watch yourselves."

"There is another bus that has just turned into the lane behind us," Darius said, looking in the rearview mirror. "It says House of Night on the side of it, too."

From one of the rear seats Johnny B called, "And it's not short. Why can't we get the normal-sized bus?"

"You ain't normal," Kramisha said.

"Your mom ain't—"

"Okay, let's get ready for school." I cut him off.

"Which means get ready for battle," Stark said.

"Park us," I told Darius.

He parked and then he and Stark and Rephaim exited the bus first, followed by the rest of us. I figured I might as well face whatever was going on, so flanked by Stevie Rae and Stark, I marched straight up to Neferet, bowed semi-respectfully to her and more respectfully to Dragon, and the Warriors. Then I said formally, "Merry meet."

"Oh, Zoey, Stevie Rae, I'm glad you and your students arrived with the other bus. It will save explanation time," Neferet said cryptically.

Before I could brilliantly say "huh?" or anything, the other bus parked next to ours and with the weird Star Trek noise they all had, its doors opened.

And my seer stone began to heat up.

Aurox exited first.

Behind him Dallas stepped off the bus. I heard Stevie Rae's shocked intake of breath. It was about then that my mouth flopped open because after Dallas a whole group of red fledglings, *the bad red fledglings*, including the totally awful Nichole and a very bruised up but still fat Kurtis kid exited the bus.

The red fledglings and Aurox lined up opposite us. I had a bizarre

West Side Story dance scene flashback. Everything was weirdly quiet until Stevie Rae, in an unnaturally high-pitched voice, said, "Dallas, what in the Sam Hill are you doin' here?"

Dallas lifted a lip. "I don't answer to you." He looked at Neferet and slowly, distinctly, fisted his right hand over his heart, bowed deeply, and said, "Merry meet, my High Priestess." All the red fledglings behind him mimicked his greeting.

Neferet smiled graciously. Her voice was warm and deceptively kind. "What a lovely greeting. Thank you, Dallas." When her emerald gaze turned from the new kids to Stevie Rae, her voice and eyes hardened. "I will answer your question, Stevie Rae. What they are doing here is the same thing you are doing here—attending classes. Oh, wait. There is a slight difference between them and your little group. Dallas and his red fledglings will be living here at the school, and I will be their High Priestess."

"Is that him?" Dallas was staring at Rephaim, who was standing beside Stevie Rae. I could practically see the anger roll off him.

"Let me introduce you. Dallas, this is Rephaim. Oh, but, you two have already met, haven't you?" Neferet sounded like she was making introductions at prom. I swear it was so darn freaky that I had to stifle the urge to ask Stark to smack me so I'd know I wasn't dreaming.

Then my gaze went to Dallas, and the fear he made me feel told me no way was I sleeping. His eyes glowed faintly red. He looked feral and very, very dangerous. I remembered when I used to think he was so cute and nice. Well, that cute, nice kid must have died when this new red vampyre with his whip-looking tattoos Changed.

At my side, Stark moved restlessly closer to me.

At Dallas's side, Aurox, who I'd been trying not to look at, moved restlessly closer to me.

"Yeah, like you said. We've met," Dallas said.

"We have." Rephaim's voice was as hard and cold as Dallas's, and it reminded me that I shouldn't underestimate him just because he smiled so sweetly at Stevie Rae.

"While I have you all together, let me be very clear about something," Neferet said, and our eyes turned to her. She looked so darn normal! Beautiful and regal and she sounded so darn reasonable that for a moment I felt a great sadness at the loss of who she could have been. "There has been unpleasantness between us in the recent past. That is over now. I will have no strife here, be you fledgling or vampyre, red or blue."

"Unpleasantness?" Stevie Rae's voice was incredulous. "They tried to kill me and Zoey!"

"Zoey *did* kill some of us!" Dallas shouted, and I was sure I heard the hum of electricity in the lines above our heads that fed the school.

"Wait, I didn't want to. Nichole and Kurtis and those guys attacked me and—"

"Enough!" Neferet's command held a frightening power that pulsed around us seeming to leach even the silver light of the risen moon. "I said the past is over. Stevie Rae and Zoey, if you cannot control yourselves then you will be expelled from this school. Dallas, the same goes for you. Aurox and the Sons of Erebus Warriors will be patrolling the halls and classrooms. If any violence breaks out they will end it. Immediately. Do I make myself clear?" No one spoke a word. Neferet's smile was cold. "Good. Now, get to class." She whirled around and, with that strange, gliding walk Neferet headed back to the main campus building and the classroom waiting there.

"There's Darkness all around her," Stark said in a voice that was low, but not low enough.

"She's totally engulfed by it," Rephaim said.

"Absolutely," Stevie Rae said. Then she looked at Dragon and the other Warriors. "Don't y'all not see it? It's like sticky spiderwebs." She jerked her thumb at Dallas and the other red fledglings. "I'll bet they can see it."

"Don't know what the hell you're talking about," Dallas said.

"Do you still have imaginary tea parties in the basement with your dollies?" Nichole asked sarcastically.

Dallas and his red fledglings laughed.

"Dallas, Neferet wants you to report to the media center. They've been having computer problems and she needs your help to straighten things out," Dragon said, stepping up to stand between our two groups. The Sons of Erebus Warriors joined him, as did Aurox.

"Shaylin, this is your class schedule. Stevie Rae can guide you around today." He handed the new fledgling a piece of paper. "Stark, Darius," Dragon continued. "Get to the stable and begin setting up for your classes. The rest of you do as the High Priestess ordered. First hour begins shortly."

"Whatever the High Priestess wants sounds good to me," Dallas said, and brushed past Rephaim with a sneer.

I watched Rephaim hold his ground. He didn't look pissed off and all Crazy Boy, like he wanted to punch a locker or anything like that, but he did look solid and strong, and he stayed protectively close to Stevie Rae.

"Let's go to class and try to ignore those idiots," I said, taking Stark's hand.

"They do not want to be ignored," Rephaim said as we walked slowly to the main campus. "They're here to cause problems."

"Stirring the shit pot," Stevie Rae said, and for some reason that made her and Rephaim smile.

Rephaim looked so totally teenage-human-boy-grinning-at-his-girlfriend that I had to remind myself he wasn't exactly what he appeared to be. I needed to remember that I'd seen Raven Mockers fight, and I knew that they were mean and dangerous, so I was wondering about him, whether him actually fighting Dallas, if it came to that, would call alive an edge of Darkness within him, when I saw the change come over his expression. One second he was smiling at Stevie Rae, and the next his face had gone still, as if he could hear a sound no one else could. Then I blinked and he seemed normal again.

"Hey, do I really get to ride horses sixth hour?" Shaylin asked, reading her schedule while she tried to keep up with us.

"If it says Equestrian Studies you do," Stevie Rae said. "See ya at lunch." She grinned once more at Rephaim, waved at the rest of us, and then went over to Shaylin. "Lemme see." She read the fledgling's schedule. "Oh, good, you have Spells and Rituals first hour. You'll like that class. I hear the new professor is cool."

"Hey, what's up with you?" Stark asked me.

"Not sure," I said quietly. "Actually, probably nothing more than the fact that I'm going to sociology class, which is taught by Neferet. Talk about stress."

"You'll be fine. She's pretending to be a professor and a High Priestess right now," he said.

"Yeah, which means she'll only humiliate me a little, versus ripping my head off with her claws," I muttered.

"If she tries, be sure to run around a lot and be scared so I can get to you in time to save you." He smiled his cocky grin at me, and I knew he was trying (unsuccessfully) to make me feel better.

"I'll keep that in mind. See you at lunch."

He kissed me, and then after one more worried look, headed toward the stables with Darius. Everyone scattered, leaving Damien, Rephaim, and me walking to class.

"You okay?" I asked Rephaim.

"Yes. Fine," he said.

I seriously didn't believe him, and I guess my sneaked peeks were super obvious because he finally stopped, sighed, and then he truly surprised me by saying, "Hey, Damien, I need to talk to Zoey. Can I meet you in class?"

Damien looked more than a little curious, but he was too polite to protest. "Sure, no problem. Don't be late, though. The professors here really get annoyed about tardiness."

"I'll make sure he hurries," I assured Damien, and then I slowed down so that Rephaim and I stayed outside the building when everyone else went in. "What's up?"

"My father is here. I can feel his presence."

"Kalona? Where?" I knew my eyes were all big and googly as I looked around us like I expected the immortal to pop out of the shadows.

"I don't know where, but I want you to know that I haven't contacted him, haven't seen him, haven't talked to him since he freed me." Rephaim shook his head. "I-I don't want you and the rest of your friends to think I'm keeping things from you."

"Okay. Well, at least that's a good thing. Do you have any idea what he wants?"

"No!"

"Okay, okay, I'm not accusing you of anything. You came to me with this, remember?"

"Yes, but I—" His face went still again. Then his eyes met mine and the sadness in them was so intense that it made my stomach ache. "He's calling me."

CHAPTER FOURTEEN

Zoey

"Calling you? What the hell do you mean? I don't hear anything." I kept gawking around expecting the boogerman to jump at me.

"No." He shook his head. "You wouldn't hear it. I don't even really *hear* it. Father can call me through the immortal blood we share. I didn't think he'd still be able to after Nyx changed me." He stared off into the distance, looking totally miserable. "But I'm not truly human. I'm still a mixture of beast and man and immortal. I still share his blood."

"Hey, it's okay. You're doing your best. I see the way you look at Stevie Rae. I know you love her. And Nyx herself forgave you."

He nodded and swept a hand across his face, which made me notice he had started to sweat. A lot.

Obviously, he noticed me noticing, and said, "It's difficult not to respond to his call. I've never resisted him before."

"Look, you stay right here. I'm gonna go get Stark and Darius and Stevie Rae. Then you can follow Kalona's call. We'll all go with you and show him that you're really one of us—that he needs to leave you alone."

"No! I don't want everyone to know he's here. Especially not Stevie Rae. She thinks I have to completely turn my back on him, but it's so hard!" He put his hands together like he was begging me to understand. "He's still my father."

Even though I wished I didn't, I was beginning to understand what he was saying. "My mom was messed up. She chose a guy over me, but deep inside I still loved her and I wanted her to love me. *Really* love

145

me. I think the hardest part about her being dead is that there isn't any chance left that she'll be my mom again."

"Then you understand," he said.

"Yeah, in a way I think I do, but I also agree with Stevie Rae. See, Rephaim, you might feel like every other kid who's had a messed-up parent, but the problem with your situation is that your dad isn't just Joe Schmoe down the block. He's a dangerous immortal who's on the wrong side in a very real battle of good versus evil."

Rephaim closed his eyes like what I'd said had physically hurt him, but he nodded and when he opened his eyes and met my gaze I could see the strength of his decision. "You're right. I have to stand up to him and make him understand that we really have gone separate ways. Come with me while I do that. Please, Zoey."

"Well, okay. Let me go get Stark and I'll—"

"Just you. I know it's stupid, but I don't want to humiliate Father, and me doing this in front of Stark would be a great insult."

"Rephaim, I can't come alone with you. Are you forgetting your dad tried to kill me?"

"Neferet held his body prisoner and forced him to follow you to the Otherworld. He didn't want to. He's never wanted to harm you. Zoey, my father has told me he will not kill you, or any High Priestess of the Goddess."

"Seriously, get a clue." I shook my head disbelievingly. "Kalona wouldn't hesitate to kill *anyone* if they stood in the way of what he wanted."

"You've been close to him since he escaped from the earth. Can you truly tell me that you have never seen a glimmer of Nyx's Warrior still within him?"

I hesitated, not wanting to remember what a fool I'd been before Heath was killed. I lifted my chin. "Kalona killed Heath because I was stupid enough to let my guard down around him."

"Heath was not a High Priestess in the service of Nyx. And you did not answer me. Speak truly. You've glimpsed what he used to be, have you not?"

For about the zillionth time I wished I was a better liar. I sighed. "Yeah, yes, okay. I thought I saw what he could have been. I thought

I saw the Warrior of Nyx," I said honestly, then added, "but I was wrong."

"I don't think you were, at least not completely. I think the Warrior is still within him. He did, after all, allow me the freedom to choose my own path."

"But he's not letting you stay free of him. He's here, calling you."

"What if he's here calling me because he misses me!" Rephaim shouted, and then wiped a hand across his tense, sweaty face. In a more controlled voice he continued, "Please, Zoey. I give you my oath that I will not allow my father to hurt you, just like I will not allow him to hurt Stevie Rae. Please come with me and bear witness that I have broken with him so that no one at the House of Night can question my loyalties." And then he said the thing that tipped me over into being Queen of Stupidville. "He hasn't seen me since I've become a boy. Maybe when he sees evidence of Nyx's forgiveness, the Warrior in him will awaken. Wouldn't Nyx want you to give her Warrior one more chance?"

I looked at him and saw what Stevie Rae must have seen that made her fall for him—basically he was a real cute boy who wanted his dad to love him. "Ah, hell," I said. "Fine. I'll go with you as long as we don't leave campus. And you should know if I get freaked or upset or scared or whatnot, Stark is gonna feel it and come running with his bow that cannot miss whatever he shoots at. And I promise you he will shoot. Nothing I can do about that."

Rephaim took my arm and started practically dragging me toward the east wall. "I won't put you in danger. You won't feel any of those things."

I was gonna say something about pigs flying, but instead I saved my breath and jogged to keep up with him.

Of course I knew where we were headed. It made sense. "The stupid tree by the stupid wall," I panted. "I don't like this at all."

"It's easy to get to and no one goes over there," Rephaim said. "That's why he's there."

"That doesn't make it any better," I said.

We sprinted across the lawn. I looked over my shoulder. I could see the gaslights of the stable that stretched toward this area of campus, and I was thinking that I probably should abdicate my Queenship in Stupidville and send out a big, scary, mental SOS to Stark when Rephaim suddenly slowed and then stopped.

I turned my attention and my gaze back to what was going on in front of me, and saw Kalona standing beside the shattered tree. His back was to us. Later I had time to think about the fact that he should have been at least facing the direction from which he knew Rephaim would be coming, but then his presence overshadowed everything, just as he knew it would. He was tall and strong and, as per usual, naked from the waist up. His incredible black wings were folded and at rest, and they looked like a god had fashioned them from pieces of the night sky.

I'd forgotten how beautiful and powerful and majestic he was. I clenched my jaw and mentally shook myself. I hadn't forgotten how dangerous he was.

"Father, I am here," Rephaim said in a voice that sounded so small and childlike that I put my hand over his where it still held on to my arm.

Kalona turned around. His amber eyes went wide. For a moment his face lost all expression and then he looked utterly stunned.

"Rephaim? Is it truly you, my son?"

I felt the quake that went through Rephaim's body and I tightened my hand over his.

"Yes, Father." His voice got stronger as he spoke. "It is me, Rephaim, your son."

I know the immortal has faked a lot of things. I know he's trafficked with Darkness and been a murderer, a liar, and a betrayer. But I think for my entire life I will remember the look on Kalona's face when he saw Rephaim that day. For an instant Kalona smiled and such pure joy suffused his entire being that I lost my grip on Rephaim. I stood there, slack jawed, and gaped at the wonder of Kalona's happiness, and realized that I saw within his expression the same love I'd seen when he'd gazed at Nyx in the Otherworld.

"Nyx forgave me," Rephaim said.

Those three words snuffed out Kalona's joy. "And then she gifted you with the form of a human boy?" the immoral said in an emotionless voice.

I could feel Rephaim's hesitation, and I knew he was going to do what I did way too often—tell the whole truth when he should keep his mouth shut—so I blurted the semi-correct short version answer for him.

"Yeah, he's a boy now and he's with us."

Kalona's amber gaze shifted to me. "Zoey, you are looking well. I thought my son was the Red One's mate. Is she sharing him with you?"

"Eew, no. It's not *that* kind of school. I'm his friend, that's all," I said, totally shoving aside the memory of how moved Kalona had been when he'd first seen Rephaim. *This is the real Kalona*, I reminded myself. "And you don't have to be such a butt. *You* called Rephaim, not the other way around."

"Yes, I called my son. Not a fledgling High Priestess."

"I asked her to come with me to speak with you," Rephaim said.

"You asked Zoey and not the Red One. Is that because she's tiring of you already?"

"No, and her name is Stevie Rae, not the Red One. I'm her mate, and I'm going to stay her mate." I liked it that all the daddy-hero-worship crap had gone out of Rephaim's voice. "That's why I answered your call, because I needed to tell you this, just like I told Nisroc, I'm walking the path of the Goddess with Stevie Rae. It's what I want. It's what I'll always want."

"Always is a very long time," Kalona said.

"Yes, I know. I spent a good portion of it doing your bidding."

"You spent it being my son!"

"No, Father. Not really. I'm beginning to understand that there is only one real difference between Darkness and Light, and that is the capacity to love. When I was doing your bidding there was obligation and fear and intimidation between us, but very little love."

I expected Kalona to blow up, but instead his shoulders slumped and he looked away as if he couldn't continue to meet Rephaim's steady gaze. "Perhaps circumstance made me ill equipped to be a father," he said slowly. "You were the product of rage and despair and lust. I think I let that shape our relationship."

I could feel the hope in Rephaim. It was like he telegraphed it through his skin and his voice. "It doesn't have to continue to shape our relationship," he said just as slowly. With a start of surprise, I realized that the two of them sounded incredibly similar. I snuck a peek at Rephaim and recognized the shape of his eyes, his mouth, his jaw, and after I saw the family resemblance I wondered how the heck I could have ever missed it. No wonder Rephaim was so gorgeous—he looked like his dad!

"You wish a new beginning between us, as well as with your new life," Kalona said.

He hadn't framed it as a question, but Rephaim answered him anyway. "Yes, Father."

Kalona looked at me. "And what of your new friends? I do not believe they would ever accept the fact that you and I are not enemies."

"Well, I can't speak for all of his new friends, but personally I don't care what kind of relationship he has with you as long as you leave the rest of us alone," I said. "Neferet is who you need to worry about. If you're really not still with her, then I can promise you *she's* not gonna accept the fact that you and Rephaim aren't enemies."

"Neferet does not control me!" Kalona's powerful voice brushed against my skin and I shivered with the familiarity of its icy touch.

"Yeah, whatever." I spoke with forced nonchalance. "I'm not talking about control. I'm talking about the fact that you and her are on the same side, and she's getting way into Darkness. She's not gonna let someone with your power stand on the sidelines."

"Neferet forfeited any possible allegiance with me when she imprisoned my body and used my spirit. You should know, Zoey Redbird, that Neferet has a new Consort."

I rolled my eyes. "Aurox isn't her Consort. He's just one of her minions."

"I wasn't speaking of her new creature. I was speaking of the white bull."

I stared at Kalona. "You're being serious."

"He is," Rephaim said.

"And why would you tell me that? We're not friends. We're not allies," I said firmly.

"We could be. We have a common enemy," Kalona said.

"I don't think we do. You're pissed off at Neferet—or at least for this split second you are. I'm fighting against Darkness in general. And that's the side you're usually on."

"He asked about new beginnings," Rephaim said.

I looked up at the really cute, really hopeful, really *naïve* boy who stood beside me. "Rephaim, Kalona isn't suddenly turning good." All I could think was: *Stevie Rae is gonna kill me if I bring him back to her with an "everything is wonderful and beautiful and perfect" attitude about his dad.* "We can't make other people what we want them to be just because we want it a bunch."

"I have no intention of being good," Kalona said. "Just as I have no express interest in being evil. I simply wish for the Tsi Sgili's downfall. She has wounded me, and I would exact my revenge."

"Okay, so just exactly what does that mean?" I asked.

"It means we have a common enemy. I will help you rid the House of Night of the Tsi Sgili who masquerades as Nyx's High Priestess and her creature, the Aurox."

"Father, will you come forward and speak to the High Council, to tell them what you know of Neferet?"

"What good would that do?" Kalona asked sharply. "I have no proof to support my words. I would accuse her of taking the white bull as Consort. She would deny it. I'm assuming she has introduced her creature as a divine gift, has she not?"

"Yeah, she has," I said. "Aurox is supposed to be a gift from Nyx."

"Let me guess—the Goddess has not appeared and denounced the creature or Neferet."

"You know that hasn't happened," I said.

"Of course it hasn't." Kalona shook his head in obvious disgust. "And because your Goddess remains silent, there is no proof from Nyx. It would be my word against Neferet's, and the Council already believes she banished me from her side. They would believe I was lying to get revenge."

"Aren't you?" I asked. "I mean, isn't that what you're saying you want, revenge?"

"I do not want her to be admonished by a ruling Council, her wrist slapped and sent to solitude in pretend service of the Goddess. I want her destroyed."

The cold hatred in his voice had me shivering again, but I couldn't argue with his logic. I didn't want to kill Neferet. Hell, I didn't want to kill anyone. But I knew in my heart of hearts that unless she was destroyed she would end up causing unimaginable pain and suffering for all of us.

"Okay, look. You need to spell it out for me. Are you talking about killing Neferet?"

"I cannot kill her, she's become immortal." His gaze held mine. "Only Neferet can cause her destruction."

My brain felt like it was going to explode. "I have no clue how to get her to do that."

"I may," Kalona said. "She consorts with the white bull. Neferet believes she can control his power. She is very wrong."

"He's the key to her destruction?" said Rephaim.

"Perhaps. We should watch and wait for a time. See what she is about, what her next move will be," Kalona said. "That will be easy with you living here at the House of Night with her. Watch her well, my son."

"We're not living here," he said before I could stop him. "I'm with Stevie Rae and Zoey and the rest of them at the depot."

"Are you? How interesting. Are all the red fledglings at the depot with you?"

"No, Neferet brought the other red fledglings, the ones who aren't part of Stevie Rae's group, to the House of Night. They're staying here now," Rephaim said.

I scowled at Rephaim and gave him a *would you please be quiet* look.

"That could be important. They tip the balance of Light and Darkness at this school."

"Yes," Rephaim said. "There is also a fledgling who can—"

"Who can keep her mouth shut and not tell everybody our business," I finished for him, giving Rephaim the stank eye.

Kalona smiled knowingly. "You do not trust me, little A-ya?"

I felt my heart freeze over. "No. I don't trust you. And don't call me that name again. I'm not A-ya."

"She's within you," he said. "I can sense her."

"She's only a piece of what makes me who I am today, so back off. Your time with her is over."

"There may come a day when you learn that past lives circle around to the present," he said.

"Why don't you hold your breath until that happens?" I asked with pretend sweetness.

Kalona laughed. "You do still amuse me."

"And you do still gross me out," I said.

"Can we not have a form of peace between us?" Rephaim said.

"We can have a truce," I said, looking at Rephaim and forcing him to meet my gaze. "But that's not peace. It's also not trusting him and telling him our business. You gotta get that straight in your head, Rephaim, or you need to leave with him right now."

"I stay with Stevie Rae," he said.

"Then remember whose side you're on," I said.

"You may rest assured that I will not let him forget that," Kalona said.

"Yeah, and you should know that Rephaim has a whole bunch of people who care about him, and we won't let him be used by you."

Kalona ignored me and spoke to his son instead. "If you need me, look to the west and follow our blood." He started to spread his wings. "Remember that you are my son, because I can assure you those around you will never forget it." He leaped into the sky and with a few powerful strokes of his wings Kalona disappeared into the night.

CHAPTER FIFTEEN

Zoey

So, I ended up cutting first hour. I mean, seriously. No way was I up to sitting there and letting Neferet take passive-aggressive shots at me after the whole Kalona/Rephaim thing. Instead I sent Rephaim to class (and told him to tell the professor he'd been in the bathroom) and then found a shadowy seat not far from the stables. I needed time to sit and think. By myself.

Kalona said he wanted a truce with us, which I figured was pretty much bullpoopie. The truth probably was that he wanted to use Rephaim to infiltrate our ranks and mess us up—and that sounded like I thought the nerd herd and I were turning into a redneck Okie paramilitary group. I sighed. Why couldn't those groups be more attractive? Which made me think about the inbred panther people on *True Blood* and how stupid Jason was. Jeesh, I needed to rewatch season three. I was totally behind on season four . . .

"Hello, Zoey. Focus," I told myself.

So, Kalona is pretending like he wants a truce. Rephaim believes him because that kid has a bad case of I-want-my-dad-to-love-me. Stevie Rae is gonna be pissed when she finds out he's been talking to Rephaim, which I totally understood. She wanted to protect Rephaim's feelings, and Kalona + a new and improved Rephaim = train wreck.

And then there was the whole bad red fledglings returning to school and pretending *not* to be raving lunatics and killers. Ugh, just ugh. Thinking about the fights in the halls that was going to cause gave me a headache.

Throw into the mix the fact that Stark still wasn't sleeping well, Neferet's new Consort was a bull (Eew, that couldn't mean what it sounded like it meant, could it?), and the Aurox kid/whatever who made me feel uber weird—scared and anxious and just downright freaked—and the whole school seemed to be a bomb waiting to explode.

I stared up at the moon. "Plus," I said quietly, as if speaking directly to the shining crescent, "in six days I have to go perform a cleansing ritual on my grandma's land because my mom was killed there."

I blinked hard. I was not going to cry. Again. I was just going to sit out here in the moonlight until it was time for me to go to drama class second hour.

As if I didn't have enough drama in my life already.

"Well," I told the moon. "At least my soul isn't shattered anymore and I'm not a sleepless Otherworld almost-ghost." Right on the heels of that cheery thought I spoke aloud the very next thing that came into my mind: "I miss Heath so much."

The words were still in the air around me when the small place in the middle of my chest began to warm. With a terrible sense of rubbernecking at an accident my gaze was pulled from the serene moon to the wall that framed the House of Night. Aurox was jogging along the school side of the wall. Even from this distance I could see that he was alert and searching for possible trouble, his gaze scanning around and up. He even looked like he was sniffing the air. He was coming toward me, though not directly so. My bench was several yards closer to the school from the wall and hidden in the shadows under the big trees, and he hadn't seen me. But he wasn't sticking to the shadows. He jogged in the open and even though the moon was not full, the night was clear and the fat crescent gave off enough silver-blue light that, as he approached, I could see his face.

Aurox was definitely what any girl would call hot. Well, any girl who didn't know he was some kind of killer creature in a boy skin suit. Then I remembered how a bunch of the fledglings had made over him after he'd killed the Raven Mocker. Guess they didn't care whether his skin was a suit or for real. It felt like something was crawling up my spine and I gave a little shudder. I cared. I cared a lot about what was beneath the skin.

His eyes were super strange. I'd noticed them before. Ironically enough, in this light they reminded me of the moon, or at least of those rocks called moonstones—only his eyes glistened, almost glowed.

My hand went slowly to my seer stone. I could feel my heartbeat speed up. *What was it about Aurox that scared me so badly?* I didn't know, but I did believe that I needed to defeat this fear. I needed to look through the seer stone and see whatever the rock revealed to me—Dark or Light, evil or good. I began to lift the stone and it was then that I noticed it.

His shadow, cast against the rocky wall of the school, did not mirror the tall, muscular body of a human guy. Aurox's shadow was that of a bull.

I must have gasped—must have made some little noise because his glowy eyes found me immediately. He changed the direction he was jogging and headed straight for me.

I slid the seer stone under my shirt and tried to keep my breathing normal and stop my heart from beating out of my chest.

When he was just a few yards away I couldn't help myself. I stood and moved around behind the wrought iron bench. I know it was silly, but somehow it felt better to have something, anything between us.

He stopped and looked at me for a few seconds without speaking. His expression was bizarrely curious, like he'd never seen a girl before and was trying to figure out what the heck I was—even though that analogy was ridiculous.

"You do not weep this night," he finally said.

"No."

"You should be in class," he said. "Neferet has ordered all fledglings to class."

"Why do you cast the shadow of a bull?" I blurted the question like a moron and then I wanted to smack my hand over my mouth. *What the hell was wrong with me?*

His brow furrowed and he looked to the spot on the ground beside him where his shadow—his very human and very normal looking shadow—turned its head in time with him.

"My shadow is not a bull," he said.

"It was a bull, before, while you were jogging beside the wall. I saw it," I said, wondering how I could sound so calm and certain when even to my own ears I seemed totally crazy.

"The bull is part of me," he said, and then he looked as surprised by his answer as I'd been by my question.

"The white bull or the black bull?" I asked.

"What color was my shadow?" he countered with.

I frowned and glanced at his dark, human shadow. "Black, of course."

"Then my bull is black," he said. "You should return to class. Neferet has commanded it."

"Zoey, is everything okay out here?"

Stark's voice made me jump. I turned my head to see him walking quickly toward me, a bow with a notched arrow held with deceptive nonchalance in his hand.

"Yeah, fine," I said. "Aurox was telling me I needed to get to class."

Stark gave Aurox a hard look. "I didn't know you were a professor at this school."

"I am following Neferet's command," Aurox said. He sounded the same as he had before Stark had shown up, but his body language had totally changed. He looked bigger, more aggressive, more dangerous.

Thankfully, the bell that signaled the end of first hour chimed. "Oh, oopsie, looks like I won't be making it to first hour. Better get to second hour on time, though." I turned my back on Aurox and went to Stark, linked my arm through his, and said, "Walk me to drama class?"

"Absolutely," he said.

Neither of us said anything to Aurox.

"He scares you," Stark said when we were out of Aurox's hearing range.

"Yeah."

Stark opened the door to the main school building and the long hallway that held most of our classrooms. It was busy, filled with fledglings changing class, but he kept his voice low and me close so that only I could hear him. "Why? Did he do something?"

"He casts the—"

My words broke off as a tall, dark-haired vampyre stepped from Neferet's classroom and into the hall before us. Stark and I stopped. At first it was hard to really believe who I was seeing, and I wanted to rub my eyes as if to clear them. Then Stark fisted his hand over his heart and bowed deeply, breaking me out of my waking dream and I followed his example while he said, "Merry meet, Thanatos."

"Ah, Stark, Zoey, merry meet. I'm pleased to see you both looking so well."

"What are you doing here?" I asked way more bluntly than I should have.

Her dark brows went up, but she looked more amused than offended. "I am here because the High Council has decided the very special fledglings," she paused and glanced at Stark, "and vampyres here deserve some additional attention."

"What does that mean?" I asked. The kids walking by us in the hall were gawking and whispering. I saw Damien's head stick out of the door to his second-hour class and his mouth formed a round, surprised "Ooooh!" when he saw Thanatos.

"It means that Monday if you cut your first-hour class, you'll be cutting one taught by Thanatos." Neferet came out of the open doorway to her classroom. She spoke with no more sternness than any normal teacher would have used with a kid who cut her class, but her eyes told a different story. I felt Stark's body tense and my guess was Darkness was all around her.

"I'd like to believe Zoey is mature enough that she has an excellent reason for not coming to class today." Thanatos smiled at Neferet, and her tone was obviously patronizing.

Neferet's face seemed to freeze. Her answering smile looked brittle. "I'd like to believe so, too. Be that as it may, Monday you will have charge of Zoey and any of those other *special* students you would like to include. There is a spare classroom down this hall and to the right. Now, if you'll excuse me I need to be sure a room is readied for your indefinite stay."

"Of course I'll excuse you, and I do apologize again for arriving with no notice, and not truly knowing how long I will be with you here at the lovely Tulsa House of Night. These are simply unusual times. Merry meet, merry part, and merry meet again, Neferet," Thanatos said.

Neferet fisted her hand over her heart and bowed her head slightly, muttering the parting words as she hurried away.

"She is not pleased that I am here," Thanatos said.

"You knew she wouldn't be," I said quietly. During our time on Skye, Stark had told me that he'd had an ally in Thanatos, so much so that he and the rest of my friends had taken the vampyre who had an affinity for death into their confidence and told her everything they'd known then about Neferet.

Thanatos nodded. "I did, though I was happy to volunteer for this mission. The very balance of good and evil in this world is in question, and I believe the answers can be found here, at this House of Night."

The bell started to chime. "Ah, hell!" I said and then added a quick, "Sorry. Uh, I'm gonna be late for class."

"Complete your classes today, Zoey. I will look forward to seeing you first hour Monday." Thanatos smiled at Stark. "Young Warrior, I have just a few bags in my car. Could you please assist me?"

"Yeah, of course," he said. He smiled and waved at me as I fisted my hand over my heart and bowed to Thanatos, and then I scampered down the hall and ducked in the drama classroom, sending Erik an *I'm really sorry* look.

He narrowed his eyes at me, but thankfully didn't say anything. Actually, he pretty much ignored me and let me sit and stare out into space and wonder if I wished the hours would hurry until the end of school, or if I should be dreading what might come next.

I was kinda leaning toward the dreading side . . .

I stared at the food on my lunch plate and, in spite of the stupid stress I was feeling, smiled. "Spaghetti." I sighed with true happiness. "And brown pop and cheesy garlic bread. Seriously, yum."

"I know. I missed the food lots." Stevie Rae grinned and moved over so that Stark and I could slide in next to her and Rephaim. I noticed Rephaim had his mouth stuffed full and was chewing rapidly. He met my eyes, smiled and, showing way too much spaghetti mumbled, "It's good."

"So, do birds eat spaghetti?" Aphrodite asked as she settled into the bench across from the four of us.

"He isn't a bird," Stevie Rae said firmly.

"Not this second he isn't," Aphrodite said.

Damien rushed up and nudged Aphrodite, who frowned at him, but scooted over. "Okay, ohmygod. I've been dying to talk to you guys. What is Thanatos doing here?"

"Hello, checked your mailbox lately?" Aphrodite said, waving around a piece of paper that looked very official and school-news-like. "My guess is you'll get the same schedule change I did. The brain-sharers got one."

The Twins joined us. "Quit calling us that," Shaunee said.

"Yeah, we don't share a brain. We share a soul. The two are way different," Erin said.

"Please, like soul-sharing is fine?" Aphrodite shook her head and rolled her eyes.

"Starting Monday Thanatos is teaching a special class first hour," I butted in before a world war could start. "We'll probably all have schedule changes."

"I do," Rephaim said with his mouth still full. "I checked it before I went into first hour."

"Oh, that's what made you so tardy," Damien said. "I didn't want to ask."

"Tardy?" Stevie Rae said. "You know the professors get annoyed at you if you're tardy."

Rephaim looked at me.

I looked at him.

He swallowed his mouthful of spaghetti. "Father was here."

"What? Kalona? Here?" Stevie Rae's voice almost squeaked the words. Kids at the nearest tables sent us curious glances.

"That's right," Aphrodite said, raising her voice and looking typically annoyed. "Barcelona is where all the best shoe shopping is—not here. Get a clue, bumpkin." Then she tilted her head down and whispered, "Not a good idea to say much about this in public—which means as in anywhere but the tunnels."

"Rephaim, are you okay?" Stevie Rae asked in a much quieter voice.

"Yes. I wasn't alone. Zoey was with me," he answered softly.

Stevie Rae blinked in surprise. "Z?"

"He's right. I was with him the whole time. It's okay. Well, as okay as it can be when He Who Cannot Be Named is involved," I whispered.

"Oh for shit's sake. This isn't Hogwarts," Aphrodite said.

"Wish it was," Erin said.

Then Shaunee did something that shocked me worse than Kalona's visit. She didn't echo her Twin. Instead, in a very small, very un-Twin-like voice she said, "You still care about him. Don't ya?"

Rephaim nodded once, just a little.

"Twin? Hogwarts?" Erin said, looking a little lost.

"Twin, this is more important." Shaunee's eyes found Rephaim again. "Dads are important."

"I didn't know you were close to your daddy," Stevie Rae said.

"I'm not," Shaunee said. "That's why I understand how important they are. Not having one who pays any attention to you doesn't mean you don't wish they were different."

"Huh," Erin said, still looking befuddled. "I didn't know that bothered you, Twin."

Shaunee shrugged and looked uncomfortable. "I don't like to talk about it much."

"Was he mean?" Erin asked Rephaim.

Rephaim glanced at me. "No, not very."

"I think Aphrodite is right. We need to talk about this when we don't have to worry about being overheard. Right now let's finish lunch and then everyone needs to go to their mailboxes and check for schedule changes, that includes the red fledglings," I said.

"Dallas's group already got theirs," Aphrodite said. "I heard them talking about it in art class."

I looked at Stevie Rae. Her face had gone real white. "We'll all be with you," I said. "And Thanatos is a powerful vampyre, a member of the High Council. She's not gonna let anything happen."

"Shekinah was Leader of the High Council, and she got killed her first day here, remember?" Stevie Rae said.

"That was by Neferet and not some douche-bag red fledgling guy," I said.

"The girls are on my nerves, too," Aphrodite said. "That Nichole bitch needs to have her hair pulled out by the roots, which are probably a different color than the rest of that mess on her head."

"I hate it when I agree with you," Stevie Rae said.

"Well, bumpkin, even you can be right sometimes."

"Can we stop now and eat the rest of our spaghetti?" I said. "There're only two more hours to get through, then we can go back to the depot and we'll have all weekend to figure this stuff out."

"That's a good idea," Damien said. "Next hour I'm checking out books and files on some of the questions we've been trying to answer. I got permission from Professor Garmy to go to the media center during Spanish class. I'm really good at conjugating verbs, and that's what she's focusing on today."

"Ugh," I said. Everyone (besides Damien) at the table nodded in agreement to my conjugating ugh, even though the Twins seemed out of synch and Erin kept giving Shaunee looks that went from annoyance to confusion and back again.

And that pretty much summed up the rest of the day: confusing, annoying, and just plain ugh.

CHAPTER SIXTEEN

Zoey

"I like his horse," I said to Lenobia.

"I like his horse, too," Lenobia said, even though she sounded like she hated to admit it.

We were standing in the corral, a little ways from the group that was clustered around Travis and his giant Percheron, Bonnie. The cowboy had been demonstrating to a very attentive audience of fledgling guys (and Darius and Rephaim and Stark) how to use a lance and a sword from horseback.

"So," Johnny B said, "Is that all she can do? Just, like, lope or whatever back and forth in a straight line?"

From on top of Bonnie the cowboy looked about a zillion feet tall. Currently, he had a long lance in his hand and I wondered for a second if he was going to skewer smart aleck, muscle-brained Johnny B. But Travis just tilted his hat back, rested the lance on his hip, and said, "My girl can do everything a smaller horse can do. She has all the gaits: walk, trot, lope, gallop." He glanced over at Lenobia and his easygoing smile turned wry. "Well, Bonnie can't turn as quick as a quarter horse. She can't run as fast and as long as a Thoroughbred. But she can tear up a trail with the best of 'em. Don't forget that she can carry me, a pile of armor and weapons, and pull down a house. All at the same time. Underestimating her would be a mistake." He shot another look at Lenobia and added, "But then underestimating females in general isn't a good idea, boy."

I covered my laugh with a cough.

Lenobia looked at me. "Don't encourage him. He's been holding fledgling court all day. The girls want to date him. The boys want to be him. He's making my head hurt."

"So you like him a little?"

I was wincing from Lenobia's frosty stare when Travis raised his voice and called, "Well, you'd have to ask the professor over there about that, but I'd be all for a little field trip."

Huh? Field trip? My ears perked up. "We go on field trips?"

"Not since we've been battling evil we haven't," Lenobia said under her breath. Then she raised her voice and started toward Bonnie and her cowboy saying, "I'm sorry, Travis, I wasn't listening. What is it you're asking?"

"One of the kids wanted to see Bonnie in action on a trail ride. I'd be happy to take some of 'em out with me and a few horses on a clear night. I grew up outside Sapulpa and know the old oil paths on the ridges there like the back o' my hand."

I saw Lenobia sucking in a breath and was sure she was getting ready to blast the cowboy into the stratosphere, when Ant, the littlest of the red fledgling kids, reached way up and, looking starstruck, patted Bonnie on her nose saying, "Wow! A trail ride? Like cowboys used to do? That'd be awesome." With obvious adoration in his eyes, he gazed at Lenobia. "Professor Lenobia, could we really?"

I think it hit me at about the same time it hit Lenobia—Ant was just asking to do some normal school stuff—to take a field trip and be a kid—versus being dead and undead and fighting immortals and the booger monsters they brought with them and worrying about saving the world.

"Perhaps. I'll have to see if I can work it into my lesson plan. There have already been several changes lately," Lenobia said in her teacher voice.

Johnny B sighed. "Changes. That'd be us undying and coming back here and messing up the schedule."

"Actually, the professor probably means me more than you," Rephaim said. "I'm the reason Stark and Darius had to start a new class here in the stables."

"Neither and both of you are right," Lenobia said crisply. "You've changed things at this House of Night, but that's not necessarily negative. I like to see change as a positive thing. It prevents stagnation. And I'm enjoying having the Warrior classes in my stables. As Travis has so aptly demonstrated today, Warriors and horses have a long, rich history together."

I saw Rephaim's surprised look and his tentative smile. Then the bell chimed and before everyone could sprint for the door Travis called out, "Whoa there, guys! No one leaves the stable until everythin's in its right place. You boys there help Stark and Darius put the weapons and targets up." Then he pointed at Rephaim and Ant. "You and you—help me get this tack off Bonnie and wipe her down. She's worked hard today."

Everyone snapped to. Lenobia hesitated, and then kinda nodded to herself, changed direction, and disappeared into her office.

Huh. So now with the approval of a tougher-than-tough vampyre professor a human cowboy was telling an ex-Raven Mocker, some undead guys, and a bunch of fledglings what to do. Huh.

By the time we rounded up all the kids, got on the short bus, and drove back to the depot it was just a little before six A.M. Even I was tired and unbelievably glad it was the weekend. I swear I didn't want to do anything but sleep, watch trash TV, and maybe do a little decorating of the tunnels. I was just thinking about my thick blue blanket (that I'd grabbed when I'd crammed my clothes and stuff from my dorm room into a cardboard box), and how nice it would feel to be curled up under it with Stark and Nala when Stevie Rae rained on my parade.

"Okay, we gotta hurry." She motioned to me, Rephaim, Stark, Darius, Aphrodite, the Twins, and Damien. "It's gonna be dawn in about an hour and a half. Rephaim and Zoey have Kalona stuff they need to tell us."

I sighed. "Okay. In the kitchen."

It took even longer for us to get the kitchen cleared of hungry fledglings and sent off to their rooms.

"This ain't gonna work good for long. We need us a place where we can have our own Council Meetings without morons all up in our business," Kramisha said, as she frowned at Johnny B who was trying to see how many Cheetos he could cram in his mouth at one time.

"Muh uh mu," Johnny B said around the Cheetos.

"Just take your silly ass outta here. We got things to discuss." She shook her head and finished shooing him and the last of the red fledglings from the kitchen. Then Kramisha faced the rest of us. "No. I ain't leavin'."

"Oh, for shit's sake, you have another poem?" Aphrodite said.

"I read in *People* magazine that negativity gives you wrinkles," Kramisha said to Aphrodite. "You may wanna consider your attitude when you look in the mirror. 'Cause I do know you love you some mirror time." She made a little "huh" noise and then her gaze went to Stevie Rae and then to me. "It come to me in Latin class."

"Latin? Seriously?" Aphrodite said. "Your English isn't even that great."

"Non scholae sed vitae discimus," Kramisha said smoothly.

There was a giant silence, then Stevie Rae said, "Dang, Latin always sounds so smart. Good job, Kramisha."

"Thank you. It nice to be 'preciated by my High Priestess. Anyway . . ." She dug around in her gihugic bag until she found her purple notepad, then she pulled it out, came over to the table, and slapped it down in front of me. "This one's for you."

"Why?" I said before I could make my mouth stop.

Kramisha shrugged. "Don't know, but you're supposed to read it."

"It would really be more helpful if you could get a little more info when these poems 'come to you,'" Aphrodite air quoted sarcastically.

"Wrinkles," Kramisha said without looking at her.

"Fine, I'll read it." I took the paper and then glanced at my gawking group. "Yes, out loud." And I read:

> *"The dividing line forms—fashioned from:*
> *Dragon's tears*
> *Missed years*
> *Overcome fears*
> *The fire and ice paradox*

Seen with True Sight
Darkness does not always equate to evil
Light does not always bring good."

As I read the last two lines my stomach squeezed. I glanced up at Kramisha. "You were right. I was supposed to read this."

"How do you know?" Stark asked.

"The last lines—the part that starts with Darkness—it's what Nyx said to me right before she kissed my forehead and filled in my crescent the day I was Marked."

"Does the rest of it mean anything to you?" Damien said.

"Well, I dunno. We all know why Dragon would be crying." Rephaim hunched his shoulders and I gave him a quick apologetic look. "The years and fears part could have to do with Dragon, too. Clearly we're gonna have to get Shaylin involved 'cause of the True Sight part, and I'm not even sure what a paradox is." I sighed. "So, in other words, no, I'm clueless about the rest of it."

"A paradox is a statement or a situation that is contradictory, but true," Damien said.

"Huh?" I said.

"Okay, an example: the paradox of war is that you have to kill people in order for people to stop being killed."

"God, I hate figurative language," Aphrodite said.

"But you are smart, my beauty. When you put your mind to something you figure it out," Darius said.

"The paradox could have something to do with Kalona and Rephaim," Shaunee suddenly spoke up.

"What do you mean?" Stevie Rae asked.

"Twin?" Erin said. "Are you okay?"

"I'm fine," Shaunee told her and then continued. "What I mean is that it's a paradoxical situation, isn't it? In order for Rephaim to prove he's changed sides and is being good now, he has to turn his back on his dad, and that's something that would usually be considered bad."

"You may have something," Damien said.

"She is fire," Aphrodite said.

I blinked. "And Kalona is ice."

"But my Twin doesn't have anything to do with Kalona," Erin said.

"Yes, she does," Rephaim said. "She understands how I feel about him, especially after today."

"Rephaim, I know you want your daddy to be a good guy and love you, but you just gotta give up on that," Stevie Rae said. I could hear the frustration in her voice.

"Please tell her about today," Rephaim said to me.

I stifled a sigh. "Kalona wants a truce with us." After the commotion of everyone being all "no way" and "oh please"—well, everyone except Shaunee and Rephaim—I went on to explain exactly what had happened between Kalona, Rephaim, and me, and summed up with, "So, no, I don't think we can trust him, but having a truce with him isn't necessarily a bad thing."

"Rephaim needs to keep our business to hisself," Kramisha added, giving Rephaim a hard look.

"Yeah, we've already talked about that. Right, Rephaim?" I said.

"I won't tell Father our secrets," Rephaim said.

"It's more than that, though," Stark said. "It's not a secret that we're living here, but that's something Kalona didn't need to know."

"If it's not a secret Father could have found out anywhere," Rephaim said.

"Yeah, maybe. But did ya ever think that maybe if he really had left Tulsa and was out west somewhere and he thought you were at the House of Night surrounded by Sons of Erebus he would have kept flying west and we'd be rid of him?" Stark said.

"That wasn't going to happen. Father wasn't going to leave me."

"He already did!" Stevie Rae suddenly blew. She stood up and wrapped her arms around herself as if she was trying to physically hold her emotions in check. "He left you when you made a choice for good. He's only come back now 'cause your brothers couldn't get you to spy for him. So now he's tryin' for himself."

"Spy?" Darius said.

Rephaim was looking at Stevie Rae as if she'd slapped him, but he answered Darius. "Yes. That is what my brothers came to ask of me. I refused right before Dragon and the Aurox creature found me."

"Okay, look, like I already said, it's clear that we shouldn't trust Kalona, but I do think that he made a valid point today. If Neferet is immortal and can only be destroyed by herself, then we definitely need help in figuring out how to push her in that direction." I paused and then added, "I also think we can trust Rephaim, even though he loves his dad."

"Kalona is a ticking time bomb," Stark said.

"So once were you. So once was I," Rephaim said.

Stevie Rae unwrapped her arms from around herself and took Rephaim's hand. "I was a time bomb, too, Rephaim, just like you guys. But all three of us made the choice for Light. Your daddy hasn't. Please, you gotta remember that."

"Again, I agree with the bumpkin," Aphrodite said.

"So do I," Erin said.

There was an obvious pause where Erin looked at Shaunee, who didn't echo her in Twin-like fashion and didn't meet her gaze.

"Well, that's a miracle. Someone call the Vatican," Aphrodite said dryly.

With the hand Stevie Rae wasn't holding, Rephaim reached out and pulled Kramisha's poem across the table. He glanced down and then read, " 'Darkness does not always equate to evil. Light does not always bring good.' Maybe things aren't exactly as they appear."

"I know one thing that is for sure and exactly as it appears," I said. "I was there in the Otherworld when Kalona asked Nyx if she would forgive him. The Goddess said only after he earned the right to ask. He hasn't earned it, Rephaim."

"Yet," Shaunee said softly.

"Yet," Rephaim echoed.

"Yet?" Erin said, shaking her head.

"All right, here's the deal: until Kalona earns the right to ask for Nyx's forgiveness, we do not trust him. We can truce with him, but it's under the heading of my enemy's enemy is my friend." I said, hoping I'd gotten that quote right. "Period, the end."

"But not trusting him doesn't mean not hoping," Shaunee said.

"No, it doesn't mean that," I said slowly, hating the resigned, sad look in my BFF's eyes as she stared at Rephaim.

"I won't let you down." Rephaim spoke first to Stevie Rae, then his gaze moved to the rest of us. "It's like Shaunee said—I can hope, but I won't trust."

"He's going to break your heart," Stevie Rae said.

"Too late to worry about that," he said. "He already did." And then a shudder rippled through Rephaim's body. I swear I saw his skin twitch. "Dawn." He stood, kissed Stevie Rae gently. "I must go. I love you."

"I'll go with—" Stevie Rae began, but then stopped herself. "No, you don't want me to. It's okay. I know it's something you have to do alone." She tiptoed and kissed him quickly. "Go on before you get caught down here."

Rephaim nodded and then sprinted from the room.

"Huh. So, he turns into a bird? Just like that?" Aphrodite said.

"Besides the fact that it hurts him and humiliates him, yeah, just like that," Stevie Rae said and, with a little sob, she bolted from the kitchen.

"Oh, for shit's sake, I was just asking. She doesn't need to be so sensitive about it."

"How would you feel if Darius turned into a bird every day?" I asked her, trying (futilely) to get her to empathize with Stevie Rae.

"Annoyed," she said. "I like to cuddle." Aphrodite seemed to be considering something, and then she added, "You know, she might try sticking him in a really, *really* big cage just before dawn. Maybe she could tame him."

We all gawked at her.

"What? It's an idea."

"One best kept to yourself," Damien said.

"So that means I should or shouldn't add it to the long shopping list I'm making for home improvements this weekend?"

"I say add it if you let me in on making the rest of the list," Kramisha said.

"I'm gonna go talk to my BFF," I said. "You two shop, but don't shop mean."

"Hey, if it's okay I'm going to bed," Stark said. "I can feel the sun dragging me down."

I forced a smile on my face and kissed him. "Sure, I'll be there in just a little while."

"Take your time. Be sure Stevie Rae's okay." With barely a glance at me he waved at the rest of the kids and walked heavily from the room.

He'd be asleep when I got to our bed. It made me feel weird, like I was suddenly having a relationship with an old man who couldn't stay awake. But I shook off the feeling, said bye to the group, and hurried to Stevie Rae's neat little room.

She was sitting on the bed bawling her eyes out and hugging Nala.

"Hey, baby girl," I said, sitting beside them and petting Nala. "Are ya takin' care of Stevie Rae?"

That made my BFF smile through her tears. "Yeah, she was in here already. She pretended to be all super grumpy, but she jumped right up on my lap and after she sneezed on me she put her paws on my chest and her face next to mine and started purrin'."

"Nal's good at her job," I said.

"Job?" Stevie Rae sniffed and grabbed a tissue from the box by the bed.

"Cat Therapist. When she's in her professional mode I like to think of her as Doctor Nal."

"Does she charge by the hour?" she asked, petting Nala who had definitely turned her purr machine on high.

"Yep. She works for catnip. Lots of it."

Stevie Rae smiled and wiped her eyes. "I'll be sure to get me a bunch."

"Wanna call your mom? Would that make you feel better?"

"Nah, she's busy getting breakfast for my brothers. I'm fine."

I gave her A Look.

"Okay, well, I'll be fine. I'm just so worried about Rephaim. I know y'all can't forget that he's a Raven Mocker, but I wish you could understand that he's really not evil anymore. Since Nyx changed him, he's just a regular boy during the sunset hours. And he doesn't know much about being a boy. Z, I'm afraid Kalona is gonna to do something that will make him mess up, and then he'll have his humanity taken away from him." She burst into noisy tears.

I pulled her into a big hug, complaining Nala and all. "No, honey! That's not gonna happen. Once the Goddess gives a gift she doesn't take it away, even if free will makes someone totally mess things up. I mean, Neferet is the perfect example. She's seriously, totally messed up and still has a bunch of Goddess-given powers. Rephaim is gonna stay a boy at night. What you have to do is decide whether you can live with the weakness that his being human brings with it."

"But love isn't a weakness," she said.

"Loving the wrong person is," I said.

Her eyes got big and round and more tears spilled over them. "Do you think it's wrong that I love him?"

"No, honey. I think it's wrong that he loves Kalona—and that makes him weak." I paused and in a small voice admitted, "I know about that. I've been there. You know I thought I loved Kalona and that made me believe he was changing."

"Yeah, I figured that."

"It took him killing Heath to wake me up," I said.

"What if it takes something terrible like that to get Rephaim to quit believing he will change?"

I sighed. "Maybe it's not so much that Rephaim thinks Kalona will change, but more that he *hopes* he will."

"Is there a difference between the two?"

"Yeah, I think there's a big difference between believing something will happen and just hoping for it," I said. "Give Rephaim a chance to deal with this. It's a hard thing, and like you said, it's all new to him. Just love him for a while and see what happens. I do believe he'd never hurt you on purpose," I said.

"I'll love him and see what happens," she agreed. Then she drew a deep breath and hugged me hard, causing Nala to grumble and squirm.

Stevie Rae and I laughed at her and spent some time settling the cat down, and then I said, "Okay, I'm gonna fall over right here if I don't get to my bed." I kissed Nala on top of the head and handed her to Stevie Rae. "Keep Dr. Nal. She's a good cuddler."

"Thanks, Z. You're the best."

I ducked out of Stevie Rae's blanket door and made my way slowly down the tunnel until I came to the pink My Little Pony blanket I'd made Stark tack up as our door. I ran my hand down the soft front of it and let myself smile as I remembered how I used to play dress up with My Little Pony and how Mom had cut some of the ponies' hair short so I'd know which were the boys and which were the girls.

Mom . . .

I closed my eyes and centered myself. "Spirit, I need you," I called softly. I felt the infilling of the element almost immediately. "This time could you stay with me a little while, just until I fall asleep?" Spirit answered my question with a rush of feeling that made me feel warm and very tired.

I ducked under the pink blanket and walked quietly to the bed. I knew he'd be asleep. I lay down beside him, pulled my blue blanket over both of us, and watched Stark for a few minutes while I let spirit lull me. He was frowning in his sleep. Under his eyelids I could see his eyes moving like he was watching a Ping-Pong match with his eyes closed. I touched his forehead gently, with just the tips of my fingers, trying to soothe away his stress. "It's okay," I whispered. "Don't have bad dreams." It seemed to work a little because he let out a long breath, his face relaxed, and he threw an arm around me so I could snuggle close while I finally fell into deep, dreamless sleep.

Kalona

At first it had been simple, even accidental, that Kalona had followed the thread of shared immortal spirit that bound him with Stark. He had slipped into the young vampyre's mind easily. But as the days multiplied and their experience in the Otherworld faded further and further into the past, Kalona found the job of invading Stark's subconscious more and more difficult.

The boy's mind was rebelling.

Kalona's invading spirit had to remain still and simply observe, or only make small suggestions to the Warrior Guardian of Zoey Redbird, or Stark's subconscious resisted and, more often than not, severed the thread that tied the two of them, ejecting Kalona's spirit in a most uncomfortable manner.

Of course it did tend to be easier if the boy was distracted by either making love to Zoey or when he was asleep and dreaming.

Initially, Kalona had preferred entering Stark as he entered Zoey. It was, indeed, pleasurable. But the sex was also a diversion the winged immortal didn't need. So as the days and nights passed, Kalona had returned to a skill he'd perfected eons ago—he entered Stark's dreams.

The immortal did not manipulate the Warrior's dreams, though, as he had done to Zoey and many others.

That would have been too obvious. Stark would have recognized what was happening. If he became cognizant of Kalona's presence the boy could borrow elemental power from Zoey and block Kalona. At the very least Stark would have been on guard against him, and then observing Stark's subconscious would have been little except a boring waste of his immortal time. Staying secret—acting subtly— that was what he must do. Yes, it was far better to lurk quietly in the recesses of Stark's mind—to whisper dark thoughts—to eavesdrop.

It was a happy coincidence that the young vampyre's dreaming mind enjoyed talking to itself. Odd, really, how Stark's subconscious tended to circle around to the same dream where he faced himself on a small piece of earth surrounded by nothingness, and talked to a mirror image of himself who was tougher and meaner than the real Stark and whom the vampyre called The Other. Stark didn't travel to The Other's presence every night, but when he did Kalona often overheard interesting pieces from the boy's day.

This night Kalona was ready to sever their tether, disgusted by a banal dream of Stark remembering happy scenes from his childhood, when the dream shifted and the child Stark grew, changed, and doubled. Kalona stilled himself and watched as the mirror images began speaking.

"Crappy day, fucknuts?"

"Yeah, and you're the turd cherry on the top of this banana split of a crap day."

"Hey, Stark, no problem. You can always count on me to keep ya

real. So why don't we talk about how today would have been lots easier if you'd manned up and hadn't been so fucking nice."

"Yeah, Other. That's one thing I can count on from you—a bad attitude."

"Yeah, fucknuts, my attitude sucks, but I don't cry about having bad days. You can count on that."

"I can also count on Zoey being in danger from people who are too damn close to her for comfort."

"Might as well spill your guts. You know I'll always play devil's advocate."

"This damn Rephaim thing is gonna bite me in the ass."

"Tell me you're not moron enough to trust him."

"I'm nice, not stupid."

"Hey, sissy boy, have you thought about the fact that if you can't trust Rephaim, then you can't trust anyone who's close to him, either."

"Like Stevie Rae. I know. I expected to have to watch her close and be sure she wasn't getting Zoey into danger, but it looks like the opposite's happening. Stevie Rae keeps pushing Rephaim to stay away from Kalona, to be safe and smart and not give his messed up dad the time of day."

"What's the problem then?"

"Shaunee."

The Other laughed. "You mean one half of the Twin duo? So, they're both causing you stress. Hey, how 'bout this—instead of crying about it you dump Zoey and make yourself the middle of a Twin sandwich. Those two bitches are hot."

"You're such a piece of shit. I'm not dumping Z. I love her. And it's not the Twins who are the problem. It's just Shaunee. Seems she has some kinda daddy complex and she's giving Rephaim fuel for his Kalona-might-change fire."

"Sounds bad. You better be on guard, fucknuts, or shit's gonna hit the fan when . . .

The scene began to fade as a beautiful white feather appeared over Stark's head.

"It's okay . . . Don't have bad dreams."

In time with the whispered words the feather softly, gently, stroked over Stark's face, soothing his furrowed brow and, like a broom with sand, sweeping away the dissipating image of The Other.

In the darkest shadows of Stark's mind, Kalona smiled and, for then, severed their nightly connection.

CHAPTER SEVENTEEN

Shaunee

"Really, Twin. Go with Kramisha and Aphrodikey. My stomach is still messed up from the Lunchables I had for breakfast. I need to stay here closer to the bathroom," Shaunee said.

"Eew, Twin, I tried to tell you Lunchables aren't a breakfast food," Erin said.

"Look, are you staying here and suckling Shauneedy, or are you coming with us? The bumpkin and the bird are upstairs heating up the car and waiting on us. We have like two-point-five minutes to get to the back door of Miss Jackson's and have Kramisha and Stevie Rae *convince* the security guy to let us in before he goes off shift and the damn store is locked up tight," Aphrodite said. "I have zero patience for Twin crap. The whole trip is already a pain in my shapely ass because I know Stevie Rae is gonna make me leave my credit card number."

"That is the right thing to do," Shaunee said.

"Whatever. *Let's go*," Aphrodite said.

"Twin, are you—" Erin began and Kramisha cut her off. "You know I hate to agree with Hateful over there, but as my momma would say, shit or get off the pot."

"Gross," Shaunee said. "Especially with the way my stomach's feeling."

"Totally," Erin agreed.

"Are you comin' or not?" Kramisha said.

"Go," Shaunee insisted. "Grab me something that has cashmere *and* fur. In red, 'cause I'm so hot. And make Aphrodite pay for it."

Erin grinned. "Done, Twin."

"Are you two gonna kiss good-bye now or what?" Aphrodite said.

Erin rolled her eyes. "Come on, Hateful. Let's shop."

"'Bout time . . ." Kramisha muttered as the three of them hurried from the kitchen.

Shaunee felt a little guilty when Erin gave her one last worried look and waved. She was frowning and staring down at the table when Zoey came in with a super rumpled looking Stark.

"Hey there, Shaunee," Z said. "You feeling better?"

"Where's Erin?" Stark asked.

"No, and shopping," Shaunee said. She didn't like the way Stark was looking at her, all disapproving and adult-like. "What's your problem?" she asked him.

"Nothin'." He shrugged nonchalantly and stuck his head in one of the fridges. "Just need some caffeine to wake up."

But even though he sounded all *whatever* he still kept with the Look, and Shaunee didn't feel like dealing. "I'm gonna go get some fresh air, then lay down. And, like Damien would say, I got homework to do." She started walking toward the exit in the corner that led up to the abandoned depot and the quickest way out.

"Hey, are you sure you're okay? You're not—"

"No!" Shaunee said quickly, Z's worried voice making her feel even guiltier. "I'm not coughing at all. Really. My stomach's just messed up. It was the old Lunchables. I knew that ham was nasty, but I love me some mini-Ritz sandwiches."

"I'll come to your room and check on you later," Z said.

"Yeah, okay, thanks," Shaunee called and escaped up the stairs and into the old ticket booth.

There she breathed easier. The depot was a mess, but she'd liked it from the very beginning—even though it was dingy and old and definitely needed some TLC. Still, it had a feel to it that reminded her of taking family trips, back before her parents had decided she wasn't interesting enough, or whatever, and quit letting her come on vacation with them.

It wasn't like she'd had a crappy life before she'd been Marked.

They'd had money. She'd gone to a cool private school back in Connecticut. She'd been popular and busy and . . . and . . .

And lonely.

Then she'd been Marked during a school trip to a summer art class or whatever during a layover at the Tulsa International Airport. Her teacher had left her behind when their plane boarded.

Crying and totally freaked, she'd called her dad. That's why his PA had put her call through to him. In the five years the woman had worked for her dad, she'd never heard Mr. Cole's daughter cry.

Shaunee had asked her dad to please send her a ticket home so she could see them before she went to a House of Night on the East Coast, preferably the one in the Hamptons.

Her dad had told her to stay in Tulsa. There was a House of Night there. Good luck and good-bye.

She hadn't seen her parents since.

They'd set up an account for her, though, and dumped money in it.

Her parents were good at believing money could fix any problem.

Actually, Shaunee was good at pretending she believed the same thing.

She walked slowly around the depot. It was cold and dark inside and, almost absently, she stopped at a pile of broken tiles that had been heaped in the center of the floor.

"Fire, come to me," Shaunee said. She inhaled and exhaled, soaking up the heat that flowed harmlessly through her body, directing it to her outstretched hands. Her fingers glowed with flickering flame. She touched the pile of tiles. "Warm 'em up." Instantly they absorbed the fire and began glowing red.

"That is certainly a useful affinity to have."

Shaunee spun around, hands raised, ready to shoot flame.

"I mean you no harm." Kalona raised his own hands, holding them and his arms open. "I have come to speak with my son, but I cannot enter the tunnels below without causing myself great pain."

Shaunee made sure she didn't look in the immortal's eyes—she remembered that he had a powerful and seductive gaze. Instead she stared over his shoulder at a spot of ceramic tile left on the ruined depot wall, pulled her element closer to herself, and in what she hoped like hell was a strong *whatever* voice said, "So you're just hiding up here?"

"Not hiding, waiting. I have been here since dusk hoping that Rephaim might come above."

"Well, you wouldn't find him here unless he was coming up to take a shower in the old locker room. This isn't the normal entrance and exit we use," Shaunee said automatically, and then she closed her mouth. *That was stupid. I shouldn't have told him our business.*

"I could not know that. I assumed you would come and go through there." He gestured to the wide front doors that looked dusty and kinda catawampus and only half on their hinges.

"Rephaim isn't here," Shaunee said. "He's shopping with Stevie Rae and those guys."

"Oh. Well, then. I . . ." Kalona paused awkwardly and Shaunee snuck a quick peek at him. He wasn't looking at her. His shoulders were slumped and he was staring at the floor. He seemed glaringly out of place and uncomfortable.

With a little start she realized he also looked a lot like Rephaim. Sure, instead of being brown and Cherokee-ish looking, Kalona was more golden. He was bigger, too. And, yeah, he had those giant black wings. But the mouth was the same. And the face was the same. Kalona glanced up at her.

Except for being amber colored, the eyes were the same, too.

Shaunee looked quickly away.

"You may meet my gaze without fear," he said. "There is a truce between us. I mean you no harm."

"No one trusts you," she said quickly and a little breathlessly.

"No one? Not even my son?"

He sounded totally defeated.

"Rephaim wants to trust you."

"Which means that he does not," Kalona said.

Shaunee did meet the immortal's gaze then. She waited, but didn't feel like he zapped her or anything. Actually, he just looked like a hot older guy with wings who seemed sad. Real sad.

"I should go," he said, and began to turn.

"Do you want me to tell Rephaim anything for you?"

He hesitated and then said, "I came here because I have been considering our common enemy, Neferet's new creature."

"Aurox," she said.

"Yes, Aurox. From what my other son told me, the creature has the ability to change form into a being that resembles a bull."

"I haven't seen him do that myself, but Zoey has," Shaunee said. "So has Rephaim."

Kalona nodded. "Then it must be truth. This means Aurox has been infused with power from an immortal, and to manifest as it has, with such a complex and complete disguise, the power used to create it had to be mighty indeed."

"That's what you want me to tell Rephaim?"

"In part. Also tell my son that power of this magnitude had to have taken a great sacrifice. Perhaps a death that was close to those in your group."

"Jack?"

"No. That boy was sacrificed by Neferet to pay her debt to Darkness for imprisoning me and forcing my spirit to the Otherworld." Kalona's voice was bitter—his anger just barely under control. "That is why I know Aurox's conception must have been the result of a death—as was my torment. Look to the sacrifice and you may discover evidence against Neferet. Causing her destruction would be more possible were she at odds with the High Council."

"I'll tell Rephaim."

"Thank you, Shaunee." Kalona said the words slowly, hesitantly, as if he was unused to the taste of them. "And tell him I said I wish him well."

"Okay, I will. Hey, uh, I think you should get a cell phone."

The winged immortal's brows went up. "Cell phone?"

"Yeah, how's Rephaim supposed to call you if he needs to talk to his dad?"

Shaunee thought Kalona almost smiled. "I do not have a cell phone."

"I guess going to the AT&T store is pretty much not an option for you."

"No." His lips tilted up even as he shook his head. "I'm not sure what I would do with my wings."

"Very true," she said. "Uh, how about a laptop? You could be on Skype."

"I do not have a laptop, either. Young fledgling, I am living in the woods on a ridge southwest of Tulsa with a flock of creatures who should not exist in the modern world. I do not have, as you would say, computer access."

Shaunee was nonplused. "I could get you a laptop. All you need is one of those remote satellite connection things and a power source, and you'll have Internet anywhere—even in the woods southwest of Tulsa. You can find electricity, can't you?"

"Yes."

"So if I got you the computer stuff, would you call your son?"

There was no hesitation Shaunee could see. "Yes," he said.

"Okay, good. Take this." She reached into the little chain mail Rebecca Minkoff shoulder purse that was her current favorite, pulled out her iPhone and threw it to Kalona. The immortal caught it without even blinking. "I'll call you when I have the laptop and stuff."

"That's very generous of you."

"Don't get emotional," she said blandly. "My parents have money. I'll just spend some of it. It's no big thing."

"I wasn't speaking of the money. I was speaking of the generosity of the friendship you are showing to my son."

Shaunee shrugged. "He's a friend of a friend—that's all. And don't get me wrong. I want my phone back."

"Yes, of course," Kalona said. Then he really smiled and Shaunee thought she'd never seen anything so amazing and joyful and totally beautiful. "Thank you, Shaunee. This time I mean it with my whole being—and that is, indeed, rare for me."

"You're welcome. Just be nice to Rephaim. He deserves a good dad."

Kalona met her gaze and she felt him look through her eyes to her heart and soul. "As do you, my fledgling friend. Fare-thee-well." Then Kalona turned and left her, exiting through the broken doors. Shaunee could hear the beat of his massive wings as he lifted into the dark evening sky.

For a long time afterward she stood there, heating the pile of broken tiles with her flame, and thinking . . .

"Twin, really. No blood coughing? You're absolutely *not* dying?" Erin's already porcelain skin had paled to crystallized snow.

"Twin. Seriously. I'm fine."

"No. If you're not dying then what the hell is wrong with you? You gave Kalona *your iPhone!*"

There was a shocked silence as the entire group that Shaunee had finally managed to get together, Erin, Zoey, Stevie Rae, Rephaim, Damien, Aphrodite, Darius, and Kramisha, paused to let the echoes of Erin's almost-shriek bounce from the tunnel walls of the kitchen.

"Well, Twin." Shaunee's voice sounded small and uber-calm in the wake of Erin's tantrum. "Like I just explained to everyone, I was upstairs and Rephaim's dad was there, too 'cause he was trying to wait around and see his kid. He told me to tell Rephaim the stuff I said. I gave him my phone so that I could actually call him and then trade it for the laptop I'm getting for him 'cause he can't go to the Apple store with those wings. Then he flew away, as per usual. That's it. I'm totally okay. The end."

"Can't he hide them wings inside one of the long black goth/cowboy coats?" Kramisha asked.

"I don't think so. They'd probably hang out of the bottom of it. Plus, he'd look, like, deformed and all humpy and probably call all sorts of unwanted attention to himself," Damien said.

"Seriously. The unwanted attention would be wearing something that's totally circa 1999 and unattractive," Aphrodite said absently as she pawed through the Miss Jackson's bag at her feet.

"Well, whether it's fashion or fear, logically speaking, I suppose he does need Shaunee to get the laptop for him," Damien concluded.

"He said that he wished me well?" was the first thing Rephaim asked after Shaunee had made her big Kalona announcement to all of them.

"Yeah." Shaunee smiled at Rephaim.

"Kalona also had information about Aurox, or at least he had an idea of where we should begin in finding out his origin," Darius said. "Zoey, I think—"

"My mom could have been the sacrifice. I know."

Shaunee blinked and then felt like she was gonna be sick. She hadn't even thought of Z's mom when Kalona had been talking about the sacrifice of someone close to them! Jack was the first person who had popped into her mind, and then there had been all that other stuff to think about. She shook her head and interrupted something Darius was saying about rituals and such.

"Z, I'm really sorry."

Zoey's face was like a question mark. "You don't need to be sorry. You just told us what happened. You didn't do anything wrong."

"Yeah, I did. I didn't even think about your mom being killed a few days ago. I was thinking about my own dad stuff and everything. I'm really sorry," she repeated.

Zoey's smile was as friendly and forgiving as it always was. "That's okay, Shaunee. It's not your fault that what's going on with Rephaim and Kalona has you upset."

"Yeah, Shaunee. We're all trying to do the best that we can. Sometimes that's not so easy," Stevie Rae said, taking Rephaim's hand in hers. "Thanks for standing up for Rephaim and caring. I 'preciate it."

"As do I," Rephaim said.

"Oh. Hey. No big thing. Yeah, I just—" Shaunee began, but Erin interrupted her in what sounded almost like a sarcastic play on their usual finish-each-other's-sentence habit.

"Yeah, I just gotta go put away the loot I got from Miss Jackson's and hang the new bead curtain I got from Pier 1. Later, everyone." Erin scooped a bunch of bags from the floor and hurried from the kitchen.

Totally confused, Shaunee watched her leave, feeling like she wasn't sure if she wanted to cry or scream.

"Go on." Zoey had come up beside her and was speaking quietly while Damien and Darius started to discuss the difference between cleansing and funeral rituals, and if there was a way that either of them could maybe be tweaked to turn into a tell-us-who-killed-her ritual.

"What?"

"Go on and talk to Erin. If anyone has any more questions about what happened I'll come find you. I don't want this to mess up your friendship," Z said, glancing at Stevie Rae. "BFF's are super important. We all need to remember that."

"Okay, thanks." Shaunee slipped from the room and hurried down the tunnel toward the very cool tunnel room she shared with her Twin. But she needn't have hurried. Erin was loaded down and just a few yards from the kitchen she'd dropped an entire giant Pier 1 bag.

"Hey, Twin," Shaunee said as she bent to pick up a shiny pillow. "It looks like a glitter explosion happened out here."

Erin didn't smile. She took the sequinned pillow from Shaunee's hands and crammed it back into an already bulging bag, saying, "I got this under control."

Shaunee touched Erin's shoulder, which felt hard and cold and lifeless. "Wait, Twin, what is it? Why are you so pissed?"

"You didn't even tell me you cared so much about your dad. You just kept it from me," Erin said, jerking her shoulder from Shaunee's touch.

"No, I didn't." Shaunee shook her head, feeling like Erin had just smacked her. "I tried to say stuff to you, but you were all, 'hey, that's in the past, Twin, let's shop' so I gave up. Don't you remember?"

"Okay, yeah, whatever. What is the big deal? I just don't get it! We've been best friends since we were both Marked—*on the same day*. Everything was fine until this daddy crap came up with Rephaim and now we're suddenly not BFFs anymore."

"Wait, I get how Rephaim's feeling and you don't, that's all. I never said we weren't BFFs anymore."

"Yeah, well, you're right. I don't get it." Erin crossed her arms. "What exactly is the issue?"

Shaunee felt like the world was pressing down on her shoulders and her best friend had suddenly become a stranger. "Erin, I miss my dad sometimes. That's all."

"Your dad? He didn't give a shit about you *years* before you were Marked. How can you miss him?"

Shaunee hesitated. She looked deep and truly *saw* Erin. "Wow. You really don't care, do you?"

"About what? About the cool crap I got for our room totally not on sale at Pier One and charged to Aphrodikey's gold card? Hell, yes. About the new stuff I just snagged from Miss Jackson's afterhours? Double hell yes I care! Alice + Olivia is the shit for the spring. I even got you a fox-lined red cashmere wrap thing that is To Die For. Oh, and I got me one, too, totally to match only in blue. We are gonna look awesome in this stuff. Perfect. We're perfect. That's what I care about. And you, too, Twin. I care about you and you care about our stuff. You always have." Erin's tirade ran out, leaving her looking kinda sad and confused. She wiped her eyes and her MAC Wonder Woman blue mascara smeared.

"No," Shaunee said slowly. "None of that's real. And, Twin, nobody's perfect. Especially not you and me."

"What the hell is it? How could Rephaim's dad change everything?" Erin shouted.

"It's been bothering me for a while, but I didn't say anything."

"Rephaim's dad or your dad?" Erin said.

"Neither, Erin. I'm not talking about either one. I'm talking about stuff in general. Like Jack dying." Shaunee felt, really, really tired.

"I cared about Jack dying! We cried and stuff."

"No, we cried, and then you got an e-mail from Danielle that had a link to Rue La La and we shopped," Shaunee said.

"So? I bought black shoes. Wait, no. *We* bought black shoes. Platforms. With pink bows and Swarovski crystals on the heels. We said it was appropriate mourning attire and that Jack would appreciate it. Then we cried some more. *We* did it. Both of us. How are you so much better than me if you did the same thing?"

Shaunee wondered how Erin could look like she was pleading and pissed at the same time.

"I'm not better than you. I didn't say that. Actually, you're better than me 'cause you're fine and I'm not. That's the bottom line. I'm not fine anymore. Not with myself and I think that means not with us, either, but I don't really know—"

"I'll tell you what, *Twin*," Erin butted in, wiping angrily at the tears that were smearing blue across her cheeks. "When you're fine again come see me. Until then find your own room and your own stuff. I don't want a roommate, or a twin, who's not fine with me." Crying silently and ignoring the things that kept spilling from her shopping bags, Erin stomped down the tunnel, leaving Shaunee standing in a pile of glittery pillows and velvet tights.

Someone cleared her throat and Shaunee jumped. It was only when Zoey handed her a wad of semi-used Kleenexes that she realized she was bawling.

"Do ya wanta talk about it?"

"Not really," Shaunee said.

"Okay, you want to be by yourself?" Zoey asked.

"I'm not sure. But I do know one thing and it's gonna sound really bad," Shaunee said with a little hiccupy sob.

"Well, then say it fast 'cause when you say it fast it gets over with and it doesn't seem so bad."

"I want to go live back at the House of Night."

There was a heavy silence, and then Zoey asked, "Does Erin want to go with you?"

"No," Shaunee said, wiping away the last of her tears. "I'm going by myself."

CHAPTER EIGHTEEN

Zoey

Sunday sucked as bad as Saturday had. Later I looked back and realized that when Erin and Shaunee split was when the whole thing started to unravel. It was weird what the two of them not speaking did to the rest of us. It was like them being pissed at each other unbalanced everyone.

"I don't know about you, but the brain-sharers are driving me crazy."

Aphrodite plopped down beside me where I was sitting on the curb that edged the old circle driveway entrance to the depot. I sighed and thought *so much for taking a second and trying to be by myself.* I scooted over to give her more room.

"Yeah, I know. It's weird them not always being together, and now Shaunee looks like she's ready to burst into tears all the time and Erin's all silent and pouting. It's super crazy down there."

"Fire and ice," Aphrodite mumbled.

My brows shot up. "You know, you may be right."

"I do not know when you're going to get a fucking clue and realize that *I'm right mostly all the time.*" Aphrodite pulled a little jeweled emery board from her Coach purse and started to file her nails. "I don't know what else that damn stupid poem means, but part of it is definitely about the brain-sharers."

"Why are you filing your nails?"

She shot me a WTF look. "Because this stupid town doesn't have enough all-night spas. Well, except for the scary ones and I just want my nails done, not my vagina. I don't want the HIV either, for that matter."

"Aphrodite, you make no sense at all sometimes."

"You are welcome for broadening your horizons. Anyway, as I was saying, what are you going to do about Tweedledee and Tweedledumber?"

"Uh, nothing. They're girlfriends. Sometimes girlfriends get mad at each other. They're gonna have to figure out a way to make up by themselves."

"Seriously? That's all you have?"

"Well, Aphrodite, what the hell do you expect me to do?"

"Did you just curse? Isn't 'hell' "—she air quoted—"a curse word?"

"How 'bout you go straight there and see?" I narrowed my eyes at her. "And for the zillionth time—*there's nothing wrong with not having a potty mouth!*"

"Yelling and cursing. Next thing I know snowballs will be flying through H E double toothpicks."

"You. Are. Hateful," I said.

"Thank you. But seriously. What are you going to do about the Twins?"

"Give them space!" I didn't mean to shout but the echo off the stone building told me otherwise. I took a deep breath and tried to stop feeling like I wanted to smother Aphrodite. "I can't be responsible every time one of my friends has issues with another of my friends. That doesn't even make sense."

"It's in a stupid but prophetic poem," she said, filing her nails.

"I still don't see how that makes me—"

I shut up as a big black Lincoln Town Car pulled through the circle entrance and stopped in front of Aphrodite and me. While we watched with unattractively open mouths, a Son of Erebus Warrior got out of the driver's seat, ignored us completely, and opened the back door of the car.

Long and lean and dressed in dark blue velvet, Thanatos took the Warrior's hand and gracefully emerged. She smiled at us and nodded acknowledgment when we bowed to her, but her attention was clearly on the depot building.

"What a lovely example of 1930s Art Deco workmanship," she said, her gaze taking in the scope of the front of the depot. "I mourned the passing of rail travel. When it finally matured it was a wonderfully relaxing way to move across this great country. Actually, it still is today. Sad that there are so few modern rail routes from which to choose. You should have visited a depot in the forties—tragedy, hope, despair, and courage all concentrated into one vibrant, living space." She continued to gaze lovingly at the old building. "Not like the horrid airports of today. They've been bleached of all romance and soul and life, especially since the tragedy of nine-eleven. So sad . . . so sad . . ."

"Uh, Thanatos, can I help you with something?" I finally asked after it became obvious that she was going to stand like, forever, and just stare at the depot.

She motioned for the Warrior to get back in the car. "Wait for me across the street in the parking garage. I will be along shortly." He bowed to her and drove away. She faced Aphrodite and me. "Ladies, I believe it is time for a change."

"A change of what?" I asked.

"Apparently a change of our entrance," Aphrodite said dryly. "Kalona came up here. Thanatos is up here. We need to put out some kind of welcome mat 'cause the whole enter-through-the-nappy basement thing is not working for us."

"Strangely put, but I think true," Thanatos said. "Which is one reason why I have, in the name of the Vampyre High Council, purchased this building for you."

I blinked in surprise and tried to formulate an appropriate response when Aphrodite said, "I hope that means renovation."

"It does," Thanatos said.

"Wait," I said. "We're not a House of Night. Why would the High Council get involved in where we're living?"

"Because we're special and cool and they don't want us to exist in a dirty hovel," Aphrodite said.

"Or because they want to control where we live and what we do," I said.

Thanatos raised her brows. "You speak with the command of a High Priestess."

"I'm not really one," I assured her. "I'm still a fledgling. Stevie Rae is the High Priestess here."

"And where is she?"

"She's with Rephaim. It'll be light soon and she likes to be with him before he changes into a bird," I said bluntly.

"And what are you?"

I frowned. "You know as much as I do about what I am. You know Stark was gifted with a Guardian Sword in the Otherworld, which means that to some extent I'm a Queen because he's my Warrior and Guardian."

"Why all the questions? I thought you were on our side," Aphrodite said.

"I'm on the side of truth," Thanatos said.

"You know Neferet is a lying bitch," Aphrodite said. "We told you that on San Clemente Island when Z was in LaLa Land."

"She means the Otherworld." I rolled my eyes at Aphrodite.

"Yeah, right, the Otherworld. Whatever," she said. "But we told you the real deal about Neferet then, and you acted like you believed us. You even helped us figure out the Skye stuff with Stark. So, what's up with you now?"

There was a super big pause, which meant there was time enough for me to wonder if Aphrodite and I had gone too far. I mean, Thanatos was a powerful, ancient vampyre, a member of the High Council whose Goddess-given affinity was death. It probably was a bad idea to question her, let alone piss her off.

"I believe what you told me when Zoey's soul was shattered was what you, all of you, thought was the truth," Thanatos finally said.

"I'm back, and we're not in Italy, but the truth hasn't changed. Neferet hasn't changed," I said.

"And yet she insists that she has been forgiven by Nyx who gifted her with Aurox as a sign of divine favor," Thanatos said.

"That's bullpoopie," I said. "Neferet hasn't changed and Aurox is no gift from Nyx."

"I do believe Neferet is hiding a truth," Thanatos said.

"That's one way of putting it," I said.

"But not the way we'd put it," Aphrodite said.

"We don't mean to be disrespectful," I added. "It's just that we've faced off against Neferet for a while now, and we've seen things that she's been careful to keep from the High Council and, really, most vampyres in general."

"But when we try to out her no one believes us because we're kids," Aphrodite said. "And a messed-up group of reject kids at that."

I raised my brows at Aphrodite and she amended, "Well, not me. I'm talking about the rest of you guys."

"That is part of the reason I'm here," Thanatos said. "To be the eyes and ears of the High Council."

"So, what exactly does it mean that the High Council has bought this building?" I asked.

"Hopefully it means I can give my mom's gold card a rest and some of us—as in those who don't need to crawl into a coffin when the sun rises—can have decent rooms up here once this building is renovated," Aphrodite said.

"It does mean that. It also means that this could become a legitimate House of Night on its own, without any ties to the original Tulsa House of Night," Thanatos explained. "The Council believes it might be wise to have a red fledgling House of Night that remains, for the most part, separate from the original."

"Okay, no. That's exactly why BA hasn't built two high schools. It'd be just too much rivalry in one district," I said. "Hating on Union and Jenks is good enough for us—and BA needs to do that with a combined front."

"What in the hell are you talking about?" Aphrodite asked.

"Broken Arrow—Union—Jenks," I said. "High schools. Too many in one town just sucks."

"Were you student council president or did you hold some other socially unacceptable position? Tulsa has like a zillion high schools and hell has not frozen over yet," Aphrodite said. "Having too many bussed kids to one school is just moronic and allows the white trash to slither in. Ugh. Just ugh."

Thankfully, Thanatos stepped between the two of us. "Human

teenage standards have never governed vampyre fledgling law. Tulsa is a middle point in the nation. It could definitely support a second House of Night. Our numbers are growing, especially with the in-rush of the red fledglings, which have been discovered in other areas as well as here."

"There are other red fledglings? I mean, besides just ours?" I said.

"Yes."

"But have any been Marked red, or have they all died and then un-died and turned red?" Aphrodite asked before I could give her a *shut up* look.

"Yours is the only red fledgling on record to date as having been Marked red," Thanatos said.

"So you know about Shaylin?" I asked, holding my breath.

"Yes. Neferet announced that she was blind before she had been Marked, and that now she has sight. She extrapolated that the poor child was broken, so she didn't need to die to receive the red Markings."

I wanted to stand up for Shaylin and say she wasn't broken, that she was special, but my gut told me to continue to keep my mouth shut about her True Sight.

"Zoey, there is no reason to hide anything from someone who is seeking the truth, unless you prefer lies and deceit," Thanatos surprised me by saying.

I met her gaze. "I don't prefer lies and deceit, but one big thing Neferet has taught me is to be careful about who I trust." And then, because my gut continued to talk to me I said the rest of what was on my mind. "I hear Neferet has a new Consort. Have you heard anything about that?"

"I have not. Zoey, are you confusing Aurox for her Consort? Whether he is or is not a gift from Nyx, Neferet has given no indication that she is romantically involved with him; he seems simply her servant."

"I'm not talking about Aurox," I kept on, even though just saying his name made my stomach feel weird. "I'm talking about the white bull."

Thanatos looked absolutely and utterly shocked. "Zoey, the worship of the white and black bulls is an ancient one, and its popularity died out centuries ago. I only have a rudimentary understanding of that religion and its past, but I can tell you that no Priestess of Nyx has ever given herself to the white bull. What you are saying would be an abomination, and it is a grave accusation." As she spoke Thanatos had become paler and paler, until finally she was so disturbed that the air around her lifted her hair and blew with agitated little gusts.

An air affinity as well as an affinity for death—that's interesting, I thought. "I'm not accusing," I said aloud. "I'm just asking you if you've heard anything about it."

"No! The High Council, as well as the vampyre community, believe Kalona, the creature Neferet convinced was Erebus on Earth, was and still is her Consort, though he has been banished from her side for one hundred years."

Aphrodite snorted. "That's bullshit. He was here with her because he thought she had control of his soul. Something got messed up, though, in the Land of the Crazy and Neferet lost control of Kalona." I thought she was going to blurt the rest of the news about Kalona hanging around wanting to truce with us to destroy Neferet, but instead Aphrodite said something smarter. "Uh, would you answer a quick question for me?"

Looking shell-shocked, Thanatos nodded.

"Okay, let's say Aurox isn't a gift from Nyx and is instead, I dunno, say, something super evil the white bull and Neferet cooked up together because they're being way inappropriate. What kind of cooking would create something like him?"

"A great sacrifice," Thanatos said.

"You mean Neferet would have to have killed someone specifically for the creation of Aurox?" Aphrodite asked.

"Yes, though I shudder at the thought of such psychopathic behavior."

"Yeah, so do we," Aphrodite said, meeting my eyes with a sad, but knowing look. "Too many people around us have died recently."

"Yeah," I echoed, feeling super sick. "Too many."

Aurox

The girl's attention came as a surprise. He was going on his nightly rounds, as per Neferet's standing command, especially assuring no Raven Mockers breached the boundary of the House of Night, when he passed close by the female dormitory building. She was standing under one of the big trees and as he drew close, she stepped directly into his path.

"Hi there." Her smile was silky. "I'm Becca. We haven't met yet, but I've been checking you out."

"Hello, Becca." Curious, he allowed her to halt him. She wasn't beautiful or unusual as were some of the other fledglings, *as was Zoey*, his mind whispered, but he shied away from the thought. This Becca fledgling had an allure about her, and her body language, how she cocked her hip and tossed back her long blond hair, said she found him pleasing. "I am Aurox."

She laughed and licked her slick pink lips. "Yeah, I know who you are. Like I said, I've been checking you out."

"And what is it you have learned from *checking me out*?" He repeated her words.

She stepped closer to him and tossed back her hair again. "That you can handle yourself in a fight, and that's a good thing these days."

She touched him then, drawing a pink painted fingernail down his chest, and that is when her emotions hit him. He could feel her desire. It was mixed with desperation and a little meanness as well. Aurox breathed deeply, inhaling the intoxicating scent of lust tinged with cruelty. A shudder of anticipation went through him as the power within began to build.

"Oooh, you're hard." Becca laughed softly, moving even closer. "Your muscles, I mean." Her desire amplified as her breasts rubbed against his chest while she leaned in to him, licked his neck, and then bit him—not hard enough to draw blood, but also not gently enough to be purely playful.

It pleased the bull within him, and the creature stirred.

"Do you like pain?" Aurox asked as he ran his hands roughly down her back. Then he dipped his head so that his teeth found the soft curve of her neck. He bit, purposefully drawing blood, though he cared less than nothing for the taste of her. "Do you like pain?" He repeated the question with her blood in his mouth, even though he could feel the answer in the rush of lust that shuddered through her.

"I like it all," Becca moaned. "Come on. Let me take a little taste. Be my Consort—be my man."

Aurox didn't think to stop her. He didn't think at all. He only felt: lust intensified by a mean, desperate spirit. Aurox let it take him over. He ground against her, closed his eyes, and gave himself to her saying words that came from deep within his subconscious—that were so instinctive and automatic that thinking and understanding had nothing to do with them. "Yes, Zo. Bite me."

"You asshole! Zoey? I'll show you some shit that will make Zoey Redbird look tame." Becca bit him. Hard. He felt the sharp pain and the warmth of his pooling blood. Then her mouth pressed against the fresh wound on his neck—but only for an instant. He felt the change in her as soon as she tasted his blood. Her anger and lust dissipated, and was replaced by raw fear.

"Oh, Goddess! No, that's not right!" Becca tried to pull away from him, but Aurox lifted her, took two strides, and backed her against the tree. "Wait, no!" Becca insisted, trying to keep her voice steady even though her fear washed over and through him, feeding him, changing him. "Stop! You don't taste right!"

The creature within him pulsed and flexed, questing to be freed to pillage and tear. He snorted and the bull echoed within the sound.

"Seriously, stop! I don't want to be with someone who's all into Zoey!"

Zoey . . .

The name echoed within him, extinguishing the bull as water on fire.

"What's going on here?"

At the sound of Dragon Lankford's voice, Aurox stepped back, releasing Becca. The girl slumped against the tree and stared fearfully up at Aurox.

"Aurox? Becca? Is there a problem between you two?" Dragon asked.

"No, only a slight misunderstanding. I believed the fledgling understood what it was she desired," Aurox said, facing the Sword Master and ignoring Becca. "I was incorrect."

She scurried out from the tree and moved to put Dragon between herself and him—her fear quickly replaced by confidence and anger. "I know what I *don't* want, and that's yet another guy who's hung up on Zoey Redbird. Here's hoping you have a thing for standing in line, 'cause there's a whole list of guys who got there before you."

"Becca, there is no reason to be crude. You know vampyres believe in freedom to choose and mutual desire. If the desire is not mutual, then choose to walk away gracefully," Dragon said firmly.

"Sounds good to me," Becca said to Dragon and then sneered in Aurox's direction. "Good f-ing bye to you, jerk." She stomped away.

"Aurox," Dragon began slowly. "Vampyre society is open to the many different roads that lead to desire and the fulfillment of passion, but you need to know that some of those roads should not be taken unless there is clear consent from all involved and a certain, deeper level of experience." Dragon's sigh made him sound old and tired. "Do you understand what it is I'm trying to explain to you?"

"I do," Aurox said. "The fledgling, Becca, has a mean spirit."

"Does she? I suppose I haven't noticed."

"I do not believe Zoey Redbird has a mean spirit," he said.

Dragon's brows lifted. "No, I do not believe she does, either. You do know that Neferet and Zoey don't get along, don't you?"

Aurox met his gaze. "They are enemies."

Dragon's gaze did not waver. "You could describe them as such, yes, though I wish circumstances were otherwise."

"You are not a follower of Neferet's," Aurox said.

The Sword Master's expression froze and his tired but open countenance shut down. "I follow myself and no one else."

"Not Nyx?"

"I won't stand against the Goddess, but I also won't stand for anyone except myself. The dragon is the only path left to me."

Aurox studied him. His emotions were veiled. The vampyre gave off nothing—not anger, not despair, not fear. Nothing. It was a puzzlement. Perhaps it was that puzzlement that had him speaking of the mystery within himself. "I said Zoey's name instead of Becca's."

Dragon's brows went up again, and his expression said he was mildly amused. "Well, Aurox, women—mean-spirited or not—do not like it when you're with one of them and speak another's name."

"But I do not know why I did it."

Dragon shrugged. "Zoey must have been on your mind."

"I did not realize it."

"Sometimes we don't."

"So, it is normal?" Aurox asked.

"Over more than one hundred years the one consistent thing I have found is that there really is no *normal* when it comes to women," Dragon said.

"Sword Master, may I ask a favor of you?"

"You may," he said.

"Do not repeat any of what happened here tonight to Neferet."

"I keep my own counsel, boy. You should remember to keep yours, too." The Sword Master clapped him on the shoulder and walked away, leaving Aurox confused, troubled, and as always, alone.

CHAPTER NINETEEN

Zoey

"This is going to be a cluster fuck of massive proportions," Aphrodite whispered to me as we stood outside the room designated as Thanatos's classroom first hour on Monday. The room was one of the biggest in the school. Actually, except for the drama classroom, which was really more like a mini-auditorium, and the auditorium itself, this was the biggest "regular" classroom in the school. *Great,* I thought, *all the more room for the explosion that's getting ready to happen.*

"It's not like we can cut this class," I muttered back to Aphrodite. Then, to the rest of my group I said, "Okay, let's go in. Don't worry. We're together so it really can't be that bad." My nerd herd, as well as Stevie Rae, Rephaim, and all of her red fledglings flanked me. Everyone nodded and looked resigned and ready for whatever was getting ready to hit the fan. I opened the door and stepped inside.

My seer stone immediately began radiating heat.

Dallas and his group were already in class, predictably filling up the back row of desks.

Aurox sat in a desk in the front row over at the far side, obviously separating himself from Dallas's group. I wondered why he wasn't hanging out with the bad guys, since he was on Neferet's team like they obviously were, but I kept my gaze carefully averted from him.

"I'm gonna try and keep a positive attitude," Stevie Rae said, ignoring the sneer Dallas was sending her and the mean laughter that wafted like cheap perfume from Nichole. She took Rephaim's hand and smiled, kissing his cheek. "Don't let them get to you."

"Good luck with that," Erin said.

Shaunee, standing several kids away from Erin, said nothing.

"He's red, and I don't mean a good red like Shaunee is," Shaylin said, peeking over my shoulder at Dallas.

I looked at her. "What do you mean?"

"I'm red?" Shaunee asked.

"Yeah," Shaylin told her. "Your color's clear and easy to understand. You're like a campfire—warm and good."

"That's real nice," Stevie Rae said.

"Thanks," Shaunee said. "That is nice."

"But what about Dallas?" Rephaim asked.

"He's red like a bomb. Like anger. Like hate," she said.

"Then I say we go down front and get as far away from him as possible," Stevie Rae said.

"Some things are harder than others to get away from," Erin said, but she wasn't looking at Dallas. She was looking at campfire-red Shaunee, who was looking at her fingernails.

"Don't be such a Negative Nancy," Stevie Rae told Erin, neatly breaking the awkward silence. Then she beamed her sweet, open smile at me. "Let's go sit up front!"

"Okay, I'll follow you," I said, even though I wanted to run screaming from the room.

"I want to run screaming from the room." Aphrodite spookily echoed my thoughts as she followed me following Stevie Rae and Rephaim.

I clamped down on the "ditto" I wanted to say and, by default, took the desk on the other side of Stevie Rae that was front and center in the room. The bell chimed and Thanatos entered from a door that led from a small office directly to the front of the room, which was raised, kinda like a stage, and had a podium smack in the middle of it with a Smart Board behind it.

"Oooh! Pretty colors!" Shaylin said from her seat behind me.

"Merry meet," Thanatos said. We all echoed her greeting. I thought she looked regal and powerful. She wore a night-colored dress that was decorated only with the silver threads of the embroidered outline of Nyx with her arms raised cupping a crescent moon. "Welcome to the first of a first. In all of our history there has never been a class quite like this one, made up of different types of fledglings, changelings, humans, and even vampyres. I stand before you representing the High Council of Vampyres which is, as long as you exist within our society, your ruling Council." Thanatos gave me a long look during the last part of her sentence. I met her gaze steadily. Hell, I agreed with her.

I just wasn't one hundred percent sure whether my group and I wanted to exist within vampyre society.

"I know you are wondering exactly what this class will entail, but I have only a partial answer to your wondering. I am here to hone and guide you on a journey that is as rare and unique as are each of you. This class will take the place of your vampyre sociology hour; therefore, I will bring to you subjects that all fledglings and vampyres must eventually attempt to understand, such as death and Darkness, Guardianship and Imprints, Light and love. But because of the unique makeup of this class there are also subjects you will bring to me, and thereby to all of us. I give you my oath that I will seek only the truth with you, and if I do not have an answer for your questioning I will do my best to discover it with you."

I thought that so far the class didn't sound too bad, and was actually starting to feel kinda at ease and curious when the poo hit the fan.

"So, let us begin seeking truth. I want each of you to spend a few moments in reflection. Then, on a piece of paper, write at least one question you would like to have answered through this class. Fold it, and after you leave I will read them. Be honest with your inquiry, without fear of censure or judgment. You need not affix your name to the question if you would rather remain anonymous."

There was a pause, and then Stevie Rae's hand went up.

"Yes, Stevie Rae," Thanatos called on her.

"I just wanna be sure we're all clear. We can ask about anything? Anything at all, without worryin' 'bout gettin' in trouble?"

Thanatos was smiling kindly at Stevie Rae, and began to respond saying, "That is an excellent—" when from the back of the room Dallas's exaggerated whisper of *"I wanna ask what a bird has that a guy don't, and why she likes it so much!"* could be heard clearly.

Stevie Rae grabbed Rephaim's hand and I knew it was to keep him from getting up to confront Dallas. Then I wasn't paying attention to my BFF or her boyfriend as Thanatos reacted. The change that came over her was fast and utterly, totally scary. She seemed to grow larger. Wind whipped around her, lifting her hair. When she spoke I was reminded of the scene in *LotR* when Galadriel gave Frodo a look at what kind of terrible dark queen she would become if she took the ring from him.

"Do you mistake me for a lesser being, Dallas?" The power of her presence shivered against us. Thanatos was so gloriously angry that she was hard to look at, so I glanced over my shoulder at Dallas. He'd pressed back into his chair as far as he could. His face was winter white.

"N-no, Professor," he stuttered.

"Call me Priestess!" Thanatos exclaimed, looking like she could throw lightning bolts and call down thunder.

"No, Priestess," he corrected quickly. "I-I didn't mean to disrespect you."

"But you meant to disrespect at least one of your classmates and here, in *my* classroom, that is unacceptable. Do you understand me, young red vampyre?"

"Yes, Priestess."

The wind died around her and Thanatos went back to looking regal instead of lethal. "Excellent," she said, and then turned her attention back to Stevie Rae. "The answer to your question is as long as you behave in a respectful manner, you may ask me anything without fearing rebuke."

"Thank you," Stevie Rae said a little breathlessly.

"All right then, you may all begin writing your questions." Thanatos paused and glanced from Rephaim to Aurox, addressing both of them with the one question. "I did not think to ask before, but as both of you are new to the, well, let us say, the academic world, do either of you need reading or writing assistance?"

Rephaim shook his head and answered first, "I don't need help. I can read and write several languages of man."

"Wow, really? I didn't know that," Stevie Rae said.

He smiled sheepishly and shrugged. "My father found it useful."

"And you, Aurox?" Thanatos prodded.

I saw him swallow and he looked nervous. "I can read and write. I-I do not know how I came by this skill, though."

"Huh, well that is interesting," Thanatos said. And then, as if people having the magickal ability to read and write was totally normal, she continued totally nonplussed. "Zoey and Stevie Rae, as you're sitting close by, please divide the room and pick up the questions from both sides for me."

Stevie Rae and I muttered our okays and then I sat there and stared at my empty piece of notebook paper. So should I ask something harmless, like a question about affinities and when is it "normal" for them to manifest? Or should I be for real and ask something I really wanted to know?

I glanced around me. Stevie Rae was writing with a very serious look on her face. Rephaim had just put his pencil down and was folding his paper in half. I got a quick look at it, but all I could see was that he'd signed his name to the question.

I'm gonna be for real, I decided and wrote: How do you get over losing your parents? I hesitated, and then signed my name to the question. I tried to check out what Stevie Rae was writing, but she was already finished and had her paper in her hand. She bounced out of her desk and started walking up and down the aisles on her side of the room, picking up papers like a pro.

I sighed and began to minesweep my side. Of course Aurox was there. The next kid in the row after Damien and Shaunee. I didn't want to meet his eyes, so instead I looked at the paper he handed me. On it, in big block letters was the question: WHAT AM I? And he'd signed it.

Totally surprised, I met his gaze. He looked back at me steadily. Then he spoke so softly only I could hear him saying, "I would like to know."

I couldn't look away from his unusual, moonstone eyes. For some moronic reason, I heard my voice whispering back, "Me, too." I snatched the paper from him and moved hastily away, trying not to think, trying just to do what I'd been told. Dallas and his group were super subdued. They barely looked at me or Stevie Rae, but I noticed they hadn't written any words on the papers I picked up from them, which was a seriously passive-aggressive bad sign. I shoved those papers to the bottom of the pile on my way back to the front of the class. Thanatos took the papers, thanked us, and then said, "I shall study your questions tonight and begin discussions on some of them tomorrow.

For the rest of the hour let us turn to a subject I believe most of you will find relevant—that of Imprinting with a mate or Consort."

I expected Thanatos to give us the standard just-say-no speech we'd been given about the Imprinting thing from day one, but I was wrong. She talked frankly about the pleasure and beauty of the proper Imprint, as well as the tragedy of one going wrong. She was interesting and funny (in a dry British kind of way). It seemed like I blinked and the bell for the end of the hour was chiming.

I hung a little behind, waiting for Aphrodite who was still in a deep but surprisingly respectful discussion with Thanatos about Imprinting. Aphrodite's point was that an Imprint wasn't based on sexuality. Thanatos was insisting, much to Aphrodite's consternation ('cause she'd Imprinted with Stevie Rae, even though it hadn't lasted very long) that sexual attraction went hand in hand with Imprinting.

Thanatos finally ended the discussion with, "Aphrodite, whether you admit a thing or not does not make it more or less true."

"I'm going to be sure Zoey gets to second hour," Aphrodite said, sounding disgruntled.

"You do that, young Prophetess." Thanatos had a smile in her voice, if not on her face. "And thank you for such a lively discussion today. I'll look forward to another one like it tomorrow."

Aphrodite nodded and frowned, and just out of earshot of Thanatos said, "Lively discussion my gorgeous ass. I'm not discussing shit about lesbian Imprints again. Ever."

"I don't think that's what she meant, Aphrodite," I said, careful to keep the smile from my face, too. "But she was right, it made for a good class—way more interesting than regular vamp soc with all of Neferet's issues."

Aphrodite opened the door. "I'm so glad I could amuse the masses and—" And we stepped into the middle of chaos.

"Bring it, birdboy!" Dallas was shouting. "You can't hide behind Stevie Rae forever!" Muscley Johnny B was pinning his arms and holding Dallas back, but he was struggling like crazy.

"I'm not hiding, you arrogant fool!" Rephaim yelled. Stevie Rae had a vise-like grip on his arm and was trying to pull him down the sidewalk away from Dallas.

"I'll get Darius and Stark," Aphrodite said, and sprinted away.

"Okay, look, you guys, stop it!" I stepped between the two guys and their growing groups.

"Butt the hell out, Zoey! This ain't your fight." Dallas turned his venom on me. "You think you're so much better than everyone else, but you don't mean shit to us." He jerked his head toward the group of his red fledglings who were standing close by, just watching and smiling.

I was surprised by how much what he said hurt my feelings. "I don't think I'm better than everyone else!"

"Don't let him get to you, Z. He's nothing but a mean, sad little boy all dressed up like a vampyre," Stevie Rae said.

"And you're nothing but a slut!" Dallas shouted at Stevie Rae.

"I told you to stop calling her that!" Rephaim tried to pull away from Stevie Rae.

"Everyone knows you're just pissed because she's not with you anymore," I told Dallas, thinking what a total and complete jerk he'd turned out to be.

"No, I'm pissed because she's with a freak of nature!" His words shot back at me. I noticed even though he was struggling and yelling, his gaze kept going back to a spot low on the wall he was inching closer and closer to. I followed his gaze and saw a single electrical outlet on the wall—one of the industrial three-pronged things.

Ah, hell!

"I'm not a freak!" Rephaim looked like he was going to explode. "I'm human!"

"Really? How 'bout we wait around until the sun comes up and let's just see how human you are." Dallas sneered and moved closer to the wall.

As nonchalantly as I could, I took a couple steps toward the outlet and wondered frantically which element would be the best to summon if I needed to fight electricity.

"That suits me fine," Rephaim was saying. "Whether it's from a human's eye or a bird's I'll be glad to watch you burn up!"

"In your dreams, you asshole!" Dallas surged forward, toward the outlet, almost getting away from Johnny B and making me stumble and fall back.

And then strong hands caught me and strong arms kept me from tumbling onto my butt. All in one motion Stark steadied me on my feet and moved me behind him and against the wall. Then he faced Dallas.

"Walk away." Stark didn't raise his voice. He sounded calm and cold and completely dangerous.

"This isn't your fight," Dallas said, but he'd already stopped struggling against Johnny B.

"If Zoey's in it, it's my fight. And you need to understand I'll win. Every time. So, walk away."

"This ends now!" Sounding like a general commanding runaway troops, Dragon Lankford and several Sons of Erebus Warriors, including Darius, burst onto the scene making a big show of standing between Dallas and Rephaim. The Sword Master's face was like a storm cloud. "Dallas, you stand there." He pointed to a place before him, then hardly glancing at Rephaim added, "And you there." Dragon pointed to an empty space beside Dallas. The two guys did what they were told, though Dallas still sent Rephaim a hateful look. Rephaim's gaze was totally focused on the Sword Master who began speaking sternly to them both.

"I will not tolerate fighting at this school. This is not a human high school. I expect you to rise above such childish, base behavior." Dragon looked from Dallas to Rephaim. "Do you understand me?"

"I do." Rephaim spoke clearly and quickly. "I do not want to be the cause of trouble."

"Then leave because as long as you're here there's gonna be trouble!" Dallas said.

"No!" Dragon hurled the word like a whip. "There will be no more trouble at this school or you will answer to me."

"He doesn't belong here," Dallas said, but his voice was subdued and he looked more pouty than dangerous.

"I agree with you, Dallas," Dragon said. "But Nyx does not. As long as the House of Night serves Nyx, we will abide by her choices, even if she chooses forgiveness when we cannot."

"Can't or won't?" Everyone's attention turned to Stevie Rae. She marched up beside Rephaim, took his hand, and faced Dragon. I thought she looked totally like a powerful High Priestess who was pissed enough to spit fire, and I was glad her element was earth and not flame. "Rephaim didn't even start this crap with Dallas. All he did was stand up for me when Dallas called me slut and whore and other stuff too awful for me to repeat. If anyone but Rephaim was standin' here you wouldn't be takin' Dallas's side."

"I can understand how Dallas and many of the students would have difficulty accepting Rephaim," Dragon said matter-of-factly.

"That is something you'll have to take up with the Goddess." Neferet's voice traveled silkily through the crowd. Everyone turned to see her standing at the head of the hallway with Thanatos beside her.

"From all reports, the Goddess has spoken on the matter of Rephaim's acceptance," Thanatos said. "Dallas, you will simply have to adhere to Nyx's decision, as will you, Sword Master."

"He's bein' accepted just fine." Stevie Rae sounded super annoyed. "Like I was tryin' to explain, it's Dallas who's causin' trouble, not Rephaim."

"And that trouble will now end," Dragon said. "I have made that clear."

"You've also made it clear that you don't want Rephaim here," Stevie Rae said.

"Our Sword Master is not required to like each of our students," Neferet said with a patronizing shake of her head. "His duty is to protect us, not mother us."

"His duty is also to be fair and honorable," Thanatos said. "Dragon Lankford, do you believe that you can be fair and honorable in your dealings with Rephaim, in spite of your personal feelings for him?"

Dragon's expression was tight, his voice strained, but his answer came with no hesitation. "I do."

"Then I accept that as your true and rightful word," Thanatos said. "As should we all."

"We should also all move on to second hour," Neferet said sharply. "*This* has taken far too much of our time." Her gaze rested disdainfully on Rephaim and Stevie Rae before she moved regally off, shooing kids before her. Dragon joined her, moving gawking students down the hallway like he was herding cattle.

"Can you see the Darkness that surrounds her and those other red fledglings?" I blinked in surprise. Stark was directing his question straight at Thanatos.

The High Council member hesitated and then slowly shook her head. "I have not trafficked with Darkness. It is not visible to me."

"I can see it," Rephaim said. "Stark's right."

"I can see it, too," Stevie Rae said quietly. "It slithers around all of them like insects, touching them and constantly hanging around." She shuddered. "It's disgusting."

"What about Dragon?" I asked. "Is it around him, too?"

It was Rephaim who answered me. "Yes and no. It is following him, but it does not wash against him like it does the others." He sighed heavily. "At least not yet it doesn't."

"It's not your fault," Stevie Rae told him earnestly. "The choices Dragon's makin' right now aren't your fault."

"I'll believe that the day he forgives me," Rephaim said. "Come on, I'll walk you to second hour."

We said our byes and see-ya-at-lunches, but Stark and I didn't go anywhere. We just stood there with Thanatos staring after Rephaim and Stevie Rae.

"The boy has a conscience," Thanatos said.

"Yeah, he does," I said.

"Then there is hope for him yet," she said.

"Can you tell that to Dragon?" Stark asked.

"Sadly, that is something Dragon Lankford is going to have to discover for himself, if the death of his mate has not caused him to completely lose who he is."

"Do you think that's happened? Do you think Dragon has completely lost himself?" I asked.

"I do," Thanatos said.

"Which means Darkness might be able to get a hold on him," Stark said. "And if our Sword Master goes over to Darkness, we're all gonna be in trouble."

"Indeed," Thanatos said.

Ah hell, I thought.

CHAPTER TWENTY

Lenobia

There were some school days when Lenobia didn't need the hour provided for each professor that was called their planning hour, which meant no students were scheduled in class with her for one solid hour.

Today was not one of those days.

Today her fifth hour planning period couldn't come soon enough or last long enough. As soon as the bell chimed to begin fifth hour she made a hasty exit from the arena. An arena that was *still* half filled with male fledglings waving swords at one another and shooting arrows at targets.

"Give Bonnie the hour off," she told Travis as she passed him. "But keep an eye on those fledglings. I don't want any of them annoying the horses."

"Yes, ma'am. Some of 'em think horses are big dogs," the cowboy said, giving the group of fledglings a steely-eyed stare. "They ain't."

"I need a break from constantly watching them. I had no idea so many non-riding fledglings were fascinated by horses." She shook her head wearily.

"Take your break. I'll have a word with Darius and Stark. They need to keep better corral on those kids."

"I couldn't agree more," Lenobia muttered and, feeling surprisingly grateful that Travis was the one heading to lecture the two Warriors, she slipped out into the cool quiet of the night.

Her bench was as empty as the busy school building was full. The breeze had kicked up and was unusually warm for late winter. Lenobia was grateful for it, and for the solitude. She sat, rolling her shoulders and inhaling then expelling a long breath.

She wasn't exactly sorry she'd welcomed the Warrior class to her domain, but the influx of fledglings—non-equestrian fledglings—was taking some getting used to. It seemed every time she turned her head an errant student wandered from the arena into her stables. So far just this day she'd found three of them gaping like young codfish at a broodmare who was perilously close to foaling and therefore restless and touchy and *not* in the mood for fish. The mare had actually tried to take a bite out of one of the boys who'd said he was *just wanting to pet her.* "Like she was, indeed, a big dog," Lenobia grumbled under her breath. But that was better than the foolish third former who'd thought it was a good idea to try to lift one of Bonnie's hooves on a bet from his friends so they could wager on *how heavy it really was.* Bonnie had spooked when one of the boys had yelped about it being a *real big paw* and the mare, completely off balanced and disconcerted, had gone down on her knees.

Thankfully, she'd been on the arena sawdust and not bruising, breaking concrete.

Travis, who had been overseeing a small group of her regular students who were learning about ground driving, had dealt with the two boys swiftly. Lenobia smiled, remembering how he'd grabbed each by the scruff of their collars and thrown them directly into a pile of Bonnie's manure that was, as he'd said, almost as big and heavy as one of her hooves. Then he'd quieted his mare with a few reassuring touches as he checked her knees, fed her one of the apple wafers he seemed to always have in his pocket, and completely nonplused, had gone back to the group of ground-driving fledglings.

He's good with the students, she thought. *Almost as good as he is with the horses.*

Truth be told, it appeared as if Travis Foster was going to be an asset to her stables. Lenobia laughed softly. Neferet was going to be sorely disappointed about that.

Her laughter died quickly, though, replaced by the stomach-rolling tension that had haunted her since she'd met Travis and his horse.

It's because he's a human, Lenobia acknowledged silently to herself. *I'm just not used to having a human male around me.*

She'd forgotten things about them. How spontaneous their laughter could be. How they could take pleasure that felt so new in things that were so old to her, like a simple sunrise. How briefly and brightly they lived.

Twenty-seven, ma'am. That's how many years he'd lived on this earth. He'd known twenty-seven years of sunrises and she'd known more than two hundred and forty of them. He would probably only know thirty or forty more years of sunrises, and then he would die.

Their lives were so brief.

Some briefer than others. Some didn't even live to see twenty-one summers, let alone enough sunrises to fill a life.

No! Lenobia's mind skittered away from that memory. The cowboy was not going to awaken those memories. She'd closed the door to them the day she'd been Marked—that terrible, wonderful day. The door wouldn't, couldn't open now or ever again.

Neferet knew some of Lenobia's past. They'd been friends once, she and the High Priestess. They'd talked and Lenobia used to believe they'd shared confidences. It had, of course, been a false friendship. Even before Kalona had emerged from the earth to stand by Neferet's side, Lenobia had begun to realize there was something very wrong with the High Priestess—something dark and disturbing.

"She's broken," Lenobia whispered to the night. "But I won't let her break me."

The door would remain closed. Always.

She heard Bonnie's heavy hoofbeats thunking solidly against the winter grass before she felt the brush of the big mare's mind. Lenobia cleared her thoughts and projected warmth and welcome. Bonnie nickered a greeting that was so low it almost did sound like it should come from what many of the students were calling her—a dinosaur, which made Lenobia laugh. She was still laughing when Travis led Bonnie up to her bench.

"No, I don't have any wafers for you." Lenobia smiled, caressing the mare's wide, soft muzzle.

"Here ya go, boss lady." Travis flipped a wafer to Lenobia as he sat on the far end of the wrought-iron-backed bench.

Lenobia caught the treat and held it out to Bonnie, who took it with surprising delicacy for such a big animal. "You know, a normal horse would founder on the amount of these things you feed her."

"She's a big girl and she likes her some cookies," Travis drawled.

As he spoke the word *cookies* the mare's ears pricked toward him. He laughed and reached across Lenobia to feed her another wafer. Lenobia shook her head. "Spoiled, spoiled, spoiled," but the smile was obvious in her voice.

Travis shrugged his broad shoulders. "I like to spoil my girl. Always have. Always will."

"That's how I feel about Mujaji." Lenobia rubbed Bonnie's broad forehead. "Some mares require special treatment."

"Oh, so with your mare it's *special treatment*. With mine it's spoiling?"

She met his gaze and saw the smile shining there. "Yes. Of course."

"Of course," he said. "And now you're remindin' me of my momma."

Lenobia lifted her brows. "I have to tell you, that sounds very odd, Mr. Foster."

He laughed aloud then, a full, joyful sound that reminded Lenobia of sunrises.

"It's a compliment, ma'am. My momma insisted on things bein' her way or the highway. Always. She was hardheaded, but it balanced because she was also almost always right."

"*Almost* always?" she said pointedly.

He laughed again. "There, see, if she was here that's exactly what she would've said."

"You miss her often, don't you," Lenobia said, studying his tanned, well-lined face. *He looks older than thirty-two, but in a pleasing way,* she thought.

"I do," he said softly.

"That says quite a lot about her," Lenobia said. "Quite a lot of good."

"Rain Foster was quite a lot of good."

Lenobia smiled and shook her head. "Rain Foster. That is an unusual name."

"Not if you were a sixties flower child," Travis said. "Lenobia, *that's* an unusual name."

Without thinking, the response tripped from her tongue. "Not if you were the daughter of an eighteenth century English lass with big dreams." The words had barely been spoken and Lenobia clamped her lips together, closing her errant mouth.

"Do you get tired of livin' for so long?"

Lenobia was taken aback. She'd expected him to be surprised and awestruck by hearing that she'd been alive for more than two hundred years. Instead he simply sounded curious. And for some reason his frank curiosity relaxed her so that she answered him with truthfulness and not with evasion. "If I didn't have my horses I think I would get very tired of living."

He nodded as if what she'd said made sense to him, but when he spoke all he said was, "Eighteenth century—that's really somethin'. A lot's changed since then."

"Not horses," she said.

"Happiness and horses," he said.

His eyes smiled into hers and she was struck again at their color, which seemed to shift and lighten. "Your eyes," she said. "They change color."

His lips tilted up. "They do. My momma used to say she could read me by their color."

Lenobia couldn't look away from him, even though anxiety rolled through her.

Thankfully, Bonnie chose then to nuzzle her. Lenobia rubbed the mare's forehead while she tried to still the cacophony of feelings this human's presence stirred. *No. I will not allow this nonsense.*

With a reinstated coolness, Lenobia looked from the mare to the cowboy. "Mr. Foster, why are you out here and not within assuring my stable is safe from prying fledglings?"

His eyes instantly darkened, returning to safe, ordinary brown. His tone went from warm to professional. "Well, ma'am, I had a talk with Darius and Stark. I do believe your horses are safe for the rest of this hour 'cause there's two very pissed-off vampyres drilling them in hand-to-hand combat—with a big focus on showing them how to knock each other off their feet." He tilted his hat up. "Seems those boys don't like it any better than you do that their fledglings are being bothersome, so they're gonna keep 'em mighty busy from now on."

"Oh. Well. That is good news," she said.

"Yep, that's how I see it, too. So I thought I'd come out here and offer you something truly pleasurable."

Was the man actually flirting with her? Lenobia squelched the nervous thrill she felt and instead leveled a cool, steady gaze on him. "I cannot think of any possible way for you to offer me pleasure."

She was sure his eyes started to lighten, but his gaze remained as steady as hers. "Well, ma'am, I assumed that would be obvious to you. I'm offerin' you a ride." He paused and then added. "On Bonnie."

"Bonnie?"

"Bonnie. My horse. The big gray girl standing right there nuzzlin' you. The one who likes cookies."

"I know who she is," Lenobia snapped.

"Thought you might like to ride her. That's why I came out here with her all saddled up for ya." When Lenobia didn't speak, he tilted his hat and looked vaguely uncomfortable. "When I need to relax—to remember to smile and breathe—I get on Bonnie and gallop her. Hard. She can move for a big girl, but it's a little like ridin' a mountain, and that makes me smile. Thought it might do the same for you." He hesitated and added, "But if you don't want to, I'll take her back inside."

Bonnie nudged her shoulder, as if offering the ride herself.

And that decided Lenobia. She'd never turned down a horse before, and no human, no matter how uncomfortable he made her, was going to cause her to start.

"I believe you could be right, Mr. Foster." She stood, took the reins from him, and flipped them over Bonnie's widely arched neck.

She could tell she'd surprised him by the way he moved. He was on his feet in an instant.

"Here, I'll give you a leg up."

"No need," she said. Lenobia turned her back to him and clucked to the mare, encouraging her to walk forward along the back side of the bench. Moving with a lithe grace that came from centuries of practice, Lenobia stepped from the ground to the seat of the bench, and then the iron backrest, easily finding the stirrup and swinging up, up, and into Bonnie's saddle. She noticed immediately that he'd shortened the stirrups of his wide Western saddle to accommodate her much shorter legs, so even though the seat was too big, it felt comfortable rather than awkward. She looked down at Travis and had to smile because he seemed so very, very far below her.

His grin answered hers. "I know."

"It's different from up here," she said.

"Yep, sure is. Take my girl out. She'll remind you to breathe and smile. Oh, and Lenobia, I'd 'preciate it if you'd stop callin' me Mr. Foster." He tipped his hat to her, added a smile and a long, slow, "If you please, ma'am."

Lenobia only raised an eyebrow at him. She gave Bonnie a squeeze with her knees and made the same kiss noise she'd heard Travis making. The mare responded with no hesitation. They moved off smoothly. The wind had continued to pick up and with the warmth this evening Lenobia was reminded of spring. She smiled. "Maybe this long, cold winter is over, Bonnie girl. Maybe spring *is* coming."

Bonnie's ears flicked back, listening, and Lenobia patted her wide neck. She pointed the mare north and rode along the stone wall past the broken tree that had been the site of so much pain, past the stables and arena. They rode, alternatively walking and trotting, all the way to the place where east joined north, in the corner of the rectangle that encompassed the campus grounds. By the time they'd reached the corner, Lenobia felt she had Bonnie's rhythm and her trust. She turned the mare so that she was pointed back in the direction from which they'd come.

"All right, my Bonnie big girl, let's see what you're made of." Lenobia leaned forward, squeezed her knees, kicked with her heels, and made a loud kiss noise while she flipped the ends of the reins on the big mare's butt.

Bonnie took off like she thought she was a quarter horse out of the roping shoots.

"Ha!" Lenobia shouted. "That's it! Let's go!"

Bonnie's huge hooves drove into the ground. Lenobia could feel the mare's powerful heartbeat. The warm night air whipped her hair back and the Horse Mistress leaned even farther forward, encouraging Bonnie to let loose—to give her everything.

The mare responded with a burst of speed that shouldn't have been possible for a creature who weighed two thousand pounds.

As the wind whistled around them, lifting Lenobia's long silver hair in time with the Percheron's mane in that magickal dance that melded horse to rider, Lenobia thought of the ancient Persian saying: *The breath of heaven is found between a horse's ears.*

"That's right! That's exactly right!" Lenobia yelled, and clung to the speeding mare's back.

Joyously, freely, wonderfully, Lenobia moved as one with Bonnie. She didn't realize she'd been laughing aloud until she pulled the mare in and circled her, finally coming to a halt, blowing and sweating, beside Travis and their bench.

"She's magnificent!" Lenobia laughed again, and leaned forward to hug Bonnie's damp neck.

"Yeah, I told ya it'd be better after that," Travis called to her, catching Bonnie's bridle and echoing Lenobia's laughter.

"What couldn't be? That's so much fun!"

"Like riding a mountain?"

"Exactly like riding a beautiful, smart, wonderful mountain!" Lenobia hugged Bonnie again. "You know what? You really do deserve all those cookies," she told the mare.

Travis just laughed.

Lenobia kicked her leg over the saddle to slide off Bonnie, but the ground was much farther away than she'd anticipated. She staggered and would have fallen had Travis not caught her elbow in his strong grip.

"Steady there . . . steady girl," he murmured, sounding like he was speaking to a spooked filly. "Ground's a long ways down. Take 'er easy or you'll have a nasty fall."

Still feeling the sweet adrenaline rush from her run with the mare, Lenobia laughed. "I don't care! The ride would be worth the fall. The ride would be worth anything!"

"Some girls are," Travis said.

Lenobia looked up at the tall cowboy. His eyes had lightened so that they weren't just hazel anymore. They were flecked with an olive green that was distinctive and light and unmistakably familiar.

Lenobia didn't think. Instinct drove her. She stepped into his embrace. It seemed Travis had stopped thinking, too, because he'd dropped Bonnie's reins and pulled Lenobia into his arms. Their lips met with a kind of desperation that was part passion, part question.

She could have stopped herself, but she didn't. She allowed it. No, more than that. Lenobia met Travis's passion with her own, and answered his question with desire and need.

The kiss went on long enough for Lenobia to recognize the taste and feel of him, and for her to admit to herself that she'd missed him—missed him desperately.

And then she began thinking again.

She only had to pull just a little and he let her slip from the warm circle of his arms.

Lenobia could feel her head shaking back and forth and her heart racing.

"No," she said, trying to get her breathing under control. "This can't be. I can't do this."

His beautiful, olive-flecked eyes looked dazed. "Lenobia, girl. Let's talk this out. There's somethin' here that we can't ignore. It's like we—"

"No!" Lenobia called the steely control that she'd commanded for centuries to her, cloaking her desire and need and fear in anger and coldness. "Do not presume. Humans are attracted to our kind. What you felt was what any man would feel if I deigned to kiss him." She forced herself to laugh, this time the sound was utterly devoid of joy. "Which is why I do not make a habit of kissing human men. It will not happen again."

Without looking at Travis or Bonnie, Lenobia strode away. Her back was to them, so they couldn't see that she pressed her hand against her mouth to keep the sob from escaping. She opened the side door to the stables so hard that it slammed against the stone building. She didn't pause. She went straight to her room that rested over her horses, closed and locked the door behind her.

Then, and only then, Lenobia allowed herself to weep.

CHAPTER TWENTY-ONE

Neferet

Things were going very well.

The red fledglings were causing problems.

Dallas hated Rephaim with an intensity that was simply lovely.

Gaea was all in a tizzy about the lawn humans. So much so that she'd forgotten to lock the side maintenance gate and one of the street people who usually frequented Cherry Street had *somehow* been compelled to stagger down Utica Street and through the unlocked gate and onto campus.

"And he'd promptly almost been carved in two by Dragon, who is seeing Raven Mockers in every shade and shadow," Neferet practically purred.

She tapped her chin contemplatively. She hated that Thanatos had invaded her House of Night. But the positive side of the High Council's interfering ways was that forcing all of those *special* students into one classroom was acting like dry twigs on coals.

"Chaos!" Neferet laughed. "It is going to cause something to ignite."

The Darkness that was her constant companion slithered closer, wrapping itself caressingly around her legs.

During the passing period the hour before, she'd overheard two of Zoey's ridiculous friends talking. It seemed the Twins, Shaunee and Erin, were having a falling-out that was affecting the entire herd.

Neferet snorted sarcastically. "Of course it would. None of them are truly strong enough to stand on their own. They huddle together like the sheep they are, trying to stay safe from the wolf." She would enjoy seeing how that little drama played itself out. "Perhaps I should befriend Erin in her time of need . . ." she mused aloud.

Neferet smiled and opened the heavy velvet drapes that usually covered the large mullioned window of her private quarters from the prying eyes of the school. She opened the window, inhaling deeply of the brisk, warm breeze. Neferet closed her eyes and opened her senses. She scented the wind for more than the familiar smells of incense from the temple and the newly cut winter grass. Neferet opened her mind to taste the aromas of emotion that roiled and lifted from the House of Night and its inhabitants.

She was intuitive in a literal and not so literal sense. At times she could, indeed, read actual thoughts. At times she could only taste emotions. If those emotions were strong enough, or the person's mind weak enough, she could even glimpse mental images—pictures of the thoughts that lived within the mind.

It was easier when she was close to the person, physically and emotionally. But it wasn't impossible to sift through the night and glean things, especially a night as filled with emotion as was this one.

Neferet concentrated.

Yes, she tasted sorrow. She sifted through it and recognized the banal emotion from Shaunee and Damien and even Dragon, though vampyres were always harder to read than fledglings or humans.

Neferet's thoughts turned to humans. She tried to inhale Aphrodite—to touch even a slight bit of emotion from the girl, and she failed. Aphrodite had always been as unreadable to her as Zoey.

"No matter." She damped her irritation. "There are other humans at play in my House tonight."

Neferet thought of Rephaim—thought of the strong lines of his face that so clearly mimicked those of his father's—thought of the infatuation that had led him to his human form . . .

Again, nothing.

She could not find Rephaim, though she knew he must be filled with readable emotions. So strange. Humans were usually such easy prey. Humans . . .

Neferet smiled as she focused her attention on a more-interesting human. The cowboy—the one she'd chosen so carefully for poor, dear, repressed Lenobia.

What was it the Horse Mistress had said when they'd first met and Lenobia had thought them friends? Ah, Neferet remembered. They'd been talking of human mates and how neither had a desire for one. Neferet hadn't admitted that they curdled her stomach— that she could never allow a human to touch her without doing him violence—never again. Instead she'd simply listened as Lenobia confessed: *I loved a human boy once. When I lost him, I almost lost myself. I can never let that happen again, so I prefer to stay away from humans altogether.*

Neferet closed her eyes, drew a deep breath, and dug her long, pointed fingernails into the palm of her left hand. As the blood welled and then dripped, she offered it to the searching shadows, thinking of the cowboy she'd planted in the soil of Lenobia's manure-ridden arena.

> *Lend Dark power to me*
> *So that his emotions I can see!*

The pain in her palm was nothing compared to the onrush of icy power she received. Neferet controlled it and focused it at the stables. She was justly rewarded. She could feel the human cowboy's warmth and compassion—his joy and desire. And then she laughed aloud because she could also feel his hurt and confusion, along with the backwash of what could only be Lenobia's heartbreak.

"It's so delicious! Everything is going according to my plans."

Absently, Neferet brushed away the more aggressive of the threads of Darkness and licked the wounds on her palm, closing them. "That is all for now. Wait until later for more." She laughed at their reluctance to quit feeding from her. She commanded them easily. *They know my true allegiance, my true sacrifice, is only for him—the white bull.* Just the thought of him—of his magnificent power—made Neferet shiver with longing. *He was all a god or goddess should be; there is much I can learn from him.*

Neferet decided it then. She would make an excuse to the much-too-curious Thanatos and leave the school before dawn. She had to be with the white bull—she needed to absorb more of his power.

She closed her eyes and breathed in the night, letting the thought of her Consort, Darkness himself, woo her. And for a moment Neferet believed she was almost happy.

Then *she* intruded. *She* always intruded.

"Seriously, Shaunee, you can't stay here."

Neferet's lip lifted in a sneer as she opened her eyes and looked down through her window to the sidewalk below. Zoey had caught the black girl by her arm and was obviously trying to stop her from going out to the parking lot.

"Look, I gave it a try, but today was hell. Really hell. So I'm gonna go get the bag I packed from the depot and left on the short bus, and I'm gonna move into my old dorm room."

"Please don't," Zoey said.

"I have to. Erin keeps hurting my feelings over and over." Neferet thought the girl was very near tears. Her weakness disgusted the Tsi Sgili. "And anyway, why does it matter?"

"It matters 'cause you're one of us!" Neferet hated the honest warmth in Zoey's voice. "You can be pissed at Erin. You can even stop being BFFs, but you can't let your whole life explode because of it."

"It's not me who's exploding. It's her," Shaunee said.

"Then be a better person. Be your own person, and maybe by doing that you can show Erin how to be your friend again."

"But not my Twin." Shaunee spoke so softly Neferet almost couldn't hear her. "I don't want to be anyone's Twin again. I just want to be myself."

Zoey smiled. "That's all you need to be. Go to sixth hour, and I promise I'll talk to Erin. You're both still part of our circle, and that has to count for something."

Shaunee nodded slowly. "'Kay. But only if you talk to her."

"I will."

Neferet sneered again as Zoey hugged the black girl who started to retrace her path toward the main school building. She expected

Zoey to walk with her, but she didn't. Instead the girl's shoulders slumped and she rubbed her forehead as if it ached. *If the little bitch stayed out of the business of her betters, she wouldn't have any worries,* Neferet thought as she watched Zoey leave the sidewalk and kick rather noisily at a tin can that the yard maintenance humans had, no doubt, left behind them. Knowing what their discarded rubbish would do to the fastidious Gaea made Neferet smile.

Zoey's can rolled to a stop against an exposed root of one of the ancient oaks that dotted the school grounds. The winter bare branches waved in another strong gust of warm wind, almost obscuring Zoey from her view—almost as if they were reaching around to protect her as the child bent to pick up the can.

Protect her . . .

Neferet's eyes widened. What if Zoey did need protecting? The trees certainly wouldn't do it—not without the annoying child calling on earth. And Zoey wouldn't know she needed to call the element if a sudden gust of wind—a sudden *accident*—caused a limb to break and fall on her.

Zoey wouldn't know what was happening until it was too late.

Without flinching, Neferet stuck her fingernail into the pink slashes that had not yet healed. She held her hand up, cupping the blood, and saying:

> *"Drink and obey*
> *The limb must do more than sway*
> *Rip it—break it—to the earth it should hurl*
> *Crush her—hurt her—kill the Zoey girl."*

Neferet braced herself for the pain that feeding Darkness brought with it, and was surprised when she felt nothing. She glanced from the tree to her palm. The sticky tendrils of Darkness quivered and writhed around her, but they did not feed.

> *What you ask tempts Fate*
> *For that the sacrifice must be great.*

The singsong words drifted through Neferet's mind, and she recognized the echo of her power Consort in them.

> *"What is it you need from me?*
> *What sacrifice must it be?"*

The answer rumbled in Neferet's mind.

> *Her life force does demand*
> *the sacrifice be equal to your command.*

Irritation filled Neferet. Zoey always caused her problems! With a mighty effort, Neferet tempered her tone so that her words would not offend her Consort.

> *"I change my request*
> *not killing her would be best.*
> *Frighten her—bruise her*
> *but leave her lifeline unbroken and pure."*

With painful abandon, the threads of Darkness descended upon the blood pooled in Neferet's hand. She did not flinch. She did not cry out. Neferet smiled and pointed at the tree.

> *"My blood from me to thee*
> *by command—so mote it be!"*

Darkness spewed from Neferet's window. Mimicking the wind, it whirled around the mighty oak's branches. Utterly captivated, Neferet watched. Zoey had picked up the can and was walking slowly away from the tree and toward the sidewalk.

But the old oak was huge and the girl was still under its canopy.

Like a whip, the tendrils of Darkness wrapped around the lowest hanging tree limb. There was a terrible, wonderful *crack!* The limb broke and hurtled down as Zoey was staring up in wide-eyed, openmouthed shock.

In spite of what her Consort had said, for an exquisite moment Neferet believed Zoey would, indeed, be killed.

And then, quite unexpectedly, a silver blur intruded on the scene. Zoey was knocked out of the way and the massive branch crashed harmlessly to the ground. As Neferet stared disbelievingly, Aurox and Zoey began to slowly unwind themselves from the tangled ball they'd become when he'd saved her from the *accident.*

With a sound of absolute disgust Neferet turned away from the window and closed the heavy drapes. "Tell my Consort that I said he could have allowed her to get a little more bruised than that." She spoke to the writhing black threads that were her constant companions, knowing they would carry if not her actual words, then their intent, to the white bull. "I think my blood was worth more than a tumble, though I can see that it was wise of him to have Aurox come to her rescue. It will make the creature appear even more heroic to silly young fledglings." Neferet's emerald eyes widened as understanding dawned. "What a delicious complication if one of the silly young fledglings who see the vessel as heroic is Zoey Redbird herself!" Darkness lapped against her legs as she left her chamber and, smiling slyly, went to find Thanatos.

Zoey

So, I'd just done a good thing—two good things actually. I'd talked Shaunee out of leaving the depot, and I'd picked up litter. I was holding the pop can thinking about how much I'd like a nice cold drink of brown pop when the wind, which had been acting crazy all night, blew a giant gust and *crack!* The gihugic branch directly above me broke off the tree. I didn't have time to do anything but gawk in silent, frozen horror—and then he hit me from the side, low and hard, like I'd seen players do a zillion times on the football field. All the air was knocked out of me and I felt like I was smothering under a ton or so of guy.

"Get off!" I gasped, trying to push his leg from around me. I flailed enough that, with a grunt, he unwrapped from on top of me. As his weight lifted I could actually suck in a breath of air. I kinda elbowed my way to a half sitting position. My mind was working slowly. At the edge of my vision I saw the big limb, still quivering from its impact with the ground. *That could've killed me,* I realized and looked up at whoever it was that I needed to send a serious thank-you to.

Moonstone eyes were staring at me. He put his hands up the instant our gazes met and took a small step backward, as if he expected me to launch an attack at him.

Warmth radiated from the seer stone that hung between my breasts. It filled my body with heat, intensified as if by the touch of Aurox's skin. It had to be my imagination, but it seemed that the stone's heat lingered everywhere in my body even after his touch was gone.

"I was patrolling."

"Yeah," I said, and looked away from him, making myself oh-so-busy brushing grass and leaves from my shirt while I tried to sort through my jumbled thoughts. "You do a lot of that."

"I saw you under the tree."

"Uh-huh." I kept brushing off grass and whatnot while my mind blared: *Aurox saved your life!*

"I wasn't going to come near you, but I heard the branch breaking. I didn't believe I was going to make it in time." His voice sounded shaky. I looked up at him then. He seemed super awkward. As I stared at him, standing there, looking out of place and dorky, I suddenly realized that no matter what else he was, at that moment Aurox was simply a boy who was as unsure of himself as any other teenage boy.

Some of the anxiety, the terrible unease that I'd felt since the first moment I'd seen him, began to fade away.

"Well, I'm glad you did make it in time." I kept my own voice calm—my emotions under control. The last thing I needed was Stark to come charging up. "And you can put your hands down. I'm not gonna bite you or anything like that."

He lowered his hands and shoved them into his jeans pockets. "I did not mean to knock you down. I did not mean to hurt you," he said.

"That limb would have done a lot worse. Plus, it was a good tackle.

Heath would have approved." I said the words and then clamped my mouth shut. Why in the hell was I talking about Heath to him?

Aurox just looked all-around confused.

I sighed. "What I mean is, thank you for saving me."

He blinked. "You are welcome."

I started to get up and he held out a hand to help me. I looked at it. It was a perfectly normal hand. It had no hoof-ness about it. I slid my hand in his. Our palms pressed together and I knew I hadn't imagined it. His touch did radiate the same heat as the seer stone.

As soon as I was on my feet I pulled my hand from his.

"Thanks," I said. "Again."

"You are welcome." He paused and almost smiled. "Again."

"I better get back to sixth hour." I broke the silence that had begun to settle between us. "I have a mare to finish grooming."

"I must continue to patrol," he said.

"So, the only class you have to go to is first hour?"

"Yes, as Neferet commands," he said.

I thought he sounded strange. Not exactly sad, but kinda resigned and still a little awkward.

"Okay, well. I'll see you first hour tomorrow." I wasn't sure what else to say. He nodded. We turned from each other and started to walk our separate ways, but something about first hour tugged at my mind and wouldn't leave me alone. I stopped and called to him. "Aurox, hang on." Looking curious, he came back to meet me beside the broken limb. "Uh, that question you wrote down today, was it for real?"

"For real?"

"Yeah, like, do you really not know what you are?" I asked.

He hesitated what felt like a long time before answering me. I could see that he was thinking and maybe weighing what he should and shouldn't tell me. I was getting ready to say something clichéd (and untrue) like, "don't worry—I won't tell anyone" when he finally spoke.

"I know what I am supposed to be. I do not know if that is all that I truly am."

Our eyes met and this time I did clearly see sadness there. "I hope Thanatos helps you find your answers."

"As do I," he said. Then he surprised me by adding, "You do not have a mean spirit, Zoey."

"Well, I'm not the nicest girl in the world, but I try not to be mean," I said.

He nodded, like what I'd said made sense to him.

"Okay, well, I'm really going now. Good luck with the rest of your patrol."

"Have a care when you walk under trees," he said, then he jogged away.

I looked up at the tree. The wind had gone from wild and crazy to gentle and barely noticeable. The old oak appeared strong and steady and totally unbreakable. As I walked back to sixth hour I thought about how deceiving appearances could be.

CHAPTER TWENTY-TWO

Zoey

I'd meant to go to back to class. Straight to sixth hour. Really. Contrary to my recent actions, I'm usually not a class cutter. I mean, it just never made much sense. Like the homework wouldn't be there when I got back to class the next day? Uh, it would, plus the lovely added bonus of being in trouble.

Let me just say ugh to in-house and all other weird ineffective high school punishment systems that stick good kids in a study hall with frequent offender/gang members. Like that's not gonna just cause more problems?

Anyway, I'd made it about halfway to the stables when Thanatos seemed to materialize from the shadows beside the sidewalk, making me jump and put my hand over my heart to be sure it didn't pound from my chest.

"I did not mean to startle you," she said.

"Yeah, well, it's been a spooky kind of a day," I said, and then remembering how the wind had swirled around her when she'd gotten pissed at Dallas, I added, "Hey, do you have an air affinity?" She lifted a brow at me, and I also remembered how super scary and powerful she was and said, "Unless it's none of my business. I don't mean to sound rude or anything."

"It is not rude to ask, and my closeness with air is no secret. It is not a true affinity. I cannot call the element, though it often manifests when I have need of it. I have long thought that air stays close to me because of my true affinity."

"Death?" Now I was really curious. "I'd think spirit would stay close to you because of your affinity."

"That does seem logical, but my affinity has only to do with helping the dead pass on, and sometimes soothing the living who have been left behind." We walked slowly, falling into an easy rhythm beside one another as we talked. "The dead move like the wind, or at least they do as they manifest to me. They are ethereal, diaphanous. They appear to have no real substance, though they are, indeed, very real."

"Like wind," I said, understanding. "It's real. It can move things. But you can't see it."

"Exactly. Why do you ask about air?"

"Well, it's been acting kinda crazy today. I wondered if you felt anything weird going on with it."

"As in it being manipulated?"

"Yeah, definitely," I said.

"No, I could not say that I have felt air being manipulated." She glanced up at the branches of the closest tree where the wind, gently, lazily, had them swaying in time to a slow, silent tune. "Seems all is quiet now."

"Yeah, it does." And I wondered if maybe it wasn't the element air that was responsible for the branch almost smooshing me. *Don't be so darn paranoid,* I reminded myself firmly. Then Thanatos's next words wiped all thoughts of weird wind and paranoia from my mind.

"Zoey, I must ask you two things: first a question, and then your forgiveness."

"You can ask me anything you want." *But I'm gonna be careful about how I answer you,* I added to myself silently. "And I don't know why you'd need my forgiveness."

"The question first, then I shall explain. I would like to ask that you join me in a class discussion tomorrow." She held up her hand to stop me as I opened my mouth to answer her with an "okay, whatever." "You should know the discussion will be about recovering from the death of a parent."

All of a sudden my throat felt really dry. I swallowed and then said, "That's gonna be hard for me to talk about 'cause I haven't gotten over my mom's death."

Thanatos nodded and then, not unkindly, said, "Yes, I realize that. But there are several other students who have also not recovered from losing a parent, though yours is the only loss, thus far, due to death."

"Huh?"

"Three other students asked the same question as did you."

"Really?"

"Yes. You must know it is a universal experience for those of us who complete the Change. We are not immortal, but we will outlive our human parents. Many of us choose to sever ties with the mortals from our childhood early in our vampyre lives. That seems to make the eventual loss less painful. Some of us maintain relationships with the people from our past—for some of us *that* makes the loss less painful."

"But it's not like either of those things for me. I'm not a vampyre, and my mom was killed—she didn't just die of old age."

"Were you very close to your mother?"

I blinked hard, not wanting to cry. "No. Not for the past three years."

"So, is your biggest struggle the manner of her death?"

I thought carefully about her question before I answered Thanatos. "I think that is part of it. I think knowing exactly what happened to her would help me have closure. But there's also the fact that now that she's gone, there's no chance she and I will be close again."

"But that chance is only over for you and her in this lifetime. If she waits in the Otherworld you could reunite there," Thanatos said. "Did she know the Goddess?"

I smiled, this time through my tears. "Mom didn't know Nyx, but Nyx knew my mom. The Goddess sent me a dream the night she died. I saw Mom being welcomed to the Otherworld."

"Well, then, that sadness should be alleviated from your spirit. All that remains is the uncertainty surrounding her death."

"Her murder," I corrected her. "Mom was killed."

There was a long silence and then she asked, "Exactly how was your mother killed?"

"The police say by druggies who were ripping off my grandma's house. Mom was there and got in the way." My voice sounded as hollow as I felt.

"No, I mean *how* was she killed? What were her wounds?"

I remembered Grandma saying that her murder had been vicious, but that Mom hadn't suffered. I also remembered the shadow that had passed over Grandma's expression when she'd told me about it. I swallowed hard again. "It was violent. That's all Grandma told me."

"Your grandmother saw her body?"

"Grandma found her."

"Zoey, is there any way your grandmother would speak with me about your mother's murder?"

"I'm sure she'd talk to you. Why? What good would that do?"

"I do not want you to become overly hopeful, but if a death is very violent the very fabric of the earth is sometimes imprinted and I can access those images of death."

"You could see how Mom was killed?"

"Perhaps. Only perhaps. But I need to question your grandmother first to know if it might even be possible."

"I can't guarantee how much Grandma will say. Right now she's observing the seven days of ritual cleansing after a death." In response to Thanatos's questioning look I explained. "Grandma's a Cherokee Wise Woman. She keeps the ancient religion and its ways."

"Then it is important that I speak with her immediately if there is any hope of resurrecting the images from your mother's death. How many days have passed since her murder?"

"She was killed last Thursday night."

Thanatos nodded. "Tomorrow will be the fifth night since her death. I need to speak with your grandmother today."

"Okay, well, I'd take you out to the lavender farm, but I know she doesn't want anyone out there until it's cleansed."

"Zoey, does your grandmother not have a cell phone?"

"Uh, yeah. You wanna call her?"

Thanatos's lips tilted up. "It is the twenty-first century, even for me."

Feeling like a moron, I rattled off Grandma's cell number while Thanatos put it in her iPhone.

"I will call her, but I would rather do so alone."

Thanatos's look said she really didn't want me to hear the kind of questions she was gonna ask Grandma, and I quickly nodded. "Yeah, I understand. That's okay with me. I need to get to sixth hour anyway."

"May I ask your forgiveness first?"

"Yeah, sure. But what for?"

"I told an untruth earlier. I would ask your forgiveness for it, and I would also ask that you keep what I am about to tell you close to your heart. Do not even share it with your Warrior or your best friend."

"Okay. I'll keep it secret."

"When Stark asked if I could see the Darkness that surrounds Neferet and Dallas's red fledglings, my answer was a lie."

I blinked. "You mean you can see Darkness?"

"I can."

I shook my head. "You need to ask Stark and Rephaim and Stevie Rae for forgiveness, too. They're the ones who can see Darkness with you—they're the ones the lie would hurt most."

"They cannot know. I have your word that you will keep this secret."

"Why? Why should I know and not them?"

Instead of a clear answer, she just started talking. "I have lived almost five centuries. For most of that time I have dealt with death daily. I have seen Darkness. I have seen its carnage, its waste, its wages. I recognize its threads and shadows all too well. Perhaps it is because I have watched it for so long that I can also see that which is its opposite—that which causes the strength of Darkness to weaken, to falter."

"What are you talking about!" I wanted to scream.

"You, Zoey Redbird. There is something about you that cannot be touched by Darkness; therefore, it is your fate to stand in the Light and lead the battle against evil."

"No. I don't want to lead any battle. You do it. Or ask Darius to.

Or even Stark. Hell, get Sgiach and the Guardians! They're all leaders. They're all Warriors who know how to fight. I don't know anything. I don't even know what to do without my mom." I ended up gasping for breath and pressing my hand against my chest. When Thanatos didn't speak, when she just held me with her dark eyes I finally managed a less crazy voice and said, "I don't want this. I just want to be a normal kid."

"That may be part of why this has fallen on your shoulders, young High Priestess, because you do *not* want it. Perhaps the power that goes with the claiming of it will not be able to corrupt you."

"Like Frodo," I whispered, more to myself than to Thanatos. "He never wanted the damn ring."

"J. R. R. Tolkien. Good books—excellent movies."

I gave her a *look* and said, "Yeah, I know. It's the twenty-first century. You probably have cable."

"I definitely have cable."

"That's cool for you, but let's go back to the Ring Bearer stuff. Uh, if I remember correctly, and I do 'cause I've seen the long extended version of the movies like a gazillion times, Frodo is basically destroyed by this ring he didn't want to bear."

"And thereby he saved his world from Darkness," Thanatos said.

I felt a freezing shiver wash down my spine. "I don't want to die. Not even to save the world."

"Death comes to us all," Thanatos said.

I shook my head again. "I'm no Ring Bearer. I'm just a kid."

"A kid who's already won her life back from Darkness, not once but several times."

"Okay, if you get that—and if you get that Neferet is on the side of Darkness 'cause *you can see it* why are you pretending like you don't?"

"I am here to settle the issue of Neferet and her true allegiance once and for all."

"Then tell the High Council about the Darkness that surrounds her!"

"And have her admonished slightly only to return, perhaps stronger, to do more evil? What if she is really the Consort of Darkness? If that is truth, then the full might of the High Council must come against her, and for that to happen we must have unequivocal proof that she is forever lost to the Goddess."

"That's why you're here. To get that proof."

"Yes."

"I won't say anything about you seeing Darkness. And I'm telling you the honest truth—get ready to see a whole bunch of it. Get ready to find your proof because I know with everything inside me that Neferet has gone over to it." I almost added that she's not even mortal anymore. But, no. That was something Thanatos needed to discover for herself. "Oh, and I forgive you. Just promise me you'll keep your eyes open and when the time comes, you'll make sure the High Council does the right thing."

"I give you my oath on it."

"Good," I said. And then while Thanatos was calling Grandma I did finally return to sixth hour.

Shaunee

She hadn't had any idea how much it would suck not to be Erin's Twin anymore. It was like that one thing—not having Erin as her BFF—changed the whole blueprint of her life.

It was so damn confusing.

When had she lost Shaunee and become Twin? She really didn't know. They'd been Marked the same day and arrived at the Tulsa House of Night the same exact hour. And they'd been friends right away. Shaunee had thought that had been because they were like soul sisters 'cause it hadn't mattered that she was black and Erin was white. That she was from Connecticut and Erin from Tulsa. They'd been *friends* and all of a sudden Shaunee hadn't felt lonely anymore. Especially 'cause she never had to be alone. Literally. She and Erin were roommates, had the same class schedule, went to the same parties, they only even dated guys who were friends.

By herself in her seat on the bus Shaunee shook her head. She could hear Erin laughing with Kramisha somewhere in the back of the bus. For a second a mean little thought snaked through her mind:

guess she's trading me in for another black girl BFF. But Shaunee stopped that crap right away. It wasn't about skin color. It never had been. It was about not being able to be alone. Which was super ironic because figuring that out had somehow put her in a position where she was alone.

"Hey, can I sit here?"

Shaunee's gaze shifted from staring out the window at the lightening pre-dawn sky to Damien standing in the aisle of the bus.

"Yeah, sure."

"Thanks." He sat beside her and dropped his heavy book bag between his feet. "I have soooo much homework. How 'bout you?"

"Yeah," she said. "I guess. Hey, did you see Zoey sixth hour?"

"Not during sixth hour. She has Equestrian Studies and I have business class, but I saw her right after school. Why? What's up?"

"Did she look okay to you?"

"Okay? Like physically okay or not-stressed-out okay?"

"She's always stressed out. I mean physically."

"Yeah, fine. What's going on?"

"Nothin'," Shaunee said. "It's just that I, uh, saw her at the beginning of sixth hour. Me and her, we talked over here by the parking lot. Then we went back to class." She studied Damien, wondering if she should tell him the truth. "Did you feel anything weird about the air tonight?"

Damien cocked his head to the side. "Nothing odd. Well, it was windy, but that's not really odd for Oklahoma. You know we're the state where *the wind comes sweeping down the plain*," he sang.

"I know that, Mr. Broadway Musical. All I'm saying is the wind was blowing *really* hard when Z and I split up, and I thought I heard something about tree limbs falling and—"

"A tree limb did fall." Stark butted in as he and Zoey slid into the seat in front of Damien and Shaunee.

"Yeah, it was all psycho-windy," Stevie Rae said, sitting beside Rephaim in the seat across the aisle from Damien. "But tellin' you that would be like tryin' to tell white about rice."

"What in the for-shit's-sake is that supposed to mean?" Aphrodite forced Z to scoot over and perched beside her as Darius did a quick head count and then got in the driver's seat and started the bus up.

"It means, Hateful, that Damien already knows it was windy today 'cause his affinity *is* wind. Just like rice *is* white. I don't even know what was hard about that analogy," Stevie Rae said.

"Just. Don't. Speak," Aphrodite told Stevie Rae.

"Rice is brown, too," Shaunee said.

Aphrodite raised a brow. "Did you just make a snarky comment without your Twin?"

"Yeah," Shaunee said, meeting her gaze steadily.

Aphrodite snorted and looked away, first saying, "It's about time."

"About the wind," Zoey said. "Yeah, it was kinda crazy tonight, and it even broke a branch from one of those old oaks." She shrugged. "Like Damien said—it's windy in Oklahoma. Hey, speaking of, Damien, did you know Thanatos had a little wind affinity?"

"Ohmygod! I'm not surprised! Did you see how uber-scary she got today when Dallas said that stupid stuff in class? I couldn't believe . . ."

Shaunee let everyone's words flow around her, but she kept watching Zoey, waiting for her to say something—anything—about what had really happened when the tree limb broke. She knew. She'd seen the whole thing.

As they bounced and bumped their way back to the depot, Shaunee realized Zoey wasn't going to say anything. *Okay, well, maybe she just told Stark what had happened—how she would've been smashed under that tree limb if Aurox hadn't saved her.* During the next lull in the conversation, which happened when they paused at a railroad crossing like Super Giant Short Bus Dorks, Shaunee blurted, "Does anyone think it's weird that Aurox goes to one class and then does nothing but patrol the school all android-like for the rest of the time?"

"There's a lot that's super weird about that guy," Aphrodite said. "But that's no surprise. He's Neferet's boy toy."

"I don't think they're having sex," Zoey said.

Shaunee studied Z. "Why not?"

"I dunno," Z said way too nonchalantly. "I guess because Neferet doesn't act like it. She acts more like he's her slave."

Stark chuckled. "Neferet acts like the world's her slave."

"I'll bet Dead Fish Eye Lady really hates it that we've all been pulled out of her class," Aphrodite said.

"You know she does, 'specially 'cause Thanatos is a real good teacher," Stevie Rae said. "And by the way, I do not appreciate you bein' so hateful about our *very* short, *very* unsexual Imprint in class today. It happened to me, too, and I can tell you that it was no pit bull at a cat party fun time for me, either."

"Please tell me you didn't just use *another* white trash analogy," Aphrodite said.

Shaunee stayed out of the argument that went on all the way from then until the moment they pulled up in front of the depot. Instead of joining in, she watched Zoey. She also watched Stark. By the time she'd exited the bus she believed two things. One was that Stark had no clue Aurox had saved Zoey's life that night. The second was that she would have never known about Aurox or Zoey or Stark if she'd still been Twin. Twin would have been too wrapped up in being the other part of someone else to really pay attention to anything or anyone else.

She didn't know what the hell was going on with Zoey and Aurox, but she knew she was going to keep her eyes and her mind open, and if she could figure it out she would. All on her own. All by herself. Which was suddenly not such a terrible thing. And for the first time since she quit completing Erin's thoughts, Shaunee smiled.

CHAPTER TWENTY-THREE

Zoey

So, I hadn't told Stark about Aurox and the tree limb thing. I mean, seriously, what was the point? Like Stark needs more stress in his life? He's still not even sleeping well because he's *still* having nightmares he refuses to tell me about but which I know about because I sleep next to him and *I'm not stupid*. Plus, the whole tree thing happened fast. No one was hurt. It's over with. Period, the end.

Well, except for one little part. That part about me making the decision to look through the seer stone at Aurox. Okay, not this second I wasn't going to. I mean, Aurox wasn't even here. But I'd decided. The second he'd touched me I'd decided.

The second he'd touched me I wasn't scared of him anymore.

I was still freaked, though.

I was silently arguing with myself about whether or not I should let Stark know I'd decided to peek at Aurox through the stone, and sorta half listening to Aphrodite and Stevie Rae arguing over tunnel renovation details (Aphrodite wanted lots of workmen and lots of glitz—Stevie Rae didn't want anyone but *our people* to even come down to the tunnels. Sigh.) when the bus pulled up to the depot and Darius opened the door.

"I'm gonna call Andolini's for a major delivery," Stevie Rae said as she and Rephaim left the bus.

"For once we can agree on something," Aphrodite said, moving over to sit on Darius's lap while the rest of us started to shuffle off the bus. "Order me one of their Santino pizzas. It's totally worth the calories. Plus, it goes perfectly with that bottle of Chianti I took from the cafeteria when I was cutting fifth—"

It happened just like that. Aphrodite was in the middle of talking about something as totally normal as cutting class and her whole body seized up. She got rigid. Her eyes rolled back in her head and *she started to cry tears of blood.* It was like she went from gorgeous, perfect girl to someone who looked barely human. Barely alive.

Darius didn't hesitate. He picked up her stiff, bloody-eyed, unseeing body and carried her from the bus. I put aside my *ohmygod* internal reaction and stood up, turning to the rest of the kids who were either gawking open-mouthed, or covering their eyes looking like they wanted to cry.

"Aphrodite's having a vision." My voice seemed to come from someone else. Someone who was calm. Stark took my hand, lending me strength. "She's gonna be fine," I continued, clinging to Stark.

"Actually, she's gonna be super pissed and mean when she comes to 'cause she really hates it when this happens to her in public," Stevie Rae said. She'd climbed halfway up the bus stairs. I noticed her eyes were kinda extra wide, but her voice also sounded totally calm and cool.

"Yeah, Stevie Rae's right," I said. "So there's no need to make a big deal out of this—now or after she comes to." I paused and, feeling like a moron, added, "Okay, I don't mean her visions aren't a big deal. I just mean she won't want to hear a bunch of 'hey, are you okays' from everyone."

"I'll go ahead and order the pizzas. Do ya think Aphrodite'll be hungry later?" Stevie Rae asked.

I thought about the last time she'd had a vision and how awful she'd felt afterward. I wanted to say what Aphrodite would really want would be a Xanax and a bottle of wine, but thought that would probably set a bad example. So I settled for, "Uh, why don't you get her one and put it in the fridge. We can nuke it later if she's hungry. Right now I'll just go check on her. She'll want water and quiet for a while."

"Okie dokie." Stevie Rae smiled and, acting absolutely normal, told the rest of the bus, "I'm takin' pizza orders from up here. Cell phone reception is crap in the tunnels. So before y'all scatter for downstairs let me know what you want, and ya better hang around so that I get it right. Speakin' of, Kramisha, could you write down what everyone wants for me, please? That'd help." She glanced at Shaunee, who was looking especially lost, and added, "Hey, do you think we could use your card for the order this time? Z and I'll be sure you get paid back."

Shaunee frowned. "Swear? Last time I totally got stuck with the bill from Queenies. Those Ultimate Egg Salad Sandwiches are awesome, but not a couple hundred dollars' worth of awesome."

"I swear." Stevie Rae narrowed her eyes, skewering the rest of the bus with the stank eye. "Y'all will pay her back."

"Yeah, okay, fine," chorused from the back of the bus.

I could have kissed my BFF. She'd totally distracted everyone from Aphrodite's horrendous and unattractive vision, *and* she'd made sure they'd be up here deciding on pizza and payback versus down in the tunnels gawking and talking about Aphrodite.

Meanwhile I pulled Stark from the bus. "We'll take a large combo," he said as we passed Stevie Rae.

"Pizza? Really?" I whispered to him, feeling like he'd just said, "Let them eat cake!" or whatever super inconsiderate thing that woman said to the masses when really important stuff was going on back in the day.

"I thought you wanted to act normal," he whispered back.

I sighed. Well, he was right. So, I told Stevie Rae, "With extra cheese and olives." Then, under my breath I added, "And thanks."

"I'll be in the kitchen when you're ready to talk," she said just as quietly, then she very loudly and very normally starting asking, "So, how many pepperonis?"

"Let's go through the depot so we can grab some water bottles from the kitchen on the way to Aphrodite's room," I told Stark when he automatically headed for the basement entrance to the tunnels. He changed direction, but still I explained (probably more to hear my calm-sounding voice than anything), "She'll be thirsty. We'll also need to grab some washcloths. I'll soak them in water and put them over her eyes."

"Do they always bleed like that?"

"Yeah, ever since she lost her Mark. Last time she had a vision she told me the pain and the blood keep getting worse and worse." I glanced at Stark. "It looked bad, didn't it?"

"She'll be okay. Darius is with her. He won't let anything happen to her." He squeezed my hand before letting me climb down ahead of him through the old ticket booth entrance to the tunnels.

"I don't think even her Warrior can protect her against this kind of stuff."

He smiled at me. "I figured out a way to protect you in the Otherworld. I think Darius can handle some visions and a little blood."

I didn't say anything else as we hurried through the kitchen, grabbing water and washcloths.

I wanted Stark to be right. I really, *really* wanted Stark to be right, but I had a bad feeling, and I hated it when that happened. It always meant something was going to go horribly, awfully, terribly wrong.

"Hey." Stark took my arm and gently tugged me to a halt just outside the glitzy gold curtain that was the latest door to Aphrodite's room. "She needs you to be okay."

"I know, you're right. It's just that the visions really hurt her, and that makes me worry."

"But they're also a gift from Nyx, and they're information we need, right?"

"Right again," I said.

His grin turned cocky. "I like it when you say I'm right."

"Don't get too used to it. You're a guy. You have a limited number of 'I'm rights'"—I air quoted—"allotted to you."

"Hey, I'll take what I can get," he said. Then he went back to serious face. "Just remember, you need to be her High Priestess now, and not her friend."

I nodded, drew a deep breath, and ducked under the gold curtain.

Okay, Aphrodite's room kept changing and getting more and more like Kim Kardashian meets Conan the Barbarian every time I went in it. This time she'd added a gold chaise lounge. No, I had no clue where she got it or how she'd gotten it down here. On the rough cement tunnel wall behind the chaise she'd hung part of Darius's throwing knife collection as decoration. She'd also hung gold beaded tassels from each of the knife hilts. Seriously. Her bed was big. Really big. Tonight the duvet was purple velvet with gold flowers stitched into it. She had millions of fluffy pillows. And her terrible Persian cat, Maleficent, had a matching cat bed that sat beside hers. Only at this moment Maleficent wasn't in her bed. She was curled protectively on Aphrodite's lap. Aphrodite was propped in the middle of her millions of pillows looking scarily pale. Darius had put a folded wet paper towel over her eyes, and it was already pink. I felt a little better when I saw that she was petting Maleficent, which meant she was conscious. But my better feeling went away as I approached the bed and the horrid cat started to yowl at me.

"Who is it?" Aphrodite's voice sounded weak and uncharacteristically frightened.

Darius touched her face. "It's Zoey and Stark, my beauty. You know I wouldn't allow anyone else within."

Stark squeezed my hand, then let go. I sent a quick, silent pray up to Nyx, *please help me be the High Priestess Aphrodite needs,* and then I stepped into the role that still felt too big a job for me to fill. "I brought some washcloths and cool water," I said briskly, moving to the side of the bed and dampening one of the cloths. "Keep your eyes closed. I'm gonna change this paper towel."

"Okay," she said.

Her eyes did stay closed. But they were still weeping blood. The scent of it came to me, and for a moment I thought I was gonna have an *ohmygod-yummy-I-want-to-eat-that* reaction. I didn't.

Aphrodite didn't smell like a human. I tried to remember how her blood had smelled last time she'd had a vision, and I drew a blank— which meant it probably hadn't been normal then, either.

I pushed that knowledge aside and sat on the bed next to her.

"I brought a bottle of water, too. Do you want a drink yet?"

"Yes. Wine. Red. Darius has it."

"My beauty, please drink water first."

"Darius, the wine helps the pain. And bring me a Xanax out of my purse while you're at it. That helps, too."

Darius didn't move. He just looked at me.

"Uh, Aphrodite, how about you choose between the Xanax and wine? Both together just don't seem healthy," I said.

"My mom does them both all the time," she snapped. Then her lips pressed into a line. Aphrodite drew a deep breath and said. "Point made. I'll stick with wine. I. Am. Not. My. Mother."

"You're definitely not your mom," I agreed. Darius looked relieved and began to open the wine. "Okay, so, while your man is letting your wine breathe I want you to drink some of this water."

Her lips curled up in what was almost her familiar sneer. "What do you know about letting wine breathe? You don't even drink."

"I watch TV. Jeesh, everyone with half a brain knows wine needs to breathe," I said, guiding her hands to the open bottle of water and helping her drink it. "How was it this time? As bad as the last?"

When it was obvious she wasn't going to answer, Darius did for her. "Worse," he said. "Maybe you should come back after she's rested."

The Zoey who was Aphrodite's friend totally agreed with him. But the Zoey who was High Priestess in Training, knew better. "She'll be drunk and exhausted for the rest of tonight and probably into tomorrow. I need to hear about this vision before she's too out of it to talk."

"Z's right," Aphrodite said before Darius could protest. "And anyway, this one was short." I was glad to see she'd drained the water bottle, but she reached out a blind hand and said, "Water's gone. Where's my wine?"

Darius brought her a wineglass that looked super simple, just crystal and a pretty shape, but it had a little Riedel mark written on the bottom, so I knew it was *nice* stemware from Williams-Sonoma. I knew that because Aphrodite had lectured me when I'd almost broken one a few days ago. (Like I care?) Anyway, Darius helped Aphrodite take a very long drink from the crystal glass. Then she exhaled slowly. "Get another bottle ready. I'll need more." He didn't even glance at me for confirmation; he just looked defeated. "And tell Stark to quit lusting after your knives. He's bowboy, not knifeboy."

"Are they super heroes now?" I asked, trying (probably unsuccessfully) to be funny.

Her lips turned up in satisfaction, and for a second she looked way too much like her cat for comfort. "Well, mine's a super hero in *lots* of ways. You'll have to decide about yours on your own."

"Vision," Stark mouthed to me from across the room where he was, indeed, checking out the ornamental knives.

"Okay, so tell me what it was about this time," I said.

"It was one of those damn death visions again. One where I was *inside* the guy getting killed."

"Guy?" I felt a little bubble of panic build. *Was it Stark?*

"Relax, it wasn't your guy or mine. It was Rephaim. I was inside him when he was killed. And, by the way," she hesitated, taking another long drink of wine. "Birdboy has some weird shit in his head."

"Give me the basics now. We'll talk about the gossipy part later," I said.

"Well, as per usual when I'm inside the person who's getting slaughtered, the vision was confusing," she said, pressing her hand over the washcloth and grimacing with pain.

"Just tell me what you remember," I prompted. "How did he die?"

"Sword almost sliced him in two. Totally gross, although his head didn't come off like yours did in that other vision."

"Well, that's nice for him," I said, not sure if I was being serious or sarcastic. "Who did the cutting in half?"

"That's where the confusion kicks in. I'm not sure who actually kills him. I am sure Dragon is there."

"Dragon kills him? Ugh. That's awful."

"Well, like I said, I'm not sure of that. I can tell you that I remember the look on Dragon's face just before the sword sliced me. He was totally shut down. He looked even worse than he's been looking recently. It's like there was no hope or light or happiness anywhere in his life, and he was crying—really bawling, like with snot and everything."

"Then Rephaim gets killed by a *sword*," I said.

"Yep," she agreed. "I know. Should be a no-brainer. Seems like Dragon did it, but it just doesn't feel one hundred percent to me, especially when you add in the bawling part and all the other confusion."

"Other confusion?"

"Yeah, bizarre shit kept flashing all around. There was something white that looked dead. There was ice that was burning a circle. There were blood and boobs everywhere, *and then* I—meaning Rephaim—was dead. The end."

I rubbed my temple where I felt a headache brewing.

"Boobs?" Stark perked up at that word.

"Yes, bowboy. Boobs. Like there was a naked woman hanging around. Literally. I didn't see her face because Rephaim was predictably mesmerized by her boobs, but I do know she had something to do with the blood and the white dead thing."

"Hey, wait," I said. "Didn't Kramisha's last poem say something about fire and ice?"

"Hmm, I'd forgotten about that. Easy for me to do because, well, fuck poetry."

"Don't be so negative," I said. "And it's not just poetry. It's prophetic poetry."

"Which makes it worse," she said.

"I remember. The poem also said something about Dragon's tears," Stark said.

"Maybe he weeps because he kills Rephaim, even after he was tasked to be his protector because he is Sword Master of our House of Night," Darius said.

"But he's not," I said. "We have our own House of Night over here, so he's not technically *our* Sword Master. Maybe that's how he rationalizes being able to kill Rephaim."

"All that sounds logical, but there's still a piece missing. That's what my gut says. I just can't see that piece. Everything except Dragon kept fading in and out of my vision, mostly because Rephaim was super focused on Stevie Rae, who was super focused on the ritual she was performing."

"Ritual? Was I there?"

"Yeah, the whole nerd herd was there. A circle was cast. You were leading things, but the ritual itself was earth centered, so Stevie Rae was playing the major part." She sucked in a breath. "Holy shit, I just realized where we were—at your grandma's lavender farm."

"Ah, hell! The cleansing ritual I'm supposed to do in a couple days. Or maybe not. Thanatos was calling Grandma about us doing something early—something that might reveal what actually happened to Mom." I paused, feeling overwhelmed by the thought of the dead white thing, the blood, and the boobs, all in the context of my mom's murder. "Does this mean I wasn't meant to find out and I shouldn't do anything at all?"

Aphrodite shrugged. "Z, I know you'll find this hard to believe because you've been Miss Front and Center in a bunch of my visions, but in this one you barely made an appearance. I just don't think this is about you at all."

"But it's at Grandma's farm."

"Yeah, but it's Rephaim getting carved up this time and not you," she said.

"Wait, isn't this good news?" Stark said, coming up to me and taking my hand.

Aphrodite snorted. "Sure, unless you're Rephaim."

Stark ignored her comment and continued, "You've seen Rephaim killed. You know where and you know who has to be there. So what if we're sure those elements don't all come together? That'll stop the death, won't it?"

"Maybe," Aphrodite said.

"Hopefully," I said.

"We need to be sure Dragon stays away from Rephaim," Darius said. "Even if he didn't actually kill him, you know for a certainty that he was present when Rephaim was killed."

"That much I do know," Aphrodite said.

"Then that's it. We keep Dragon and Rephaim separate, even if that means Rephaim doesn't come with the rest of us when we go to Grandma's farm."

"If I go, Rephaim goes."

Stark, Darius, and I turned to see Stevie Rae and Rephaim ducking under the blanket and coming into the room. Aphrodite frowned, but kept the washcloth on her eyes.

"Her vision was about Rephaim." Stevie Rae didn't say it like a question, but I answered her anyway. "Yeah. He dies."

"How? Who does it?" Stevie Rae's voice was hard. She looked ready to take on the world.

"Not sure," Aphrodite spoke up. "It was from birdboy's point of view, which means the whole damn thing was confusing."

"But we know it happens at Grandma's farm and that Dragon is there," I said. "Which is why we were saying Rephaim should stay here when we all go out there, *if* we all still go out there."

"We will," Stark said. "You can't let this stop the ritual you were going to do for your mom."

"It's not for her," I said miserably. "She's dead. That won't change."

"That's right," he said. "It's for you and your grandma, which is more important than doing something for a dead woman." He glanced at Rephaim and Stevie Rae. "The ritual needs to happen, but Rephaim doesn't need to be there and be in danger. It would be smartest if, like Z was saying, he stayed here."

"So that someone, like Dragon, can sneak up on him when he's all alone? I don't think so," Stevie Rae said.

"I do not understand," Rephaim said.

I sighed. "Aphrodite gets visions of deaths. Sometimes they're real clear and easy to keep from happening. Sometimes they're confusing."

"Because I'm inside the person who's getting killed. That's how it was with you. And, speaking of, flying seems scary. No matter what your birdbrain thinks."

"It is not scary when you have wings," Rephaim said, sounding matter-of-fact.

"Huh," I said.

"No," Stevie Rae spoke up. "Keep whatever you found inside his head to yourself. It's not anyone's business."

"She was inside my head?" Rephaim was obviously confused squared.

"In a vision I was. It won't happen again. I hope. And there was something else hanging around the vision besides Dragon. It was a bull, or at least the shadow of a bull."

"Shadow of a bull?" My stomach felt sick. "Was that the dead white thing you saw?"

"No. That was definitely something else."

"Did you see what color it was?"

"Zoey, shadows are only one color," she said.

"Aurox," Stark said.

"Did you see Aurox?" I asked quickly.

"Nope. Just the bull shadow. And for the record, I agree with you and Stark and Darius—birdboy should stay away from Dragon. If that means he stays here, then that's what should happen. Now, may I please have a refill on my wine and some rest?"

"I don't think it's good for you to drink while you're bleedin' like that." Stevie Rae said.

"Don't question me. I'm a professional," Aphrodite said.

"What does that even mean?" I asked.

"It means my beauty is done talking and needs to sleep," Darius said.

"The pizza should be here soon," Stevie Rae said. "I got you one."

"If I'm still awake when it gets here I'll eat it," Aphrodite said. Then she took the washcloth off her eyes and blinked them slowly open. I was prepared. I'd seen this before. Rephaim, however, was not.

"By all the gods! You do weep blood," he said.

She turned her red-tinged gaze to him. "Yeah. Even I know it's terrible symbolism. Birdboy, you need to remember this. I got this damn vision because there was a message in it for you. Keep your ass safe. Stay away from pointy objects, and if that means you need to stay away from Dragon Lankford, then do it."

"For how long?" he asked her. "How long must I hide from this vampyre?"

She shook her head. "I got a warning, not a timeline."

"I'd rather not hide."

"I'd rather not have you dead," Stevie Rae said.

"I'd rather sleep," Aphrodite said.

"All right, let's go," I said. I handed Darius my last bottle of water. "Try to make her drink this between glasses of wine."

"I'm right here. You don't have to talk about me like I can't hear you." She made a toasting gesture with her glass and then drained it.

"You're under the influence, so I'm ignoring you," I said. "Get some rest. I'll talk to you later."

We moved from Aphrodite's room, Rephaim and Stevie Rae holding hands and talking in low voices to each other as we made our way up through the tunnels and outside where we were going to wait for a very confused delivery boy who I was going to be sure got an excellent tip.

"What do you think about the vision?" Stark asked, putting his arm around me and holding me close to him.

"I think Stevie Rae is going to be a problem. She's going to try to protect Rephaim so much that she's gonna end up getting him killed."

Stark nodded and looked grim. "That's how Darkness works. It turns love into something bad."

His words surprised me. He sounded so cynical, so old. "Stark, Darkness can't turn love into anything. Love is the only thing that lasts through Darkness and death and destruction. You know that—or you used to."

He stopped then and all of a sudden I was in his arms and he was holding me so tight that he almost stopped my breath.

"What is it?" I whispered to him. "What's wrong?"

"Sometimes I think I should have been the one to die and Heath should have been the one who stayed with you. He believed in love a lot more than I do."

"I don't think the amount of belief you have is what's important. I think it's what you have belief in that matters."

"Then we'll be okay because I believe in you," he said.

I wrapped my arms around him and held on, trying to reassure him and myself with touch when words just didn't seem to be enough.

CHAPTER TWENTY-FOUR

Neferet

How goes the pursuit of chaos, my heartless one? The white bull's deep voice echoed through her mind.

Neferet turned almost in a complete circle before she caught sight of his luminous, magickal coat, his massive horns, his cloven hoofs. He was approaching her from behind the tomb over which the statue of an angelic young girl looked down, head bowed. Time had crumbled one of her stone hands and Neferet thought her expression made it seem as if the angel had given part of herself as an offering, perhaps to the white bull.

The thought made Neferet burn with jealousy.

She walked to meet her bull, moving slowly, languorously. Neferet knew she was beautiful, yet still she felt compelled to pull power from the surrounding shadows to enhance herself. Her long, thick hair glistened, much like the liquid silk of her black gown. She'd chosen it because it reminded her of Darkness—reminded her of her bull.

Neferet stopped before him and dropped gracefully to her knees. "The pursuit of chaos goes well, my lord."

So, I am your lord? How interesting.

Neferet tilted her head back and smiled seductively up at the massive god. "Would you rather I call you my Consort?"

Ah, the naming of a thing. There is power in it.

"There is, indeed." Neferet lifted her hand and touched one of his thick horns. It glistened like opals.

I approve of your name for the vessel. Aurox, after the great and mighty auroch bulls of old. There is something fitting and right in that name.

"I am glad you approve, my lord," she said, thinking that still he hadn't said whether she could or could not call him Consort.

And how does he serve you, this creature created through an imperfect sacrifice?

"He serves me well. I see no imperfection when I look at him, only a gracious gift from you."

You will remember that I warned you, though, will you not? The vessel may be cracked.

"The vessel himself is unimportant," Neferet said dismissively. "He is simply a means to an end." She stood and moved closer to him. "We need not waste precious moments speaking of Aurox. He will serve me, and serve me well—or he will cease to exist."

You cast aside my gifts so easily?

"Oh, no, my lord!" she assured him. "I simply listen to you and hear your warning. Can we not speak of something more pleasurable than an empty vessel?"

You mentioned Consort. It brought to mind something I would like to show you—something you might, perhaps, find interesting.

"I am yours to command, my lord." Neferet curtseyed.

The enormous incarnation of Darkness knelt, offering his back to her. *Come, my heartless one.*

Neferet climbed astride him. His coat was ice—slick and cold and impenetrable. He carried her into the night, sliding inhumanly fast through shadows, riding the currents of night, using the hidden, horrible things that always, always did his bidding, until he finally halted in the thickest shadows under ancient, winter nude trees on a ridge southwest of Tulsa.

"Where are we?" Neferet shivered as she clung to him.

Quietly, my heartless one. Observe silently. Watch. Listen.

Neferet watched, listened, and very soon what she believed to be a tall, muscular man descended from one of three stilted wooden shacks that sat atop the ridge before her. He walked to the edge of the ridge and sat on a huge, flat sandstone boulder.

It was only after he sat that she saw his wings. *Kalona!* She thought his name, did not speak it, but the bull answered her. *Yes, it is your old Consort, Kalona. Let us move closer. Let us observe. The night* around them rippled and reformed, cloaking the bull and Neferet eerily, so that it seemed they were only part of the fabric of shadows and the lazy mist that had suddenly begun to unfurl over the ridge.

Neferet held her breath as the bull moved silently and invisibly closer to Kalona, so close that she could see over his broad shoulder and realized he was holding a cellular phone. He began touching the screen, and Neferet could see it light up. The winged immortal hesitated, his finger hovering indecisively.

Do you know what you are seeing?

Neferet stared at Kalona. His shoulders slumped. He rubbed his forehead. He bowed his head as if in defeat and finally, reluctantly, placed the phone gently on the rock beside him.

No, Neferet thought. *I do not know what I'm seeing.*

Kalona, fallen Warrior of Nyx, longs for someone who is absent from him. Someone he does not have the courage to contact.

Me? She couldn't stop the thought.

The bull's humorless laughter drifted through her mind. *No, my heartless one. Your old Consort longs for the company of his son.*

Rephaim! Neferet's anger began to build. *He longs for that boy?*

He does, though he has not yet put words to the feeling. Do you know what that means?

Neferet thought before she spoke. She discarded jealously and envy and all the trappings of mortal love. Then, and only then did she truly understand. *Yes. It means Kalona has a very big weakness.*

It does, indeed.

They began to fade away from the ridge, slipping from shadow to shadow, riding the night. Neferet stroked the bull's neck, thought about new possibilities, and smiled.

Rephaim

"We gotta talk about Aphrodite's vision," Stevie Rae said.

Rephaim took one of her curls and twirled it around a finger. When he'd completely captured it, he tugged playfully. "You talk. I will touch your hair."

She smiled, but gently pushed his hand away. "Rephaim, stop. Be serious. Aphrodite's vision is scary."

"Did you not tell me Aphrodite foretold Zoey's death? Twice. As well as her grandmother's? Each time the foretelling of those deaths made it possible for them to have been averted." Rephaim caressed her cheek and kissed her gently before saying, "We will use this vision to avert my death as well."

"'Kay. That sounds good to me." She nuzzled his hand with her cheek. "But we gotta be clear about somethin'. Dragon's some kinda key, so you really do need to stay away from him."

"Yes. I know." He caressed the side of her head, loving the softness of her hair, and let his fingers trail slowly down her neck and shoulder.

"Rephaim, please listen to me." Stevie Rae took his face between her hands and made him stop touching her hair and her skin.

"I'm listening to you." Reluctantly, he focused his attention on her words.

"I've been thinkin' that maybe I was wrong. Maybe you do need to stay here and not go to school, and for sure not go to whatever ritual we do out at Z's g-ma's farm, or at least you need to stay away until we figure out more of the details about Aphrodite's vision."

Rephaim took her hands from his face and held them in his own. "Stevie Rae, if I begin hiding now, when will it end?"

"I don't know, but I do know you'll be alive."

"There are worse things than death. Being trapped by your fear of it is one of those things." He smiled. "Actually, I find the whole thing curiously positive. The vision means that I am truly human."

"What the heck do you mean? Of course you're human."

"I look human, or at least I do until the sun rises. Being mortal makes me truly what I appear to be."

"But doesn't knowing your immortal blood is gone make you sad?"

"No, it makes me a little more normal."

Stevie Rae's bright blue eyes widened. "You know what else it makes you? *Not* being part of Kalona's blood anymore."

Rephaim tried to understand Stevie Rae's denial of his father. He really did, but he couldn't help the defensive, almost angry feeling that came over him when she tried to push him away from the winged immortal.

"Do you believe it takes more than blood to make a father?" He spoke slowly, trying to reason through his feelings and find the truth beneath them.

"Yep, absolutely," she said.

"Then it stands to reason that the absence of blood does not automatically *unmake* a father, too." Before she could rebut what he was saying, he continued, "Kalona is immortal, but I was by his side long enough to glimpse humanity within that immortality."

"Rephaim, I don't want to argue about your daddy. I know you think I hate him, but that's not it. I hate that he hurts you."

"I understand that." He pulled her into his arms and kissed the top of her head, breathing in the sweet, familiar scent of girl and shampoo and soap. "But you must let me find my own way in this. He is my father. Nothing will change that."

"Okay, I'll try to lay off the speeches about staying away from Kalona, but I want you to promise me you'll think about staying away from Dragon—at least for a little while."

"That is an easy promise to make. I already try to avoid the Sword Master because I know the sight of me causes him pain, but I will not hide. I cannot hide from Dragon any more than I can hide from my father."

She pulled back and looked at him. "We're in this together, aren't we?"

He met her gaze. "We are. Always."

"All right. Let's stay together, even if it's dangerous. I'll protect you," she said.

"And I will protect you," he agreed. Rephaim kissed her then, long and slow. He held her close for just a few moments more, letting her scent and her sweetness blanket him.

"You have to go now?" She spoke with her face buried in his chest.

"You know I do."

"I'm gonna quit asking that I go up there with you 'cause I know you don't want me to, but I want you to know that if you ever change your mind I'll be with you until the very end. 'Cause even when you're a bird, you're *my* bird."

That made him chuckle. "I never thought of it like that, but I am your bird, and your bird needs to go out to the morning sky and stretch his wings."

"Okie dokie." He liked that she let go of him first and beamed an enthusiastic, if not totally believable smile at him. "I'll be here when you fly home."

"Good, because I will always fly home to you." He kissed her quickly, pulled on his shirt, and left their room. He was glad he'd left before his skin started that awful prickling. He hated the panicked feeling it gave him to run through the tunnels, yearning harder and harder for the aboveground world and the beckoning sky.

Just a little way from the last tunnel junction before the basement exit, he saw something move within the shadows and he automatically took a defensive stance.

"Hey, relax. It's just me."

He did relax as he recognized Shaunee's voice, followed closely by the girl herself as she emerged from the right-hand branch of the tunnel. She looked disheveled and was carrying a large plastic basket.

"Hello, Shaunee," he said. "Are you well?"

"Yeah, I guess. I have one more load of my stuff to haul from Erin's room to my new place down there." She pointed her thumb behind her at the darkness. "And, yes, I know I'm gonna have to string lights."

"*You* need light?"

She grinned, held up her hand, palm flat, blew on it, and a little flame appeared, dancing merrily. "Well, not really, but anyone who wants to come visit probably does."

"I'll help you do that tomorrow if you'd like," he heard himself saying, and then suddenly wished he hadn't. What if she was like most of the other fledglings, and really didn't want much to do with him?

He needn't have been worried. Shaunee didn't reject him. Actually, her grin got bigger. "That'd be awesome. I was gonna try to put some up when I brought back the last load of stuff, but moving sucks and all I really want to do is curl up on my very comfy new bed and rewatch the last episode of *Game of Thrones* on my iPad. I really like me some Daenerys."

"Stevie Rae and I have been watching that, too. You know it has ravens in it."

"Yeah, and dragons and dead things and a cool dwarf, which should be all whatthefuckery and crazy, which it is but in a good way." She bit her lip and looked like she was trying to decide whether to say more, so Rephaim just stood there, waiting, even when his skin began to tingle. Finally, Shaunee said in a very small voice, "Erin never liked it. She said it was too *Dungeons and Dragons* dorkified, and I agreed out loud with her, but I used to sneak and watch it while she was sleeping."

Rephaim wasn't sure how he should respond to that. He didn't really understand why the two girls used to need to act as if they were one person, so he also found it difficult to understand why they both, in their own ways, seemed so upset and lost now. "Maybe you could watch it with Stevie Rae and me when the new season begins?" he offered.

"Would Stevie Rae make buttered popcorn? She used to make awesome buttered popcorn."

"She still does, so yes, I'm saying she will make the popcorn. With butter."

"Oooh, yum. I'm in. And, thanks, Rephaim."

"You are welcome. I must go now . . ." he trailed off as he began moving away from her toward the basement exit to above.

"Hey, I heard about Aphrodite's vision. I just wanta say I hope you don't get dead."

"I hope I don't get dead, either." He paused, and then added, "If something does happen to me, would you call that phone you gave Father and tell him?"

"Yeah, of course. But nothing's gonna happen to you. I hope. And, plus, you don't have to get dead—you can call that phone whenever you want to, you know, just to talk to him."

Rephaim realized he'd never even thought of something so simple, so mundane, so normal—to just call his father. "I will. Soon," he said, and he meant it. "I'll see you after sunset."

"See ya," she called.

Then Rephaim did have to hurry through the last part of the tunnel and rush up the iron ladder and through the basement, but he didn't mind. His last thought before the raven and the sky overtook his human mind was that he was glad Shaunee and Erin had stopped being one person because Shaunee, all by herself, was a nice girl. And along with Damien and maybe even Zoey, they might possibly be the first true friends he'd ever had . . .

Kalona

There was something about the night that wouldn't let him rest. His sons were asleep, warm and safe and nesting in the three hunters' blinds. He should have been sleeping, too. Instead he found himself out on the ridge, sitting on a huge, flat-topped boulder, thinking.

The iPhone was in his hand. He considered the modern world and the strange magick it had developed. He couldn't decide if he liked it better than the ancient world. Certainly, it was more comfortable. Absolutely, it was more complicated. But better? Kalona tended to believe it was not.

He looked at the phone. The fledgling had given it so that he could contact Rephaim, yet the boy was not listed in the contacts. *Silly, useless thing,* he thought. And then, on second thought, he realized Stevie Rae was in the contact list. Contact the Red One and he would contact his son.

He did not want to speak with the Red One. She was at the root of his problems. Had she not interfered, Rephaim would be here, by his side, as was the proper order of things.

Or Rephaim would be dead after bleeding out, broken and alone that terrible night. And would that not have been a better, more fitting end for my son than to be shackled to a young vampyre and her unforgiving Goddess?

The thoughts had barely formed in his head when Kalona regretted them.

No, it would not be better if Rephaim had died.

And Nyx was not unforgiving. She'd forgiven his son. It was only him she refused to forgive.

Kalona spoke to the heavens, "It is ironic that in doing my son a kindness, you have done me a cruelty. You've taken from me the last creature in this world that truly loved me." His voice was lost quickly to the night and he was completely alone. Goddess, he was tired of being alone!

He missed Rephaim's company.

Kalona's shoulders slumped.

It was then that he felt the presence of Darkness. It was subtle and well cloaked, but Kalona had known Darkness too long, both battling against it and fighting beside it, to be fooled.

Kalona put the phone away from him and schooled his features to an impassive, neutral mask. He had no idea why the white bull was lurking this night, but he knew his presence portended great trouble and tribulations for this world and, perhaps, even for him.

He understood something Neferet was too intoxicated by power to realize: the incarnation of Darkness could never truly be an ally. The white bull had only one objective: to destroy and consume the black bull. He would use anything or anyone to gain his objective, just as he would destroy anything or anyone who got in his way.

If Neferet believed she was his Consort, she was utterly, completely incorrect. The white bull of Darkness did not have Consorts—it had conquests.

The presence dissipated and Kalona breathed a sigh of relief. Then he straightened, considering. *Neferet? Did I sense her presence, too?*

He glanced down at the iPhone. How long had they been watching him? What had they heard? What did they know?

Was Rephaim in danger?

Kalona surged to his feet and launched himself into the sky. His mighty wings beat against the night as he rode the air currents swiftly and silently, heading east into the pre-dawn glooming.

He reached the depot moments before sunrise, landing on the gravely ground near the railroad tracks, well away from the high front entrance that Shaunee had already explained to him was unused. Kalona was pacing, staring at an old metal grate and silently cursing the fact that he'd left the damned phone on the rock when the rusting grate was pushed aside and his son ran from the building.

Kalona began to move toward him, relieved beyond words that they boy was whole and well, when his son's mouth opened and he shrieked—a terrible sound to hear. Then he watched Rephaim's body shiver, writhe, morph *and a raven burst forth from the skin of the boy!*

Moving on instinct alone, Kalona took to the sky following the raven. The immortal stayed well aloft, high above the prying eyes of the city, though in truth the raven spent very little time in the city. Instead he flew west and a little south, eerily following the same path Kalona had taken. It wasn't long before the raven was on the ridge perched in an old oak whose branches spread like a protective giant around the hunters' blinds. There Rephaim the Raven stayed, only occasionally feeding, sometimes climbing the sky, but always, always circling back to the ridge.

As sunset approached the bird flew. This time he did not circle, but instead he faced the east and made wing toward Tulsa. Kalona followed and as the sun dipped below the horizon, the raven landed just outside the basement entrance to the depot. The bird shrieked a cry that changed into a shout of agony, and then there was Rephaim, naked, breathing hard, and on his knees.

Kalona backed into the shadows and watched his son dress and then the sound of metal grating being moved had them both looking.

"You're back! Yeah!" The Red One hurled herself into his son's arms. He caught her and held her close, laughing and kissing her. Hand in hand the two of them disappeared inside the basement of the building.

Kalona, suddenly weak-kneed and feeling unimaginably old, sat upon the rusted railway track and spoke aloud to the night and to the Goddess that was its personification.

"You forgave him, and yet still you make him suffer as a beast. Why? Because he is paying for my transgressions? Damn you, Nyx. Damn you."

CHAPTER TWENTY-FIVE

Zoey

So, I was nervous about first hour and what Thanatos was gonna say about losing a parent—specifically my mom—but the day was starting out really well. For the first time in a really long time Stark was awake before me, and so I got woken up with kisses and him calling me Sleeping Beauty. He wolfed down the most ginormic bowl full of Cap'n Crunch I'd ever seen, and in the parking lot outside the depot he was messing around with Darius, doing a little mock boxing match while kids were filling up the short bus.

I was already on the bus watching him out the window with what I'm sure was a goofy happy smile on my face when Aphrodite emerged from the depot. I was surprised to see her 'cause I figured she'd be so hungover and exhausted that she would definitely not be going to school today. She squinted and then put on sunglasses, even though it was 7:30 P.M. and there was no sun at all.

"She don't look good," Kramisha said from her seat behind me.

"How can you tell from this far away?"

"She got flats on and her hair's in a ponytail. That girl never wears flats and her hair usually looks like Barbie," Kramisha said. "I mean regular Barbie and not none of those weird dolls like Tennis Barbie or Go to the Gym Barbie."

"Everyone knows Barbie doesn't have to work out to keep her kick-ass body," Shaunee said.

"Bull truth," Stevie Rae said.

"Huh?" I said, totally befuddled.

"Just trust us. Aphrodite don't look good," Kramisha repeated.

"She doesn't even have any lip gloss on. Bad sign," Erin said.

"If she doesn't have on any eye makeup, Hell has officially frozen over," Shaunee said, which was interesting because that's as close as she'd gotten to a Twin comment in days.

I glanced at Shaunee, who was sitting in the front seat of the bus, as far away from Erin's place in the back as she could get. Shaunee was digging in her purse like she'd misplaced a tube of one of MAC's seasonal lipsticks that you buy and fall in love with AND THEN THEY DISCONTINUE IT BECAUSE THEY REALLY HATE US AND WANT US TO BE CRAZY.

Anyway, I was sure Shaunee's cheeks looked pink. So, was she embarrassed about the kinda accidental Twin comment she had made, or excited about it? I didn't have much time to consider which it could be because Aphrodite climbed into the bus and sat heavily in the first seat behind the driver's chair, which was directly in front of me.

"Coffee," she croaked. "I told Darius we have to swing the short bus through Starbucks at Utica on the way. I'm going to die if I don't get an uber-sweet caramel double espresso coffee drink and a giant slab of their blueberry coffee cake."

"Them's a lot of calories," Kramisha told her.

"If you try to stop me I will kill you dead," Aphrodite said.

"I think your hair looks good like that," Shaunee told her.

"For shit's sake, I don't need the pity of half a brain-sharer. I do not feel that damn bad."

Shaunee skewered her with a look. "I'm not half of anything and I'm not giving you any pity. I was just sayin' I like your hair 'cause you usually don't wear it like that, but if you're too much of a bitch to accept a compliment then you can fuck yourself."

The entire bus inhaled a giant breath. The silence was total and frightening. I wasn't sure whether I should summon elements or run. Then Aphrodite pulled her sunglasses down her nose and looked over their rims at Shaunee. Her eyes were pink-tinged and bruised and just all-around horrendously unattractive, but they were shining with humor. "I think I like you using a brain of your own."

"Yeah, well, I haven't decided if I like you at all, but your hair still looks good."

"Huh," Aphrodite said.

"Huh," Shaunee said.

We all breathed a long sigh of relief.

And that's pretty much how the day proceeded. Stark was back to his old, charming, sexy, totally fabulous self. When I asked what the heck had gotten into him he said, "Z, I slept like a log and I feel like Superman today!" Seriously. Superman. And, apparently, he meant it 'cause he was zooming around everywhere, laughing and being a total guy.

He was the cutest thing I'd seen since that Trololo Cat YouTube video.

So, before school was cool. The ride to school was even okay. Well, Aphrodite was grumpy, but that was pretty much normal. Plus, she was actually talking to Shaunee, which was nice 'cause it was obvious Shaunee wasn't sure who she was now that she wasn't one half of the Twin team. And we did stop at Starbucks on the way. I know fledglings aren't supposed to feel caffeine highs anymore, but it definitely seemed like we were all buzzing by the time we pulled into the House of Night.

Of course once we got to school everything else was, as Stevie Rae would've said, as under control as herding cats.

It all started with first hour. Okay, I hadn't actually forgotten Thanatos was going to use me as an example for her how-do-we-deal-with-losing-parents class project or whatever. I'd just kinda misplaced the memory of it, which probably had to do with Stark being so dang adorable and me being so dang happy he was acting like himself again.

And maybe I hadn't wanted to remember. Maybe I'd just wanted to not be momless and heartbroken for a little while.

Anyway, my selective amnesia didn't last more than just about two-point-five seconds after I stepped into first hour and followed Stevie Rae and Rephaim up front. Aurox was there, just where he'd been yesterday. He met my gaze for an instant before he looked away. Then I remembered what was up—that class wasn't just going to be me being entertained or me daydreaming. Class was gonna be, well, *me*. That totally made my stomach clench and suddenly I was nervous and anxious and wishing I'd gotten permission to go to the bathroom or the nurse or anywhere except class.

It was only later that I realized my seer stone, for the first time, hadn't heated up at the sight of him because, of course, Thanatos started to talk, which totally distracted me by putting the cherry on top of my anxiety sundae.

"I read your questions and found a common theme in many of them," she said. "Quite a few of you expressed a desire to discuss how to deal with the loss of your parents. The truth is if you complete the Change and become vampyres, you will inevitably lose not just your parents, but all of your mortal contemporaries because, as you already know, although vampyres are not immortal we are definitely longer lived than humans. So, to help us delve into this subject I have solicited the aid of the only one of your peers who has lost a parent, as well as a mate, to death—Zoey Redbird."

I wanted to die.

Everyone was quiet and paying attention, even the jerky red fledgling back row that surrounded Dallas.

"First, let me begin with a word of encouragement," Thanatos said. "As you know, my affinity is death. I often guide spirits in their crossing from this world to the Otherworld, so I can tell each of you with certainty that there is an Otherworld waiting for us. I have not traveled there, but Zoey has." She smiled encouragement to me. "I believe you have seen both your mate and your mother joyously welcomed into Nyx's realm."

"Yes." I realized my voice was way too soft, so I cleared my throat and tried again, louder. "Yes, I saw my mom welcomed by Nyx, and I actually spent time there with Heath."

"And is it a beautiful place?"

I felt a little of the sickness leave my stomach as I remembered the good part. "Yeah, it's awesome. Even when my soul was shattered and I was super messed up, I could feel the peace and happiness in the Goddess Grove." *I just couldn't reach it for myself,* I added silently.

Stevie Rae's hand went up. "Yes, Stevie Rae." Thanatos called on her.

"Is it okay if we ask questions?"

"Zoey?" Thanatos's wise gaze turned to me.

"Yeah, sure, I guess."

"Then go ahead and ask your question, Red High Priestess." Thanatos's gaze took in the entire class. "But let us remember the rules of civility that are always in effect in my classroom."

There was a pause and then Stevie Rae asked me, "Uh, so, the Otherworld, it's a big grove?"

I was surprised by her question and her obvious curiosity—then I realized she'd never asked me much of anything about the Otherworld. Really, outside of Sgiach, and mentioning it when I'd led the ritual for Jack, I really hadn't talked about it hardly at all.

"Well, yeah, but I know there are a bunch of different parts of the Otherworld. Like when I first found Heath he was fishing off a dock that was on a really pretty lake." Even though missing him made me sad, the memory made me smile. "Heath loved to fish. I mean, seriously loved it. So, that's where I first found him, but when we needed to be safe we went to the Goddess Grove. That was in a different part of the Otherworld."

Damien's hand went up and Thanatos called on him.

"I know you didn't see Jack up there, but are you saying that you believe there are places in the Otherworld that are specific to each of us?"

I thought about it for a second, and then nodded. "Yeah, I think that's a good way of describing it. Jack is probably in the arts and crafts section."

Damien smiled through his tears. "He wanted to be a fashion designer. He's in the *Project Runway* section."

"Oooh! Nice section," I heard from somewhere behind me and a few kids laughed softly.

Hesitantly, Aurox's hand went up. After Thanatos called his name, he turned so that he could meet my gaze. "You said there are different parts of the Otherworld. Do you think there is a part that is a place of punishment?"

His strange, moon-colored eyes were filled with an unspoken anguish, and I knew his question came from a place that was deeper than curiosity and that my answer would mean more than just providing random school information. *Please, Nyx give me the words; let my answer be true.*

I drew a long breath and found spirit within me. I held to the element that was closest to my heart and trusted that through it my Goddess would guide my words. As I started speaking I noticed how quiet it had gotten in the room and I could practically feel the back-row kids holding their breaths.

"I saw things in the Otherworld that were scary and not nice, but they were outside forces and not from the Goddess. Did I see a place of punishment? No, but what I did see was Heath moving on to another realm of the Otherworld. He believed he was going to be reborn from that part of the realm. While he was leaving he told me that, even though he was moving on, our love stayed with him." I paused and had to blink hard and wipe at one tear that had somehow escaped. "What my gut tells me is that Nyx isn't a Goddess of punishment, but it wouldn't surprise me if really hateful people are reborn in a way that either makes up for the awfulness of their past lives, or teaches them something they didn't learn before."

"You mean like someone who was a wife beater gets reborn as a woman?" Shaunee said.

"How about as a woman in a burka in Afghanistan?" Aphrodite added with a sarcastic lift of an eyebrow.

"Yeah, that is kinda what I mean," I said. "But I think the what and where and who would be up to the Goddess."

"Do you think it's ever up to the person?" Aurox asked me.

"I hope so," I said earnestly, thinking of Heath and my mom.

"So, knowing beyond any doubt that there is an Otherworld and that our loved ones can find their way to it, even if they aren't vampyres, or even fledglings, is some comfort to us as we outlive the mortals in our lives. That does not mean losing a parent is ever easy. Zoey, I know this is painful, but could you share with us what it is that is most difficult for you about your mother's death?"

I nodded and opened my mouth to say something about the fact that now she can't ever make up for the way she un-mom-ed me over the past three years, but the words wouldn't come.

"Take your time," Thanatos said.

Stevie Rae reached over and took my hand. Squeezing it, she whispered, "It's okay, just pretend like there's no one here except us. You can tell me."

I looked at my BFF and blurted, "It's so awful that I don't know what really happened to her."

"Why do you think that is what saddens you the most?"

From the stage Thanatos asked the question, but I kept looking at Stevie Rae. She smiled and said, "How come it would be better if you knew what happened to your momma?"

"Because someone needs to pay for what was done to her," I told my BFF.

"Vengeance?" Thanatos asked.

Then I did look at her. "No. Justice," I said firmly.

"It is admirable as well as understandable for you to desire justice. Let this be a lesson to the rest of you—there is a distinct difference between wanting to gain revenge and exact vengeance, and wanting the truth to shine forth so that justice for all is illuminated." Thanatos met my gaze. "I believe I can help give you the truth, so that you will be able to get justice for your mother and closure for yourself."

"What do you mean?"

"I spoke with your grandmother. Today is the fifth night after your mother's death. I explained to her that five is an important number in our belief system—it represents the elements and our closeness to them. She has agreed to pause her traditional cleansing on this, the fifth night. It is not a certainty, but with the elemental power held by your circle and your connection to the one whose death we seek to reveal, I believe I can illuminate the truth of your mother's murder if you are willing to cast your circle and witness what it reveals."

"I'm willing." I felt sick, but I knew I had to go through with this.

"There is more," Thanatos said. She looked from me to Stevie Rae. "Zoey will cast the circle. I will be there to invoke the presence of death, but the spell that invokes death hinges upon you."

"Me?" Stevie Rae squeaked.

"It is your element in which this deed was imprinted. It is through your element the truth of it will be revealed." Thanatos's gaze sought out each member of my circle as she continued explaining. "This spell will not be pleasant. Zoey's mother was murdered. If we are successful, we will witness that horrendous act. You must each be willing participants, focused and aware of what it is you are agreeing to."

"I'm willing," Stevie Rae said immediately.

"Me, too . . . Yep, I'm in . . . I'm willing," came from Shaunee and Damien and Erin.

"Then it is decided. We leave as soon as first hour is over. If I call your name you will assemble in the parking lot and prepare yourself for the ritual and spell. If I do not call your name please proceed to your second-hour class. Your homework will be an essay on loss—and that homework will be due from those participating in the ritual as well as those of you who do not. The students joining me are: Zoey, Stevie Rae, Damien, Shaunee, Erin, and Aphrodite. The rest of you may begin working on your essays. Good day to you, and blessed be." Thanatos bowed formally to her classroom and then went to sit behind her desk.

My mouth flopped open. As Grandma would have said, this whole thing flummoxed me.

Aphrodite plopped down in the desk beside me and hissed a whisper. "Talk to Thanatos. Be sure she doesn't let Dragon go with us." She paused, tilted her head, and gawked at Stevie Rae and Rephaim, who totally had their heads together and were talking like a mile a minute. "Unless I'm wrong—and I'm never wrong—she's gonna insist birdboy goes with us, which is no surprise because I can promise you Darius won't let me go without him. But having Rephaim with us means Dragon can't go or, according to my vision, he's gonna get sliced in two."

"Hell!" I said.

"Cursing?" Aphrodite said.

"No. It's a place. I didn't send anyone there," I said.

"Grow up," she said.

"Screw you," I said, succinctly.

Aphrodite laughed, which totally took the Big Girl sting from my almost-curse. I sighed and as the bell chimed, got out of my desk and walked slowly but resolutely up to Thanatos.

From her seat behind her desk Thanatos glanced up, but her eyes didn't go to me. Instead she glanced around me and called, "Aurox, a moment please."

Aurox had been leaving class, but he stopped and turned. "You want me, Priestess?"

"I want to give you an answer to your question."

"Uh, I'll wait outside so you two can—"

"There is no need for you to leave." Thanatos cut me off. "My answer is the same for whomever is asking the question."

"I do not understand," Aurox said.

Actually, neither did I. His question was "What am I?" How could there be only one answer for that question?

"I believe you will understand when you hear me out. The question of what we are can only be answered by ourselves. We each decide what we are by the life choices we make. How we were made, who are parents are, where we are from, the color of our skin, who we choose to love, all those things do not define us. Our actions define us, and will keep defining us until even after death."

I saw surprise in Aurox's expression. "The past does not matter?"

"The past matters a great deal, especially if we don't learn from it. But the future need not be dictated by the past."

"I decide what I am?" He spoke slowly, as if he was working through a riddle.

"Yes."

"Thank you, Priestess."

"You are welcome and you may be excused now."

He fisted his hand over his heart and bowed deeply to her before leaving the room.

I was looking after him, still thinking about the surprise I'd seen in Aurox when Thanatos spoke to me. "Zoey, I know this ritual and the spell casting will be difficult for you, but I believe it will also give you closure."

"Yeah, me, too." Feeling a little like a kid caught with her hand in the cookie jar, I spoke quickly, my eyes turning to Thanatos. "I mean, I don't want to do it. I don't want to see what happened to Mom, but I figure I keep replaying it in my imagination anyway. The truth will at least stop my imagination."

"It will do that," she said.

"So, this ritual—who all will be there?"

"Those I named already. I would imagine your Guardian will accompany you, as will Aphrodite's Darius. And I will be there. Follow your instincts, Zoey. Is there anyone else you request?"

Aurox's presence seemed to linger in the room with us and I shook my head. "No, I don't want to request anyone else. My circle and our Warriors are all that I need, but there is someone I *don't* want there." She raised her eyebrows and I continued. "Dragon Lankford. He hates Rephaim, and he's pretty much acting as Stevie Rae's Warrior, so he should be with her." I made a quick decision, *Thanatos should know*, and added, "Plus, yesterday Aphrodite had a vision that showed Dragon totally involved with Rephaim being skewered by a sword. I'd rather that didn't happen during my mom's reveal ritual."

"Dragon Lankford has been tasked with protecting this school and its students. If he allows, or takes part in, Rephaim being injured a great injustice will have been committed and he must be brought to task quickly and—"

"Wait, stop." I interrupted her. "I don't want this spell to be some kind of setup for Dragon to get in trouble. I don't want any of that drama to touch what's happened to my mom. Her murder is drama enough. Can't you just help me be sure Dragon's not there? We'll deal with his issues later."

Thanatos bowed her head slightly. "You have a valid point, and you are right to remind me. Your mother's death is not the appropriate venue to test Dragon or to illuminate his failings. I shall see that he does not accompany us."

"Thanks," I said.

"Thank me when the ritual and spellcasting is over. I've found quite often that the dead reveal things that should have been kept hidden from the living."

And on that ominous note I left death's classroom and made my way to the parking lot and to a future none of us would have been able to predict.

Neferet

When the bell chimed to end first hour Neferet moved nonchalantly to the doorway of her classroom. Under the guise of saying good-bye to what was left of the class after Thanatos had culled it for her own *special* first hour, Neferet positioned herself so that she could watch the High Council member's students as they departed.

Dallas, now would be a lovely time to orchestrate another altercation.

No sooner had the thought formed in her mind then the young red vampyre himself moved into her view. He wasn't posturing or provoking. Neferet frowned. He and his ragged group of compatriots were slinking from Thanatos's first hour as if they were dogs with their tails tucked between their legs.

Then Zoey's group, minus Zoey, she noted, hurried from class all moving in the same direction. *The same direction?* Most of them had different second-hour classes. No matter how sheep-like they were, they should not all be traveling together.

Aurox emerged and Neferet smiled.

As if he could feel her gaze the vessel looked her way.

"Come to me," she mouthed the words and gestured to her office. Neferet didn't wait to see if the vessel complied. She knew he would do as commanded.

"Yes, Priestess," he said, standing before her desk. "You called?"

"Did anything unusual happen first hour?"

"Unusual, Priestess?"

Neferet barely contained her irritation. *Must he be so stupid?* "Yes, unusual! I noticed Dallas and his group seemed unusually reserved, and many of the other students, those closest to Zoey Redbird, left together as if they had somewhere to go that was not their second-hour class."

"Your observation is correct, Priestess. Thanatos intends to oversee Zoey and her circle performing a ritual so that she may then cast a spell invoking death. Her intent is for Zoey to witness the truth of her mother's death and thereby to attain closure."

"What?" Neferet felt as if her mind was going to explode.

"Yes, Priestess. Thanatos is using Zoey as an example of how all fledglings and vampyres can overcome the loss of a parent."

Neferet lifted her hand, palm out, and the threads of Darkness swarmed to her. Aurox took a step back, obviously uncomfortable with her tumultuous emotions. She made a conscious effort to control herself and the sticky tendrils quieted.

"Where is this spellcasting taking place?"

"At the site of Zoey's mother's murder."

Through clenched teeth Neferet managed to say, "When? When is this happening?"

"They are gathering to leave now, Priestess."

"And you are quite certain Thanatos is accompanying them?"

"Yes, Priestess."

"May all the immortals be damned!" Neferet almost spat the curse. "A reveal ritual. It must be accompanied by the casting of a very specific spell . . ." She drummed her pointed fingernails on her desk, thinking. "It would have to be earth-based, as it is within that specific plot of earth that the death would have been Imprinted. It is Stevie Rae then, and not Zoey who must be impeded." She turned her attention back to Aurox. "This is my command: you will thwart this ritual and the casting of the death spell. Do whatever you must to stop it, even if you must kill, although I do not want the death to be one of the Priestesses." She grimaced in annoyance. "Unfortunately, the price of a Priestess's death is too costly, especially as I don't have an equitable sacrifice to offer," she muttered, almost to herself. Then she caught the vessel's moonstone gaze with her own. "Do *not* kill a Priestess. I'd prefer *no one* realize you were there, but if you cannot stop the spell without giving yourself away, then do what you must. Your command is that the ritual and its spellwork go awry, so that Thanatos cannot reveal the manner of Zoey's mother's death. Do you understand me?"

"I do, Priestess."

"Then get out of here and do as I command. If you are discovered do not expect me to rescue you. Expect me to forget we ever had this conversation."

When he simply stood there staring at her, she said, "What is it? Why are you not already obeying my orders?"

"I do not know where to go, Priestess. How do I reach the location of the ritual?"

Neferet squelched the urge to smite him to his knees with Darkness. Instead she scribbled an address on a notepad, tore it off, and handed it to him. "Use the GPS as I've showed you before. This is the address. It couldn't be easier if I conjured you there."

He bowed, clutching the paper. "As you command, Priestess," he said, leaving the room.

"And be careful they do not see you arriving!"

"Yes, Priestess," he said before closing the door behind him.

Neferet watched him go. "I wish he was smarter," she whispered to the dark tendrils that crawled up her arms and caressed her wrists. "Oh, but you are, aren't you? Go with him. Strengthen him. Watch him. Be quite sure he does not falter in obeying my *simple* commands. Then return and tell me everything." The tendrils hesitated. Neferet sighed and, with a quick flick of her forefinger, she sliced the inside of her bicep and ground her teeth as Darkness fed from her. Shortly, she waved them away and licked the shallow wound closed. "Go now. You've taken your payment. Do my bidding,"

The shadows slithered from her and Neferet, content, called for her assistant to bring her a glass of wine laced with blood.

"Find some virgin's blood this time," she snapped when the young vampyre answered her summons. "The other is simply too common, and I have a feeling a celebration will soon be in order."

"Yes, Priestess, as you command." The assistant bowed and scurried out.

"That is right." Neferet spoke aloud to the listening shadows. "All will be as I command. And someday soon they will not call me Priestess, but Goddess. Someday *very* soon . . ."

Neferet laughed.

CHAPTER TWENTY-SIX

Dragon

A Sword Master notices everything. It's part of what makes him successful—what keeps him alive. Though it didn't take his preternatural abilities of observation for Dragon Lankford to know something was going on with Zoey's inner group. It only took following his instincts and asking one simple question.

Shortly after second hour was underway Dragon instructed his students to begin their warm-up exercises, and told them he would return momentarily. Instinct had been niggling at him, driving him, prodding him, worrying him. Darius and Stark were talented Warriors—both more than capable in their specialized areas of weaponry. Darius was probably the most gifted knife thrower Dragon had ever known, and Stark's infallibility with bow and arrow was, indeed, awe inspiring.

Neither of those abilities meant they should be in charge of training young, impressionable fledglings. Teaching was a gift in itself, and Dragon very much doubted that two such youthful vampyres had the experience and wisdom needed to be true professors.

She had been young when she was made a professor, so very young. That was how he'd met her—his mate—his life—his own. He knew what Anastasia would say were she here. She would smile kindly and remind him that he should not judge others harshly because of their youth—that once he had known how that felt. She would remind him that he was in the perfect position to mentor the youths—to be sure they developed into worthy Warriors and exceptional teachers.

But Anastasia was as dead as the past and because of that his life was utterly changed. Dragon did not want to supervise or mentor or oversee young professors, especially in light of the fact that they had begun this extra class so that he would not have to suffer the presence of the Raven Mocker turned boy. But Dragon was finding that duty was an odd thing. Even though he had stepped away from the path he'd walked with his mate and his Goddess, it seemed he had not become entirely free of the bonds that tied him to honor and responsibility.

So, begrudgingly, Dragon gave in to the instinct that was telling him to check on the young Warriors and made the short trek from the field house to the arena of Lenobia's stables where Stark and Darius had set up their Warrior training.

As soon as he placed foot inside the sawdust arena, Dragon knew he'd been right to be concerned. The two vampyres weren't conducting training—the human stable man was. Lenobia was nowhere to be seen, and the two Warriors were following Aphrodite *from* the stables. Dragon shook his head in disgust.

"Darius!" he called. The young vampyre paused, gestured for Stark and Aphrodite to go ahead, and then he hurried over to Dragon. "Why is a human leading your class?"

"It cannot be avoided," Darius said. "Stark and I must escort Aphrodite and Zoey."

"Escort them? Where?"

Dragon could see that Darius was not comfortable discussing the subject with him, but he really had very little choice. No matter their differing views on Rephaim and Neferet and some of the new red fledglings, Dragon was still Darius's ranking Warrior, and as thus he owed the Sword Master an answer.

"Thanatos is going to lead Zoey and her circle in a ritual at her grandmother's farm. The spell involved is supposed to reveal the manner of her mother's death."

Dragon felt the shock of it—this was major spellwork, and one that entailed some measure of danger, even if the threat was more emotional than physical. *I should have been informed. I should have been included.*

Dragon kept his thoughts veiled and only asked, "Why now, during school hours, is this ritual taking place?"

"This is the fifth night after her murder."

Dragon nodded, understanding. "One night for each of the elements. Four would be incomplete. Six would be too late. It must be tonight."

"Yes, that is how Thanatos explained it, too." Darius added, obviously uncomfortable, "May I have leave to go, Sword Master? My Prophetess awaits."

"Yes, you may."

Darius bowed and Dragon watched him go. Then, with a grim set to his handsome face, Dragon Lankford changed direction and made his way quickly to the classroom Thanatos had made her own.

He was relieved to see the High Priestess was still there, looking through one of the cupboards in the rear of the room and gathering candles and herbs, which she placed carefully in a large spellwork basket that was all too familiar to him. It had been Anastasia's favorite.

The sight of it made him feel raw and exposed. Nevertheless, he cleared his throat and said, "Priestess, may I have a word with you?"

Thanatos turned at the sound of his voice. "Certainly, Sword Master."

"Darius tells me you are leading Zoey's circle in a reveal ritual and some major spellwork at her grandmother's farm."

Though he didn't frame the words in a question, Thanatos nodded. "Yes."

"Priestess, I was under the impression that you are aware that I am Leader of the Sons of Erebus at this House of Night."

"I am aware of your position here, Sword Master," she agreed.

"Then, though I do not mean to admonish you or show you disrespect, I must ask your reasons for not informing me of and including me in an undertaking of such rare importance as well as danger."

Thanatos hesitated, and then she nodded, as if agreeing with him. "You are correct, because of your position at this school I should have informed you of my plans. I did not for a very simple reason: I decided that your presence at the ritual would be a distraction; therefore, I did not include you and did not inform you. I apologize if that seems I did not respect your position. That was not my intention."

"A distraction? Why would I be a distraction?"

"As Stevie Rae's Consort and protector, Rephaim will be attending the ritual."

Thoroughly annoyed Dragon retorted, "What does Rephaim have to do with me being a distraction?"

"If you harm the Consort of the Priestess who embodies the earth element, that will definitely distract her from performing her very pivotal part in the reveal ritual, and it will hinder the spellwork to follow."

"I would be there to protect our students. Not to harm them." Dragon forced the words through clenched teeth.

"And yet Aphrodite has been given a vision wherein you appear to be harming Rephaim."

"I would not do that unless he was endangering the other students!"

"Be that as it may, your presence would be a distraction. Dragon, two other Warriors will be present, and the power of Zoey's circle will be strong. The students are protected. And, Sword Master, let me add that I have seen a deep, disturbing change in you since the death of your mate."

"I grieve her loss."

"Sword Master, I think the truth is that you *are* lost. And even were Rephaim not going to be at the ritual, I would not want you present."

"Then I will leave you so as not to be a distraction." Dragon spun on his heels, but before he could exit the room, Thanatos's words snared him. "Please let me explain. I would not want you present at any ritual wherein a spell was cast to reveal the truth about death with the intent to bring about justice and closure. I do not mean to insult you, but I sense that you are in such conflict in your own life that your presence would simply go against the very heart of the spell."

As if her words had formed a wall before him, Dragon stopped. He did not turn to look at the High Priestess. In a voice he hardly recognized as his own, he spoke. "My presence would go against the very heart of the spell. Is that what you said to me?"

"I spoke the truth to you as I know it."

"Is that all you wish to say to me, Priestess?" He still did not turn to look at her.

"Yes, except that I wish you to blessed be, Sword Master."

Dragon didn't bow to her. He didn't fist his hand over his heart in respect. He could not. If he didn't get away so that he could think Dragon felt as if he would explode. He stumbled out into the hallway and started moving blindly. Ignoring the curious glances from students, he made his way from the main House of Night building and stumbled outside.

Memories bombarded him. Words swirled around and around through his mind. He'd been present when a different Warrior had been kept from attending another Priestess so, so many years ago, but he could hear Anastasia's voice as clearly as if she'd just spoken the words.

I do not mean to insult you, but I cannot cast a peace spell while I'm being guarded by a Warrior. It simply goes against the very heart of the spell . . .

The High Priestess at Tower Grove House of Night had agreed with her young professor of Spells and Rituals and commanded that Dragon escort Anastasia in place of a vampyre Warrior. He'd been tasked with protecting her that night—with watching over her while she cast a peace spell in the heart of St. Louis.

And he'd failed Anastasia.

Oh, she'd lived. She'd not been killed *that* night, but Dragon had allowed evil to escape his sword. That same evil, one hundred and seventy-seven years later, had murdered his love, his life, his own.

Dragon was breathing hard. He was leaning against something that felt cool and soothing to the heat that boiled in his body. Blinking, he looked up and realized where his feet had taken him. Dragon was leaning against the statue of Nyx that stood before her temple. As he gazed at the Goddess's marble face, the whispering wind blew the clouds from the moon and silver light caressed Nyx, illuminating her eyes.

She seemed, for a heartbeat, alive and looking at him with such a terrible sense of sadness that it made his heart, which he'd thought had been broken into so many pieces that it would never feel again, ache.

It was then that Dragon understood what he must do.

"I am going to the ritual. I'll watch and not interfere—unless evil tries to strike again. If it does, this time I give you my oath I will cut it down."

Zoey

"Are you sure we shouldn't ask Shaylin to come?" Stevie Rae asked. She was sitting with Rephaim in their usual place on the bus while we waited for Thanatos to join us.

"I really think it's not right for her to come," I said. "She's only been Marked for just a few days. She hasn't had time to even settle in as a fledgling, let alone figure out her True Sight thing."

"Plus, we're not advertising that she has True Sight," Aphrodite said. "The less people know about our business, the better."

"She was part of Kramisha's poem, though," Stevie Rae said.

"We don't know that for sure. The poem said"—I squinted, like that could help my memory and then, mostly accurately I recited—"the poem said, 'Seen with True Sight, Darkness doesn't equate to evil, and Light doesn't always bring good.' What if the True Sight part is the same as most of Kramisha's poems—meant to be symbolic and not literal?"

"Goddess, I hate poetry," Aphrodite said.

"Kramisha's not comin', either?" Stevie Rae said, sounding weirdly whiny. "Shouldn't we get her?"

"No, Stevie Rae, we need to stick with our circle—our core group," I said.

"The Herd of Nerd, plus the guys and moi," Aphrodite said. "Bumpkin, what's your issue? It's not like we haven't taken on the world before and come out mostly ahead."

"You sound scared," Damien said.

Stevie Rae glanced behind me where Damien was sitting midway back with Erin.

"I am scared," she admitted softly.

"Do not be scared." Rephaim slid his arm around her. "Aphrodite's vision has forewarned us. Nothing will happen to me."

"Uh, I'm not so sure being scared isn't smart." I spoke up, letting my gut help me reason through my thoughts. "I'm gonna see how my mom was killed. That scares me, so I know I'm gonna have to be ready for something terrible and super hard to watch. Aphrodite had a vision of Rephaim's death, probably during the ritual we're getting ready to go do. I think it's okay if Stevie Rae is scared, you should be scared, too, Rephaim—just enough so you'll both be prepared and ready for bad stuff if it happens."

"I'm frightened," Damien admitted. "Jack's death is still too raw, too close, and thinking about seeing another death frightens me."

"We'll all be with you," I told him. "We're all in this together."

"I'm scared. I've never circled without being a Twin," Shaunee blurted.

There was a very uncomfortable silence, and then from the middle of the bus Erin said, "I'm still here. I'm still water to your fire. You won't be alone."

"We all need to be scared safe, not scared stupid," I said, feeling incredibly relieved that the Twins were kinda sorta talking.

"Fear can be beneficial if it is tempered with common sense and courage." We jumped as Thanatos seemed to magickally appear in the front of the bus. She was holding a ginormic spellwork basket and wearing a long, hooded cloak that was a beautiful sapphire blue color. She looked powerful and ancient and scary. Then she smiled, and her scary changed to somehow include us and I relaxed just a little bit.

"We're all here," I said after I swallowed down the heart that was in my throat. "We're ready."

"You are *almost* ready. Before we leave campus I have to task each of the five circle members. Because it is a reveal ritual, and the spell I cast will allow those present to see that which has been hidden, each of you must bring to the altar something that reveals a truth about yourself that is usually hidden."

"Oh, boy." I sighed.

"Take a moment to think about what it is you need to reveal about yourself, and then go collect something to symbolize it. Quickly. We must complete our ritual and set the spell this night, before it passes midnight and a new day begins."

Shaunee was the first of us to get up. She looked determined as she hurried off the bus. Damien followed her. Then Stevie Rae. Then Erin. I had a sudden thought, and dug through my purse. In the bottom of it, with the used Kleenexes, topless ChapStick, and purse crud, I found it. Satisfied, I looked up to see Stark, Darius, Rephaim, and Aphrodite all gawking at me.

"Do you need help figuring out this assignment?" Aphrodite said, only semi-sarcastically.

"Zoey already has what she needs with her," Thanatos said.

"Yeah. She's right. I do." I had the very immature urge to stick my tongue out at Aphrodite, which I didn't do (of course). Instead I settled for crossing my arms and looking smug.

We didn't have long to wait for my circle to come back. Stevie Rae was first. She looked unusually frowny. She wasn't carrying anything, but when she sat down I saw her rest her hand over one of her front jeans pockets, as if she was protecting something there.

Damien left with his man purse and came back with it. He gave Thanatos an overly perky smile and said, "Mission accomplished!"

Shaunee came back next. She didn't say anything. She just went back to her seat and resumed staring out the window.

Erin finally came back. She was carrying a little thermal sack. The kind high-end grocers (like Petty's at Utica Square) give you to carry home ice cream and frozen stuff. "What?" She snapped at us. "I'm back. We're ready. Let's go."

Thanatos quelled Erin's outburst with one hard look, which sent the half of an ex-Twin skulking to the back of the bus. Then she told Darius, "Take us to the lavender farm of Sylvia Redbird." Darius pulled the short bus out of the House of Night campus. I expected Thanatos to sit down (uh, like a normal teacher) and bounce along with the rest of us. Instead she took a firm hold of the handicapped (sigh) rail with one hand, and with the other she reached into her

super-loaded spellwork basket and pulled out a big bundle of something that looked like a bunch of weeds that had clusters of little
white flowers just like I'd seen at the side of the road and in Oklahoma fields and ditches about a thousand times.

"As you all know, we are going to perform a reveal ritual, and I am
going to cast a spell invoking death that will, hopefully, illuminate
images from the past, specifically those of Zoey's mother's murder. It
is a difficult ritual and a complex spell." Thanatos had been speaking
to all of us, but now she turned her attention to Stevie Rae. "As I
mentioned before, earth is the key to unlocking this spell. The suc-
cess of the vision rests on the power of your connection to the earth,
as well as the commitment of the circle to bringing alive the images
of the events of the past."

"I'm real connected to earth. Promise," Stevie Rae said.

Thanatos's lips tilted up. "That is an excellent beginning."

"I think my circle is real committed to this ritual, too," I said.

I heard my friends around me echoing my words with yeses and
uh-huhs.

"What's with the weeds?" Aphrodite asked.

Thanatos shook one plant free of the others and held it up so we
could see it. Like I'd thought to begin with, it was just a plain old
weed that had a bunch of ordinary, but kinda pretty, white flowers
clustered at the end of it, a little like baby's breath.

"This is not a weed. It is a wonderful wild flower called angelica.
Its properties are unusually strong and pure. It is a flower of communication. When used in spellwork its nature is to reveal what is
hidden to the conscious eye. During tonight's ritual you, my young
Red High Priestess, are going to wear a crown woven by your friends
of this magickal flower."

"Ooooh! That's super cool!"

Thanatos handed the bundle of wildflowers to Stevie Rae. "Pass
these out. The rest of you braid the plants you get together into a
circle. Stevie Rae will stack the circles on her head before the ritual."

"Braid?" Stark muttered.

Stevie Rae dropped a bunch of *flowers* in our laps. I raised my
brows at Stark. "Yep," I said. "Braid. Death orders it."

"Well, in that case . . ." He sighed and started to awkwardly braid the long stems together.

While we all braided (even Rephaim, who actually seemed to have some kind of weird gift with knotwork and ended up doing a cool intricate braid *and* helping Stark with the mess he was working on) Thanatos walked up and down the aisle of the bus and talked to us. It was weirdly like being in a mobile classroom.

"From the moment our feet touch the earth of our ritual site, we must concentrate on the intent of our spell. Try to wipe the rest of the world from your minds. Concentrate only on one small thing— that we be allowed to see the truth of Linda Heffer's death."

"Murder," I heard myself saying. "She didn't just die. She was killed." Thanatos turned and her gaze met mine. She nodded. "I stand corrected. We are seeking truth, and so we must speak the truth. Your mother did not die of old age or disease. She was murdered. We are asking to be allowed to witness it."

"Thanks," I said, and then went back to braiding.

"It is fortuitous that the murder took place on a lavender farm. Lavender is a powerful magick herb. It has cleansing properties, but at its purest lavender is the embodiment of tranquility. It calms and soothes. It evokes peace and tranquility."

"Why is that good? Z's mom was killed in the middle of what amounts to a giant mound of lavender. Looks like its calming stuff didn't work too well," Aphrodite said.

"An herb cannot force the actions of someone who is committed to their destructive path. Lavender could not have saved Zoey's mother. But the fact that she was killed surrounded by land that nurtures lavender means that the earth itself is uneasy with the violence committed on a space intended for peace."

"And that's good for us because . . ." I asked, feeling more than a little dense.

"Because the land will want to be rid of the violence inflicted upon it. It should give the images over eagerly, if not easily."

"Why not easily?" Damien said.

"Rituals and spells that deal with great emotion are never easy," Thanatos said. "Death spells are particularly tricky. Death rarely cooperates, even when we just want to glimpse it versus embrace it fully."

"So when my momma used to say nothin' good ever comes easy, she was tellin' the truth," Stevie Rae said.

"She was," Thanatos said. "So, let us continue to prepare. The spell will have three parts. The first will take place between here and the physical site of our ritual. It is known as the Releasing. In order for us to be successful tonight we must all be of one accord with our intent. Clear your minds. Concentrate."

"On death?" Stevie Rae asked.

"No, on truth. Concentrate on our shared desire to seek and find the truth tonight."

"True Sight."

I didn't realize I'd spoken the words out loud until Thanatos nodded and said, "Yes, indeed. True Sight is an excellent way to put it. Tonight we wish to see with true sight."

Thanatos moved to the back of the bus to check on Erin's angelica braiding. I felt eyes on me and looked up from my own wildflower wreath to see Aphrodite and Stevie Rae staring at me.

"Tonight, 'seen with True Sight,'" Aphrodite quoted quietly. "'Darkness does not always equate to evil. Light does not always bring good.'"

"I told you we should have brought Kramisha," Stevie Rae whispered.

"I think we should have brought a damn tank," Stark said.

"*Clear your minds!*" I practically hissed the whisper, giving all of them a hard look. Then I went back to braiding.

I tried to clear my mind.

I tried to think about truth.

But I was too young—too scared—too worried. So the truth I found myself concentrating on was simple, but definitely not what Thanatos meant:

The truth is I need my mom and I'd give just about anything to have her alive and on my side again.

CHAPTER TWENTY-SEVEN

Aurox

Aurox left the House of Night campus quickly, being sure he was well ahead of the school bus. It was, by human standards, very late and the roads were nearly empty. He was glad for the directions from the voice in his vehicle. Glad that he had time to drive and think without the worry of being discovered following an all too diligent Darius.

Neferet had ordered that he thwart the forthcoming ritual and the death spell Thanatos meant to cast, though she'd made it clear he wasn't to kill any of the Priestesses in doing so. Aurox was not surprised that he was grateful for that one small caveat. For a moment while Neferet had been speaking her commands to him he'd believed she was going to task him with murdering Zoey. The thought had made him feel sick, although according to Priestess he did not have the ability to *feel* anything. He was a vessel. The emotions of others fueled his strength, but once used, the feelings were meant to dissipate.

Then why, since the moment he'd been alone with Zoey when she'd been weeping about her mother's death, did he still feel sadness, a deep, pressing despair, guilt, and recently something else, something new? Aurox felt loneliness.

He could almost hear Priestess's mocking laughter.

"Yes, I feel!" he shouted, and his voice echoed within the speeding vehicle, as if he was alone in a cave—always alone. "I do feel, even though Priestess says I do not." He smashed his fist in the dashboard, not minding that his knuckles split and the leather dented. "I feel *her* sadness. I feel *her* fear. I feel *her* loneliness. Why? Why does Zoey Redbird make me feel?"

We each decide what we are by the life choices we make. Thanatos's voice seemed to be there with him in the car. *Our actions define us, and will keep defining us until even after death.*

"I was created to serve Neferet." Could Thanatos be correct, even for a creature such as him?

More of the High Priestess's words came to him as if answering his question.

". . . the future need not be dictated by the past."

The voice in the car spoke then, dissipating Thanatos's wisdom. It told him to turn right and within half a mile he was to arrive at his destination. Aurox completed the turn, but then he steered the car through the ditch and did not stop it until he was sure it was parked well away from passing headlights and prying eyes. He got out of the car and, moving silently and quickly, Aurox paralleled the quaint gravel lane, which led to a modest home.

Aurox halted before he came to the home, and not just because he needed to use the concealment of the small orchard adjacent to the house and the large lavender field that framed it. He halted because of the sight of the scorched circle within the winter-sleeping herbs. He knew that burning. It was not from fire that the land was charred and the lavender destroyed. It was from a cold burn—a frigid destruction.

Darkness has been here. Aurox told himself. And then he understood. *Neferet and the white bull did this deed. They killed Zoey Redbird's mother.*

Something slipped inside him then, as if a wheel that had been stuck, struggling in the muck and the mud, had finally broken free. Aurox's legs felt weak, and he sat heavily with his back leaning against the rough bark of one of the trees, waiting . . . watching . . . but doing nothing.

Dragon

Looking up Zoey's home address had been quick and easy. Her grandmother's farm was only an hour or so away. He waited until the school bus left campus, and then followed slowly, being certain the ever-vigilant Darius did not notice him in the rearview mirror. Dragon didn't need to stay close to the bus. He knew where he was going. He knew what he must do.

Duty was everything.

His task was to keep the school and its students safe.

A dragon protects its own.

That's all he had left—the dragon.

> *"Your death has broken me*
> *The dragon is all I have left to be."*

His own words taunted him. "I was telling you the truth!" he shouted to the emptiness. "Anastasia, you're gone. I have nothing left except the dragon and my duty."

> *"If you are not my mate, kind and true,*
> *how will I ever again find you?"*

Anastasia's answer seemed to drift around him, bringing with it the fecund scent of the land bordering the mighty Mississippi River and a warm brush of humid, summer breezes where sunflowers nodded their heavy heads as if in approval.

"No!" he shouted, dispelling the memory. "That's all gone. *You're* gone. I have nothing left. I didn't make this choice, your Goddess did when she let you be taken from me because all those years ago I was merciful." He shook his head. "I will not make that same mistake again."

Ignoring the emptiness inside him, Dragon Lankford drove on.

Zoey

As we got closer and closer to Grandma's house I got more and more nervous. My stomach was killing me. I had a headache. My angelica wreath was crap. Stark had to help me finish it. Seriously. Stark. And that boy is not what you'd call skilled at braiding.

My mom is the truth. That's all I know.

"Remember," Thanatos said as we turned down Grandma's familiar lane. "Intent is important. We are here to reveal the truth so that we might bring about justice for a life cut short. Nothing more. Nothing less." She looked at me. "You can do this. You do not lack courage."

"Are you sure?"

She smiled just a little. "Your soul was shattered. That should have been a death sentence, yet you lived *and* you returned to yourself, bringing your Warrior with you. That has never before been done. You do not lack courage," she repeated.

Stark squeezed my hand. I nodded my head like I was agreeing with her, but inside I was shrieking a different truth: *If I'd been really courageous I would have been able to save Heath and my soul wouldn't have ever shattered and Stark wouldn't have needed rescuing!*

Thankfully, before any of that could slip out of my mouth and mess up everything Thanatos was trying to help us do, Darius stopped the bus and opened the door.

We all just sat there. Finally, Thanatos said, "Zoey, you must touch the earth first. It is your mother who was killed here."

I got up and, still clutching Stark's hand, climbed down the bus stairs.

We'd parked in front of Grandma's house. The bus looked weirdly out of place in the little gravel parking lot beside Grandma's Jeep.

I guess because I knew Grandma wasn't staying in her house during the seven-day cleansing ritual, I'd expected it to be dark and strange looking, but it was the opposite. Every room was lit. The place was so bright that I had to squint to look at it straight on. The windows twinkled like the glass had been newly polished. The big front porch was alight, too, showing comfy rocking chairs and little lemonade-ready tables.

And then Grandma was there, pulling me into her arms and filling my world with the scent of my childhood.

"Oh, *u-we-tsi-a-ge-ya,* it does my heart great joy to see you!" she said after she and I finally were able to let loose of each other.

She was wearing her favorite buckskin dress. I knew it was so old that she and her mom had worked together on the purple and green beadwork that decorated the bodice. She'd often told me the story of how when she was a girl, she'd traded one of the Wise Women of her tribe a belt she'd spent all one winter beading for the shells and glass beads that she'd threaded into the fringe on the sleeves and hem. I remembered when the dress was so pure white that I thought it looked like the clouds, but now it had yellowed. That should have made it old and shabby, but it didn't. To my eyes it made it look well loved and valuable beyond any price tag in a store or an auction war on eBay.

I also couldn't help but notice Grandma had lost weight and there were dark shadows under her expressive eyes.

"How are you doing, Grandma?"

"Better now, my daughter. And after tonight's ritual, I believe I will be even better yet." Grandma fisted her hand over her heart and respectfully bowed to Thanatos. "Blessed be, High Priestess."

"Blessed be, Sylvia Redbird. It is a pleasure to meet you face-to-face. I only wish it could be under different circumstances."

"As do I. I would love to sit and chat with Death," Grandma said, with a hint of the old sparkle in her eyes.

"You honor me," Thanatos said. "Though I do not claim to be Death. I only have an affinity for her."

"Her?" Grandma asked.

"It is a mother who brings each of us into this world. Does it not stand to reason it would be a mother who calls us to pass from this world as well?"

"Huh. I'd never thought of it like that," Shaunee said.

"It makes it seem kinda nice," Stevie Rae said.

"That depends on your mother," Aphrodite said.

"No, Prophetess. It depends on *the Mother,*" Thanatos corrected.

"Well, that's good news," Damien said. "My mom wasn't the nightmare Aphrodite's was, but she wasn't exactly nurturing, either."

"This conversation is interesting and everything, but shouldn't we be focusing on the spell?" Stark said. "Isn't anything else asking for problems?"

"Young Warrior, you are correct," Thanatos said. "Let us begin. Sylvia, please lead us to the spot where you discovered your daughter's body."

"Very well." Grandma only had to walk a few feet from where we were. The spot was super obvious. There, at the edge of the lavender field that flanked the north side of Grandma's house, backing to her lawn, was a perfect circle of burned plants. The entire ground was blackened and dead and horrible. Even the plants that framed the circle looked blighted and dying.

"There is no blood," Thanatos said, holding up her hand so that none of us actually entered the circle of destruction.

"That was one of the oddities the sheriff and his deputies could not explain," Grandma said.

Thanatos moved so that she stood directly in front of Grandma. She rested a hand on her shoulder, and I saw Grandma take a deep, gasping breath, as if the High Priestess had infused her with energy through her touch.

"I understand this is difficult. But the question is necessary. Exactly what was the manner of your daughter's death?"

Grandma drew another breath and then said in a clear, strong voice, "My daughter's throat was slit."

"Yet they found no blood on the earth surrounding her body?"

"No. None here. None on the porch. None in the house."

"And in her body itself? Was there blood remaining in her body?"

"The coroner's report said no. He also said it was impossible. That something more than just a neck slash happened to Linda, but all he had were questions and no answers. That's all anyone has had."

"Sylvia Redbird, we are here to get answers if you are strong enough to see them."

Grandma lifted her chin. "I am."

"Then so mote it be. All vampyre rituals begin with an altar to our Goddess at their center," Thanatos told us. I was thinking that we all already knew that, and then her next words stopped the question in my mind. "Sylvia, I would ask that you form the altar at the heart of this ritual. Are you willing to do that?"

"I am."

"Then so be it. You will enter the tainted ground at my side and show me exactly where you found your child. That will be the site of our altar and the center, the heart and spirit of our circle." She glanced at the rest of us. "No one else come within. Nyx's circle is not yet cast, but our intention is clearly set on this space. You will only cross its boundaries as each element is called." She looked from Stark to Darius and Rephaim. "Warriors, form a triangle outside and surround the circle." Thanatos pointed straight ahead of her. "Rephaim, that direction is north. Your place is there. Stark, take the position in the east. Darius, your place is west."

"Where do you want me?" Aphrodite asked.

"Outside the circle protecting the only position that remains—to the south."

"She is not a Warrior," Darius said.

"No, she is something more powerful, a Prophetess of our Goddess. Do you doubt her strength?"

Aphrodite put her fists on her hips and raised a blond brow at him.

"No. I would never doubt her strength," Darius said. And with a bow to Thanatos, he, Aphrodite, and the other Warriors moved to their places outside the circle.

Thanatos took Grandma's hand and, carrying her spellwork basket, she said, "Are you ready, Sylvia?"

Grandma nodded and said yes in Cherokee. "*Uh.*"

Together they stepped into the circle of destruction. Grandma led Thanatos to a spot just a little south of the center. She pointed. "Here was my daughter."

"Sit where your child once lay. Face north, the direction of the element earth, and represent the spirit of Nyx in this, a circle we would reclaim from destruction and through revealed truth make it our own."

Grandma nodded solemnly. She sat with a grace that had her buckskin dress fluttering softly. She was facing north, with her back to us, but I could see her chin was lifted and her shoulders were square and proud.

At that moment I was so proud of her I thought my heart would burst.

Thanatos placed her basket beside Grandma. She opened it and took out a beautiful piece of velvet fabric made of the same material as her cloak. She shook out the square and placed it on the ground in front of Grandma. Then she pulled out the angelica wreaths we'd braided. I was surprised by how beautiful they looked all stacked together, with the white flowers almost glowing against the sapphire velvet. Next she lifted a black velvet bag that I was sure I'd seen Anastasia using in class. If I was right, it would be filled with salt. She placed it and the five candles that represented each of the elements on the cloth, too. All were within reach of Grandma.

Thanatos faced us. Her voice carried easily in the night as if even the bugs and birds around us had paused to listen.

"The casting of this circle will be unusual, as our ritual is really a spell within a ritual within a circle, though we will begin with air and end with spirit. When I call each of you, approach our altar. Give Sylvia the item that symbolizes the truth about yourself you wish to reveal. Speak your truth to her. In turn she will give you the proper candle. Then move to your spot around the circle."

"Are you going to call the elements then?" I asked, not sure if I was leading the casting of the circle or not.

"You and I will both cast this circle, young Priestess," she said. "I will incant the spell and bind it with salt. You will light the candles. My intent is that when spirit is called and the circle set, the next words I speak will, with the help of all the elements—especially earth—cast our spell and invoke Death."

"Okay," I said. I looked at my friends and they nodded. "We're ready."

"Damien, come to the altar and represent your element, air."

I heard Damien take a deep breath before he stepped inside the circle of ruined lavender and approached Grandma.

"What is it you wish to reveal to spirit?" Thanatos asked.

Damien reached into the man purse he always had slung over his shoulder and pulled out a MAC pressed powder compact. He opened it and the moonlight caught it, showing a fragmented surface and a shattered reflection. As he gave it to Grandma he said, "I brought a broken mirror because even though I might look and act like I'm okay, I secretly wonder if Jack's death has forever broken something inside me."

Grandma placed the compact on the altar cloth and then gave Damien the yellow air candle. She touched his hand as she did and said, "I hear you, child." Damien moved to Grandma's right and took the eastern place at the edge of the circle.

"My turn," Shaunee said softly, and then she went to Grandma. When she reached her she gave her a long white feather she'd been cupping in her hand. "This feather symbolizes that even though I've been afraid to be alone for a really long time, I want to be free of that fear."

Grandma placed the feather beside Damien's broken mirror and gave Shaunee her red candle. "I hear you, child," she said, touching her hand gently, kindly, just as she had Damien.

Erin didn't say anything. She walked quickly to Grandma and handed her the little insulated bag she'd brought on the bus. Grandma opened it, reached in, and pulled out an ice cube.

"This is me inside. I'm frozen, like I don't really have any feelings."

Grandma took the ice and added it to the other items on the altar cloth. She gave Erin her blue candle, touching her gently and saying, "I hear you, child." Blank-faced, Erin moved to the western edge of the circle.

"Wish me luck," Stevie Rae whispered.

"Luck," I said softly.

She went to Grandma and smiled down at her. "Hi, Grandma."

"Hello, child of the earth." Grandma returned her smile. "What do you wish to reveal to me?"

Stevie Rae took a piece of paper out of her jeans pocket. It was black, like the construction paper we used to get in grade school to cut stuff out of during art class. She gave it to Grandma saying, "This paper is like my fear of losing Rephaim to something dark and scary that I don't really understand."

Grandma unfolded the black paper and smoothed it onto the altar cloth. She gave Stevie Rae the green candle, a soft touch, and said, "I hear you, child."

Before Stevie Rae took her place in the north, Thanatos picked up the braided circles of angelica and placed them on Stevie Rae's head.

"The truth reveal from earth through thee. So we shall ask, and so mote it be."

"Thank you. I'll do my best," Stevie Rae said solemnly, and then she took her place in the circle.

It was my turn. *Nyx, please help me be strong enough to handle what I see tonight.* I went to Grandma. She smiled and said, "What is it you have to reveal to me, *u-we-tsi-a-ge-ya*?"

I'd left my purse on the bus, but first I'd taken my symbol thing out of it. From my jeans pocket I brought out a hair tie. It was one of those wrapped rubber bands that weren't supposed to pull out your hair when you used them, but they never really worked. I handed it to Grandma. "Almost all the time now I feel like I'm being pulled in a bunch of different directions by a bunch of different people. I think sometimes I'm going to snap like a rubber band and shatter all over again. This time forever."

Grandma slowly placed my hair tie on the altar cloth. When she gave me my purple candle she cupped my hands with both of hers. Her voice shook only a little when she said, "I hear you, child."

I stepped behind Grandma then, staying in the center of the circle, and looked to Thanatos for my next move.

From the spellwork basket the High Priestess took a long box of wooden matches. She lifted the bag of salt and told me, "You may leave your candle on the altar. Your grandmother serves as keeper of the spirit until you evoke your element."

I put the candle in the middle of the little circle Grandma had made of the things we'd each given her. I bent and kissed her soft cheek. "No matter what we see tonight, remember that I love you and that we still have each other," I said.

Grandma hugged me and I thought she was going to kiss my cheek. Instead she whispered, "*U-we-tsi-a-ge-ya*, beware. I feel eyes watching from the shadows."

Before I could say anything, Thanatos was giving me the matches as well as my final instructions. "I will stay to your left so that you lead the physical casting of the circle, but as we approach each element I will call it. The reveal spell is woven within the elemental call. As we move around the circle I will bind the spell with salt and, if she listens, invoke Death." Thanatos raised her voice, directing her words to my waiting friends. "With a circle this strong I would expect quite a tangible response to my invocation. Prepare yourselves, and remember, this ritual is not something done to you, but rather done with you." Then she lifted her hands and intoned, *"Let us begin as we intend to end—we seek the truth so that this land, these people, can mend."*

Together Thanatos and I walked to Damien who was clutching his yellow candle with both hands and looking as nervous as I felt.

All right, here we go, I thought. *Please help me, Nyx. I can't do this without you.*

CHAPTER TWENTY-EIGHT

Neferet

The shadows were agitated. Something was very wrong.

"Read the next chapter in your sociology book. I have business to which I must attend." Neferet snapped the command to her very surprised-looking fifth hour students before hurrying from the classroom. She cloaked herself in mist and darkness so that prying eyes and all too curious professors would not witness her passage as she hurried to her private chamber. There she quickly slashed her hand. Cupping her palm she held it out in offering. "Drink! Tell me what is amiss!"

The tendrils of Darkness swarmed her blood, latching onto her leach-like. As they fed, whispered words from many different voices filled her mind.

> *The vessel does nothing to hinder earth*
> *Joined with spirit the death vision will be given rebirth*

"What?" Anger filled Neferet. "Is Aurox not there? Was he too stupid to find the farm?"

> *The vessel is there*
> *He watches without care*

"Force him to act! Make him stop the damn ritual!" The tendril voices all babbled at once, forming a stew of confusion in her mind.

She closed her palm and slapped them away. "Do as I command! You've had your blood."

The myriad of whispering voices were abruptly cut off as the specter of the white bull materialized in the middle of her chamber. The image was transparent and not fully formed, but his voice, powerful and obviously irritated, blasted through her mind. *I have told you before your sacrifice must be equal to the command!*

With an effort, Neferet stifled her own anger and, with soft, placating words she spoke to the ghostly apparition, "But the vessel was a gift from you. Why would it take a great sacrifice to control a creature created from Darkness? I don't even understand why he is deviating from my command."

I warned you at his creation that the sacrifice used to form him was not perfect and so the vessel would be flawed.

"Well, I can tell you that recently I've begun to doubt his intelligence."

It could be he is thinking for himself rather than not at all.

"So, he's lazy? I gave him a task and he's doing nothing!" Neferet paused, controlled her temper, and then sighed dramatically. "It isn't that I mind so much for myself, but it seems disrespectful to you."

Ah, my heartless one, it touches me that your concern is on my behalf. Perhaps the vessel does need prompting.

"If you prompt him, you would have my thanks." Neferet curtseyed deeply to the apparition.

For you, my threads will force his actions. Still, they require an appropriate sacrifice.

Trying not to sound as annoyed as she felt, Neferet said, "Very well. What sacrifice do they require?"

The vessel is a beast, thus a beast must be sacrificed to control it.

"A beast? A Raven Mocker?"

No, the sacrifice must be a creature allied with you.

Neferet felt ill. "Skylar? I must sacrifice my cat?"

If it troubles you so, choose another. There are many felines about this place, are there not . . .

With those words, the specter of the white bull wavered and then dissipated. With a look of cold determination, Neferet took the razor-edged athame from her dresser, opened the door to her chamber, and began summoning the perfect sacrifice. It would not be Skylar—he was not a Warrior's cat. His death wouldn't be imbued with the appropriate violence. No, there was only one feline whose death would suit this need. Cloaked in mist and shadow, Neferet glided into the night . . .

Zoey

"Come air, sweet, soft touch of Nyx breath divine."

From the very first sentence of Thanatos's spell, I knew that this wasn't going to be like any circle I'd ever before experienced. First of all, the High Priestess's voice had changed. It wasn't that she shouted or anything like that, but there was something about the singsong cadence of the spell that lent power to her voice so that her words seemed to be alive and surrounding us. As she continued to speak that power bled out into the space around us. It sizzled across my skin and down my body. I could see Damien's gooseflesh raised on his arms, and I knew the others were being affected by it, too.

> *"Blow from this place concealing shadows past*
> *It is death's shade to view we do incline*
> *Death revealed through this circle spell we cast."*

With a flourish of her hands Thanatos gestured for Damien to lift his candle. The Priestess nodded at me and I struck the match, lit the wick, and said, "Air, please join our circle."

There was a mighty *whoosh!* and whipping wind swirled around us, lifting my hair and making Thanatos's cloak billow.

"To fire," she told me, and I walked doceil or clockwise to Shaunee. Her brown eyes were big and round, and she was staring behind us. Remembering Grandma's warning, I glanced back and gasped in astonishment. A glowing length of scarlet light snaked from Damien, outlining the circle and tracing our path from him to Shaunee.

I was used to the silver thread that often appeared when I cast a circle, but this was different. Yeah, it was powerful, but it also felt ominous. I didn't know if Thanatos saw it or not; I didn't know if it was a good or bad sign that it was there, but I didn't want to interrupt the High Priestess's spell as she was already beginning the fire invocation.

> *"Come fire, your blaze must be strong, sure, and true*
> *Strike, burn, destroy what would prevent our sight*
> *Force violent death revealed to us anew*
> *Your illumating flame expose with truth's light."*

At her gesture, Shaunee lifted the red candle and I lit it saying, "Fire, please join our circle."

It was as if we were suddenly standing inside an inferno. Flames shot from Shaunee's body, filling the already charred circle, but this fire didn't add to the destruction. Instead I heard a massive hissing and from everywhere that had been dead and blighted mist lifted, as if fire had met ice and not earth.

Then air joined fire and the flames and mist flew up into the sky to streak and flash.

"Lightning." Shaunee's voice sounded hushed and awed. "Air mixed with fire is making lightning."

"To water," Thanatos said.

The thick rope of glowing scarlet followed us.

When we stopped in front of Erin I thought she looked scared, but she nodded and said, "Bring it on. I'm ready."

Thanatos spoke:

> *"Come water, flow throughout this circle space*
> *With tide of truth wash clear sight-stealing time*
> *Allowing us to see death's tear-streaked face*
> *Violence cleansed sets us free of evil's grime."*

Erin lifted the candle to meet my match as I said, "Water, please join our circle."

There was a roar as if we'd suddenly been transported into the middle of a waterfall. The night turned brilliant shades of blue and turquoise and sapphire—all the colors of water. The element gushed into the blackened circle. Water swirled around like an angry whirl-pool and then, just like air and fire, it gushed straight up into the lightning-streaked sky. Clouds billowed and roiled—thunder clapped, growling with such fierceness that I cringed.

"No," Erin said quickly. "Water's not mad at us."

"Neither is fire," Shaunee said.

"Nor wind," Damien added.

"The elements are outraged at the act that was committed here," Thanatos said. "Prepare yourself, circle. We move to earth."

With thunderclouds multiplying above us and lightning illuminating the gathering storm, I moved to stand in front of Stevie Rae.

"Time to cowboy up," she said.

Thanatos nodded and spoke the earth invocation:

> *"Come earth, rich, verdant truly Goddess blessed*
> *Your bosom nurtures and keeps this spell's key*
> *Open here and dark death will be confessed*
> *For the wound in your heart, justice we'll see."*

Stevie Rae lifted the green candle to my flame. "Earth, please join our circle."

The ground beneath our feet began shaking as if we were standing in the middle of an earthquake. I couldn't help the little shriek that slipped from my mouth.

"Zoey!" Stark yelled. I could see him staggering, trying to reach the circle, which was now completely ringed with a thick rope of red.

"Wait, it's okay!" Stevie Rae shouted above the cacophony of angry elements. "Like the other element, earth isn't mad at us. It's not gonna hurt us. Look, it's making the ground new."

I looked down and saw that she was right. The ground that had been washed clean by water had shifted, rolled, until instead of ashes and the remnants of blighted plants, the rich red Oklahoma earth lay newly exposed.

"See, it's being made right," Stevie Rae said. As she spoke, the tremors gentled and then stopped completely.

"We must finish the circle and the spell," Thanatos said. "Call spirit, Zoey. Now."

Aurox

From his hidden place within the orchard Aurox watched the glowing scarlet circle form. Its power was awe-inspiring; the might of the elements was incredible to behold. He could feel the emotions air, fire, water, and earth evoked in the fledglings and vampyre who embodied them. Joy and courage and righteous indignation filled the circle and boiled over to wash through him.

Aurox could use the energy to change—to morph into the creature that would emerge from him, attack Rephaim as had been his command from Neferet, and most certainly disrupt the spell the High Priestess had almost fully cast.

He stared at Zoey. Radiant, she turned to the old woman who sat in the middle of the circle. Aurox knew once Thanatos evoked the final element, spirit, and Zoey lit the purple candle, the circle would be complete and the reveal spell would be set fully into motion.

If it was going to be stopped he had to act now.

He stood, warring with himself.

I was created to serve Neferet. She serves Darkness.

Before him the elemental Light of the Goddess glistened and expanded, so clean and bright, especially compared to what had been soiled by Darkness and destruction.

I should not stop this! Deep within him his spirit was crying out for him not to hinder. Instead to wait, to bear witness, to—

Pain exploded through Aurox as tendrils of Darkness whipped around him. Thick and sticky they spread, web-like, across his body. Aurox gasped as his skin began absorbing things, melting into the creature that rested within him, and awakening it. Helpless to stop himself, Aurox felt the bull emerge. The creature took control of his body. *I knew only one thing, Neferet's last command: attack Rephaim.*

Head lowered, glistening, deadly horns fully formed, Aurox charged Rephaim.

Zoey

Thanatos and I moved slowly and carefully to stand before Grandma, who was sitting, unharmed, in the center of the elemental tumult. Her face was pale, but her hands were completely steady as she lifted the purple candle.

Thanatos began the spirit invocation:

> *"Come spirit, faithful, eternal and wise*
> *Sealed with salt we ask the truth to reveal*
> *Lost years, wasted tears you felt Linda's cries*
> *Darkness be gone! Spirit's strength we shall feel."*

I was striking the match to light the purple candle when Stevie Rae's shout disrupted everything.

"Rephaim! Look out!"

I glanced up in time to see Dragon Lankford burst out of the shadows. Sword upraised, he was sprinting toward Rephaim.

"Trust me!" Dragon yelled. "Get down!"

"No!" Stevie Rae screamed.

Rephaim didn't hesitate. Not even for an instant. He dropped to his knees as if he was sacrificing himself to Dragon's sword. I wanted to puke. I heard Aphrodite shriek something about *I told you so!* but I couldn't look at her. I was absolutely sure the Sword Master was going to cut the boy in two. I couldn't stop staring at the train wreck that was happening to Rephaim.

Dragon leaped over Rephaim's kneeling body and with a terrible screeching sound his sword collided with the razor edge of the bull-like creature's horns. At the last moment he managed to deflect the deathblow from Rephaim, but the creature's momentum was too much—his body was too powerful. Not even Dragon could stop the impact. Rephaim disappeared, not gored but knocked aside with such force that he was airborne for what seemed like ages, and when he finally landed it was far from our circle and he did not move.

"Oh, Goddess, no!" Stevie Rae sobbed. "Rephaim!"

I saw that she was turning, moving to step out of the circle and go to Rephaim.

"Do not break the circle! It is what Darkness wants; do that and any sacrifice here is made for nothing!" I couldn't see Aphrodite, but in her voice echoed a majesty that I knew Stevie Rae recognized because instead of breaking the circle she dropped to her knees, exactly as Rephaim had only moments before. Stevie Rae bowed her head and, in a broken voice said, "Nyx, I trust in your mercy. Please, protect my Rephaim."

The bull-thing turned and, tearing the earth with his hooves, he charged Rephaim again.

Dragon Lankford moved almost as preternaturally fast as the creature. He was there in time, standing between death and Rephaim. Lifting his sword he said, "A Sword Master of Nyx is here. I will protect Rephaim."

Dragon clashed with the beast again. It battered him back, but in doing so Dragon was moving him away from Rephaim's unconscious body. Then, snarling a frightening sound, the creature turned its head so that I could see its bestial face—and I felt like I'd been kicked in the gut. The creature's eyes glowed with moonstones. I knew the thing was Aurox—fully changed and absolutely, totally, no longer human.

"Warriors, rally to me!" Dragon shouted as he faced Aurox's next attack.

"Zoey, you must summon spirit and light the candle!" Thanatos grabbed my shoulders, turned me to face her and shook me. Hard. "Dragon will battle the beast. We must hold true to the circle and complete the spell or there is no hope for any of them."

Any of them? Where was Stark? Where was Darius? I looked wildly around. My gaze passed over and through them before I actually understood what I saw. They were there, both of them, standing in the positions they had taken before we'd begun casting the circle, but they couldn't help Dragon. They couldn't even help themselves. Darius and Stark, my Warrior, my Guardian, were frozen zombies. Mouths open in silent screams of agony their eyes stared sightlessly at nothing.

"Threads of Darkness encase them," Thanatos said, still gripping my shoulders. "Open the circle so that I may complete the spell. We need the power of Death and all five elements to battle this evil."

"Zoeybird, do as she says." Grandma lifted the purple candle.

With shaking hands I lit the match and yelled, "Spirit, join our circle!"

Thanatos raised her arms. Flinging salt around us she spoke the final words of the spell:

> *"Death's dark door I command open to me*
> *The truth Darkness has hidden we shall see!"*

The scarlet rope expanded and with a deafening roar it funneled up and up, creating a chaos of glowing red that illuminated the bruised storm clouds filling the swollen sky above us.

"Keep control of your elements! Remember our intent!" Thanatos yelled. "Begin with air!"

Damien lifted both of his hands and in a strong, sure voice called, "Air, blow from this place concealing shadows past!"

A gale blew from Damien. It captured the chaotic red glow and changed it into a cone of swirling, concentrated energy.

"Fire!" Thanatos commanded.

Shaunee lifted her hands, shouting, "Fire, strike, burn, destroy what would prevent our sight!"

Lightning sizzled, magnet-like, drawn to the center of the glowing cone.

"Water!"

Erin's arms weren't lifted. Instead she was pointing to the spot where Grandma had found Mom's body. "Water, with tide of truth wash clear sight-stealing time!"

Crack! A bolt spiked from the sky, striking the ground. As the earth opened, water rushed up from it, rippling in the red earth like a pool of blood.

"Earth!"

Stevie Rae, still on her knees, was staring at the battle Dragon waged with Aurox, watching it circle ever closer and closer to Rephaim's still body. She was crying and her voice shook, but her words rang across the circle, carried by the power of her heartache. "Earth, your bosom nurtures and keeps this spell's key."

The water rippled. Images lifted from the pool's depths as if the earth was vomiting them, but they wavered and were unclear, just unrecognizable glimpses of faces and vaguely human forms.

"Spirit!" Thanatos called.

My mouth opened and through me, spirit recited the correct words from the revealing spell. "Lost years, wasted tears you felt my mom's cries. Spirit, release the truth before our eyes!"

Instantly, everything outside the circle—Aurox and Dragon, Darius and Stark and Aphrodite—ceased to exist for me. The only thing that was real was what was being revealed within the pool. The water cleared and, as if it was happening before my eyes I saw my mom on Grandma's front porch. She answered the door, smiling but looking kinda confused. Then the scene expanded and the point of view changed and I could see Neferet, naked, standing on the other side of the open door, asking if Sylvia Redbird was home. I heard Grandma sob and I wanted to run to the pool of water, to stand between it and Grandma—to try and shield her from the grisly, unbearable vision I knew it was going to expose.

But I couldn't move.

"No, wait." Panicked, I looked down. The red glow that had outlined our circle had expanded. It carpeted the entire space, engulfing each of us. "This is too much! I don't want Grandma to—"

"You cannot stop it," Thanatos said. "Death has put this spell in motion. Only death can release us."

Grandma managed to lift her arm. She slid her hand in mine. Trapped by the power of death unleashed through the elements, we saw everything. Neferet bound my mother with sticky, whip-like threads of black and then she slit her throat and let the threads drag her from the porch. In the middle of a blighted circle, the white bull of Darkness drank from her until the threads surrounding him were swollen and bloated. After Mom was dead and drained of blood, Neferet, laughing, mounted the beast and they disappeared together.

"It is true," Thanatos said. "Neferet's Consort is Darkness."

Then Stevie Rae cried, "Help Rephaim! The bull's gonna kill him!" I looked from the disappearing vision in the pool to Stevie Rae. I only had time to wonder why the hell she was on her cell phone before the world around me exploded into sound and blood.

CHAPTER TWENTY-NINE

Kalona

Rephaim hadn't told him. His son had let him believe the Goddess had forgiven him, and in doing so she'd gifted him with the form of a human boy.

Rephaim hadn't mentioned that he'd been condemned to be a bird, a beast who could only long for something that was, with a creature's mind, forever unattainable.

"At least for the hours of daylight it is unattainable," Kalona said, pacing across the top of the ridge.

"Help you, we will?"

Kalona's anger exploded at the hissing, semi-human sound of his *other* son's voice. He turned on Nisroc, raising his hand to cuff him into silence. The Raven Mockers who were clustered around scurried back, out of his reach. Nisroc cringed, but remained near and did not try to escape his father's wrath.

Mid-swing, Kalona hesitated. He let his fist drop to his side. He stared at his silent son who crouched, waiting for the blow.

"Why?" Kalona allowed the desperation he was feeling to be heard in his voice. "Why would you want to help me?"

Nisroc raised his head. There was confusion in his red gaze. "You are Father."

"But I have not been a good father," Kalona heard himself say.

Nisroc's gaze remained steady on his. "That mattersss not. Ssstill you are Father."

Utterly defeated, Kalona could only shake his head, and in a voice gentled by emotions he barely understood, he said, "You cannot help me with this." Kalona gestured to the sky. "Go on. It is full dark now. You may stretch your wings and ride the sky without being seen. Just be back before dawn."

They didn't hesitate. They leaped from the ridge, and with raven cries took to the sky.

He didn't realize Nisroc had not left with the rest of them until he spoke. His son's voice was unusually soft. Perhaps it was the softness of it that made him sound so human. "Help you, I would."

Kalona looked at his son. "Thank you," he said.

Nisroc bowed his head as if his father's words were as tangible as the blow he'd almost received.

Kalona cleared his throat, and looked away from the creature he'd created in anger and lust. "Go on. Join your brothers. I command it of you."

"Yesss, Father."

Kalona listened to Nisroc's wings beat against the wind. He tilted his head up so that he could watch his son disappear into the night.

It was when he was alone that the phone began to ring. Feeling decidedly foolish, he lifted the thing from the rock he'd left it on the night before. The display said STEVIE RAE. Without hesitation Kalona tapped the accept button and put the phone to his ear.

"Help Rephaim! The bull's gonna kill him!" The Red One's voice shouted above a terrible swell of sounds.

There was a crackle of static and the connection went dead.

Kalona's body was moving before his mind fully processed his decision. He launched himself into the air, gathering with him the ethereal wisps that drifted from the Otherworld to form invisible currents in the mortal sky.

"I call upon the power of the spirit of ancient immortals, which is mine by birthright to command. Take me to the blood of my blood, the son of my spirit. Take me to Rephaim!"

Zoey

"Help Rephaim! The bull's gonna kill him!" Stevie Rae screamed and dropped the phone, which was instantly engulfed in the scarlet glow. She tried to get to her feet and go to Rephaim, but her body was trapped within the circle's power. Desperately, she yelled at me, "Close the circle! Let me help him!"

I didn't hesitate. We'd seen the truth of Mom's murder. The circle could be closed. "Spirit, earth, water, fire, air—I release you!"

But my words made no difference. The red glow still imprisoned us.

"What's happening?" Stevie Rae was sobbing and struggling futilely to stand.

"Death has put this spell in motion," Thanatos repeated. She sounded sad, resigned. "Only death can release it."

"You represent death. You release us!" I said.

"I cannot." She looked old and defeated. "Forgive me."

"No! That's not good enough. You have to—"

Before I could complete the words, Aurox lowered his horrible head to charge at Rephaim again. Bleeding and battered, Dragon Lankford staggered between the boy and the creature, taking the blow meant for Rephaim. Aurox's horn caught Dragon in the middle of his chest, lifting him off his feet as the bull gored completely through the Sword Master. Aurox stepped back, shaking his head so that Dragon's body came loose and slid to the ground. We watched Dragon shudder, cough, and with his last breath he looked toward our circle and said, "If only death can release you, then my death releases you . . ."

Aurox roared his victory and circled around Dragon to resume his attack on Rephaim.

But Dragon's death changed everything. The red glow lifted from the circle. It went so high that it seemed to touch the moon. In the sky it exploded and a pure silver mist fell back to earth bathing everything gently in a warm, spring-scented rain.

The instant she was released Stevie Rae ran forward, calling, "Earth, come to me! Protect Rephaim!"

But the green glow that appeared instantly around Rephaim wasn't needed. As the silver rain washed over the bull, the creature's body jerked and twitched and then stumbled. I blinked and wiped my face, trying to clear my vision, but I realized there was nothing wrong with my sight. The bull-thing *was* melting, changing, shifting, and within moments Aurox, the boy who'd saved me from the falling branch, was standing in his place.

He blinked several times and looked around as if he was confused, as if he didn't know where he was.

"Stay away from him!" Stevie Rae snarled at Aurox as she stood between him and Rephaim. Her hands were glowing green.

Aurox took a hesitant step back, shaking his head. He was looking around, still obvious dazed. I saw the moment his gaze found Dragon's gored body.

"No!" Aurox said. "No." He looked from the Sword Master's battered body and his gaze found me. "Zoey! I *chose* a different future. I did!"

Then Stark and Darius were there, descending on him with swords raised. Aurox was still shaking his head and saying over and over again, "I chose a new future . . . I chose a new future . . ." but no matter what his words said, I could see that his body was beginning to ripple again. He was shifting back into the bull. Stark and Darius were going to kill him.

Darkness does not always equate to evil; light does not always bring good. See with true sight, child . . . see with true sight . . .

Nyx's voice filled my mind and I knew what I had to do. I lifted the seer stone from where it hung between my breasts, drew a deep breath, and looked through it at Aurox.

Seen through the stone the boy's body radiated a moonstone glow from its center, near his heart. The glow expanded until it shielded Aurox completely. And then I realized what the glow actually was—it was the image of another body, one that was ghostly, ethereal, and it wasn't so much shielding Aurox as overshadowing him because it was so bright.

And familiar.

"Heath!" I screamed his name. Aurox, already partially changed into the creature, swung his head around to look at me. The glowing vision of Heath moved with him and, just for an instant, our gazes met. I saw Heath's eyes widen in surprise. "Earth!" I borrowed from the elemental energy Stevie Rae had already manifested. "Protect Aurox. Don't let Stark and Darius hurt him!" Some of the green glow that hovered around Rephaim spread through the ground and then lifted in front of Aurox, forming a wall between him and the two Warriors.

"Zoey, what in the hell are you doing?" Stark said, trying to get around the wall of protection.

"I know what I'm doing," I told Stark, but my gaze never left Aurox. But Aurox wasn't human anymore. The creature was fully formed and the image of Heath was gone. The beast roared with rage and agony and despair, dropped his head, and charged directly at me.

I know it was moronic, but I didn't move. Instead I kept staring into his eyes and sounding way more calm and certain than I felt as I said, "You won't hurt me. I know you won't."

At the last instant Aurox veered to the side. Missing my body by inches, he passed so close to me that I could smell the blood and death on him, and feel the brush of his skin. Then he disappeared into the night.

I don't know whether it was adrenaline or stupidity that had kept me on my feet up 'til then, but both suddenly deserted me and I went down smack on my butt. The green wall disappeared and Stark ran to me.

"Are you hurt? Are you okay? What the hell is wrong with you?" Stark crouched beside me and fired questions at me as he ran his hands all over my body. "Are you bleeding?"

I grabbed his hands, holding tight to him, hoping he couldn't tell how badly my own hands were shaking. "I'm fine. Really."

"You're stupid. Really," Aphrodite said, looking down her nose at me. "Seriously, Z. It's either that or you're delusional. Bullboy is not Heath."

"Hell no he's not Heath," Stark said, looking at Aphrodite like she'd lost her mind.

So he didn't hear me. Good, maybe no one else heard me. I can handle

Aphrodite. Later. Just then I ignored her, which was easy because Grandma was hurrying up looking as worried as Stark. "Did he harm you?"

I tugged on Stark's hands and he helped me up. Then I hugged Grandma. "No, I'm okay."

She gave me a reassuring squeeze and *didn't* call me stupid. Instead she said, "Rephaim is not."

"Uh-oh." Damien, Erin, and Shaunee had joined Stevie Rae where she knelt at Rephaim's side. We started over to them. Under her breath, Aphrodite said, "This is gonna be bad. *Really* bad."

I meant to keep my eyes from looking at Dragon's body, but they didn't listen to me. He'd fallen not far from Rephaim. Just seeing his face I would have thought he was sleeping. I mean, except for the trickle of blood from the corner of his mouth he actually looked more at peace than he had since Anastasia's death. It was his body that was a disaster. Both arms had wounds in them. Aurox's horn had ripped through the fabric of his pants leaving one of his thighs a hamburger meat–looking mess. His chest was a terrible thing to see. His ribs had splintered around the hole. From his chest down, blood was everywhere.

I was standing there, staring, when Thanatos's velvet cloak swirled into view. She'd unclasped the brooch that held it over her shoulders and, with a flourish, the High Priestess covered Dragon's body. She had an odd expression on her face, and I was trying to figure out what was going on, when she spoke.

"You may move on now. You were destined to either die this night with your oath reclaimed, your path true—or to emerge from this night with your body alive, but your spirit dead to all that is honorable." Thanatos smiled, and I realized her expression looked odd because she was talking to the air *above* Dragon's body. "By sacrificing yourself for Rephaim you found mercy again, and through it, our Goddess." Thanatos made a sweeping gesture up with her arm, and I thought she looked incredibly graceful and totally beautiful. "There is your path. Move on to the Otherworld and your new future."

Then I gasped as the sky above Thanatos shivered. Night parted and a familiar tree came into view. It was green and lush, a rowan and hawthorn twined together. The pieces of cloth that were tied to its massive umbrella of branches kept changing colors and lengths as they waved gently in a warm breeze that smelled of earth and moss and springtime.

"The Goddess's hanging tree," Stark whispered.

"You can see it, too?" I murmured to him.

"Yeah," he said.

"So can I," Aphrodite said.

"As can I," Darius said—and all around me my friends nodded and whispered and stared in wonderment as a girl stepped from behind the tree. She was blond and smiling, and looked super gorgeous in a long skirt the color of blue topaz that had glass beads and shells and white leather fringe all around its hem and the neckline of the sleeveless, matching top. She was carrying a single sunflower.

"It's Anastasia!" Damien said.

"She's so young," I blurted, and then closed my mouth, worried that I'd say something to shatter the vision.

But Anastasia didn't seem to see us. Her attention was completely captivated by the young man who strode into view. His hair was long and thick and tied back and his brown eyes sparkled with unshed tears.

"It's Dragon," Shaunee said.

"No," Thanatos corrected her. "It's Bryan, her Bryan."

The young Bryan Lankford touched Anastasia's face reverently. "My own," he said.

"*My* own," she said. "I knew you would find yourself again."

"And in doing so, I found you." Smiling, he pulled her into his arms and as their lips met the sky shimmered again and the doorway to the Otherworld closed.

Stark handed me a balled-up Kleenex he pulled from his jeans pocket. I blew my nose.

"Is Rephaim gonna die now, too?"

Stevie Rae's question pulled us firmly back to earth. I turned to see that she was still kneeling beside Rephaim. I was close enough now to see that he was bleeding from a deep gash in his head. He looked pale and still—too still.

"Your affinity is Death," Stevie Rae continued. Wiping tears from her face with the back of her hand, she stared at Thanatos. "So, tell me the truth. Is Rephaim gonna die?"

There was a giant whooshing sound and Kalona dropped from the sky. Stark and Darius instantly raised their weapons and moved to stand between Aphrodite and me, and the immortal. But Kalona didn't even glance at us. He hurried to Rephaim.

"You're too late!" Stevie Rae yelled at him. "I called, but you came too late."

Kalona looked from his son to Stevie Rae. "I did not hesitate. I came at your call." Then he utterly shocked me by kneeling beside Stevie Rae. Slowly, he reached around her and touched his son's face. "He lives."

"Not for long," Thanatos said gently. "Take what time is left to say your farewells. Death has marked Rephaim for her own."

Kalona's amber gaze seemed to skewer the High Priestess. The power in his voice was as terrible as was his grief. "Death cannot have him! He is *my* son, and I am an immortal. He cannot die."

"Did you not renounce him and name him no longer your child?"

The pain that flashed across Kalona's face was heartbreaking. I could see that he was trying to speak, but the words wouldn't come.

Stevie Rae touched the immortal's arm. His gaze turned to her.

"We all say things we don't mean sometimes, 'specially when we're mad. If you didn't mean it, why don't you try just sayin' you're sorry?" She looked from the immortal to his son. "Tell Rephaim. Maybe he'll hear you." Then she scooted back, leaving Kalona by himself, kneeling beside Rephaim.

Kalona leaned forward and pulled his son to him, so that Rephaim rested across his lap. The immortal looked down at him for what seemed like a very long time and then, in a voice unsteady with emotion he said, "Rephaim, I am sorry. You are my son. You will always be my son. Forgive me for my anger and my foolishness." And then Nyx's fallen Warrior closed his eyes, bowed his head, and added, "Goddess, please. Do not let him pay for my mistakes."

A single tear tracked down Kalona's cheek and fell onto Rephaim's forehead and the bloody wound that gaped there. There was a flash of light, so brilliant and pure that I was blinded for a moment. As I blinked the dots from my vision I saw Rephaim take a deep breath and open his eyes. The gash on his forehead was gone. He looked a little baffled. Kalona moved awkwardly to help him sit up on his own, which Rephaim did easily. Rephaim's smile was tentative, but he sounded perfectly normal when he said, "Hello, Father. When did you get here?"

Stevie Rae wrapped her arms around Rephaim and hugged him hard, but her face was tilted up so that it was obvious she was speaking to Kalona when she said, "Just in time. Your daddy got here just in time."

Kalona stood. At that moment he wasn't an alluring, powerful, downright scary immortal. He was just a dad who didn't have a clue what to say to his kid.

"The Red One—" Kalona paused, and then began again. "Stevie Rae called. I came."

First Rephaim smiled, and then his happiness faltered as he obviously remembered. "Dragon. Where is he? He wasn't trying to hurt me. I know he wasn't."

Stevie Rae bit her lip. Tears spilled from her eyes as she said, "Yeah, we know. Dragon saved you from Aurox."

"Aurox? Neferet's creature? He was here?" Kalona asked.

"He was. He tried to kill your son and disrupt the reveal ritual. Dragon Lankford gave his life to save him," Thanatos said.

All of our eyes went to Dragon's shrouded body.

I didn't know what to say. How the hell was I going to explain to them that I'd really seen Heath's soul inside Aurox? And what the hell was I going to do about it?

"You must know that Neferet has allied herself with Darkness," Kalona said.

"I do," Thanatos agreed. "And the Vampyre High Council will now know it, as well."

"What's going to happen?" I asked Thanatos.

"Neferet will be stripped of her title of High Priestess and shunned by all vampyres," Thanatos said.

"She will fight," Kalona said grimly. "And she has powerful allies in Darkness, her creature, and the Red Ones who follow her."

"Then we will defend ourselves," Thanatos said.

"Does that mean you are staying in Tulsa? Or are you going to return to your Italian isle and leave these children to battle Darkness?" Kalona asked.

Thanatos narrowed her eyes at him. "The Tulsa House of Night has a new High Priestess, and she is Death."

Kalona stared at Thanatos, then he looked from her to his son. I could see the indecision on his face and I figured he was getting ready to fly away—actually the thought passed my mind that even though he'd said sorry to Rephaim and seemed to have a truce with us, we couldn't *really* be sure he wasn't still involved with Neferet. I mean, I'd believed in him before and Heath had died because of it.

But when the immortal finally moved it wasn't because he was flying away. He strode over to Thanatos, and then he knelt on one knee and said, "It seems your House of Night will also need a new Sword Master. I pledge myself body, heart, and soul to protect you, High Priestess. I believe it is just that I serve as Death's Warrior. Will you accept my oath?"

"Holy shit!" I heard Aphrodite murmur.

Beside me Stark moved restlessly and I saw him share a *look* with Darius.

"I do accept your oath, Kalona, and I will hold it as binding."

Kalona bowed his head and fisted his hand over his heart saying, "Thank you, High Priestess." When he stood, his gaze went directly to his son.

Rephaim's smile was brilliant, even though his face was washed with tears. "You did the right thing," he told his father.

Kalona nodded. "Yes. At last."

"Well, then. Shall we return to our House of Night and see what awaits us there?" Thanatos asked.

We all nodded, even though I know I wasn't the only one whose stomach hurt and who absolutely wanted to run screaming *from* whatever we were going to find back in Tulsa.

But none of us ran. None of us said much of anything as we followed Death and her winged Warrior to the bus. Darius and Stark carried Dragon's cloak-wrapped body. I kissed Grandma good-bye and stared out of the bus's window as we drove past the circle that had been blighted by Darkness and which was now filled to bursting with lavender plants in full, beautiful bloom.

"Wait," I called to Darius. "Stop the bus."

I opened my window and heard my friends all do the same. Then, as one, we breathed deeply, inhaling the magickal scent of reblessed lavender.

"Look!" Stevie Rae cried, pointing above the circle.

I looked up and there, hovering, was our Goddess. She was dressed in robes the color of night and wore a headdress decorated with stars. Her smile took in us all, and with the fragrance of the flowers, her words drifted through the bus:

Hold to the memory of the healing that happened here this night.
You will need that strength and peace for the upcoming fight.

I closed my eyes, bowed my head and thought, *ah, hell . . .*

THE END

For now . . .